Beyond Conviction

C.J. Watson

Publishing Information

First published 2023, C.J. Watson. Amazon Kindle Direct Publishing

ISBN: 978-0-6458017-1-2

Visit CJWatson.info to find additional information, features, author interviews and news of any author events, and you can sign up for e-newsletters. Be the first to hear about new releases!

A catalogue record for this book is available from the National Library of Australia

Acknowledgments

Am I the only one who ever reads these kinds of pages? It would be understandable, given most authors have a simple 'For X' as their thank you. But I always loved how a thank you section could provide a window into the author's personality. Derek Landy is my favourite example of this, so I'll include him here as well. Either way, buckle up, dear reader, as we have a lot of thanks to get through and not a lot of pages to do it.

Thank you to April and Cryptic studios for the inspiration to this book's predecessor.

Thank you to Baby, for, in your own way, forcing my hand into seriously rewriting said predecessor.

Thank you to Beautiful and your feathery alchemical muses. Looks like I beat you to it, but I'll look forward to the day your name is in all the headlines. I was first, but I've no doubt you'll be better.

Thank you to my 'co-authors' Delilah, Millie and Luna, who frequently supervised the writing of this novel and ensured I never had a cold lap throughout the process.

A huge thank you to my Gorgeous, Angharad, for all your love, support, and bringing unending light into my life. This book wouldn't be what it is without you.

Thank you to my editor, Annie Jenkinson of Just Copyeditors, for translating my self-aggrandising prose into something resembling coherent thought.

Thank you to Yahya Khajehi for taking my primary school-level scribbles and turning them into such amazing cover art.

Thank you to my favourite childhood authors, such as John Flanagan, Emily Rodda, Joseph Delaney and too many others to list, for igniting my love of reading.

Thank you to my favourite teen and adult authors, such as Terry Goodkind, Saxon Andrew, and all the others I lack the space to list, for inspiring me throughout.

An equally big thank you to the not-so-amazing authors, who for obvious reasons shall go unnamed, for making me wonder how certain works/drafts ever made it past the first beta reader, let alone all the way through to publishing. You brought the impossible ideal of authorship back down into the real world, making me think *I could do a better job than this!* And so, here I am, hopefully putting my money where my mouth is.

Thank you to any aspiring authors taking inspiration from my pages. It took the writing of multiple full-length novels before I was able to produce a story worthy of sharing. Don't be intimidated, as the task might seem daunting. But if you have love in your heart for your characters, stories and worlds, you can do it too.

And finally, thank you, dear reader. I have reserved a special place for you in the afterword, for the depth of my gratitude cannot be compressed down into a single witty sentence.

TABLE OF CONTENTS

Literature gives us the opportunity to experience lives, perspectives, and worlds different from our own.

Though remember, friend, a good story has many readings…and this is but one.

- *Extra History*

One: Hope from a Bleak Future

The large concrete structure of the spaceport sat in stark contrast against the verdant, vibrant fields surrounding it.

"Melons, six dols," Ellie called lightly at the few passersby, a bright, welcoming smile on her face.

It was market day on the farm world Adroa, not that it was easy to tell. The cracked streets surrounding the spaceport were nearly deserted, only a handful of people milling about the single row of stalls, though enough to be considered a crowd on their tiny fringe colony.

"Ugh…" Alayna grunted beside her, chin resting on the wooden countertop, an expression of abject boredom on her face. "Why do you need me here? Why can't I just lie under the cart until it's time to go home?"

Ellie leaned over, lightly placing her fingertips on Alayna's shoulders.

"Because the sales we make today are what will feed us for the rest of the year," Ellie said sympathetically. "I know you don't think being here helps, but it does, and I need every little bit we can get. So, sit up, straighten your back, and please, show them that beautiful smile of yours."

Alayna rolled her eyes so hard that Ellie thought they may pop out of her head and clatter to the countertop below. But still, the young girl sat up, posed herself on the chair, and donned her cocky, 'vixen' smile that Ellie had only ever seen Alayna pull off. Looking side-on at those walking by, Alayna caught the attention of a few.

Turning back, Ellie let out a start at the man she hadn't realised was there. He had managed to sidle up quietly.

"Oh, I'm sorry Mr Magonihue, I didn't see you."

The man just grunted.

"Well, I've come to trade," he said in a scratchy voice. The man was old, very old, his skin tanned a dark brown from years of working in the fields, looking like antique leather in places. His jowls hung down either side of his mouth, giving his face a distinct, bulldog-like appearance while his absurdly tiny eyes sat back under a heavy brow set in a permanent frown.

"Of course!" Ellie said welcomingly. "The rains have made our crop extra sweet this year. Our watermelons are six dols while our snow and butterfly—"

"Save your sales patter!" he snapped. "I don't have any dols! I'll trade you half a kilo of last year's jerky for a couple melons. And that's as good as my offer gets. Take it or leave it. I haven't come here to barter anything different."

Ellie hesitated.

"I'm… sorry, Mr Magonihue, but it's been a lean year for everyone, even with the rains. If we could keep things to dols—"

He snapped again, "Don't turn your nose up at a trade, melon girl. I need the juice for me grubs, and even a blind snout herder could see you need the protein," he growled, placing both hands on the edge of the counter, dangerously close to Alayna.

Ellie's chest fell as she discreetly turned to Alayna; she had cocked her head to glare her own special brand of death at the old man. Ellie couldn't help but run her eyes up and down the slender girl's body. Fierce as she was, Ellie could close her hand around Alayna's arm and have her thumb and forefinger touch. Her lithe figure bordered on skeletal as she sat side-on in the chair. Ellie's head dropped momentarily, reluctantly admitting the old man wasn't wrong. Meat was a luxury they couldn't regularly afford, even if it was year-old jerky. Things were different out in the frontier.

"If you would be so kind as to raise that to a full kilo," Ellie said hesitantly, fearful of the old man flying into a rage at the plea. "Then I'll let you walk away with the two biggest watermelons you can carry. Would that be... acceptable?"

The old man grunted in displeasure. Though the fruits were sweet, he was decidedly sour about the notion of the proposed arrangement. Still, he reached into his coat and placed a small silver scale on the counter. Placing a disposable bag on top, he pulled out a cloth sack and began ladling in the small strips of dried meat with his unclean fingers.

As the bag neared full, he began taking strips back out and swapping them for smaller or larger pieces until the scales displayed *exactly* one kilo. Closing the bag, he handed it to Ellie before snatching the scales, promptly stashing them back inside his coat.

"Thank you, Mr Magonihue. Please, take whichever you like," Ellie said, motioning politely to the line of wooden crates propped up at forty-five-degree angles beside them.

The old man just grunted, looking over the fruits to grab two of the largest looking specimens before puttering off. Not so much as a thank you or goodbye. He did not glance back.

"Each of those was worth at least eight dols," Alayna complained.

"Yet both of them combined still wouldn't be enough to buy a kilo of meat on a normal day," Ellie pointed out, the doubt in her voice evident to even herself as she weighed up the costs. Her tone was subdued, soft. It was not that she criticised her customer—anyone who purchased anything at all was revered to some degree—but it was growing so much harder to get by.

"Which is why he just short-changed you. You trusted *his* scales? They were probably rigged to read higher than the actual weight."

"Enough," Ellie chided, her voice gaining just a touch of steel. "Mr Magonihue might be an old sourpuss, but he's a man of honour. Scepticism is a good thing to have, Alayna, but you really must improve at reading people's characters. It does not serve you to believe everyone might swindle you. It is a negative trait."

Alayna grumbled something under her breath.

"What was that?" Ellie asked, setting her hands on her hips.

"Nothing," Alayna answered before quickly looking away.

Ellie stood there a few moments longer, eventually letting her hands slip from her hips and returning to the small bag on the counter. Sifting through the pieces to ensure none were too far gone, she removed a small sliver and held it out to Alayna.

Alayna hesitated for a moment.

Ellie could almost read her thoughts as she was no doubt picturing the slivers of meat running through the old man's dirty fingers. Ultimately, her belly won the battle, and she took the jerky, popping it into her mouth without a word. Ellie carefully closed the bag again, stashing it beneath the counter.

Hours passed with only a handful more sales to speak of.

The star that was their sun, with its bright coronal ejections tracing visible loops about its surface, was halfway beyond the horizon before it was time to pack up.

"Come help me take down the stall, please," Ellie asked Alayna in her usual quiet voice.

Stepping around the counter, she counted their remaining stock. Overall, they'd sold about a third of what they'd brought. Ellie's shoulders dropped. Even as the only melon farmer on the entire planet, it was challenging to sell the sweet fruit to the kind of hard-trodden, highly practical people of Adroa.

With a light sigh, she turned to Alayna.

"Let's load them back onto the cart while we wait for Jonathan. We'll bring them back for export tomorrow."

Alayna scoffed.

"And let that dirty pirate captain pay us cents for what he's going to sell for dols and then keep the difference because of his made-up 'shipping costs?'"

"He's not a pirate," Ellie lied. "And Alayna, please, you must watch what you say aloud. He's the only way we can get *anything* for what we have. Even a few dols are better than letting them rot in the cupboard. And if you keep burning all our bridges, we'll have nowhere left to turn," she pleaded. "Those who burn their bridges end up drowning in the river."

Alayna's brow furrowed as she crossed her arms over her chest. Her foot tapped angrily for a few moments, then she turned suddenly, grabbing the nearest crate to stomp away towards their cart.

Ellie quietly accepted the younger girl's anger and started loading the crates.

Their shadows grew long, stretching out across the field behind them. Tall grasses waved in the wind as the curved ground turned into rolling hills disappearing into the far-off horizon.

The light was giving its last life as Ellie switched on their single electric lantern. As the pool of light wrapped around them, a short, silent figure exited the darkness. The boy's shock of short, dark hair stood in stark contrast to Alayna's flowing, fiery red tresses that reached all the way down to the back of her thighs. The sack hanging over the boy's shoulder was draping worryingly. He stopped in front of Ellie, head bowed.

"I'm sorry," his small voice said in a whisper, the words seemingly unwilling to cross even the short distance between them, his eyes watering immediately. Ellie heard Alayna groan behind her as she knelt and placed both hands on his shoulders.

"What happened?" Ellie asked, her voice full of concern.

"No one would sell to me, not at the prices I offered. I tried asking, but they said no…" He'd trailed off.

Ellie gently took the sack from his shoulder.

He surrendered it without even the slightest resistance as she lowered it to the ground between them. "I tried to haggle and to argue. Really, I did. I didn't let them walk all over me, just like you said. But I still had to pay more, or else I wouldn't have been able to get anything. Then you—we—would've had nothing at all, and then—"

His voice was tiny, almost like that of a kitten mewing. It carried a permanent falter, as if always on the verge of bursting into tears.

Ellie drew open the sack and leaned forward, peering inside. A few heads of lettuce sat atop a bed of unwashed potatoes alongside a single pack of rice and some scattered yams and ears of corn.

"Are you kidding me?" Alayna exclaimed as she stomped over towards them. She snatched the sack out of Ellie's hand to look inside. "Jonathan, this is a *fraction* of what you were supposed to get!" she said in a disgusted tone, throwing the top of the sack down.

"What do you think we can do with this? It won't even be enough to feed one, let alone—"

"I'm sorry," he said.

"Can't you ever grow a spine! They only charge you that much because they know they can get away with it when it's you!"

"I'm sorry," he said, his head dropping even further. "I try. I really d-do…"

"We're going to be eating marshweed for months because you can't ever put your foot down!" she exclaimed.

"I'm sorry," his voice said, resigned in monotone acceptance.

"Alayna," Ellie began. "Don't be so harsh all the time. Like he says, he—"

"I'm sorry, I'm sorry," Alayna parroted. "Is that *all* you ever have to say for yourself! Being sorry doesn't feed us, Jonathan. It doesn't save us from the swarms when the bullets run out! What are you gonna do when the Rike come crashing through the door? Just roll over and let them eat you because you're too *polite* to put up a fight?"

"I'm sorry."

"Say something else!" she shouted. "Stop saying you're sorry! You make me want to scream!"

"I'm... sorry—"

And now, Alayna did scream. She screamed in rage and frustration, throwing her arms up in the air. Then she stormed off to climb into the back of the cart, drawing her knees up to her chest and crossing her arms around them, deliberately facing her back towards Ellie and Jonathan.

Jonathan's small frame shook like a leaf. He ought to have been relieved she had wandered away, that he had escaped a further tongue lashing. Instead, he only seemed miserable that she had gone in such a manner, and that *sorry* hadn't worked. It never did work, never would. But just like those paltry vegetables, it was all he ever had.

Ellie wrapped her arms around him and pulled him forward, burying his face in her bosom as she stroked the back of his head. Tears left silent trails as they tumbled down his cheeks. Jonathan made no attempt to wipe them.

"Tomorrow, we'll all go to the export and see if we can make any last-minute trades," Ellie said softly. "I'm sure people will be willing to sell lower when they're about to sign away their excess, and you'll have another chance to show us what you can do. We'll be fine, okay? It will all work out; you'll see."

The small frame of Jonathan was nodding against her chest, slow and hesitant. She placed her hands on his shoulders again and gently pushed him back, letting him stand on his own two feet. He wiped at his tears with the back of his hand as Ellie led him toward the cart. The air around them seemed to tighten as they passed by Alayna. It was as if she were walking past a ticking bomb, where the slightest bump might cause it to go off.

She was cautious in her approach, reaching over the cart's edge as little as she could as her fingers searched around. Feeling her hand close around the smooth Polyplast she was looking for, Ellie pulled a short, stocky rifle out from where it lay on the bed.

Pressing a rubberised button worn thin by age and use, she checked the weapon's charge. A battery icon lit up on a small screen, where the firearm's butt raised to meet the main body.

Three segments lit up, leaving two more with a hollow outline. Handling it carefully, the lethal potential of its boxy form still making her nervous, Ellie slung the rifle across her shoulder. Alayna was pointedly ignoring her, so Ellie was able to back away without incident. She and Jonathan both trod carefully as they moved towards the front.

Together, they lifted the yoke running horizontally to the cart's central shaft and began pulling it along. Neither made any mention of Alayna's extra weight as she rode in the back.

The journey home took several hours, the paved roads around the spaceport quickly disappearing far behind them. The path they walked was simply a trail of flattened grass skirting the property lines of the sparse farms. Not a word was said among the three as the cart rattled along. Though their lantern cast a pale island of light around them, it did nothing to illuminate the world.

No, that job was left to the magnificence of Sulaya.

Ellie raised her head, breathing deeply, a chill wind blowing across the grass. Bathed in the pale blue light of Adroa's sister planet, the frozen ball of ice sat so impossibly huge in the sky that Ellie could make out its weather patterns with her naked eye.

Something seemed to open up in her chest as her heart fluttered, for a moment allowing herself to forget their food situation and just enjoy *being*. It might be a hard life out past the borders of the Conviction, teetering on the very edge of colonised space. But at least out here, there was room, there was air, and she could *breathe*.

The sky was open above them, with fields, rivers, and the occasional homestead all they could see. The slow drifting of clouds and gentle waves of windswept grass spoke to something deep within her soul and in this moment, she could almost be convinced to drop everything and just sit, staring off into the world and her clean night sky.

She was drawn from her moment by movement in the night; far off to her right, the lights of the Jackdaws' farm just about came into view. No doubt it was Mr Jackdaw and his eldest son Alex who were in the two mechs roaming across their fields, the beams of their headlights piercing out into the night. Mr Jackdaw piloted his four-legged, twenty-tonne mech slowly through his lines of crops. The large, multi-barrelled chain guns on top shone in the moonlight, still and locked in place, no doubt getting in some last-minute harvesting ahead of the export tomorrow.

His son in the smaller, bipedal mech followed along behind, its shoulder cannon stowed back, pointing skyward as the mech sifted through the soil.

Ellie was tempted to wave but the giant mechs were too distant, distinguishable through the clear night air, but otherwise focused on their task. The sight of them alone was reassuring.

Accepting the fleeting feeling of security for what it was, she turned back to face the front, Ellie focusing all her efforts on pushing ahead as they were nearing home. The hill on which she'd built their homestead became visible as they crested a slight rise before continuing down the curved, meandering track.

Reaching the base, they began their seemingly interminable climb towards the peak of their hill. Ellie had to dig in her feet and brace against the weight as she and Jonathan hauled the load up the entire way.

At the top, Ellie let out a sigh of relief as their tiny container home came into view. They rolled towards it, passing their field of tilled ground, covered in their melon plants' snaking vines and thick leaves. As they neared the front of their house, they passed their lone auto-turret, standing an eternal, patient vigil at the foot of their field. The automated weapon spun towards them, assessing them with its sensors to ensure they weren't secretly a Rike swarm in disguise. After a moment, it seemed satisfied they were human, turning away and continuing to scan the area.

Bringing the cart to a stop, Ellie kicked out the stand from under the yoke, resting it on the ground.

Alayna got up immediately, grabbed one of the crates and headed straight inside, avoiding them both. The door beeped and unlocked as she approached, the lights coming on as she disappeared within. Jonathan slowly followed, taking a crate from the back, heaving it inside.

Ellie took a moment to walk over to the turret, checking its status with concern. At her touch, a small image projected from its base. A blueprinted, almost wireframe image of the turret showed its internals while a tall bar next to it gave its power levels. All parts reported as 'Ok'.

The few solar panels on their home's angled roof had charged the battery to almost full. It would last through the night and into the morning, but that meant there hadn't been enough to overflow into the house. They wouldn't be able to run the heaters tonight. An important thought, it turned out, as Ellie realised her breath was fogging in the air, the night's chill truly beginning to set in.

With Jonathan and Alayna having continued to unload most of the crates, she pulled the cart around to the side of the house and picked up the last remaining pair. Climbing the few stairs leading up to the porch and doorway, Ellie stepped inside and kicked the front door closed.

"Lock," she said to the door. It beeped, sounding the hard metal *schlinct* of the bolts sliding into place. She stacked the crates atop those already laid by the door and stepped back, rolling her shoulders to loosen them, wriggling her toes to get the blood flowing after the long, cold walk.

Ellie looked around. This house was a simple rectangle, its entryway sitting sandwiched between the kitchen on the left and the living room on the right. A tight, spiral staircase rose from the floor at the back of the entryway to lead up to their diminutive bedroom, the ensuite of which acted as their bathroom. Their only furniture consisted of a two-cushion sofa in the living room and a small, triangular corner table in the kitchen. "Don't get settled yet, please. Dinner in twenty minutes," Ellie called lightly up the staircase where the two had disappeared.

Ellie began packing away what they had brought back in the sack, ensuring everything was carefully stored in the pantry or cold box to prevent any unseen rot from spreading. Her mouth twitched with worry as she stepped back, unable to stop herself from imagining the impact that losing even a small quantity of their stores would have.

She was especially careful of the jerky. Keeping a small pinch separate, she moved the rest to a cloth sack and drew the opening tightly closed.

Working in the small kitchen, Ellie drew one of their watermelons from the crates and cut it in half, hollowing it out and pressing the fruit through a strainer with her hand. Ellie put the leftover pulp to one side and sliced the rind into small cubes. Peeling one of the ears of corn, she then sliced off half the kernels and put the other half away. She poured everything into their one big pot and placed it onto their induction burner.

She carefully checked the remaining power for the house; each minute of actual cooking would deplete what little power they had remaining, so she could only hope it would be sunny tomorrow. Their batteries would then manage to recharge, and the captain of the export ship would be in a far better mood if he didn't have to ride down through thick cloud cover.

Ellie turned off the burner the moment the pot reached a rolling boil. Taking care to let none spill, she ladled the thin soup into three waiting bowls.

Finally, Ellie carefully sprinkled two of them with a few pieces of jerky and set the other bowl aside for herself. "Okay, dinner's ready. Come downstairs please," she called softly. The siblings appeared, clomping down the stairs and walking over. Ellie handed them both their bowls before taking hers. Jonathan hesitated, seeing he had some small pieces of the precious meat while Ellie was bereft of such a luxury. He moved to spoon at least a portion or two over to her, but she placed her hand over Jonathan's, gently pressing it back down. He looked up at her with sad eyes, and Ellie smiled at him in what she hoped was a reassuring way.

Jonathan dropped his head in quiet acceptance and wordlessly shuffled away.

The three ate together. Alayna leaned against the kitchen counter while Ellie and Jonathan sat at their small corner table. When they were done, Alayna washed the bowls and spoons while Jonathan handled the pot.

Ellie moved to coax them towards bed once the washing had been done, Alayna going away upstairs without complaint. Jonathan, however, lagged behind. Stepping up to him, Ellie ran her fingers gently through his hair, ruffling the fibres and feeling them slide across her palm. They felt soft, silky, and … She opened her mouth to speak when suddenly, he threw his arms around her in a shaky hug as if uncertain whether or not it would be welcomed. Everything about him always seemed unsure, and it was sad to see. Of course, she would always welcome his hug, especially when he needed hers so badly.

"I'm sorry I didn't get more," he whispered.

"Shhh," Ellie hushed him. "We'll make up for it tomorrow, okay?" She gave him a fond squeeze, holding him tight, relishing how his tremors calmed at her touch. "I love you. And you know I'll be needing your help to get everything moved and loaded. You help in so many ways, so don't you go worrying about anything, d'you hear?" She spoke softly as she stroked his face in an almost motherly fashion. He should have nodded in agreement—but he did not. "I need you to get your rest, so you can lift and move and pull the cart. You can do that for me, can't you?"

Jonathan looked up at her, electric blue eyes reflecting her own. His mouth quivered as he tried to resist the urge to break into tears. He nodded.

"I will," he said quietly. "I promise."

She smiled at him, brushing the fringe of his unruly hair to one side. "Then head to bed, and I'll see you in the morning, okay? Nothing is worth worrying about. You'll see."

Ellie pulled him into another, tighter hug, resting her chin on the top of his head until she felt his shaking slow again before stopping completely. With a kiss on Jonathan's forehead, Ellie turned him around and gently pushed him towards the stairs. The soft pad of his footsteps on the cold metal stairs faded, cutting off entirely at the sound of the bedroom door closing.

In the sudden silence, the emptiness around her crashed in from all sides, this quietness making her painfully aware she'd been left alone once again.

She took a step forward and stopped. All at once, the day had come to a close, the seemingly endless work consuming her waking hours suddenly ended. There was simply nothing left that could be done tonight.

Slowly, Ellie moved quietly over to the door. She manually unlocked it, slipping through into the cold beyond. The small porch was lit by the inside glow and she moved to the railing, stepping up onto the handrail and grasping the edge of the roof from below. With a deftness borne of repeated practice, Ellie was able to swing her leg up and over the slanted edge, climbing up the rest of the way gingerly, mock roofing tiles groaning ever so slightly under her weight.

She rose to her feet.

Careful not to slip in the moonlight, she walked forward to the beam of the tiny house. The triangular roof sitting atop the squared shipping container provided the space for the bedroom and ensuite beneath.

Ellie shivered in the cold breeze. Yet as she sat high on the peak of the roof, she couldn't help but feel as if all the luxury the universe could offer was spoiling her.

Great grass fields sloped away from her in all directions, countless rivers running and sparkling in Sulaya's wondrous light. The sky was so open above her, cast in a blanket of stars so thick it was hard to believe it was real. The breeze was so cold, crisp, and clean that Ellie was sure she could open her mouth and bite a thin layer of ice straight out of the air.

This was the kind of thing she used to only dream about in the dank, crowded hive world from which she had come.

She scrunched her eyes and shook her head, waving away the claustrophobic memories before they had even the faintest chance to enter her mind, instead focusing on the landscape and on letting her eyes follow the glittering rivers and occasional tree that pierced an open field, also the forests far to the west and the mountains beyond those. Straight ahead, far, far on the horizon, she could just make out the tell-tale crescent of the ocean. She'd long wanted to see it, having never had the opportunity before, but the trek would be several days there and back again. Ellie might have time, but she had no reasonable way to gather and transport the supplies necessary to make such a journey. Still, even without knowing the specifics of how, if things worked out tomorrow, she would find some way to make it out there and finally see that vast expanse about which she'd been dreaming for so long.

From her vantage point, she could make out the waft of smoke rising from a thick clump of neatly planted trees signalling the Lindens' homestead. The lights from Mr Jackdaw's mech still moved about some distance past that. Despite the hardships, Ellie was grateful for her small place in the universe nestled between two caring neighbours, sitting on her little house atop her equally little hill.

It's worth everything it's taken to get here.

As the thought occurred, it was appropriate that her eyes settled on the one mark of destruction on the landscape.

Bellator Peak, a striking pillar of barren cliff suddenly pierced the smooth, flat valley surrounding it as though some great, angry god had punched up from the underworld beneath and lifted the ground towards the sky but failing to make it through. The formation was large, but too small to be considered a mesa. Would that technically make it a butte?

But unlike the natural buttes of which Ellie was aware, Bellator Peak was missing the surrounding pile of dirt, rocks and boulders. What had happened to the rest of the rock and earth formed part of the mystery as the stark mountainsides dropped away straight to the valley floor, the surrounding landscape simply continuing as if it wasn't there.

The lonely mountain stood as a stark sentinel against the night, distinctly out of place in the vista in which it sat. And yet, Ellie had always felt herself drawing a strange kind of comfort from it. This was a night on which the temperature had continued to drop, Ellie realised as she shivered, her breath now fogging even more heavily in front of her.

Wrapping her arms about herself, she stood, taking one last moment to drink in the air and scenery before the cold drove her back to the shelter of indoors. Then climbing down, she gingerly opened the front door and slipped inside, feeling guilty for her little adventure.

Ellie stifled the urge to dwell on it, brushing past the thoughts before they could take root and spread. Instead, she decided to move into the living room and make sure the metal window shutters that clung to the outside of their home were closed all the way. Finding them secure, and with only the faintest of slits allowing light and vision to pass through, she reached to the back of her head to release her captive hair from its confining ponytail. Sighing lightly to herself, she unslung the rifle then changed from her white, market day sundress into her thin pyjamas.

Ellie knelt, sweeping the bright blonde locks of hair that had fallen across her face to one side. Then, carefully lifting the rifle from where she'd placed it, she laid it flat on the floor to run parallel to the edge of the sofa. Hopefully—or at least so the idea went— Ellie would be able to roll over and grab the weapon in the darkness without having to feel around for it; it would be lying there quietly waiting for her, like some old friend on whom she could always rely. Though as she looked side-on at the shutters outside the window, she hoped that she wouldn't need to, the same as she did every night.

Climbing onto the sofa itself, Ellie sank into the mercifully soft cushions; her hip crooked in that uncomfortable way it usually did as it dropped into the thin void where their two edges met. But even with the slight discomfort, she was just glad to be lying down. Taking the blanket that had been draped across the back, she wrapped it tightly about her form.

Now, she allowed herself a moment to shiver as she settled in, resting her head and using the sofa's armrest as a makeshift pillow.

"Lights off, please."

With a click, darkness fell across her as the lights winked out. Within a few moments, her eyes adjusted to the dim glow from outside, the shutters letting in just the thinnest lines of light to cast against the interior. Ellie tried to relax, willing sleep to come to her exhausted body. But after a few minutes in which she began to drift off, her attention snapped back.

Familiar, rhythmic sounds were breaking in through the night. Ellie rolled over, doing her best *not* to hear it. The sounds might be disconcerting to someone fresh from the Conviction, but this was the frontier.

Things were different here.

Two: No Shelter

Ellie was so used to the chimes of her alarm that she woke as soon as the first chord played.

"Stop, please," she said, cutting off the intrusive sound. Once it stopped, she dropped her head back onto the armrest.

Ellie could feel the desperate want clawing at her chest, the urge to roll over and close her eyes tight. But if she were to give in to that urge, she would be unlikely to get back up again, able to sleep for another year if left to her own devices.

Forcing herself upright, she swung her legs over the edge, placing her feet on the cold floor and swearing she could feel the heat evaporating from her skin as the blanket slipped from her shoulders and fell to the wayside. Bracing one arm against the seat cushion, the other against her leg, Ellie leaned forward to hang her head in complete exhaustion.

"Perimeter check," she said into the silence, her voice still heavy with sleep.

"No disturbances," the house assistant responded in a polite, unhurried manner.

Ellie sighed a little, finally permitting herself to let out a small amount of tension she hadn't realised she was holding. The constant worry of waking up to a Rike swarm looking at her hungrily through the gaps in the shutters was as unlikely as it was irrational. But that never stopped her heart from beating faster until she knew the perimeter hadn't been disturbed.

"W-weather, please," she said, beginning to shiver as she stood from the sofa.

The cold pressed in from all sides as she padded over to the window where she carefully leaned towards the glass, peeping through the slits in the shutters on the other side. The perimeter check may have been clear, but the house only had basic sensors, and something could still sneak past undetected. A swarm was unmissable, a blighted scar slicing across the landscape as hundreds of thousands of Rike piled over each other in a frenzy.

Yet single Rike out hunting alone were known to be quick, quiet, and far stealthier than when paired with their countless brethren. Whether the scouts were a different breed or due to some inherent herd mentality, lone Rike seemed far more intelligent than their swarm counterparts.

Ellie didn't see any movement as she scrutinised the world from behind her protective barrier. Moving her hand to grasp a small lever sticking out of the wall, she pressed her palm into the metal and pushed it upwards. The shutters opened halfway, allowing her a better view.

"Current temperature is negative two degrees Celsius," the assistant responded. "The forecast for today is sunny with light cloud cover. It is predicted to be eighteen degrees at midday and twelve degrees in the evening. The current crop growth rate is expected to be low."

Outside, the soil was firm, no tracks or signs it had been churned up anywhere. The small status light of their turret was still shining a faint green in the dim light. Ellie opened the shutters before crossing her arms, holding herself while she shivered a moment.

Arms still crossed, she turned back into the room.

"Bat-battery?" she asked.

"Seven percent."

"Air heater on, please," she said into the room.

Ellie went to stand directly in front of a small grille on the wall. With it set to be a sunny day, it would surely be okay to spare the power, at least enough to mitigate the risk of hypothermia. Warm air began to blow out of the grille as the simple air heater powered on, a small fan blowing air over heated electric coils. Arguably, this was the most inefficient method of heating, but ceramic pad-style heaters were hard enough to find on a frontier world at all, let alone for someone like herself. Grabbing the blanket, she held it up behind her like a cape to try and capture as much warmth as possible.

Leaning forward, Ellie pressed her forehead against the cold wall, standing there for a few minutes as she tried to throw off the last shackles of sleep. Her shoulders sagged as the weariness hung in her bones like a chill.

Still, this day was to be an important one. As the light from outside continued to brighten, she had to face the fact that there was work to be done.

With a deep sniff, Ellie pushed off the wall, wrapping the blanket around herself and hugging it tightly like a makeshift gown. Returning to the lounge, she bent down to fish the rifle's charging cable out from underneath. Plugging it in, the weapon's status lights illuminated in response. It would drain the house battery further but, Ellie reasoned, exposure would take three hours to kill them. More if luck were to be on their side, whereas having to deal with a Rike unarmed would drop their life expectancy to about three seconds, regardless of luck.

She slid the entire rifle back into its place. Standing, she moved over to the kitchen to prepare breakfast.

Ellie cut slices off a loaf of truly stale bread. Tearing the hard, crumbling pieces apart, she dumped them into the pot, adding a few spoons of oats at risk of becoming mouldy in the changing weather. She topped them with water, spending even more of their precious power bringing the mix to a boil. Then she mashed everything together to make a simple porridge.

In the cold, quiet morning, standing in their tiny house with nothing but a pot of what could be considered gruel, Ellie couldn't escape the rising feelings of guilt, her spirits plummeting as she looked at the bland mixture. It wasn't much. In fact, it was barely anything. But it was all they had. It was all *she* had.

At least it will give them something warm in their bellies.

Ellie clung to the thought as she carefully ladled the mixture into two bowls, then scraped the pot sides repeatedly until they were nearly bare, with as much of it sitting in the bowls as she could. Taking the dirtied ladle, she smeared what little porridge was still clinging to it around the inside of a third bowl. She placed the bowl in the sink and checked the time.

Ellie had let the two sleep in as long as she could. Moving forward, she paused as she passed by the entryway for a moment. Ellie tried to do the math, weighing up all the work that needed to be done; could she handle the day's duties by herself? Her lips tightened in shame; no, she couldn't take care of it alone, not if they were to make it through the season. The two teenagers would have to endure the same cold manual labour she did.

"Alayna, Jonathan, time to get up," she called up the stairs.

After a few moments, no signs of movement had come.

"Play their alarm, please," she said softly, bringing the sweet melody of light music drifting down from the bedroom, increasing in volume as it continued to play.

"Oh, for Pete's sake, be quiet!" Ellie heard Alayna shout, cutting off the music abruptly.

"Alayna, Jonathan, breakfast's ready. Come down please," she called again. This time, there came the unmistakable shuffling thumps of the two trying to extricate themselves from bed.

Ellie moved back into the living room and changed into her field clothes. The short-sleeved top was the thickest thing she owned, keeping her as warm as could be hoped, and resistant to the mud in which she frequently worked. A wrap-around skirt extended halfway down her thighs, allowing her to bend and kneel without restricting her movement.

A pair of tall socks reached most of the way to her knees, providing just a little more warmth and protecting her shins from the ground.

The *clomp* of half-asleep footfalls announced the arrival of the two teenagers. Alayna made her way down first, walking straight over to stand beside Ellie. Alayna pressed her back up against the heater grille and let out a jittering shudder.

"You'd best eat your breakfast soon; it won't stay warm much longer," Ellie said as she put her slightly wavy hair up into its usual loose ponytail.

"In a minute," Alayna replied, seemingly content to let the porridge go cold if it meant she could continue to stand there, burning a hole through her chest.

"Umm…" Ellie heard Jonathan say as he brought over the two steaming bowls, confused as to who to give them to. Ellie shook her head.

"I've had mine." Ellie lied, motioning to the sink with the dirty bowl as she finished doing up her hair. "You two eat up then come help me, please. There's a lot we need to do today."

Jonathan seemed unsure for a moment, holding his bowl guiltily. But seeing the dirty dish in the sink seemed enough to convince him he wasn't being greedy, and he began eating.

Ellie pulled down on the bottom of her skirt as if nothing was out of the ordinary. With it straightened, she moved towards the front door and prepared to begin the day.

"Unlock, please," she said, hearing the *schlinct* of the bolts retracting. She twisted the handle and opened the door just enough to stick her head out, looking both ways to take advantage of a much better view than the opened window provided. Nothing seemed out of place.

She opened the door the rest of the way.

"Heater off, please," Ellie said as she stepped outside, followed by the sound of Alayna making an annoyed start as she closed the door behind her. As much as Ellie would have liked to keep it on for Alayna, the heat would soon be blown away by the chill breeze once they started moving everything into the cart. And they couldn't afford to throw away power, no matter how cold or tired they were.

Straightening up, Ellie circled to the side of the house and picked up a number of the stacked crates, moving them over to the edge of their field and taking one from the top. She stepped lightly as she began making her way inwards, moving in a slow, meandering pattern, looking for any fruits they might have missed the day before.

Export was the day most of the prominent farmers managed to earn their income, at least those who had hundreds of acres to their name, as well as herds of livestock and the enormous mechs with which to defend them. The trading they did would comprise entire orders of magnitude ahead of what Ellie and her melons could achieve on any market day.

The large farmers might buy from smaller farmers like herself to fill any gaps or shortcomings in the following months. But generally, today was the day everyone would be rushing to unload everything they could, working out what to do with whatever was left.

With enough land and enough mechanisation, one *could* make a decent living out on the frontier. But it would take more than Ellie could currently manage with her small, eight-square-acre plot.

Kneeling, she checked under broad leaves as the sun fully crested the horizon. Dirt clung to her bare knees as she stood, Ellie brushing off the worst of it before moving on.

She had hoped their salvation would have come from the exotic snow melons she'd developed, having worked so hard to ensure the heavy melons would thrive during Adroa's cold winters. Their persistent growth had saved them from starvation for the past few years and given them a much-needed source of calories and vitamins. But no one was generally interested in them once the novelty of a blue melon with the internal texture of shaved ice wore off.

Though even with marshweed to supplement, the melons wouldn't have been enough to sustain them, even if Ellie had been able to grow enough.

Now Ellie had a new variety, one she had been labouring over with her little genetics kit for years. Testing and failing and testing and failing, an endless cycle. She'd finally managed to grow a usable harvest; now, she just hoped it would pay off.

Over the next several hours, she picked her way across their entire field. Only a handful had been missed of all the plants she'd checked. What she'd collected only took up half of the crate she had brought. Ellie supposed she should be glad to have done such a thorough job previously, yet a cold lump was weighing heavy in her chest.

It's not much, but we had even less to sell last year, and we survived. We'll be fine, Ellie tried to assure herself. But the stone weighing down the pit of her stomach remained.

By the time she'd worked her way back to the house, the sun had risen about a hand's width above the horizon. Jonathan and Alayna had used the time to move their harvest onto the cart. The crates were stacked evenly, each crate holding varying numbers of melons, depending on their type. The stacks combined only came to about Ellie's head.

Even fully loaded, their little cart was laughable compared to the literal *tonnes* of wheat and vegetables her neighbours would be exporting.

But still, it *was* more than they'd had last year. Ellie couldn't help but feel the stone in her chest lighten just a little.

"Good work, you two," Ellie said with an uplifting lilt to her voice. "Thank you both for working so hard." She brushed Jonathan's hair out of his face and straightened Alayna's fringe. The latter lightly slapped her hand away and looked to the side in embarrassment.

"Come on, wash up and we'll go," she said, sliding her crate on top as the two moved indoors. Following them, Ellie closed the door behind her before calling up the stairs where they'd disappeared.

"Jonathan, make sure you brush your hair. And Alayna, *please* wear your red outfit for me."

Sounds of disgruntled indignity echoed down from the bedroom as Alayna complained in a muffled voice. It was astonishing how much boiling rage that girl could communicate with nothing but cut-off words and ticked-off mouth noises!

Still, Ellie left the two to their work as she moved to the kitchen. Wetting her hand, she removed as much of the dirt as she could, though without a full shower and scrub, a light brown patch remained over each knee where some dirt had stubbornly sunk into the natural lines of her skin and refused to budge. The dark brown offered a stark contrast to her otherwise naturally pale skin. Ellie's lips pursed. It'd just have to do.

Walking over to the living room, she closed the shutters and changed her outfit. Raising it above her head, Ellie slipped her arms through their holes and pulled it down. The fabric of the white, breezy summer dress was light and thin, a single piece with wide shoulder straps and a less-than-modest neckline, its material hugging her feminine form closely.

She drew a flat, second strip of material high around her waist, tightening it to accentuate her hourglass figure. The dress reached down as far as her upper thighs, ending in a short skirt and leaving her legs bare. Ellie wasn't above using feminine charms to endear herself for better trade deals. Though, on the frontier, that did carry a modicum of risk.

Especially if Hunter Jay is around, Ellie thought.

Which, given the day, he almost certainly would be. But then, so would everyone else.

As Ellie made the final touches to her dress and hair, heavy footsteps sounded, stomping down the spiral staircase. Turning around, she gasped.

"Alayna, you look beautiful," Ellie said with sincerity as she took in the girl, who screwed her face up into a pout. She wore her only feminine outfit, a simple, salmon-pink dress with flat shoulders and a high, squared neckline. A wide black belt around her waist divided her upper and lower body while underneath, a pleated skirt hung to the girl's knees.

Ellies' fingers twitched a little; Alayna was still wearing her battered brown work boots. Ellie weighed the situation in her mind, deciding to let it be. Getting this wolverine of a girl into any dress was usually an exercise in futility, even something as plain and square as it was.

"I don't see why we always have to bother with this dog and pony show," Alayna complained as she crossed her arms over her chest. "It feels like we're just pomping ourselves up for ugly old farmers."

Ellie walked over and placed a hand on the younger girl's shoulder.

"That's because we are, in a way…" Ellie said gently. "Pretty girls are more likely to get better prices. I know it's not right, Alayna, but we need to make the absolute best of the day, and our wellbeing depends on us putting our pride to one side and doing our utmost."

"This is our last chance of the season to get anything but marshweed. I know how much you don't like it, but I also know you like trudging through the bog even less." Ellie began running her fingers through Alayna's hair, a habit she'd developed as the girl was always frustrated with it constantly devolving into a scraggly tangle, despite her relentless efforts to the contrary. Ellie tugged out the knots until Alayna started growing restless.

"I'll handle Captain Slackvore with Jonathan. I just need you to go around to the other farmers and get the best prices you can beforehand, okay? It's what's going to get us through. So please, I know it hurts, but don't forget to lean forward a little and push your elbows together. Use what Mum gave you," Ellie finished as she lightly kissed Alayna's forehead.

Alayna seethed below Ellie.

"Well, Mum already gave everything to you," she grumbled as she leaned forward and headbutted Ellie's admittedly ample chest in indignation. "I just got the leftovers."

"Shhh, you're only sixteen; you're just beginning to grow into a woman. They'll get bigger—"

As long as we can get you enough to eat, Ellie thought. Though, to be fair, the lean diet wasn't impacting her in that department overly so.

"Ahhhh!" Alayna recoiled. "Stop. I don't want to talk about it," she said, turning away and crossing her arms.

"Okay," Ellie said, voice full of understanding. "Let's get Jonathan and then we'll leave."

"I'm, I'm here," a quiet voice said hesitantly.

Ellie turned around to see Jonathan already standing there. She hadn't even heard him come down the stairs. He wore his nice white shirt and straight black pants.

"All right then," Ellie said, ushering them out the door. "Let's make our way to the spaceport and see what we can get."

Locking up, the three walked over to their cart and picked up the yoke. With the wind blowing, an open sky above and a comfortingly heavy cart behind, they took off on the long walk to the centre of town.

Their travel was well-paced and relatively uneventful. The fields were empty, their harvests taken in and no signs of the hulking mechs moving about. The pilots and their families were making their way to the spaceport, just as the three of them were.

As they trundled up to the bustling concrete structure, Ellie couldn't help but marvel at the scale of the larger harvests. Lines of shipping containers, each as big as her home, were organised into neat, stacked rows ready to be loaded. Each dwarfed the size of the three of them and their little handcart.

They made their way to the bottom of the main boarding ramp, off to one side. Once the ship had landed, the captain would come out and bargain with the larger farmers before their line would begin to move. They were set to wait a while.

"Alayna, hold out your hand," Ellie said in a hushed tone as they stepped out from under the yoke. The younger girl turned her head towards Ellie questioningly but did as she was asked. Ellie held her palm over Alayna's.

"I need you to take this and go speak with the other farmers while Jonathan and I wait here for the captain," she said as two blue rings appeared over the back of their hands, confirming the transfer.

"That's a hundred and seventy-three dols. I need you to stretch it as far as you possibly can. Take whatever you can get. It doesn't matter what as long as there's a lot of it. Can you do that for me?" Ellie asked.

Alayna looked up to meet her eyes. Her gaze hardened in determination and her fist tightened. She nodded with a surprising air of authority.

Ellie pulled the small girl into a tight hug, holding her there for a long moment, before eventually letting her wriggle out of her grasp. Ellie placed a hand against the side of Alayna's face, making sure their eyes met for what she was about to say.

"And please, *please*, just remember to be nice. We have to live with these people, Alayna. Burning our friends and neighbours won't help. They're good people just trying to feed their families as well." Her tone was, for once, serious. Ellie loved the girl to bits, but Alayna had the temperament of a speared dragon, which could cause her to be aggressive and argumentative. She might irreversibly damage the relationships they had with the other colonists, which was why she'd kept her close on market day and sent Jonathan to begin with.

Yet the face that looked back at her wasn't righteous or indignant; it was determined. Ellie had trusted her with every last dol they had, the balance hovering in her vision reduced to mere cents. Alayna shifted her body language, crossing her arms and raising one to hold her chin. She smirked and looked up at Ellie with her confident 'vixen' expression, the one so alluring that all the boys her age couldn't help but be drawn in by it, despite the danger it'd put them in.

"I'll get us enough food to last the season," she said. "I promise." The girl extracted herself from under Ellie's hands and stepped away, moving off.

Even if everything else goes wrong, we'll just have to eat marshweed. We'll still survive; we'll still be okay.

Doubt clawed at her, however, as she watched Alayna's thin legs move beneath her skirt and felt Jonathan huddling close, trying to share warmth without touching her, without being a 'bother'.

As Alayna disappeared into the crowds, she turned back. Leaning forward slightly, she squeezed her elbows together over her waist, causing her chest to pop. She gave them a final wink before turning and walking off. Ellie gave a small sigh of relief. Alayna could be charming when she *wanted* to be, and at least had no trouble standing up for herself.

"Ellie? Ellie White!" She heard her name called and had to pivot her expression as much as her body as an enormous bear of a man swept her off her feet. Her ribs seemed to compress as she was crushed into an affectionate bear hug.

"Hello, Mister Mathews." She gasped as the air was squeezed from her.

"Tannis, put that poor girl down!" a second, feminine voice said.

Ellie felt it as the enormous man jumped before delicately placing her back on the ground with a sheepish and apologetic grin.

"I'm so sorry, Ellie. Are you okay?" Mrs Mathews came up and immediately started to fuss over Ellie, pulling the hem of her dress straight as she apologised.

"You look stunning in that dress; how have you *been,* dear?"

Tannis Mathews was nothing short of gigantic, towering over Ellie to block out the sun, with her head barely reaching his chest. A bushy brown beard and thick, heavy muscles bulged beneath his too-small shirt as the buttons struggled to keep the ends together. Equally bushy eyebrows provided a fair amount of shade for the pair of kind, pale blue eyes sitting beneath.

Despite his intimidating size, a bright smile beamed down at her, light dancing in his eyes. Before Ellie could catch her breath to properly respond, Mrs Mathews stepped forward and drew her into a tight hug of her own. Ellie's face rested in the crook of the woman's neck.

Mrs Mathews was the kind of beautiful that made every girl green with envy. Tall and slender, she towered easily a head above Ellie. Her pale skin was flawless, her raven black hair hanging straight down, parting like water over her shoulders and framing a delicate, symmetrical face. She carried the same infectious smile as her husband.

Pulling her back by the shoulders, Mrs Mathews tugged at the frills of Ellie's dress and tucked away loose strands of hair. The mannerisms were motherly and caring, similar to the way Ellie played with Alayna's and Jonathan's hair.

"Ellie, you look gorgeous. I don't know what's brighter, the sun, or you in that dress."

Ellie couldn't help but drop her eyes bashfully as her lips tightened into a small smile. The couple had such an easy and genuine manner to them that it was hard to take their words as anything but completely earnest.

"T-thank you, Mrs Mathews," Ellie stuttered. "You look beautiful today, as ever. How are Jonesy and Kayla and Phillip and… Uhm... " Ellie cut out as she desperately tried to remember the rest of the family. She loved the Mathews, but they just had so *many* children.

Mrs Mathews laughed good-naturedly, the light tone pleasant to the ear.

"Oh, don't worry darling. I forget them myself half the time," she said. "The boys are all off getting the harvest ready for loading, while Kayla and Marionette are walking around and seeing if anyone is up for any last-minute trades."

"And how are you, my boy?" Tannis said suddenly, voice booming from his barrel chest with a friendly grin. He kneeled and slapped Jonathan on the back good-naturedly, almost knocking the small boy off his feet. Tannis' facial expression turned abashed as he steadied him with a whispered, "Sorry, lad".

Jonathan looked to Ellie as if asking for permission to speak. She offered a small, reassuring smile, hoping it would encourage him to speak on his own.

"Ah, it's fine, Mr Mathews. I'm fine, thank you for asking."

Tannis straightened to his full, towering height, patting Jonathan on the shoulder. "That's my boy. With an attitude like that and with these good manners, you'll go far."

Jonathan's face showed how he doubted it, his expression seeming to say, *it's not all about me though, is it? I can be as polite as you like and still, nothing much comes my way. This is my lot in life.*

"Speaking of trading," Mrs Mathews said. "It looks like you've had quite the harvest this year. Would you perhaps be willing to sell a few before the captain arrives for export?"

"Oh! Y-yes, of course." Ellie was listening to herself stuttering in surprise. She turned to appraise her cart as if she'd just become aware of it. "Which would you be interested in?"

"Well, I know how proud you are of your butterfly melons. And Jace absolutely loves making snow cones out of your snowmelons. And you love a good slice of watermelon when you're out in the fields, don't you, darling?"

"That I do, my love," Tannis rumbled back as he leaned forward to tickle his wife's face with his beard. Mrs Mathews placed her hand on his chin to push his face away, clearly used to her husband's antics.

"So, between all of us," Mrs Mathews continued. "I'd say, a crate of each if that's all right with you?"

All right… Is it all right? Ellie's face brightened as if she couldn't believe her luck.

"Oh, of course! That'll be…" Ellie did the maths in her head. Each crate could hold roughly two watermelons, three ice melons, or four butterfly melons. "Thirty-five dols if that's okay?"

"Of course, it is, darling," Mrs Mathews said as she held out her hand. Ellie lifted hers in kind, facing their palms together until the thin holographic rings appeared, hovering over the backs of both of their hands and confirming the transaction.

"Please, take whichever you like," Ellie said with gratitude as she motioned to the cart.

Tannis stepped up and made a show of selecting, scratching his beard in thought and picking up a pair of crates to weigh in each hand.

"Yes, yes. I see, ahh," he muttered in a loud whisper, continuing his performance.

Mrs Mathews simply stood there elegantly, back posed in perfect posture. She glanced at Ellie and their eyes locked together. Her look said it all.

Please forgive my idiot husband. And he'll not help himself to more than we're due.

Ellie couldn't help but smile. The Mathews were good people, and the relationship they had with each other was the kind Ellie hoped she would one day have as well.

"Why Ellie, I have to say, in my expert opinion, these are simply the best melons on the planet!" Mr Mathews exclaimed as he hoisted three stacked crates onto his shoulder. Despite Ellie knowing from experience just how much they could weigh, the big man held all of them up on one arm with ease.

"Shall we return to our brood, my love?" he asked jovially as he walked back to stand by his wife.

"Of course, dear. Ellie, Jonathan," Mrs Mathews said, turning to address the two of them. "It's been wonderful seeing you again. Next time you're on our side of the colony you *must* drop by for dinner. Your sister too." She pulled Jonathan into a hug, unabashedly planting his face into her chest as only a mother could do. Ellie saw the momentary panic in Jonathan's movements, before he just went limp and waited patiently to be released.

"I know the boys would love to have you over," Mrs Mathews said with a sly, conspiratorial tone and a wink to Ellie.

"Oh, thank you!" Ellie said as it was her turn for a farewell hug. "I was hoping to come by in a few weeks anyhow. Collect some of the plants by the river and maybe drop in on the Sayers while we're there."

The moment the words left Ellie's mouth, a giant spear of ice pierced the mood. Both the Mathews flinched, their mannerisms turning uneasy before looking at each other, their expressions unreadable.

"Ellie…" Mrs Mathews began quietly, her hands wringing together. "Have you been onto the colonies' intranet lately?"

Ellie felt something drain from her, a feeling of dread looming.

"N-no," she stuttered. "I try every now and then. But what with the weather, and the transmitter taking up so much power, and being so busy, I—"

They must have seen the fear in her expression. She could feel her own eyes going wide, her hand rising defensively. Mrs Mathews shared a distressed look with her husband. Ellie felt Jonathan nudging closer, hiding behind her nervously, the way a distressed young dog took refuge behind its master.

"Ellie," Tannis said with a pained tone, his mouth set in a hard line that did nothing to hide the sadness in his eyes. "The Sayers' farm was overrun by a swarm."

"We heard their distress call, and I jumped in slugger with the boys right behind me. But by the time we got there…"

He trailed off momentarily, shaking his head, appearing to overthink what he was trying to say.

"Brendan had stood his ground, protecting his own. We found him by the house. Sharlot's magazines were dry and their turrets were in pieces. Everyone but him made it to their shelter, but the bugs... Well, they'd already dug it up and cracked it open. They're all... the entire family…" The big man sagged heavily, wilting before her eyes.

Ellie's tension drew as taut as it could go, ringing as if plucked by a thin, spidery leg.

"But…b-but, they weren't on the outer edge? Their farm was relatively inward?" she questioned in despair, hoping in a futile way they'd say it was a joke or they'd somehow got it wrong.

The Sayers were good people, just like the Mathews. They were the ones who had taken her in and sheltered her the first night she'd arrived on Adroa, a fifteen-year-old girl with two nine-year-olds in tow, reeking of a ship's bowels and with the stink of a distant hive world clinging to her skin. Nothing to her name but a small shipping container she had no way of moving.

It was Brendan Sayer and his mech, Sharlot, who had carried them and their home to where it now rested.

His wife Maryanne, a standoffish and stern, but still kind woman, had helped her sort out her claim.

A weight of sadness was pressing down on her shoulders, hollowing out her insides.

"The outer farms were far enough apart that they just swarmed through without meeting any opposition. The Sayers' place was the first homestead they came across," Tannis said, sympathy heavy in his voice. "There hasn't been a big lure out that way for some time. I don't know whether it was because of that, because they'd already happened to have dug out the shelter anyway, or there was some other reason. But by the time me and the boys arrived, they'd already begun constructing a nest."

That caused Ellie's head to snap up to meet his eyes. The nests, the half-mountain-sized structures of hardened slime and clay, were where the Rike spawned, only existing far out in the unsettled regions of the colony and past the boundary separating claimed land from the wilds of the planet, known as 'the outer edge'. Left alone long enough, they would eventually send out large swarm expeditions to create new nests.

The big lure Tannis had mentioned was a gathering of farmers and their mechs who, together, used an artificial, electronic lure to draw the Rike out of their hive and into the open. It was one of the few ways to outright destroy a hive, or at least keep the Rikes' numbers down.

Ellie had taken part in a big lure once before, helping organise equipment and keeping the logistics in order. Even though she hadn't taken part in the fight itself, she could still remember the thundering booms vibrating through the ground, bright flashes lighting up the night and the sweet, acrid scent of gunpowder on the wind.

The farmers on the outer edge had the largest claims, most mechanisation and potent defences, acting as an informal bulwark against the Rike attacks. Between them and her neighbours such as the Lindens, Ellie relied on that 'herd protection' mentality to keep them safe. Her solitary turret and metal shutters would do nothing to protect them against anything more than a stray Rike scout hunting through the night. Given that nearly all the heavy guns were pointing outwards, if the Rike managed to form a nest inside the colony, it would be catastrophic for her and all the other smaller farms.

"Thank you for telling me," Ellie said to the Mathews. "I'm sorry if it put a dampener on the mood." Her voice was soft and resolute, determined to grieve for the Sayers in her own time. They deserved to be remembered and felt for, but there would soon be months of downtime to do just that. Right now, she needed to be the bright, happy girl that people loved, so she could make sure Alayna and Jonathan wouldn't starve. She had a responsibility to care for the children, and mourning wouldn't take that away anytime soon.

Stamping down on the welling feelings of sadness and worry, Ellie pushed them to the side to be processed later. She forced a small smile.

"It really was good to see you through," she told the Mathews. "Tell everyone we said hello and hope to visit soon."

Both the Mathews gave her a sympathetic look, Mrs Mathews also offering another tight hug before stepping away and pulling Jonathan into the same. Mr Mathews leaned in to drape his arm over Ellie's back and pull her in, still supporting all three crates with the other. Once he released her, he clapped Jonathan on the back, much more gently this time, before the couple moved off. They turned back for a final wave before disappearing into the bustle.

"A swarm?" Jonathan asked nervously behind her.

Ellie turned. She cupped his face gently with both her hands and raised his chin. She let go and started straightening his hair, brushing loose strands back into place almost idly.

"Don't worry," she soothed. "We're right towards the centre of the colony. Plus, we have the Jackdaws and Lindens right next to us. We'll be fine."

But her reassurances betrayed the slightest sense of nervousness in their tone.

Her words also didn't seem to stop the timid boy from dropping his head back down. Almost simultaneously, she began to feel vibrations in the air. Only one thing could it be…

She turned her head skyward, aware of Jonathan doing the same, almost as if they were one. A black, blocky object was clearly visible against the bright blue sky, growing rapidly as was the thrumming in the air. The ship's powerful engines and gravity repulsors slowed its freefall as it dropped towards the spaceport like a meteor, leaving multiple trails of smoke and fire in its wake. Numerous downwards-pointing rocket nozzles belched black exhaust as they added their strength to the fight against gravity.

The noise rose, intensity heightening until Ellie could feel it vibrating the hollow spaces in her chest. She placed both hands on Jonathan's shoulders, instinctively pulling him against her. The ship was descending fast and Ellie was beginning to be fearful; had something gone wrong? The pirate ship crew surely lacked the same training or even care as commercial pilots. Had the captain ordered them to descend too aggressively, eager to begin making his profits, and were they now unable to recover as a consequence?

The ship was dwarfing Ellie's field of view, casting a deep shadow across the area. Ellie swore she could smell the burnt propellants of the chemical engines moments before the downward rockets cut out, the thrum of the repulsors rupturing into an ear-splitting roar like standing directly behind a jet engine at full throttle. A full-body push pressed into Ellie as the ship's fields pushed against her and everything else nearby.

The ship stalled noticeably, its descent slowing to a crawl just a few hundred metres above the spaceport platform, though Ellie was having trouble accurately gauging distances given the scales involved.

The enormous ship was coloured an off-black, shades of dark grey mixed together, pitted with the sickly reds and yellows of rust at random points. Several large landing feet extended from the centre of the mass as it continued to lower itself. They disappeared over the lip of the platform before the impact of the touchdown transmitted through the ground, sending a vast tremor through the beleaguered Ellie.

What would have been a major event on almost any other planet had practically no effect on the crowds surrounding her, though plenty of winces and glares were cast towards the behemoth now teetering on the almost comically undersized spaceport. But as the roar spun down and dissipated, replaced with the whines of hydraulic rams, the people around her continued on their way.

Ellie lifted her arms to fix her hair and straighten her dress.

"Is it just me or was that a lot closer than in other years?" she asked Jonathan with an amused tone. She was trying to lighten the mood, perhaps more as a coping mechanism now the tension she was feeling began to ease.

"It was...it was closer, I think?" Jonathan answered in an unsure tone.

"Well, I'm sure Alayna enjoyed it. She always loves watching it descend—"

Ellie's words trailed off as she wobbled on her feet. Jonathan flinched in alarm and gently gripped her arm to steady her.

"Sorry, Jonathan, I'm fine." The strength returned to her legs.

"H-headaches again?" Jonathan asked nervously, fixing her with wide eyes as he let her go.

"Yes, don't worry," Ellie said, raising a hand to rub her eyes.

She always seemed to get headaches around large crowds. Was it the noise, heat, or combined sensory overload? Whatever it was, Adroa had suited her beautifully in that regard. With so few people around, her headaches had nearly disappeared since arriving all those years ago.

Ellie shuddered, remembering her homeworld. Living in the pits of a human hive whilst being sensitive to crowds was a special kind of hell.

"It's just a little too crowded for me I think," Ellie said, lowering her hand back down and turning to Jonathan with a small smile. "And I'm sure that rumpus Captain Slackvore just made didn't help—"

Ellie was cut off a second time as a scream pierced the air. Her head snapped up immediately. The scream began as one of genuine fear, its tone crying for help but quickly shifting, ending in a tone of anger and outrage.

While at first it could have been any of the young girls on the planet, Ellie knew only one who was able to shift that suddenly and carry the promise of so much vengeful, flesh-rending *wrath*.

She began to run.

Three: A Dangerous New Friend

Ellie broke into a sprint before realising what she was doing, heading in the vague direction from which she'd heard the scream originate.

Heads were turning, some people moving away while others moved forward, the source of the disturbance becoming obvious as she ran. Indistinct shrieks morphed into understandable words as Ellie crossed the concrete brim of the spaceport.

A knot of people was forming around the source of the noise as Ellie dove forward, apologising without direction as she pushed through in a panic. By now, she could clearly make out Alayna cursing a torrent of obscenities strong enough to scour the rust off the ship and make even the seasoned pirates reconsider their life choices.

As she finally broke through the frontline, Ellie immediately froze; Alayna had her feet planted as she was loosely surrounded by a group of large men, screaming death at one in particular. That man was none other than Hunter-Jay. A wide, leering grin left the hog of a man looking like a cat that had just eaten the fattest canary it had ever seen.

The next few moments happened before Ellie could react.

Alayna squared off against Hunter as one of his men rushed in from behind. Ice pierced Ellie's soul as the man wrapped his arms around Alayna's waist and picked her up. Alayna's eyes went wide with shock and disbelief, the movement signalling the others to close in around her.

"DON'T YOU TOUCH ME!" Alayna screamed in a high-pitched shrill, the end of her sentence devolving into a crazed banshee shriek. Her arm rose, fingers curling as she slashed back down. The first man who'd rushed forward from beside Hunter screamed as she clawed his face. Sharp nails raked against soft skin, opening up several long gashes immediately spurting blood. The man dropped to his knees screaming, clutching at his ruined face with shaking hands. It was as though her fingernails had acted as tiny penknives.

The viciousness of the attack caused all those around her to hesitate, stunning the crowd to silence, looking on in shock. How could she do such a thing? From where did she even get the strength—or the courage? But the frail-looking girl wasn't done. With her arm still swinging, she grabbed for the shoulder of the lackey holding her. Using it for leverage, she spun around inside his grip, pulling herself upwards. He let out a pitched cry of shock and desperate agony as Alayna sank her teeth into the side of his neck.

His grip loosened immediately as he tried to pull her off, jerking and kicking as his finger gripped the cloth of her dress. But Alayna wasn't coming loose. Ellie could see the girl visibly straining as she grabbed onto him, bringing her knees up against his chest and using the purchase to push herself back, ripping at his neck.

Ellie's stun was beginning to wear off, her heart hammering in fear. Heat began to spread out into her limbs, but it all seemed to be happening in slow motion.

The wounded lackey was similarly clawing, trying to give back as good as he got from the diminutive girl, beating his fists against Alayna now. He spun on his heels, fighting to keep his balance as he desperately tried to pry her loose. Blood was pouring down his neck to soak into his shirt. One thing was certain; he would never have expected such a bitter struggle. Not with her, anyway.

"*HELP!*" *he* shrieked in panic to his companions, who had yet to be released from their frozen hold.

Jonathan rocketed past Ellie as if fired from a cannon. He sprinted towards the pair as the lackey desperately wrenched on Alayna's hair. When Jonathan was a few paces away, he launched into a flying leap, pulling his arms up to protect his head as he bodyslammed into the man's side.

The small boy clearly had no plans beyond an all-out assault. The force was enough to send the larger man sprawling as Jonathan bounced off, hitting the concrete hard and scraping himself along the ground.

The sudden jerk was enough to rip Alayna free, the attacker knocked out from under her. She tripped as she landed unevenly, pulled forward by the force before recovering just enough to remain on her feet.

Alayna slowly turned to face Hunter. With visible venom, she spat out what looked like an enormous blood clot that splatted wetly against the ground.

The severed chunk of neck glistened in the sun between them, Alayna wiping at her mouth, the quantity of blood enough to smear up her entire forearm.

She fixed Hunter with a wild, wide-eyed glare. His smug grin had disappeared, even the confident Hunters' eyes having widened slightly. As Alayna stood there heaving, though, his surprised expression quickly turned to one of contempt.

No one moved except for the two men rocking on the ground, clutching their injuries. No one seemed to know how to react to the skinny, twig-armed girl who had, in seconds, taken out two fully grown men. Men who, combined, likely came in at eight times her weight.

Ellie began to step forward. One foot in front of the other.

One.

Two.

"Now, now, girlie, that wasn't very polite, was it?" Hunter said in his gravelly drawl as he began to move forward. "Not a nice, ladylike way to behave."

Alayna reared up like a viper, her face every bit as furious. Yet it wasn't dissuading Hunter at all.

"Those are my boys right there. I'll be down two workers because you couldn't take a *joke*. Why, with all the work and business I'm going to lose, not to mention who's going to pay for their recovery, I think I'm well in my right to demand… *compensation*."

The final word came out so oily, so slick with a perverted inflection, that even Ellie was surprised by how fast she crossed the distance. Ellie inserted herself between Hunter and Alayna, feeling a strange sense of suspended calm as her heart hammered in her chest, her stomach beginning doing backflips.

A sly grin spread across Hunter's face as he looked down at her.

"Melon girl, you arrived just in time," he said.

A wave of violation washed over Ellie as his eyes slid up and down her form. She turned her head away, her face burning red.

"I was just discussing with your little sister here how she would pay for all this unfair damage she's caused to me and my boys. The lost work, covering their expenses while they're being treated, not to mention the pain and anguish she's inflicted." Hunter's voice was smooth, almost charismatic, with a sickly tone resembling 'reasonable'. Ellie swallowed hard, all too aware of the intentions behind his manner.

"How...how much do you think that would be?" Ellie asked, unable to meet his gaze and instead staring at a patch of ground off to the side. Alayna made a start behind her, so she stepped back discreetly, pressing her heel down on the girl's toes. Alayna made an indignant noise as if about to speak up, so Ellie leaned back and pressed down harder. She was hoping to hide the small girl behind her only slightly larger frame, pleading in her mind for Alayna to keep quiet.

The moment Hunter's teeth were visible through his smile, Ellie juddered, racked with consternation. Were they about to lose what little they had?

"Oh, once all is said and done, I'd imagine the cost would come to several thousand dols…" He leered.

Ellie stayed glacially still, fearful of making the situation any worse. But inside, the floor was opening up beneath her.

Several thousand dols! We'll never pay that off.

As she did the math, the true scope of what was happening grew suddenly clear.

Even with no interest, which she didn't trust Hunter not to demand, it'd take her years to pay off a debt like that. Her mind immediately began throwing up ideas on how they could escape, where they could run if she were to just grab Alayna and Jonathan, bargain or stow away on Slackvore's ship and flee.

Of course, it was unfair. Of course, *Hunter* would take a situation like this and turn it into an opportunity of barely veiled exploitation. But what could she do? There were no wardens or law keepers from whom Ellie could seek protection. And even if she were to hide with one of her neighbours, feeling as though she was preying on their sympathy, Hunter would most likely burn their entire homestead to the ground.

Then Ellie would be responsible for their destroyed lives as well.

"Unless, of course, you were to come along to my place one night."

He leaned in, towering over her and getting so close she could smell the marshweed liquor he brewed on his thick breath.

"I'll break out the good stuff; we can lie down by the fire and…get to know each other. *Thoroughly.* That'll be nice, won't it?" Hunter breathed the last word with such anticipation it almost made her retch.

Ellie's mouth set into a hard line as she resisted the urge. She didn't want to turn her head towards the pig of a man standing before her. But, slowly, dragging her eyes from the spot of ground at which they'd been staring, she turned to face him, head still bowed.

Ellie held no illusions as to what he had in mind. Even without his reputation amongst the farmers, his lecherous gaze and smug grin told her everything she needed to know. Had all her years of successfully slipping away from him finally come to an end?

"There we go," he said in a satisfied tone. Alayna stirred behind Ellie, so she pressed down even harder to keep the girl quiet.

"What's one night in the face of a few thousand dols? Why, you might even enjoy yourself. I'm quite the gentleman, you know. I don't know why you ever said no up until now."

Because you're a violent, foul-smelling, self-entitled prick who only wants me for my breasts! Ellie thought with uncharacteristic venom.

Ellie could feel her eyes begin to burn, a cold acceptance of what she'd have to do forming in the pit of her stomach. She forced her chin to start rising, to look up and meet his gaze when a soft clap jerked her head all the way up. Her eyes widened.

"Easy friend, plenty of space out here on the frontier; no need to crowd in like that." The bright and welcoming voice carried from a figure who had just slapped his hand on Hunter's shoulder.

Ellie jerked back, impacting Alayna behind her, forcing the small girl to backpedal a step in surprise. Even Hunter flinched from the newcomer, an instinctive reaction, one that had been drilled into them from the earliest days of life to the visage that stood before them.

Standing within arm's reach of them, almost halfway between Ellie and Hunter, was the intimidating sight of an armed Conviction soldier.

The sharpened, matte black combat armour of the Conviction military was unmistakable. From his heavy combat boots, bladed pauldrons and spiked knuckles, his silhouette alone was identification enough. A thread of nervousness stretched taut in Ellie's stomach as a wave of fear washed over her. The only way someone on a hive world ever came across a soldier of the Conviction was when the riots became so bad, they overcame even the heavy hand of the wardens. The Conviction sent in their soldiers to 'restore order through means of rapid depopulation', also known as slaughtering everything in sight.

The inset eyes and geometric face masks of the Conviction helmets were drilled into every child as things to be feared. To stare one down was to abandon whatever mob justice you were partaking in and run or face a painful and unceremonious death. So, this soldier must have been one of the Conviction.

Ellie blinked. *Or was he?*

This soldier wasn't wearing a helmet. Where his rank and unit insignia would typically be over his left breast were only opaque scrape marks, as if they had been sanded away, his wavy, well-kept, bleached-blond hair neatly framing a handsome face. A friendly smile and intrigued, kind eyes looked out toward her and Alayna.

"Pardon the intrusion, Miss. I couldn't help but notice what was happening, and figured I'd step in." He turned his head to look directly at them both. "Perhaps the two of you wouldn't mind stepping over here?" the newcomer continued, motioning lightly to a spot behind him that would put himself between them and Hunter. The stranger was smiling, but his eyes intently focused on Ellie's, the meaning behind his gaze immediate and unspoken.

Recovering with a spit as he overcame his initial shock, Hunter spoke up suddenly.

"Step in? Well, you better step the hell out of it! Fancy yourself the new sheriff outsider?" Hunter snapped, slapping the hand off his shoulder as he visibly collected himself from his earlier shock.

"Not at all," the newcomer replied coolly, seemingly unfazed by Hunter's tone as he turned back to face him. "Jake Ardent, private security. I hear you're having a bug problem," he finished, holding out his hand for Hunter to shake.

Ellie wanted to move, to grasp at the stranger's offer and retreat to the protection his gaze had promised. But she was rooted to the ground as Hunter bristled at the outstretched hand, baring his teeth.

"Well, *Jake Ardent, Private Security—*" Hunter spat in boiling anger.

Hunter suddenly choked, trailing off as his red face looked fit to burst. Ellie was sure he was about to tip over the edge into an explosive rage.

At what felt like the last moment, Hunter visibly reined in whatever he was going to say. He took a breath and slowly released the tension that had hunched his shoulders, settling back onto his heels. Hunter smiled, raising his hand to slick back the strands of greasy hair that had come loose. When he spoke again, his tone was much more even, carrying its usual slimy inflection.

"Let me do something that's not common around here, *friend*, and give you something for free," he began. "A demonstration of how we deal with people who're caught sticking their noses in other people's debt negotiations. *Boys!*" Hunter raised his voice on the last word, snapping his fingers. His remaining uninjured cronies circled around to back up their boss.

Hunter stepped forward.

"Seriously…" the newcomer apparently called Jake deadpanned in a tone of disbelief, as if he'd just watched his cat throw up on the new white carpet.

Hunter pulled back, winding up for a full-body strike before snapping forward, throwing a punch aimed at Jake's head. Ellie jerked at the sound of the ensuing impact.

But instead of Hunter's fist impacting Jake's face as Ellie expected, Jake caught Hunter's throw by the forearm and guided it to the side, simultaneously taking a diagonal step forward. Jake now stood beside Hunter, holding his forearm tightly as it extended off to Jake's side. Hunter was caught off-balance, pulled forward onto his toes.

"You want to rethink that?" Jake asked in a cold tone, his smile gone.

"Burn and die!" Hunter screamed, his face reddening with embarrassment.

Ellie only narrowly avoided being bowled over as one of Hunter's men charged past her. She cried out in alarm before she could stop herself.

All at once, with a fluidity that seemed entirely out of place in this fight, Jake began to move. He jerked Hunter's arm forward, pivoting on the spot, slamming the flattened palm of his other hand on the back of Hunter's elbow. A sickening *crack* echoed into the distance. Hunter began screaming hysterically as his arm snapped in the wrong direction.

Jake leaned hard, dragging Hunter into the path of his charging goon. Whether it was his boss's screaming or the unexpected resistance, the man hesitated. It proved costly as Jake let go of Hunter and slammed a powerful kick into his flank, bodily launching the bulkier Hunter into the hesitating goon. Both men crashed to the cold, hard concrete in a tangle of limbs.

Jake spun to meet the rush of another of Hunter's men, bringing his fists up to the height of his face in a guard position. Ellie thought he was going to trade blows with the charging man. Yet just before the man could fully cross the distance, Jake's foot suddenly shot upwards. Jake's whole upper body leaned back, his foot delivering a crushingly strong kick into the attacker's groin. The man cried out in pain, doubling over as his hands slapped down instinctively.

Ellie winced as Jake stepped forward, bringing his fist up into the man's gut. Conviction soldiers had pointed, triangular spikes integrated into their armour that extended just past their knuckles, formidable weapons they used to great effect to remind unruly citizens that a warden's baton was a kindness in comparison.

The impact lifted the man off his feet, puncturing multiple holes into his sternum. Ellie was sure she heard ribs breaking as the man collapsed onto his knees, screaming. An instant later, Jake's armoured foot cracked into the side of his head, causing the man to do a half spin as he was thrown sideways. The attacker went slack, impacting the ground in a limp heap.

He was no longer moving, lying slumped in an unnatural position.

Two of Hunter's men remained, standing beside each other. Both wore expressions of shock and fear as they stood in mismatched fighting stances, looking as though they'd made them up on the spot.

"What are you doing? Get him!" Hunter screamed at them from the ground, causing them both to jump.

Despite Hunter's order, one man took a step back. The other lacked the same amount of sense. He set his chin, pulling one arm all the way back behind him and he roared, charging forward.

The man ran straight towards Jake.

Ellie knew something was very wrong when Jake made no move to defend himself, simply watching the man charge. When the man reached Jake, he planted his feet, twisted his waist, and brought his arm up from beneath with all the force he could muster. The man's movements were slow, almost ungainly, but Jake made no attempt to block.

The man's fist came up from beneath, impacting the hardened armour plates covering Jake's stomach. Jake was rocked back on his heels as a wet *crunch* sounded. The man squealed like a snout as all the bones in his hand shattered.

"No *shit,"* Jake said incredulously.

Jake's arm snapped forward lightning fast, burying two armoured fingers deep into the man's eye sockets. The attacker let out a horrific, high-pitched shriek, falling back a step. With space now between them, Jake raised a leg and stomped straight onto the man's knee. His shriek rose in pitch as a second loud *crunch* hit Ellie's ears, causing her to flinch as the man's leg folded over in the wrong direction. The man collapsed to the ground, clutching his face, choking on a strangled scream.

Jake straightened, stretching his fingers briefly before balling them back into fists. He looked side-on at Hunter's one remaining goon.

The man stood, eyes wide, flicking between Jake and the injured man, looking terrified. Jake stood still for a long moment, piercing eyes never leaving the opponent. Finally, Hunter's last goon decided he wasn't going to win today and held up both his hands in a placating gesture.

Jake paused, considering the aggressor before nodding in a direction, dismissing him.

To what little credit Ellie could give the man, he did at least run to one of his companions, picking him up and dragging him away instead of immediately fleeing.

Ellie stood, shielding Alayna protectively as Jake's armoured form turned back to them. She could feel a latticework of ice taking hold within her. Despite all appearances, it wasn't the black, spiked combat armour, a symbol of the Conviction. It wasn't the sidearm or large knife that remained holstered around his waist, or the deadly-looking rifle clamped to his back. It wasn't even the fact he'd just knocked Hunter, known scourge of the colony and three of his goons to the ground whilst staring down a fourth.

No, it was the complete lack of thought or hesitation in his actions that was pressing to the forefront of her mind. The other men's attacks now seemed slow, clumsy even, whereas Jake had been direct, brutal, and uncompromising. He'd shattered Hunter's elbow, breaking a second man's ribs before gouging out the eyes of a third without so much as a change in expression. He'd flowed into the attacks with a singular, utilitarian purpose, his movements almost dance-like in their ease and practice.

Yet, despite the fear and uncertainty causing her heart to hammer in her chest, something about the kindness in his expression caused her to hesitate.

His eyes were full of concern, and he looked at her with genuine care, as if worried for her.

But the moment was fleeting as he turned to face the crowd directly. It had grown significantly.

"My sincere and utmost apologies," Jake's voice boomed out. "This was not how I had anticipated being introduced. To make up for the trouble I've caused, I'd like to offer you all a free armed response in recompense for my actions." He turned from side to side, addressing as much of the gathered crowd as he could. "I appreciate your forgiveness and look forward to meeting each of you individually."

With that, he turned away from the crowd, stepping towards Ellie, a definite note of dismissal in his last words. The crowd stayed in place a few moments longer, but with the excitement over, people began to lose interest. There were many long stares at Hunter's men still on the ground, though none stepped forward to offer assistance as they broke off.

"Sorry to steal your thunder," Jake said quietly to Ellie as he leaned in sideways. "I figured you wouldn't mind if I drew the attention away from you. Keep people talking about how it ended so they forget how it…"—he trailed off as his eyes shifted from her to Alayna—"...began."

He stood with an easy confidence, his manner open and welcoming. His eyes met hers whenever he spoke, staying steady and avoiding the usual down-then-up flick.

"Oh, th-thank you…" Ellie stammered, still trying to fully comprehend exactly what had happened in the past few minutes.

Her eyes snapped open now the adrenaline and danger were beginning to fade.

"Jonathan!" Ellie called out in a worried voice as she spun, eyes darting side to side, looking for the injured boy.

No answer came, only movement behind her as Jake moved away. She turned to watch him stride over to a small form, quivering on the ground.

"Come on, big man, you're all right," she heard him say in a soft tone, his voice carrying across the short distance as he crouched, holding out his hand to the small boy.

"Don't *touch* him!" Alayna snapped. There came the sharp impact of the girl's bony shoulder as she barged past.

Jake's head turned as Alayna came up beside him and more or less coiled herself around Jonathan. Ellie couldn't hear exactly what she was saying as she alternated from glaring daggers at the armoured Jake and whispering to the shaking Jonathan.

Jake retracted his hand and slowly stood, stepping back a few paces and out of Alayna's danger zone. She still shot him the occasional glare but quickly turned her attention back to Jonathan, a rare display of care from the wolverine of a girl.

Ellie began to step towards them as Jake passed in the opposite direction, their eyes meeting.

Well, this has been an interesting day, his expression seemed to say.

It's not normally this eventful. Ellie thought back, shocked at how readily the thought came, directed towards him.

Whether Jake received the message or not, via her facial muscles or some spontaneous telepathy Ellie just developed, his expression turned amused before he broke eye contact with her and moved on.

The moment they passed, Ellie stopped in her tracks, conflicted in her thoughts and still trying to parcel and process the events in sequence. She needed to make sure Jonathan and Alayna were all right. But the two were already together, and Alayna was in the middle of showing some very rare care and even affection towards him. That would go further towards mending Jonathan than anything Ellie could ever do.

And she did need to thank Jake properly. Her mind was still flooded with images of what she would have had to do and endure to pay off Hunter's debt. She could nearly taste his reek in her mouth.

With a look towards Alayna and Jonathan, just to assure herself the two of them would be fine for the next few minutes, Ellie turned back around, jerking in surprise to see Jake had lowered to one knee beside Hunter.

"I'll admit, I thought you would have had enough of a survival instinct to know not to pick a fight with someone armed, and armoured, in full battle kit. It seems I may have overestimated you," Ellie heard him say in a tone that rooted her to the spot. There was nothing aggressive or antagonistic about it, but something lying beneath the words was very, very cold.

"Then let me make this extremely clear, so I can be sure there are no misunderstandings." Ellie watched him lean in just a little closer, the two men's faces a hand's breadth apart.

"If you come near any of those three again, or you pull some stupid stunt to try and collect on that 'debt' you were spouting off about, and I promise, no matter where you run on this little *blip* of a planet, you won't make it to see the next sunrise."

Eyes that a moment ago had been so full of friendliness and welcome, had turned hard and unforgiving. Jake's tone dripped with disdain. The switch was jarring, his gaze silently promising a level of pain and violence that caused even Hunter to pause. A shiver jolted right up her spine.

Ellie straightened instinctively as Jake rose, holding a hand out to Hunter. Hunter glared at him, using his good arm to drag himself away before clumsily climbing to his feet.

Jake watched him go, an amused smile and a quirk of an eyebrow spreading across his face. He turned back in Ellie's direction; she could swear she saw a slight hitch in his movements as he realised she was standing there, watching. But the movement was so small and over so quickly, she genuinely wasn't sure whether she had imagined it.

Jake moved to stand in front of her, Ellie dropping her gaze fearfully, unable to meet his eyes. His body shifted as if he'd tilted his head. After a long moment, she heard him chuckle, a slight edge of nervousness playing in the sound.

"Sorry if I scared you, or the others. Not exactly how I planned to go introducing myself when arriving." He raised one hand to scratch the back of his head.

Ellie instinctively followed the movement, her gaze rising along the armour with its sharpened corners and geometric edges. It wasn't until she was this close that she realised not only was the place over the left breast scraped bare. The other Conviction iconography all over the armour had also been removed, assuming it had even been there to begin with.

"But still. I don't think we've been properly introduced." Something in his voice compelled her to look upwards, to meet his eyes as he spoke to her. A nervousness, almost a bashfulness.

A pair of vibrant green eyes looked back down at her. A handsome face with light skin and a strong jawline sat beneath a shock of brushed, bleach-blonde hair. Of all the other things happening around them, Ellie suddenly became very aware of the dirt still clinging to her knees.

She was behaving like a deer caught in headlights. Alayna had been ripping the throat out of a man a few minutes ago. She'd more or less had to sell herself to Hunter just to make sure they could survive. Then Jake, the dangerously handsome and mysterious newcomer, had intervened and gone from friendly to terrifying, to nervous. Ellie was beginning to breathe faster as it all became a bit... Well, a bit much.

How's a girl supposed to deal with this all at once?

But, as a few memories flashed across her mind, she did what she always did. She just kept going.

"Jake Ardent, private security. I may have mentioned that earlier," he said, holding out a hand.

"Ellie. Ellie White." She politely shook his hand. "Um, b-best melon farmer on Adroa," Ellie stammered nervously, feeling almost foolish. She had only used the title as a joke before but had no other equivalent to match Jake's private security moniker.

"Well, nice to meet you, best melon farmer Ellie," he responded with a bright smile. Her cheeks flushed red in embarrassment before Jake began looking around at the dissipating crowds.

"Looks like things are wrapping up here. Would you mind if I were to walk you back to your harvest?"

"Why?"

Ellie jumped as she heard Alayna snap out the question from behind. She turned to see Alayna standing there, glaring daggers with Jonathan standing quietly beside her.

"You want to take Ellie on a 'night out' too? Think you can swoop in and save us and collect a nice 'hero's reward'?" Alayna spat. "Looks like you're all the same, you supposed knights in shining armour."

"Not at all, Spitfire," Jake responded smoothly, a good-natured grin lighting up his eyes in complete defiance of Alayna's accusatory tone. "Though I do appreciate the pragmatic questioning of my motives. I suppose that's part of a necessary survival instinct, given what I've seen of this place…" His voice trailed off, shooting a furtive glance over his shoulder to where Hunter and his gang were limping away, dragging their wounded with them.

"We were fine before you arrived; I could have handled them all myself. Why don't you just leave?"

"Alayna!" Ellie snapped.

Jake regarded the smaller girl with a wry smile and a raised eyebrow.

"I have no doubt you could have handled them," he said with a chuckle. "And I also understand I'm new here, the 'outsider' at the moment. If my leaving makes you more comfortable, then that's what I'll do," he said, nodding respectfully to Alayna.

Something inside Ellie dropped a little; it was not that she thought they needed protection from Hunter or his men. Not at the moment, at least. But there was something to be said for walking through the crowds with someone so new and…. intimidating. Especially with his sudden appearance and unexplained Conviction-issued equipment, a curiosity burned in her mind and she was longing to walk and talk with him.

The more Ellie thought about it, the more she wished Jake would stay.

"I'm sure we'll see each other around," Jake continued, addressing the three of them, though he made the most eye contact with her. "I've got a nice parcel of land and am moving in. So not only will you have a new neighbour, but I'll also be offering my services once I get set up. It'll be interesting to see how bad the Rike swarms are here. But on that note, Ellie—" he said, causing her to jump as he addressed her directly. "Please, take this."

He held out a thin metal card to her.

Ellie hesitated a moment before carefully reaching out. The card looked to be made from polished stainless steel, a clean, angular ship design etched into its surface above elegant lettering.

Sentinel Security.

In one corner, a circle had been stamped into its surface.

"If you're ever in trouble, press that button," Jake said, pointing to the circle. "And I'll be there before you know it. It doesn't matter if it's a scout, an entire swarm or...something else," he said. He didn't even need to glance in Hunter's direction for Ellie to understand what 'something else' he was referring to.

"Oh...thank you, Jake?" she said in question, unsure how to address him. But he had already called her by her first name, and somehow, 'Mr Ardent' just didn't feel right. Ellie let out a silent sigh of relief as he chuckled.

"Jake is fine," he said, amused. "In the meantime, I'm sure you have a harvest to return to. I'll see you around," he finished with a polite smile, raising two fingers to his head and flicking them forward in a mock salute. Spinning on his heel, he set his back to them and strode confidently away.

Ellie watched him go until his back disappeared amidst the dissipating crowds.

"Who did he think *he* was?" Alayna seethed. "We didn't need his help."

"Alayna, please," Ellie said quietly as she turned to run her fingers through the smaller girl's hair and scratch away at the spots of dried blood that still clung to her face. "Remember what I told you about burning bridges. Not everyone is hostile or trying to tear you apart."

She moved her hand under the girl's chin to lift it by her fingertips.

"I know you can't help being paranoid. But we might have made a friend today. Please don't chase him off until he gives you reason to," Ellie continued.

"Having said that, I *am* proud of you," Ellie said. "And you too, Jonathan," she added, turning to the boy. Ellie ran her nails through Jonathan's hair as with Alayna, using the opportunity to look closely at the scrapes he'd taken.

"Whatever people might think, they'll at least hesitate before thinking they can do what they like with you," Ellie said lightly. "Now, are the two of you okay?" Ellie asked, turning to look at both as she stroked Jonathan's face.

"I'm fine," Alayna said grumpily, crossing her arms and looking away. Ellie felt Jonathan nod in her hand.

"All right then. Let's get back to the cart. We still have everything we need to do today."

"You go," Alayna said, twisting at the waist, grabbing the back of her dress skirt and lifting it to scrub at her face, removing the last few traces of blood. She winced a moment as her hand passed over her cheekbone, the area now reddened and beginning to swell from the beating she'd taken at the start of the fight.

"I didn't get anything done before that asshole got in my way. I still have everything you gave me so I'll trade for what I can and meet you back at the cart."

"Alayna…" Ellie began.

But the girl had already gone, dropping the hem of her skirt and breaking off from them. Her tense mannerisms melted into her confident stride before she was lost behind the loose wall of people and produce.

Ellie sighed quietly.

It's so hard to know if I'm doing things right.

Placing her hand between Jonathan's shoulder blades, she pressed him forward.

"Come on, let's get back to the cart."

The pair began walking, but Jonathan started shaking the moment Alayna disappeared from view. Ellie put her arm around his shoulder as they moved along. She worked her mind hard, trying to think of something to take his mind off Alayna's absence, anything to distract the boy that wasn't about the fight or the blood.

"What…do you think a Conviction soldier is doing here?" she asked.

Jonathan didn't respond immediately, continuing to walk in lockstep with her. Ellie eventually sensed that he wanted to say something. The words just weren't coming forth, smothered in his throat before given any real presence.

"Hmm?" Ellie asked, concern in her voice. "Come on," she said encouragingly. "You always work things out so much faster than I do. You don't have any ideas?"

Ellie could tell something was simmering in the back of his mind, behind all the timidity and the thousand-yard stares. He had an incredibly sharp mind; he was usually just too afraid to use it.

"I think…" Jonathan said quietly. "He's a deserter? He has the armour. But…" he trailed off.

"But?" Ellie prompted. She rubbed his back reassuringly, not wanting to lose the momentum and knowing he'd close back up if she didn't keep gently leading him.

"But, the Conviction doesn't have deserters? Soldiers are soldiers for life, aren't they?" he asked. "I thought, maybe, he might be a pirate or gang leader who managed to kill—"

Jonathan paused as if in fear of the next words before quickly changing his wording. A line of worry creased Ellie's forehead.

Maybe this wasn't the best topic.

But then, Jonathan was speaking again.

"…who managed to *beat* a soldier and take his armour, but that seems even less likely. You don't think he's here to…" He trailed off, looking away towards the ground.

Ellie rubbed her hands up and down his back again, a nervous feeling arising in her chest. She hadn't given it much thought with everything that had happened, was still happening. Yet it made complete sense that Jake would be a deserter, and Ellie had subconsciously accepted it as fact the moment Jonathan had said it. Now, already she wasn't so sure, but she couldn't offer up an alternative. Was he seeing something she wasn't?

"Don't think he's here to...what, Jonathan?" she asked softly. It took a moment before Jonathan reluctantly replied.

"To conquer us?" he asked, looking up to meet her gaze, fear and worry in his demeanour.

Ellie was silent momentarily before a small smile crossed her face. She tried to hide it but was only partially successful.

To conquer them? The Conviction certainly had a track record in that regard. But to send a single soldier to the very edge of known space, to conquer a tiny little farming colony of only a few hundred? There were thousands of other colonies in the outer reaches alone that were not only closer to their space, but far, far more valuable. Even if the Conviction launched a campaign to conquer the entire frontier, it would be a long, long time before they made it out this far.

Adroa held no value beyond a breathable atmosphere and fertile soil. It orbited a dim star in a typical system without strategic or cultural significance. The only things even mildly interesting about the entire system were Adroa and Sulaya themselves. The two planets interlocked, orbiting each other like a pair of binary stars as they followed an otherwise normal path around their sun. Sulaya wasn't even habitable; Adroa had stolen her atmosphere millions of years ago. Binary planets might be rare, but they weren't unheard of.

That can't be it.

And yet, she couldn't stop herself from replaying everything within her mind, looking at it all with new scrutiny. Jake's friendly smile, his seemingly genuine care. Was it all a ruse to gain their trust? Ellie found herself second-guessing everything, looking at it in a new light. Was the sudden change she'd witnessed a glimpse of what was truly underneath or was he just a good person towards whom she was levelling unfair accusations, even if only in her mind?

Her expression must have changed, giving away her thoughts. Jonathan bumped into her slightly, in that quiet way he used to get her attention.

Ellie shook herself and quickly put on a smile.

"It's okay; I was just thinking. Don't worry," she said reassuringly. She reached out to put her hand on his shoulder, pulling the frail boy against her.

"I don't think the Conviction would have any interest in Adroa. There's nothing past us but the vast emptiness of unexplored space. And there are thousands of richer, more valuable colonies between them and us. I'm sure Jake is just a deserter and he's come out here to hide."

Jonathan looked up at her, uncertainty and fear in his expression. But he seemed to accept her answer as the most logical for now, and instead, turned his gaze to stare at something ahead. Ellie turned to follow his line of sight to their cart nearby.

It hadn't moved, but the crowds around it had.

They walked over quickly, Ellie's mouth setting in worry as she counted over the crates. With a sigh of relief, she saw everything was accounted for.

With one or two exceptions such as Hunter and his gang, everyone on the colony had come to Adroa to get out from under the rule of the Conviction. Most were young, hard-working and honest families. Theft, at least, was something Ellie rarely had to worry about.

"Okay," Ellie said with a relieved tone, turning to Jonathan. "Help me with the cart. The captain will be out by now, so we better start making our way up."

Four: High Score

Ellie saw the captain was indeed out as they crested the top of the ramp to the spaceport's main platform. It was next to impossible to miss him and his distinctly booming voice as it carried across the distance.

Ellie could see he'd already dealt with many of the larger farmers as large stacks of shipping containers were being loaded up the ship's ramp by their respective mechs.

It was surprising, however, to see a number of the ship's heavy loaders carrying many separate payloads out of the cargo hold. Giant construction haulers floated by above them with a throaty rumble. Of course, Ellie expected some offloading; it was the one delivery of the year that brought people whatever they may need from off-world. But as quadrupedal loaders stomped past the two of them and their little cart, Ellie could make out construction supplies, large metal and plasteel plates, as well as bags of instant cement stacked high atop one another. Even some large panels of framed glass moved past, reflecting the world in their mirrored finish.

Ellie tilted her head in curiosity. Almost all the buildings outside the area immediately surrounding the spaceport were earthen or wooden or else small, prefabricated dwellings like her own, a necessity of self-reliance on the tiny fringe colony. Metal for building material was used almost exclusively for swarm bunkers.

Not that it did the Sayers much good.

Ellie screwed her eyes shut, turning her head away from the procession and batting away the thoughts. Emotions welled deep down as she'd yet to fully process her grief over the loss of the Sayers and the multitude of emotions between which she'd been flung during her ordeal with Hunter.

But right now, Ellie couldn't afford to let it affect her mood. She slammed the window shut on the emotional storm clouds gathering in the distance, simultaneously trying to harden her heart and soften her smile. Soon, she would have all the time she needed to process her emotions. But now was the critical moment that would determine what she would be able to feed Jonathan and Alayna for the next *year*.

Ellie nudged the cart and Jonathan along, pulling to one side and joining the short line of smaller farms shuffling forward bit by bit. Even at the back of the line, only a handful of people stood ahead of them.

"Are you okay with taking the cart the rest of the way?" Ellie turned to ask Jonathan softly.

Jonathan simply nodded, taking the full weight of the yoke so Ellie could slip under. Facing her back to the line ahead, Ellie tugged on the bottom of her skirt and straightened all the frills along its edges. She took care to pull up and position her bosom as well as she could, letting her natural curves accentuate the fullness of her chest and the graceful silhouette of her neck.

Reaching up, she quickly retied her ponytail, ensuring it looked fresh and making sure her fringe was swooping down just low enough to cover one eye perfectly.

"How do I look?" Ellie asked.

"You look… You look good," Jonathan replied.

Ellie smiled at him, running her fingers through his hair one last time to straighten it neatly.

Ellie took position next to him, doing her best to stand easy and look casual. They shuffled along as the line progressed. Ellie did her best to discreetly listen to the deals the other farmers were cutting with the captain, specifically the prices they were negotiating for their goods so she'd have an idea of the window in which she had to manoeuvre. The captain held a monopoly over their prices as their primary link to space, excluding the occasional prospector or explorer. They were prices that could be decided on his whim and were affected by his mood. What they were able to negotiate the year before was no guarantee of what they'd get today.

But try as she might, their voices naturally dropped to an almost conspiratorial level when it came to actual negotiation. Ellie could make out the sounds, but not the words. The distance, noise of the heavy machinery and general bustle of the area proved too much for her ears to overcome.

"Captain, *please*. The colour is only due to nitrates in the soil. Trees can't be rotated like other crops; the fruits more than make up for it in their extra size and juiciness from the rains!"

Ellie turned her head slightly, careful not to look over-interested in the scene playing out. The farmer ahead of her had raised his volume, a distinct note of desperation and pleading entering his voice.

A cold stone dropped in Ellie's stomach. The farmer had just made a grave mistake, tipping his hand and letting his desperation show. No one liked a charity case except for the captain, and even then, only for all the wrong reasons.

"Ah, Mr Thomas, how many years have we been trading? I *fully* understand the difficulty of farming, and if it were up to me, I'd be paying you all *twice* the asking price currently on the market," the captain replied, his words sympathetic, but his smile predatory. His tone indicated he knew that everyone else was aware of what he was doing. And yet he'd put on the theatrics anyway because there was nothing anyone could do about it.

"But the only ones I can sell it to are the colonies that don't grow enough for themselves. Why, the cost of fuel alone to fly your produce all the way to Etheria, or even Newgate Station, let alone the cost of crew and maintenance… Imagine if I were to go to all of that expense, only for half the stock to rot on the shelves for not being 'pink' enough," he said, holding up one of Mr Thomas's Pink Lady apples that was almost entirely a pale yellow.

"Why, such a thing would *ruin* me. And then how would you or the rest of the colony feel when I have to close up shop and can't make a run next year, or any other year, for that matter?"

"But…" Mr Thomas began, indignant but unsure of his footing.

"Now listen here. I can offer you twelve dols per tonne," he continued as if Mr Thomas hadn't said anything at all. "That seems more than fair; since each apple is, as you said, *so much larger* than last year's, it should be much easier to hit that same weight with fewer fruits. Oh, and no need to thank me directly. Just keep it to yourself that I cut you such a good deal, yes?" he finished in that slimy, coy tone.

Ellie tried not to baulk, very aware she would already be in the captain's peripheral vision. Twelve dols a tonne was nothing short of thinly veiled robbery.

Mr Thomas seethed, clearly backed into a corner.

"You're a wretched bastard, Captain," he said in earnest, holding out his hand.

The captain smiled.

"Why thank you. I take that as a compliment. Wouldn't make it out here to buy up your slop if I wasn't," he said, nodding once.

Two blue circles appeared over the backs of their hands to confirm the transaction. The light had barely dissipated before Mr Thomas snatched his hand away and stormed off, a dark cloud hanging over his expression.

Grabbing his coat with both hands, the captain pulled down to straighten it before turning to acknowledge Ellie.

Captain Slackvore was a complete dichotomy of character. He wore a long, brown trench coat, tattered in places and well-weathered. Its creases ran deep, and its surface was cracked from years of use. Yet underneath, he wore vibrant, tailored pants and a complexly embroidered vest, the material a shimmering purple interlaced with intricate floral patterns, and its shades perpetually shifting from slightly lighter to slightly darker than the rest of the outfit. Equally ornate boots with black velvet trim worked together with a dark, wide-brimmed Stetson to vertically frame the odd man.

A slimy smile that always made Ellie feel as if she was on the wrong end of a bad deal she couldn't understand hung below a pair of cunning, calculating eyes. His exact age was unclear. Older than Ellie for sure, but still far younger than one would expect of a man running a pirate crew. Then again, the man exuded a fierceness not difficult to pick up on.

"Melon girl!" he bellowed in welcome, a deep, booming voice scratched raw by the various questionable spirits Ellie knew the crew brewed, and occasionally sold.

"Captain Slackvore! It is so good to see you!" Ellie responded with a bright smile and a light, excited tone. Stepping forward, she threw her arms around his shoulders and pressed her entire body tightly against his, pretending the scene with Mr Thomas hadn't just happened.

"It always feels like an age between your visits," she said, pulling away. She planted her feet, ensuring she was standing with proper posture, then she met his eyes dead-on. Ellie knew from experience that with men like him, you had to show you were deserving of respect or they would devour you whole.

"How is the trade business? I always get so worried thinking about you running such valuable cargo with all those pirates out there."

Slackvore let out a baritone chuckle.

"Oh, not to worry, they all know to steer clear when *my* crew and I enter a system," he said with a dark grin. "I'm more interested in you. Another year on the farthest corners of colonised space. The Rike haven't been causing you too much trouble?"

"Not at all," Ellie said lightly. "I'm nested between two powerful neighbours that keep the swarms away, and we're capable of handling the few stray Rike that somehow make it through." Ellie raised her arm to place a hand on her chest. "Honestly, I don't know why everyone makes such a big deal of the Rikes. They barely disturb me."

Slackvore's eyes followed the movement of her hand. When she moved it away, his eyes remained on her cleavage. She discreetly clasped her hands and pulled her arms in, pressing certain assets together and making them pop in a way that numbed men's brains.

Ellie tried to focus inward, to push back the strain in her throat and calm her rapidly beating heart. Showtime had begun, and she had exactly one chance to get this right. Slackvore might have an inflated sense of self-worth, but he was by no means stupid. The pressure weighed down on her as she desperately tried to ignore it.

"So, I wouldn't worry about us, Captain; we're well protected and quite at ease."

To Ellie, it sounded as if she was able to keep her tone just as light and deniably flirty as before, despite the strain in her throat. But as she spoke, Slackvore's eyes narrowed suspiciously.

Heat was rising to her head, accompanied by the small beads of sweat beginning to form under her hair.

"But if you are fine, and I am fine—" She mentally kicked herself at the stilted dialogue, her desperation to move on rising. "Then may I interest you in some of the produce behind me?"

Ellie turned her head, trying to use the flush she knew she must have to her advantage.

"After all, I did bring it all this way, just for you," she said, reaching up to idly play with a free strand of hair. Her emotions still raged dangerously inside. Ellie shunted them back, locking them down with as much determination as she could muster.

The captain smiled a wide, toothy grin.

"Of course!" he said, looking over her cart. "Though, such a *small* harvest. I feel downright terrible that I might not be able to make your trip worth the time."

This, at least, Ellie had been expecting.

"I know I may not have the *biggest* harvest," Ellie emphasised as she bowed slightly to him, giving him a clear view of her weighty cleavage. She kept her eyes down so he could feel as though he was stealing a glimpse, as if she didn't know exactly where he was looking.

"But all my melons are hand-reared, nurtured from the time they are saplings, given all the care and attention in the world, to grow into the largest, sweetest fruits you'll find anywhere on the frontier. This year especially, since I've finally managed to cultivate a, if I may say so, delicious new variety I call 'Butterfly Melons'."

Ellie straightened slowly and deliberately, giving the captain time to pretend he was looking elsewhere.

"I'd be….so grateful if you'd try one," Ellie said shyly as she averted her gaze, tilting her head and laying it on thick.

"Well now." Slackvore leaned in a little, lowering his voice as if they were sharing a personal, intimate moment. So close she could feel the heat of his breath against her cheek. "What kind of ship's Captain would I be if I refused such a reasonable request?"

Hook. Line. Sinker.

Ellie suppressed a large smile, stealing a longing glance towards him before turning about.

The moment she'd turned away, Ellie gave a very Alayna-like eye roll. *Captain* Slackvore evidently thought he was being clever, subtly inserting his title into the conversation.

I suppose this is the part where my poor inner farm girl throws a hand to her head and falls hopelessly in love.

Ellie chided herself internally. That wasn't the state of mind she should be in right now, especially as she was so highly strung already. Ellie needed to be confident, flirty, and seemingly open to his advances to shake as much money out of the dirty old pirate as possible.

To that end, she swung her hips as she walked to one side of the cart; gently running a hand over Jonathan's shoulder as he stood by the yoke, diligently doing his best to be invisible. Ellie selected one of the golden, basketball-sized fruits, holding it tightly against her as she walked back with it in both arms.

Ellie held out the melon to the captain. When he reached out to take it, she moved her hands to rest lightly over his.

"If…if I may," she said, stepping closer.

The butterfly melon was smooth, but not completely circular. Its edges bulged in eight directions as if someone had taken a balloon and tied a string too tightly around it, looking almost like a pumpkin or garlic clove. The segments curved inwards, meeting at the top and bottom, with the top having the stub of a vine poking out from it. Ellie guided one of Slackvore's hands to the top, before slipping her own away, her movements slow and longing. Slackvore might have been holding an entirely new fruit in his hands, unique in all the universe, but his gaze was fixed squarely on her.

Good.

"Carving melons has always been one of the main obstacles stopping people from eating them. The rinds are so thick you usually need a large knife and a thick chopping block to get through them. They're fine once cut, but they're more challenging to eat than, say, a banana or an apple. And certainly not something children can prepare for themselves. One of my main goals when cultivating my Butterfly Melons was to fix that problem. If you'd be so kind as to press your fingers into the top, you should feel the flesh give way a little, which will give you enough purchase to just—"

Ellie raised her hands, curling her fingers and motioning like she was ripping something in half.

Slackvore looked to the melon, back to her, then back to the melon. Playing along, he did as she asked, gripping the melon by its vine stub for purchase. He dug his finger into the top and pulled as instructed, visibly jumping as an entire section came away with a wet snap; it left him gripping a neat slice in one hand, long, juicy strands still connecting it to the main body.

Ellie's excitement was growing as Slackvore gave a final tug, lifting the slice to glisten wetly in the sun.

"The area directly by the vine has been carefully cultivated to be soft enough to pierce with your fingers, but the rest of the rind is still thick enough to resist damage during shipping. These fruits don't bruise or mar, and with just a wipe down, they display beautifully anywhere across the Conviction. Even after months of travel in a ship's hold. And that is ignoring their main selling point."

Ellie decided to play off her excitement and risk overstepping her bounds just a little. She understood Slackvore had to keep an air of authority about him at all times and was fiercely protective of his personal space. But he hadn't seemed to mind when she'd guided his hand before. And besides, how would it look to his crew working about them if he *did* reject a beautiful woman who was only trying to get close to him?

So, Ellie stepped in close, very close, as she tried to force a blush onto her face. Her movements were slow and deliberate, and she looked down as if in embarrassment again, able to feel his breath on her forehead as they were barely a hand's width apart. Ellie delicately placed her hands over his and gently tugged, guiding the slice towards his face.

"Would you mind having a taste?" Ellie asked, bashful.

Slackvore paused to take in the aroma.

Ellie couldn't help but feel a swell of hope as his eyes fluttered. Raising the fruit the last little way, Slackvore took a bite, his eyes opening wide. Now was the time to press the advantage.

"The internal taste and consistency is like the softest parts of a mango. The sweetness is due to being mixed with peach, mangosteen and just a touch of blood orange. The plant reproduces outside the fruit so there are no hidden seeds. It took seasons of trial and error, but I finally modified the plant's xylem and phloem to grow near microscopic, meaning there is no pulp or pith. And just this year, with the help of the rains, I was finally able to grow them to a size worth selling. They are, without a doubt, the most complex, most time, effort and resource-intensive plants I have ever cultivated, grown specifically to take the intergalactic market by storm. I'm the only producer in the whole universe. And I'm selling, directly, to you, *Captain*."

She'd unwittingly been growing short of breath. As she finished, the bottom dropped out of her stomach to be replaced with a flock of nervous butterflies, their wings tickling her insides as hope warred with dread.

Ellie looked to Slackvore. An electric jolt shot through her as she realised something: he was smiling.

Fair enough, it was like a pit viper smiling at a cornered mouse, but a smile, nonetheless.

"Ellie White, this is why you have always been my favourite farmer," Slackvore exclaimed, raising the bitten melon slice into the air. "If this doesn't shut those spoilt interbrats up, nothing will!" A touch of venom entered his tone.

Seeming to have forgotten himself for a moment, he lowered back down, leaning towards Ellie, looking her dead in the eye with a predatory grin.

"I'll give you three dols *per melon*. How many do you have?"

Ellie was completely bewildered, her eyes widening. Slackvore had never made such a direct or generous offer to her before.

"E-eight crates, thirty-two individual melons. It's a low number because it's the first year they've been a viable harvest," Ellie stuttered and over-explained, kicking herself. She needed to rein it in, or Slackvore would take advantage of her in other ways. The man always had a knack for extracting his pound of flesh. Literally, at times, depending on who he was dealing with.

"Perfect," he almost growled in a dark tone, looking off to the side, smiling at something Ellie couldn't see.

"I'll be happy to help load them up once we confirm prices for my water and snow melons," Ellie said, bowing her head and doing a slight curtsey, hoping to draw his attention back to their other business. Alas, Slackvore was having none of it.

"Yes, yes," he said, waving dismissively, seemingly losing all interest in her and appearing more than a modicum annoyed at being pulled from his thoughts. "What was the price the previous year?"

"Th-thirty-eight cents per watermelon, forty-one per snow?" Ellie choked in surprise.

"Deal," Slackvore said immediately, holding out his hand.

Ellie blinked.

No way.

Ellie carefully stepped forward to raise her hand under his. The movement seemed painfully slow as her mind screamed desperately to hurry before he could back out. This was amazing, remarkable… exciting! She felt as if in a dreamworld where every wish came true.

Slackvore didn't even yank his hand away at the last moment like she was almost expecting. Instead, the blue circles appeared over the backs of their hands, confirming their transaction.

Ellie's eyes widened as the numbers rose in her field of vision. She couldn't believe she'd just got away with it.

Fair enough, Ellie hadn't technically lied. Slackvore hadn't specified *which* previous year, so she'd chosen the one with the highest prices.

"It was a pleasure doing business with you, Captain," Ellie said calmly and sweetly. "I hope your voyages are pleasant and you find success with my melons."

"Hmm?" Slackvore scratched his chin absentmindedly, almost as if he'd forgotten she was there. His face jerked as he seemed to snap out of it, his regular greasy smile returning a moment later.

"Of course, Ms White. Here, let me get that for you." Raising his hand, he motioned with two fingers. A handful of crew members came running up, causing Jonathan to jump as they began unloading the crates from their little cart.

"Now that you've fleeced me for all I'm worth," he continued, locking eyes with her and dropping to an almost sultry tone. "Why don't you go see our good friend Breacher? He should still be camped out by the bottom of the ramp if the flathead hasn't walked off to find a concrete wall to bash his skull against. I've brought many useful items to sell; you could go giving me back all those dols you just stole." He winked.

"I'm sure your prices would be more than fair," Ellie said politely, lying through her teeth.

Ellie stepped forward, wrapping Slackvore in a tight hug, once again pressing her whole body against him as tightly as she could. Ellie always did her best to ensure he enjoyed the experience, planting positive associations into his mind when thinking about her, reinforcing the idea for next year.

"Until next year, Captain. Stay safe." Ellie stepped back, bowing her head deeply. Turning, she stepped away, decisively cutting off any drawn-out goodbyes. Running her hand along Jonathan's shoulder as she passed, the frail boy diligently brought about the now empty cart and followed beside her. Ellie kept deliberately swinging her hips as she moved out of

Slackvore's field of vision. Jonathan didn't need to be told to stay to the side, not behind her blocking the view. Despite having never openly discussed it, Jonathan always seemed to know exactly what she was doing. Instinctively, he did everything he could to support her.

After a few minutes of walking, they crossed over the top of the ramp, making their way down the long slope. Ellie couldn't stop herself from staring in disbelief at the semi-transparent numbers hovering in her vision. They kept timing out and disappearing, and she kept calling them back up.

This is more than we've ever had before. Ever, ever, ever!

Ellie had worked tirelessly on her Butterfly Melons, inputting many years of genetic manipulation using a starter kit she'd stolen off some far-off station during transit, then slaving over alleles until everything combined just the way she wanted. She'd really believed they would sell, that they held such unique properties.

But in the back of her mind was always a niggling doubt keeping her reality in check. They'd be too hard, the crop would fail, they'd turn sour or infertile or any number of other scenarios that would ruin everything, just like it always did. Nothing could ever seem to go right, let alone the runaway success she'd just experienced. With Slackvore of all people!

As they neared the bottom of the ramp, Ellie turned to Jonathan.

"Jonathan, leave the cart with me. I need you to run off, find Alayna, and bring her back here."

Jonathan tilted his head slightly in surprise.

"Are…are you sure?" he asked.

"Yes," Ellie said firmly, laying her hand on the yoke and lifting it slightly. "Now go. *Run,"* she urged.

Jonathan stood there a moment, still uncertain, staring into her face as if searching for confirmation. Ellie kept her expression serious. When Jonathan realised this wasn't a joke or a test, he turned. Jonathan planted his feet, looked out to the surrounding crowd and launched forward. His skinny legs pumped hard as he sprinted off, head turning this way and that, looking for Alayna.

Ellie sighed, stepping around the yoke and holding up the now much lighter cart. Jonathan might not always be the most capable in certain situations, but she could always trust him to give his best in anything she asked. Ellie wasn't quite sure where she'd be without him. The thought brought with it an unwanted sombreness. She batted at the storm pressing against her window.

Not yet. Not yet, she told it.

Ellie might have finished with Slackvore, but the day was not over, far from it. She grasped the surprise and hope that had taken root in her chest and used it as a ward against the negative feelings. Relaxing her stance, Ellie began pulling the cart forward. Around one side of the ramp, a large stall had been set up.

Ellie had to pause and manoeuvre around the many mechs and loaders still moving huge containers of produce. Even in the relative bustle, Ellie was able to spot her quarry from a distance.

Breacher stood looking bored out of his mind behind the counter. Several other crew members worked the shelves beside him, leaving Breacher to stare blankly into space.

Ellie hadn't heard the story of how he had earned the name 'Breacher', but she could make an educated guess. The bald man was nothing short of monolithic, an enormous slab of meat and muscle, supposedly acting as Slackvore's quartermaster. It wasn't difficult to imagine him taking up an entire doorway, charging through and acting as a meat shield for the men coming in behind him, two or three abreast. He surpassed even Tannis Mathews in size. But where Mr Mathews was a down-to-earth farmer with kind eyes and soft edges over his strong arms, Breacher's skin looked stretched to bursting over bulging, sinewy muscles.

The overly defined cordage was a clear indicator of deep muscle manipulation taken well past what would have been the Conviction's legal limit.

Ellie was sure if Breacher and Mr Mathews ever came to wrestle, the mountains would be shaken loose from their foundations.

Pausing for a deep breath, she took a moment to prepare herself, needing to play a different character for Breacher. Ellie might not have to put so much effort into trying to outmanoeuvre a slimy viper as with Slackvore, but it was offset by the sheer amount of energy she would need to put into her performance.

"Breacher!" Ellie squealed excitedly.

She dropped the yoke and rushed forward as the man turned at the sound of her voice, his face lighting up the moment he saw her. Ellie sprinted the last few metres to the stall. Without breaking stride, she leapt on top of the counter, using it to launch herself at him. She impacted Breacher dead on, wrapping her arms around his thick neck and squeezing tightly.

"How have you been? How have you *been*? I've missed you so much; I have so much to tell you!" Ellie exclaimed excitedly in the highest, girliest voice she could manage. The trunks that Breacher called arms closed around her as he burst out laughing. Thankfully, the near-crushing hug took on most of her weight as wrapping her arms around Breacher's neck left Ellie's feet dangling, barely even reaching his knees.

"Melon girl! How have you been?" Breacher's voice was so deep, Ellie swore she could hear it echoing around inside his chest. It gave her the impression of some great, slumbering beast buried far beneath the planet's surface. Its voice resonating from the deep, bouncing off the slick stone walls of underground caverns. Holding him this tight, Ellie could feel it vibrating her eyeballs when he spoke.

"Fantastic!" Ellie exclaimed. "The rains have been beautiful this season. And a new strain of melon I've worked so hard on really impressed the captain. I'm just so..." Ellie worked herself up until she let out a squeal.

"And then I get to see my favourite goliath in all the frontier. Oh, I love export day *so much!*" Ellie injected as much exuberance into her mannerisms as she could.

The big man chuckled.

"That's wonderful! It's always great hearing how your year went." Breacher hugged even tighter. Ellie endured as much as she could but had to politely motion and push away as her spine felt just about to pop. There was no doubt in Ellie's mind the big man could snap her like a twig if he wanted. Thankfully, he placed her back on top of the counter, still intact.

Now safely on the counter, Ellie crouched to lower herself back to the ground, taking advantage of the position to hide the desperation with which she sucked huge gulps of air into her lungs.

"There are so many things I can't wait to tell you. But you first, you first! I want to hear all about your adventures through space and the wild frontier. I almost never hear about anything on this little farm planet," Ellie said, encouraging him to speak first. And speak he did. Breacher began telling her about his year and the 'adventures' he'd had along the way. About life on a ship like the Blister Fang and the rugged, untamed nature of the frontier. Some of it was even new.

As he spoke, Ellie delicately leaned forward, resting her elbows on the counter and letting certain assets pronounce themselves against the fit of her dress. She nodded, smiled, and acted just a little flirty, telling her own stories as the conversation shifted back and forth, but always trying to keep the big man talking about himself, her eyes wide in wonder. And in deviousness…

Ellie was used to people stealing glances at her. Watching her from the corner of their eye as she walked past. Her natural form tended to draw a lot of attention, mostly, but not exclusively, from men. But most people would at least act with some level of finesse or decorum, both of which seemed entirely beyond the giant. Whenever Ellie took the reins of conversation, Breacher stood there, staring decidedly lower than her eyes, jaw hanging loose.

He was harmless enough, but Ellie still had to hide her amusement. The man was about as bright as a bag of rocks and as subtle as a brick in a blender.

That did at least make it easier for Ellie. Breacher ate up her 'excited schoolgirl' character whole and unquestioningly, including the wrapper, carton, and probably the whole shelf on which it sat.

After a while of conversing back and forth, Ellie decided to press on. Her heart rate rose as she grew nervous. Had Slackvore communicated how much he'd paid her? Would Breacher know how much she had to bargain with? Ellie had never had this much to trade with before, and a fear that she might lose it all began to creep up her spine.

Ellie giggled as he finished a story, leaning languidly to one side and freeing up an arm to motion to the piles of stock behind him.

"And what have you brought with you this year? I don't suppose you were able to get that spa bath, were you?" Ellie smiled, referencing a conversation from previous years.

"'fraid not. I did find a nice one on Calcetti, but the captain got crabby about storage space when I tried to bring it aboard," he said with an amused smile. "Though I'm sure we'll have something you can use."

As Breacher moved to run down the various items they had available, Ellie's focus snapped to one in particular. As they spoke, she'd been eyeing the various bins and wares stacked on quick-collapse shelving, half of it looking as though the crew had just raided a junkyard and brought back the first items they'd found. But with Breacher moving out of the way, a whole new section had been revealed to her.

Ellie listened to Breacher as he pointed out an assortment of objects, the other crew within the stall instinctively ducking as he swung his arms around. They seemed to have a near-supernatural sense of where the giant was at all times. Ellie wasn't entirely sure how many other worlds the Blister Fang stopped at, but she imagined it would only take being thrown into the shelving once or twice by an idle sweep of Breacher's arm for the crew to develop the skill.

Looking at what was available, Ellie pointed to a small auxiliary battery, asking to see it so it didn't seem like she was too eager for the item she actually wanted. Breacher handed it over and Ellie inspected it idly, flipping it in her hand and trying to look interested.

"This could do," she said. Tapping it in her hand, Ellie let her eyes casually sweep over the shelves, finally settling on what she'd spotted earlier.

"Would it be too much trouble if I could see that as well, Breacher?" Ellie asked, pointing.

"Nothing's too much bother for you," Breacher responded with a grin, turning around to pick up the package and deposit it on the counter.

The fact it was still in what looked like its original box was nothing short of a miracle, though the cardboard had been worn to tatters, to the point the graphics were barely distinguishable. Huge rips in the corners were held together with copious amounts of brown packing tape.

Ellie reached in, feeling her hands land on cool metal, the smooth form reassuring her rapidly beating heart. Ellie lifted, pulling the small wind turbine from its box.

"Oh, don't you have some...character," Ellie said for Breacher's benefit, rubbing the ball of her hand along its length like she was trying to buff off some of the encrusted dirt. "Do you have any idea if this still works?" she asked.

Turning it sceptically, the weight was nevertheless reassuring in her hands. It had clearly seen many years in the sun and gone through its fair share of repairs. It bore mounting brackets for four fins. However, at some point, someone had crudely drilled through the housing to be able to mount just three roughly equal distances apart. Ellie was careful not to let the metal burrs cut into her skin. She'd have to sell her soul to borrow someone's auto-doc if she caught tetanus.

Placing it gently on the counter, she tipped the box towards her, seeing three blades loose inside. Two looked as if they may have been original, the other a discoloured copper pipe with a piece of sheet metal welded to it, hammered into a vague curve to catch the wind.

"It should. Can't imagine I would have bought it if it didn't," Breacher replied.

"It's... it's just it doesn't look as though it does..." Ellie led, picking it up again and holding it out to him.

"Yeah, it doesn't, does it?" he said, taking the smooth cone shape. Where Ellie needed two hands to properly support it, Breacher took it in one as though he didn't even register the weight.

"One of the runts might have got it," he growled, turning towards the other crew in the stall, looking as though about to storm off.

"Oh but, could we test it first? I don't want to go getting anyone in trouble!" Ellie said quickly. The turbine may have survived years of outdoor life, weathering sun, storms, and wind. But if Breacher stomped off and started berating one of the crew, Ellie was sure it would *not* survive the violent shaking it would receive as he argued. Assuming it wasn't used as a cudgel to bludgeon someone outright.

"Hmm, I suppose we could," Breacher said, still eying off the other crew, who all seemed to be finding excuses to duck behind shelves or boxes.

"Please?" Ellie said sweetly, turning her body side on and discretely fluttering her eyelashes at him.

Breacher paused, a big, dopey grin spreading across his face as he seemed to zone out momentarily.

"Uh...okay," he said airily.

Oh Breacher... How gullible you are. I love you for it!

Ellie almost felt guilty for playing him like she was, but she reminded herself that getting this wind turbine would provide year-round energy, even throughout the night. It would solve all their power problems, keeping the turret charged and allowing her to run the heater during winter. Alayna and Jonathan wouldn't have to freeze during the colder months, shivering against her as they balled up on the sofa. Suddenly, Ellie didn't feel so guilty.

Breacher searched around for a few moments. He pulled out what Ellie assumed, given the context, was an electrical measuring device. Breacher put the main body of the turbine down and slid off the outer shell. He began sticking two long, metal probes against various areas, periodically pausing to spin the main shaft with his hand.

Ellie stood by, watching him work, somewhat surprised he seemed to know what he was doing. Ellie had no idea what was happening exactly, but the sight of the probes and wires dug a deep memory out of the recesses of her mind.

One memory was where she was holding open a metal flap as her father spliced into some protected conduit. The fear experienced in the eternal night of the hive world's lower levels echoed faintly even now. But the promise of free, unlimited power overruled the danger of getting caught by the city's wardens.

Funny how so many of her problems were caused, and resolved, by power.

Beep.

The meter let out a little electric sound. Breacher held the probes in place with one hand and spun the shaft with the other. The device let out a long, warbled tone the entire time he spun it.

"And there it is. It works," Breacher said.

"Oh, I'm so glad," Ellie replied, fixing him with a genuinely happy smile. "This would keep us warm during the winter!"

Ellie immediately kicked herself. The pirate crew were not the kind of people you let know what was important to you. You would get no sympathy, only extortion as Slackvore had proven, time and time again.

Breacher didn't seem to react to her slip. No greasy smile spread across his face like she could picture happening with Slackvore.

"I'd rather just huddle around a roaring fire if you ask me. But I'm glad it'll be of use to you." Breacher said obliviously, slipping the outer shell back into place and returning the whole assembly to its box.

"I suppose we should talk prices then. It would be so wonderfully useful, but I don't have much to spare," Ellie said, trying to force an embarrassed tone into her voice.

"Well, I can't think of anyone I'd prefer to have it. So let's say… Six hundred and fifty dols." Breacher said after a moment's consideration.

"Oh goodness," Ellie exclaimed, straightening and placing a hand against her chest in shock. "I'd need three years of harvests to afford that."

Breacher looked confused momentarily, as if what she'd said made no sense.

"Well, how much *do* you have?" he asked, scratching his head.

Ellie took a moment, running multiple expressions across her face as if she were in deep consideration, hesitating, reaching out with a hand, only to draw it back again.

"I could afford… a hundred and twenty dols? Would that be enough?" Ellie asked with a worried tone.

Breacher frowned.

"Sorry, Ellie," he said slowly. "The captain would have my head if I sold it for that low. We do have to haul this half again the width of the Conviction just to make it out here. Can't go giving it away like that."

Ellie visibly wilted, sagging against the counter.

"I see," she said sorrowfully. "That's understandable, and I certainly wouldn't want to go getting you in trouble or taking advantage of the captain. Maybe I could borrow from the neighbours or…" she trailed off.

After a long moment, Ellie continued.

"What's the absolute minimum you *could* go, Breacher?" she asked, looking up as if searching for hope. He looked down to meet her eyes. He stood there, considering for several long heartbeats, mouth set in a hard line.

"Two hundred and thirty," he said. "As long as I make *some* profit off it, the captain shouldn't go venting me out the airlock. *Shouldn't,"* he emphasised.

Ellie turned to look around, eyes scanning the crowd for options. To her immense surprise and satisfaction, Jonathan and Alayna were standing a small distance away, watching her. Ellie gasped audibly before waving and calling out, "Alayna! Come over here, quick!"

The skinny girl came rushing towards her, and Ellie couldn't help but notice the sack she carried over her shoulder swung heavily as she did so.

"What? What is—" The girl didn't have time to finish as Ellie wrapped her arm around the girl's shoulder and jerked her to face away from Breacher, pressing their heads together and forming a two-person scrum.

"Hold out your hand," Ellie hissed as she tugged the top of her own dress as low as it would go.

Alayna, confused, still did as she was asked. Ellie laid her palm flat over Alayna's, the two blue rings appearing as she transferred funds to Alayna.

"What!" Alayna exclaimed with a start.

"Shhh, we need it!" Ellie said at a conspicuous volume before releasing the girl. Twirling on the spot, the bottom of her dress fanning out as she did so, Ellie exclaimed, "two hundred and twenty-six!"

"Two hundred and twenty-six dols, Breacher. Is that enough? It's all we have. Goodness me, I'm so sorry; let me think where I can get the four."

Ellie grabbed the edges of the counter with her hands, leaning forwards while arching her back as if about to give birth in a distressed state. She bobbed with nervous energy, trying to wear a most dismayed and worried expression.

Of course, the nervous bobbing was causing certain parts of her to bounce more than others, and with the lowest neckline she could manage, she may as well have been pointing a neon sign to her cleavage.

The big man stood there, slack-jawed for a long moment. Ellie waited, expecting a delay until his mental processes kicked in and he spoke again. Except he didn't speak when Ellie expected him to. She waited a little longer, then a little longer again. A few minutes had passed before Ellie thought she might have broken the simple man and stopped bouncing.

"Breacher?" she asked shyly, a touch of nervousness in her voice.

Breacher leaned back, the spell breaking slowly, to finally meet her eyes again. He seemed shocked to see her. Then the man's mouth tightened to a thin line, and he seemed to come to a decision.

"Of course, it is; what kind of man would I be if I said no?"

"Oh, Breacher! Thank you, thank you, thank you!" Ellie squealed and pulled the big man down into a hug by the scruff of his shirt. "You've no idea how much of a difference this will make!" Ellie said honestly, now the deal had been done.

Pulling back, she scooped up the box with the turbine and its blades and held it tightly against her chest.

"I always knew you were a good man Breacher, but I can't tell you how much I appreciate it," she said sweetly, holding out her hand. Breacher held out his as well, the blue circles flashing briefly as Ellie transferred every dol in her account. Ellie also made sure to transfer the extra few cents until her funds were completely zeroed out. This would cause a minor alert to appear in Breacher's vision alerting him that her account was empty, and he'd be at risk of criminal prosecution if he attempted to withdraw any further. Though there weren't exactly any wardens around to enforce it. A small trick Ellie had used to her advantage multiple times before.

"Thank you so much again Breacher, thank you so much," Ellie said, bowing repeatedly as she began backing away.

"Oh, yes. You're welcome," Breacher said, surprise entering his eyes as he realised she was leaving. The big man looked conflicted for a long moment as if wrestling with some dilemma. Eventually, his brows set, and he called after her.

"Perhaps we could grab dinner before we take off?"

"Oh, I'd have loved to but I'm sorry, Breacher; you know how it is. I need to get home and install this before nightfall. Next year though?" Ellie said, still bowing and backing away, hoping to hide behind her schoolgirl character's exuberance, reinforced by her genuine excitement.

"Safe travels, Breacher; thank you so much," she called one final time as she cast her biggest, brightest smile too.

Ellie continued to back away until she passed Alayna, grabbing the thin girl by the hand and pulling her away. Ellie turned and began to walk quickly, motioning for Jonathan to follow. She was keenly aware she'd pushed it a little far, but the risk had been worth it. There came a buzzing excitement in the pit of her stomach, feeling triumphant for the first time since...well, possibly for the first time ever. Ellie seemed to have successfully swindled the swindlers, scoring a perfect game like never before. She needed to get home and end the day, as it could only go downhill from here. She didn't know what Alayna had managed to get, but it didn't matter; she'd eat marshweed from now until the next harvest if it meant getting cleanly away.

"Come on you two, we're leaving," Ellie said as she hurried them along.

"But I'm not done getting us food!" Alayna protested.

"It doesn't matter. I'm quite sure you've done an amazing job, but we're getting out of here before Breacher comes chasing after us with a flower bouquet. Now put that in the cart and help pull."

Jonathan paused for just a moment as Alayna, still eyeing Ellie sceptically, lifted the sack into the back and tied it closed with a loose knot. Ellie carefully placed the turbine box down, bracing it in the corner. She angled their rifle as a makeshift buttress to hold it in place and prevent it from sliding around. Ellie couldn't help but check again and confirm the turbine was actually there with all its blades. She was still having difficulty believing she'd done it.

"So, are you not going to tell me what's just happened?" Alayna asked pointedly.

"Shush, not now, later," Ellie replied, eager to be on their way.

Stepping around the corners, Ellie and Jonathan lined up against the yoke and began to pull away from the spaceport. After a moment of deliberate sulking, Alayna seemed to sense Ellie's energy. Alayna scoffed in displeasure, before stepping in and pressing hard against the yoke. Jonathan followed Alayna's lead, seeing how much effort the redhead put in. Together, the three of them began making good time towards home.

Five: A Cold Night's Tears

It was just hitting sunset by the time they trundled up to their small container home. Ellie had begun to relax; as the distance behind them increased, it seemed less and less likely some of the crew would come screaming after them.

Ellie wanted to breathe a sigh of relief, but dared not until the wind turbine was installed and generating power.

"I need you two to help me with this," Ellie said as they rested the cart on its stand. "Jonathan, can you get a thick branch from the firewood pile, straight as you can find. Alayna, could you please bring me the spare turret cable? Do you know where it is?"

Jonathan headed around the house dutifully. Alayna scoffed.

"Of course, I know where it is!" she snapped indignantly, walking off.

Ellie moved around to pull the turbine from the box. She sat in the rear of the cart, carefully attaching the fins and eyeing up their roof until both Jonathan and Alayna returned.

Installing the turbine took only a little time, just enough for the yellows and oranges of sunset to deepen to the blues and purples of twilight.

Ellie climbed down from the roof, dragging the cable behind her. She was ready to make the final connection. She'd mounted the turbine to the thick, solid branch Jonathan had found and lashed it to a pointed corner on one side of the roof. It now stood as the tallest part of their home, free to spin in all directions and held together by dried and tightly wound melon vines. Many, many paranoid knots held it firmly in place.

"Okay. Here we go. Are we ready?" Ellie asked, holding the end of their only spare power cable in her hand.

"Y-ye—" Jonathan began.

"YES!" Alayna interrupted impatiently.

"Okay then. Here goes," Ellie said as she firmly slotted the plug into the small power distribution unit mounted on the side of their house. It slid in with a final *thunk*. A small yellow light began blinking next to it, turning a solid green after just a few moments. Ellie rushed inside, running over to their house assistant's display and navigating to the power status.

Her heart jumped as there it was. The house assistant had recognised the turbine and automatically integrated it into their systems. It sat listed with a graph and numbers showing how many volts and amps it was providing, all working as it should.

"It works!" Ellie exclaimed with relief, turning to hug Alayna and Jonathan, who had followed her. "It works; it actually works!"

A giddy, light feeling fluttered around the pit of her stomach as if her whole torso had suddenly emptied out. Despite all logic to the contrary, in the back of her mind, Ellie had still been waiting for the hammer to drop, for the sword of Damocles to come falling down and bring ruin upon their heads. That was what reality always was. Despite her best efforts and determined resistance to hope, it was always a disappointment. More pain and agony were always waiting around the corner, always handing out only enough mercy to keep them clinging to life and extending their torment.

And yet, here they were. Slackvore hadn't bankrupted them, Breacher hadn't forced her into an arranged marriage, the crew hadn't come chasing after them and the wind turbine hadn't caught fire the moment it was plugged in. The extra power was going to solve so many of their problems. It was as if life was opening up like a book before her. Tears of joy came streaming down her face. She sighed as Jonathan delicately wrapped his arms around her waist, and even Alayna stood there, letting Ellie hold her without complaint.

With this, they'd be able to keep the turret charged permanently, running the heaters in winter and even powering the transmitter. Ellie wouldn't have to scrape by on the minimum cooking time, risking giving them all botulism to ensure they weren't ripped apart by Rike in the night. Such a sense of euphoric relief washed over her that her knees began to shake, and she sagged forward.

Ellie hadn't acknowledged how much her head had been spinning, both Alayna and Jonathan letting out a surprised start as they caught her. The two quickly guided her to the lounge, where she sat heavily.

"Ellie, are you okay?" Jonathan asked nervously.

"Yes, yes! I'm fine," she answered with a genuine smile. "It's just been an emotional day."

Jonathan stood, looking lost.

"Go get her a glass of water!" Alayna snapped.

Jonathan jumped, before turning quickly towards the kitchen.

Alayna sat beside Ellie.

Ellie wanted to reach over and straighten Alayna's straps and hair, but while her mind and chest turned light and giddy, her arms were now incredibly heavy.

Alayna turned and eyed Ellie up and down for a long moment.

The young girl turned, facing rigidly forward.

"I'll cook dinner tonight," Alayna loudly announced.

"Alayna, you don't have to—"

"I'M COOKING!" she snapped, suddenly standing. "Just…" Alayna said in a softer tone, lowering her hands from shoulder level down to her waist. "Lie down or something," she finished, motioning along the length of the sofa.

Ellie complied. After all, she was still dizzy, and once Alayna set her mind on something, Ellie would have better luck stopping a volcano from erupting than dissuading the girl. Ellie lay her head down on the armrest, stretching out. She'd just relax a moment and recover until dinner was ready.

It felt as though she'd barely closed her eyes, a soft fuzz slowly surrounding her consciousness, before a misplaced thump yanked her attention back to the present. Ellie opened her eyes again, only to find herself shrouded in darkness.

Ellie sat up, her blanket falling from her shoulders. She looked about; the gaps in the shutters let in a soft, pale light that washed over their quaint living space.

Ellie rose slowly, swinging her legs over the edge of the cushions. She hadn't realised how much her muscles ached as she stretched. From what Ellie could see through the shutters, the colours of the sunset were well and truly gone. Dropping her eyes, Ellie saw a bowl and a tall glass of water set before her. She must have slept completely through dinner.

Reaching out, Ellie took the bowl in her hands, some residual warmth seeped through its edges, promising she hadn't been out *too* long. Ellie gripped the spoon poking out the side, and after a quick mix, she lifted it to her mouth.

Ellie was momentarily taken aback as she swallowed a thick dollop of potato soup. The texture rolled down her throat, hitting her stomach with a blooming heat. It lacked any of the milk or butter for which the recipe would traditionally call, their cold box being insufficient to keep dairy from going rancid. But even in the darkness, Ellie could make out a small sprinkling of dried jerky throughout the soup, its unmistakable salty meatiness making up for the deficit with its flavour. What had Alayna been able to procure to justify using so many potatoes in a single dish? Her curiosity didn't stop her from eating heartily.

With the last clink of metal on ceramic as she scraped the final blob away, Ellie sat back and sighed, feeling an odd sense of calm and evenness as she sat there in the quiet dark.

Their home wasn't large, and lacked basics such as a stove and even refrigeration. They sat on a small parcel of land, risking every day an attack from the Rike always one bad harvest away from starvation. Or at least a diet of marshweed, just a slower, more painful version of the same fate.

And yet, it didn't have the perpetual reek of the lower levels of a hive city. No roaming gangs were threatening to drag them from their beds, nor was their entire existence given as rent to some faceless landlord they would never know. What little they did have, out here on a distant frontier, was truly *theirs*.

Ellie stood, carefully picking up the bowl and glass and walking them over to the sink. Two more sets rested in the drying rack, quiet and still.

They're going to have a much better life here, she thought, leaning on the counter.

If Ellie was honest with herself, their ending up here was more a result of what they were running from than any deliberate plan. Almost.

They could have ended up on some transit station, or any number of semi-settled worlds with developed infrastructure. But then they'd have lived their entire lives from the gutter, squeaking by at the bare minimum forever. Their only chance at upward mobility was to start from somewhere no one else wanted to be, no one with the means to get there anyway. Ellie still remembered the terrifying moment when she'd had to make an unexpected choice: to jump ship and take her young siblings to a potentially hostile planet or spend forever hoping for a chance that would likely never come. She knew then that she was probably making the right choice. But with the struggle they'd experienced, the slow decline, the years of labour and uncertainty, only now did it feel as if Jonathan and Alayna might actually have a future.

Ellie took a deep breath. She turned and moved towards the door, unlocking it, then slipping out into the cold night air. As she climbed to the roof, she was almost surprised to see their wind turbine still spinning, slowly turning side to side in the gentle breeze. Ellie couldn't keep her eyes off it. Even as she sat atop the peak of their roof, wanting to look out over the valley, her gaze was drawn back.

Such a small thing. Such a small, simple thing. A few magnets, some coils of copper and a few other bits and pieces, and yet it represented such a milestone. With its power, they would be safer, healthier, and more comfortable. Ellie had spent so long struggling just to get the necessities of their survival that she could barely process it. And they still had their farm; there would be more melons to sell next year, and the year after that, and the year after that. They finally had a stable foundation beneath them, and could at last start accelerating away from simply surviving. Things were only going to get better from here.

Unless we end up like the Sayers.

Something tickled her cheek. She reached up with one hand, and her fingers came away wet. Her throat tightened, and her face screwed up. Ellie fought it for a moment, before finally letting her walls down. The storm she'd been holding back all day finally broke through. For the first time in a long while, Ellie let herself genuinely cry.

She cried for the Sayers, good people undeserving of what had happened to them. She cried for having to almost sell herself to Hunter, and for the shock of what had followed. She cried for the unbelievability of besting Slackvore, and the luck she'd had with Breacher. She cried for Jonathan and Alayna, for everything they had been through, and their future that suddenly seemed so bright. And last, she cried and cried for herself because for the first time she could remember, she didn't quite feel like a total failure.

Ellie cried so hard for so long that when she stopped, her breathing ragged and her head aching, she was sure it was only because her body had no more liquid left to give.

As she took long, shuddering breaths that misted in the air before her, Ellie looked upward. Her face was hot and puffy, and she'd made a complete mess of her hands and forearms. But for once, Ellie felt *better*. After all, she could see the stars now. She hadn't seen those for the first time until she was a teenager.

Forcefully wrestling the last of her emotions into submission, Ellie lowered her eyes to the landscape, to the rolling green hills, fields, and rivers glittering in the moonlight. Even Bellator Peak was standing silent sentinel—

That's new... Ellie thought.

In the distance, atop Bellator Peak, sat a new structure. A long, thin spire rose from its top, reaching high into the air. A single row of windows lined the tower near its apex, glowing with soft light from within. A compound spread out from its base, widening towards the bottom and spreading to cover the top of Bellator Peak, extending over its edges. Great struts supported the platform from beneath, anchored into the stone edges of the butte, a ring of tall walls circling its outer edge. A large structure sat behind the walls, against the tower's base.

Ellie was far too distant to make out any specific detail, yet she couldn't help but feel her curiosity perk up. Was this what those construction supplies she'd seen earlier were for?

On that thought, Ellie looked towards the spaceport. The flat concrete top sat visible in the night, empty. Had she slept through the ship taking off? How tired had she been?

As it turned out, very. For no sooner did the thought occur to Ellie than her shoulders sagged in exhaustion. Not only had she been pushing herself throughout the day to keep herself together and put forward a high-energy, enthusiastic front, but the long cry had drained her emotionally and physically, all on top of the last few frantic weeks of harvesting and preparing for market day and export. Ellie stood wearily, shooting one last look at the spaceport, at Bellator Peak, and at their turbine before slowly climbing down.

Slipping inside, Ellie locked the door behind her, making a point of double-checking the status of the turret and the shutters before finally moving towards the lounge. As she reached under to pull out their rifle's charge cable, it was already in place and plugged in. As she drew her hand back, a thought occurred to her.

"Set the heater to turn on tomorrow morning, please," she said quietly.

"What time would you like the heater set to?" the disembodied voice of the house assistant asked politely.

"Whenever I start to wake up?" Ellie replied, a small smile tugging at her mouth as she looked forward to waking in total warmth and comfort.

The house assistant chimed in acknowledgement as Ellie changed into her pyjamas and made herself comfortable. Pulling her blanket tight, she let out a long yawn before settling down. She began drifting off almost immediately, full of hope for what tomorrow would bring.

***

It had been several hours since sundown when a dark figure walked across the field, paying no mind to the vines of melon plants it was crushing beneath its feet. The solitary turret spun towards it as the automated weapon became aware of its presence. After a long moment, the barrels turned away, satisfied it was not a Rike. The figure continued past the turret, unbothered by the proximity even as it was appraised, approaching the tiny home.

It leant forward at the window as if trying to peer through the metal shutters. After a moment, it straightened again before striding around the side of the house.

Crouching down next to the empty cart and modest pile of firewood, the figure pulled a small black box from within its cloak. The device fitted easily in the figure's palm. Pressing the device onto the wall, it remained in place even as the figure withdrew its hands. With a few button presses, the device began transmitting an ultrasonic tone far too high for any human to hear. Its task now complete, the figure stood. It seemed to consider the wall with hatred, dark eyes glinting as if it able to see right through the corrugated metal. After a long moment, it turned and strode away into the night.

Tens of kilometres away, a Rike raised its head to the sky, thick, bony claws gouging into the dirt. It let out an enraged, guttural scream from deep within its throat, followed in kind by its many thousands of brethren. Almost as one, they began to move.

Six: Enemy at the Gates

The first Ellie knew of something being wrong was the high-pitched shriek of the house alarm tearing her from sleep. She shot upwards, heart leaping from her chest as the booming of their turret opening fire shook the place.

"Jonathan! Alayna!" Ellie screamed as she rolled off the sofa, diving for their rifle. Her hand closed around the hard Polyplast, knuckles white as the screeching of Rike tore through the night. The harsh, guttural sounds reached across the distance to rip into her soul. This wasn't the polite but insistent tone of their assistant detecting a stray scout at the edge of their sensors. This was the house screaming bloody murder at a threat it had no hope of combating.

There came the sound of a slamming door and pounding feet as Alayna and Jonathan came running down the stairs. The briefest moment of relief at seeing them was quickly torn away as she rushed to the window. Ellie thought she might have to point the rifle through the shutters and help their turret fight a hunting party. But her heart leapt into her throat as she took in the scene playing out beyond.

Bodies littered their field. Slumped, carapaced forms hunched over, claws stark and unmoving as they shone in the pale light. Yet despite the numbers already lying dead and bleeding into their field, still more were coming. Their turret swung wildly from side to side, dispatching Rike with inhuman efficiency as they charged forward. They leapt over their dead, tearing apart the ground as they bound forward with animalistic intent. Too many, moving too fast.

No sooner could Ellie make out an individual, its form taking shape out of the darkness, than it would come skidding to a lifeless halt, pushing forward a mound of freshly churned earth as it carved a furrow through the rich soil. But even given all the ammo in the world, their little turret wouldn't hold for long. In the distance, the dark ground *seethed* with the mass of countless Rike.

"What's happening?" Alayna screamed over the deafening sound.

Ellie ignored her as she sprinted past, panic rising to consume her as she slammed into the wall to stop herself, bashing their assistant's display with a finger. Ellie vaguely registered the turret's ammo counter dropping faster than she could read as she stabbed the button for their transmitter. It lit up a solid green, indicating it was active.

For a horrible moment, Ellie tried to speak, to say something, *anything*. But her throat closed, strangling her voice before it could be given life. Fear constricted her neck so tight she struggled to suck in enough air to remain conscious. Her vision swam as she became light-headed.

The Rike are coming for us. Does anyone read? Can you bring your mechs and your bombs? Can you please save us!

The words were clear in her mind; she knew what she had to say. Tears rolled down her cheek as their turret continued to fire, but the desperate panic clawing at her had frozen her completely.

"ELLIE!" Alayna screeched behind her.

"Help," Ellie said in a strangled tone, pushing against the block in her throat before finally managing to gasp, "HELP! This is Ellie White! The Rike are attacking my farm! Mr Jackdaw, Mrs Linden, can you hear me? Please, please, please, please…" Ellie was beginning to break down, comprehending how terrified she was. How inadequate she was…

She wouldn't be able to protect Alayna and Jonathan with just her little rifle.

A change in sound caused Ellie's head to jerk up, and she rushed with Jonathan and Alayna to the window. The powerful booming of the turret had stopped, its ammunition running dry. Ellie always knew a single drum wouldn't be enough to hold back anything but the occasional scout. But she'd had to choose between having ammunition as a contingency or food to keep them fed through a long winter. Ellie screwed her eyes shut in a moment of frustration.

Had she really made the wrong choice? Yet still, their turret continued to fire, the booms becoming replaced with multiple *brrt-zaps* as the turret switched to using its power supply to superheat the air at the back of its barrel, throwing the semi-liquid matter forward as a searingly hot plasma bolt.

Ellie watched in horror as the tide quickly changed, a plasma bolt hitting the side of a charging Rike, splashing against its carapace and burning through with a hiss, edges glowing red like newly forged metal. The Rike shrieked in rage, but continued to charge until a second bolt struck its forehead, the bolt burning through the thinner head plate into its skull. With the plasma bolts having less stopping power than a supersonic slug, the perimeter their turret had already been struggling to maintain began to collapse.

"Ellie! Ellie, it's Julie; Michael and the boys are on their way, do you read?" A tinny voice came from the assistant's display. Ellie ran over.

"Yes! Yes, I read, Mrs Linden; thank you, thank you!" Ellie said desperately.

"They'll be there in ten minutes, hun; just hang on, you hear?" Mrs Linden replied as if Ellie had just been struck in the chest.

"Oh, no, no, no, no! We're not going to last that long. They're right out—"

"Ellie, ELLIE!" Jonathan began pulling at her, desperately trying to get her to turn around. Ellie turned to him as he held up a flat piece of metal to her face. Jake's card…

Jake's card!

Ellie snatched it from his hands.

"Good job, Jonathan," Ellie said throatily. With a shaking hand, she pressed the etched circle in the corner of the card. Surprisingly, the edges of the circle lit up, spreading across the lettering until the card was glowing a rich blue. But nothing else happened.

Ellie pressed the circle again, flipping the card around in her hands but nothing changed; it simply remained lit as Ellie's stomach dropped out.

She leapt up in terror as something heavy slammed against the house, causing her to drop the card.

"Get back!" Ellie screamed at Jonathan and Alayna, the scrabbling of bone against metal filling the air. Mrs Linden's cries faded into the stream of noise. The cracks of light from outside were blotted out as multiple forms moved about. Alayna broke off and dashed to the kitchen. Before Ellie could call out to her, the shriek of tortured metal split the night as one of the shutters was torn from its housing. Light flooded in and Ellie could see the scuttling, skittering form of a Rike tearing at the remaining shutters.

Ellie raised the rifle with shaking hands, eyes wide with panic as the sounds of the house alarm, the screech and growls of the Rike and the thundering of thousands of sharpened hooves merged into one calamitous roar. Without really thinking about where she was aiming, Ellie pulled the trigger. Glass shattered as the plasma bolt shot out of the rifle and through the window. The Rike screeched in inhuman agony, pulling back desperately against its claw, now melted into the partially molten metal. It continued to try and rip its claw free with such force that, with a sickeningly wet crack, the entire front half of its limb snapped off, leaving sinewy trails to glisten in the light.

Even with the pain of losing a limb, it did not retreat. Instead, the Rike thrashed against the shutters repeatedly, splattering purple blood into the room from its amputated stump in a blind rage. Ellie had just enough time to register the sight of long, jagged fangs biting down on a second shutter before it too was torn away. The Rike disappeared into the space beyond for just a moment, before slamming back into the shutters. The Rike's force, weight, and sheer rage bent them inwards as it clawed through the gap. Claw-tipped arms flailed viciously, searching for purchase as it dragged itself halfway into the living room.

Ellie fired again. And again, the Rike screeched, enraged as the bolt struck its flank. The mottled red surface sizzled and popped, burning away in a cloud of discoloured smoke. It turned its head to fix its gaze on Ellie, beady eyes burning with pure hatred.

Ellie prepared to fire again when a banshee shriek every bit as furious and full of hate as the wails of a thousand Rike knocked her off guard. Alayna charged forward, brandishing their kitchen knife. Ellie watched as the small girl dove forward to drive the knife right between a pair of armoured plates, deep into the Rike's neck.

The walls reverberated with the sounds of screaming as the Rike tried to claw its way further inside, trapped between the twisted shutters. Alayna withdrew the knife and struck again, and again, and again. Blood spurted out and covered her as she screamed, her face morphing into a fierce grimace of rage. Ellie stepped back in fear as the thin girl took on a visage of a vengeful, demonic spawn just broken through the gates of hell.

The Rike continued to screech and wail, each one getting weaker than the last. It finally stopped altogether, hanging limply from the shutters, knife buried to the hilt in its neck.

"Alayna…" Ellie could see the girl's chest heaving with heavy breaths that billowed clouds of mist into the cold night air. Her hands were covered in purple blood up to her elbows as she held the knife in a shaking grip, hair and eyes wild as she gritted her teeth and bared them at her kill.

"Alayna...come here!" Ellie said in desperation, taking a step forward and lowering the rifle. Alayna turned to her, Ellie shuddering involuntarily as the girl's eyes showed the full extent of the berserker rage pumping through her veins.

But they were interrupted as a second heavy form slammed against the house, then a third, then a fourth. Multiple Rike began screaming as they tried to crawl through the gaps in the shutters, pushing each other aside, clawing at their dead brother.

"Alayna!" Ellie screamed, raising the rifle. The girl did not need to be told as she immediately dove away from the window. The body of the first Rike was ripped back through the shutters just as Alayna impacted the floor. Ellie fired, and fired, and fired again, pulling the trigger as quickly as she could line up the muzzle again after each shot. The *pop-zip* of the rifle drowned out the alarm, the room filling with the acrid stink of burning flesh and chitin.

Alayna combat crawled across the floor towards her, standing back up to take position beside Ellie as they backed away, the Rike momentarily held at bay by the weight of their own bodies. Their wild thrashings and the smell of seared meat seemed to whip them into a blood frenzy. No sooner did one pull its way through the gap than it was hauled back out by its brethren, each one all too eager to be the first to get in and tear them to pieces. Ellie couldn't even tell if their turret was firing anymore as more and more Rike began to pile against the window.

"I love you!"

The sound carried to her ears, bringing the revelation that Ellie had heard herself desperately cry the words out, the whole house groaning against the weight of the Rike.

Distantly, a roaring began to build in her ears as her back pressed against the far wall, barely able to feel the trigger beneath her finger anymore.

But the roaring continued to get louder and louder, overtaking the shrieks, wails and house alarm before metamorphosing into something physical. It wasn't just the blood roaring in her ears.

Suddenly, the Rike by the window exploded in blood, bone, and viscera, coating the inside of the house and causing Ellie to jerk away as some of it flew into her eyes. The heavy, thundering boom of cannon fire cut through the still screeching alarm, faster and more potent than their turret. And rising above that, the screaming wail of jet engines pushed into the red.

"Get out, get out now!" a voice roared over electronic speakers, a tone of urgency permeating the authoritarian bark. A familiar manner triggered recognition deep within Ellie's chest.

Before she could fully process what she was doing, moving on sheer survival instinct and terror, Ellie dropped the rifle, grabbing Alayna and Jonathan's hands and pulling them forward. The front door swung open automatically as the house assistant cleared the way for their escape.

The first thing that hit Ellie was the cold. The second was the sheer number of bodies on the ground, both moving and still. Floodlights shone from an aircraft flying low overhead as the bright streaks of its weapons fire tore groups of Rike apart.

Their loyal little turret somehow still fired into the madness. As Ellie looked out across their farm, she was hit by a wall of terror as a panic unlike anything she had ever known engulfed her. Beyond their turret, at the far end of their fields, flowing up the hill like a tide and seeming to consume the ground itself, the leading edge of an entire Rike swarm cascaded forward. Ellie barely registered she'd moved before she was pulling at Alayna and Jonathan, sprinting around and away from the house, her lungs immediately burning as they ran down the hill.

Years of poor nutrition and a threadbare diet had left her body desiccated to the point where even the adrenalin was having a hard time keeping her muscles going. But by Sulaya, it was trying, causing her heart to hammer frantically as they continued down the side of their hill that faced inwards towards the colony. The long, moist grass tugged against their legs as they ran.

In the distance, movement caught Ellie's eye, her vision snapping into focus; she could see lights! Yes, there were floodlights each moving about, coming from the direction of the Lindens' farm. It had to be the Lindens in their powerful mechs. It had to be!

If they could just reach them, they'd be safe.

Behind her, Ellie could still hear the screaming of the Rike and the booms of the cannon. She looked over her shoulder, her stomach flipping. Almost in slow motion, Ellie watched their entire house uproot, their little shipping container home breaking free of its foundations by the sheer weight of biomass ramming into it, sending Rike bodies spilling over all sides like a wave crashing around a rock as it began to tip. Their turbine was the last Ellie saw of their home before it disappeared behind the crest of the hill, blades still spinning as it broke free of its mast and went crashing into the swarm below.

Ellie kept running, her mind simultaneously ablaze and numb, still gripping her two siblings tightly. She couldn't think about tomorrow now. Right now, they had to run, to get away, to reach the lights. Ellie kept pulling Alayna and Jonathan along until the roar began to build in her ears again, the sound growing closer until the small V-shaped aircraft flew backwards over their heads, a powerful rush of air washing over them as it fired back in the direction from which they had come. It spun in the air as its two down-facing engines gimballed back and forth for stability. It ceased firing, lowering to hover just above the ground a few metres in front of them.

"Get on!" the authoritative voice boomed out once more.

"Let GO!" Alayna screamed and tore her hand free from Ellie's grip. The moment she was released, the girl began to speed away ahead of her. Jonathan's grip perceptibly shifted in her hand as well as he, too, overtook. But rather than let go, his grip tightened as the thin, flighty boy began to pull her along at an even greater speed.

Alayna was the first to reach the craft, jumping out of the grass and slamming into its side, causing the small aircraft to rock slightly. Following just behind, Ellie had a quick moment of panic, no idea what to actually do. The small aircraft looked to be single-seated, with no way for them to climb inside. Alayna was standing on a thin protrusion extending from the craft's underside. It looked as though it may have been designed for people to ride along externally, but Ellie was terrified their weight would be too much and unbalance the relatively small craft. Though with the Rike at her back, Ellie had no choice but to put thought to the side and launch herself as high as she could, bodyslamming the aircraft's hull.

Her flattened palm stuck momentarily to the smooth glass of the cockpit as her feet found footing on the flat metal protrusion, but the force of her rebound was too great. The grip of her palm gave way, and she was suddenly tipping backwards in a moment of terrifying clarity, her equilibrium slowly tipping too far for her to recover from, sending her falling. The engine's roar was deafening as the entire craft tilted in the opposite direction, trying to catch her.

Ellie's arm jerked taut; Jonathan was still grasping her hand! The motion caused her to spin halfway around, facing back the way they'd come. Long furrows were being dug into the grass as multiple Rike bounded towards them, their forms surfacing and disappearing like sharks breaching the ocean's waves.

A hand gripped her shoulder and spun her back towards the craft. Alayna had grabbed her, holding the aircraft with one hand, reaching out with the other. Together, Alayna and Jonathan hauled Ellie back up, where she was able to grab a metal handle built into the main body.

"Hold on!" the voice boomed as the engines flared, vibrations shaking around her insides as they began pulling away from the ground. Ellie looked over her shoulder as she pressed herself flat against the fuselage. A Rike leapt out from the grass after them, jumping high on its powerful hind legs. A high shriek of teeth scraping metal caused a bolt of lightning to shoot up Ellie's spine as the Rike's frontmost fangs made contact with the skid on which they were standing.

For a terrifying moment, Ellie was hyper-aware of her bare foot a hair's breadth from the monster's powerful jaws. It let out a guttural, shrieking growl at the three of them.

"FUCK YOU!" Alayna screamed in panicked rage, slamming her heel down between its eyes.

The Rike, barely holding on as it was, was thrown free, peeling off lines of paint as it was sent shrieking to crash back to the ground below.

Alayna spat after it, but Ellie could see the girl shaking.

The craft rapidly gained altitude, and the other Rike fell short as they tried to leap after them. Despite the relative distance, it was still much, much too close for comfort.

"We're not done yet. I'll be as quick as I can, but I need you to hold on, okay?" the voice said over the roar of the engines.

"Okay!" Ellie screamed in return. Between the engines and the wind whipping past, had the pilot even heard her? She turned her head to look out past the nose of the craft as they flew towards the lights in the distance.

As they approached and circled, Ellie could make out it was indeed the Lindens. Michael Linden with his daughter and two sons, each piloting their individual farming mech.

"Attention, convoy. A Rike host is advancing over the hill west by southwest, several thousand strong, area effect weapons recommended. LAC weapons platform will remain on station, callsign bluebird one. Be advised, carrying precious cargo," the voice boomed out to the mechs below.

"Boy, if you're trying to tell me to use my *big* bangers on a swarm, you're about as late as a summer snowfall. Just get behind us and catch any that get by. And keep Ellie and the others safe, or you'll be dealing with more than some angry critters!" The drawl of Michael Linden's voice boomed back over his own speakers.

Ellie watched the hill as the pilot pulled back. She couldn't see their house anymore, just the rapidly flattening grass as a wave of Rike swarmed forward.

As they passed some threshold Ellie wasn't able to distinguish, the Lindens opened fire. Grenades were launched from their tubes with throaty *whumps*, flying in wide arcs before impacting in fiery explosions. Large, multibarrelled chainguns opened up and strafed the oncoming rush of bodies. Smoke began to rise and fill the air as the grass caught fire in several places.

A Rike managed to make it through the fire and charged one of the bipedal mechs. It leapt from the grass, jaws snapping. The mech's pilot saw it at the last moment, spinning at the waist and bringing its backhand around from where it held a large excavation shovel. The Rike was blown into a chunky paste, the full force of the multi-tonne machine splattering it, spraying the area with a wide arc of purple blood. The hollow, reverberating echo of metal impacting bone reached Ellie even over the surrounding din, sounding distressingly gong-like.

The craft they were on began shaking violently as it added its strength to the firing line. The heavy thumps of its chin cannon firing sent painful impacts through her feet as the scream of missiles launching past her head blew her hair about. Ellie remained conscious of her grip, losing sensation in her fingers as she held on tightly in the cold night air. Turning her head to look at Jonathan and Alayna, both were clinging just as tightly as she was.

The noise and explosions continued for so long that it took a moment before Ellie registered the sudden quiet as they stopped. No more machine guns or grenade launchers. No more explosions or screeches or alarms. Even the roar of the engines was almost muted as they hovered in place, Ellie's ears ringing fiercely.

"Was that it?" Michael Linden's voice broke the silence after a few moments.

"Negative; the main host was easily in the tens of thousands," the pilot replied. Now given just a moment to process her thoughts, Ellie realised it was, in fact, Jake's voice.

"Well, that sure wasn't thousands of them, boy; where are they!" Michael Linden said with a touch of agitation.

"I don't know. Stand by," Jake replied.

There came a lurch as the craft tipped forward, engines changing pitch as they climbed back up the hill. Now, they were flying much higher than before, edging forward cautiously, well beyond the reach of anything on the ground. Ellie couldn't help but still feel a flitter of panic. Some of the larger Rike hives were known to spawn species that could fly. Given the size of the swarm they'd encountered, there was a very real chance they had come from one such hive.

Yet as they rose above the crest, it was just as silent as before. Ellie couldn't see what was happening; the body of the aircraft was between her and the top of the hill as Jake flew a long, slow circle around their house.

Or where it used to be.

Ellie screwed her eyes shut, gripping a little tighter as she tried to throw away the thought.

Eventually, the large circle they were following brought them back around to the Lindens.

"The Rike host has retreated. I'm not detecting anything left in the area," Ellie heard Jake say over the speakers.

"What? The Rike don't retreat once they're on the hunt, boy!" Michael Linden replied, stomping his mech for emphasis. "Are you sure your sensors are working?"

"They're working fine. I'm not detecting any living Rike at all," Jake said calmly. "Listen, return to your farm and make sure you sleep with one eye open tonight. I have to get Ellie and the others out of the cold before they freeze. Call me if you see anything else and need help. We'll continue this tomorrow," Jake finished.

"Now hold on just a damn minute!" Michael boomed back. "I don't know who the hell you are, and I don't care how many missiles you got stuffed into that fancy flyer of yours. Ellie and her kin ain't going nowhere they don't want to."

"It is currently negative six degrees," Jake began coolly. "The longer we stand here arguing, the more likely they're going to get hypothermia. I've taken them under my protection, I'll be able to get them to my home faster than you can, and I have some level of medical training. Right now, I'm their best option." A note of warning overlay his tone.

Ellie craned her neck to look down over her shoulder, seeing all the Lindens pointing weapons in their direction.

Mr Linden let out an unhappy growl over his speakers before addressing her directly.

"Ellie, give us a wave if you're okay to head off. We won't let him take you if you don't want to go. You must say what you want."

Ellie wasn't sure what to make of the situation as the craft rotated slightly to face her towards the Lindens. Jake had chased off Hunter, but that was about the only interaction they'd had. She'd known the Lindens for years and knew they'd look after them for a few days.

But what about beyond that?

How could she possibly consider the future at that moment? Her thinking was both hyper panicked and yet woefully slow as pain nipped at her from all directions. As the freezing wind bit into her, and with Jonathan and Alayna clinging to the craft beside her, Ellie could only think of getting out of that wretched cold as soon as possible.

Bracing herself against the craft so she could free up a hand, Ellie swung her arm up and down in a wide, slow wave.

Michael grunted as his weapons lowered back towards the ground.

"All right. But if we don't hear anything by tomorrow, we'll come looking for them, and you can bet we won't be politely knocking at your door, you hear?" Michael said gruffly.

"Acknowledged," Jake responded, seemingly unperturbed.

As they began to pull away, Ellie wanted to reach out, wanting to thank the Lindens for coming to help, for answering her cry and for doing their best to save her. For spending so much on them in the form of ammunition and putting themselves at risk to keep her family safe…

But they were already beyond her reach. Her line of sight turned with Jake's aircraft, to be taken up entirely by the valley at night.

Seven: Nothing is Free

Ellie no longer held much in the way of expectations anymore. Though if they were not heading to the Lindens, she had no idea where else they may be heading.

The wind picked up as the craft gained speed. Ellie turned her head to the front and saw they were flying straight towards the shining new compound sitting atop Bellator Peak.

The flight couldn't have taken more than a few minutes. Yet by the time the bottom of the skids touched down on the roof of the central spire, Ellie's fingers, toes, ears, nose and lungs were either screaming at her, or had already transitioned into that deep, distinct pain of frostbite taking hold in living cells.

There was a metallic *thump* of some heavy lock, the glass canopy of Jake's craft lifting before sliding back along its length. Jake set his hand on the side of his craft and vaulted out of the cockpit.

"Are all of you okay?" Jake asked with a note of concern. Taking off his helmet, Ellie could make out a worried expression as he evaluated the three of them clinging to the side of his aircraft.

"D-do we, do we look okay?" Alayna snapped at him, shivering hard.

"Okay, fair enough, stupid question. At least your tongue hasn't frozen yet," Jake said, stepping towards them. "Quick, let's get you inside before that damage becomes permanent."

Reaching up, Jake plucked Jonathan off the side of the craft like a small barnacle; the boy seemed to weigh almost nothing in his arms. Placing Jonathan down, Jake turned towards Ellie and held out his hand like a gallant suitor. The distance between the metal skid upon which she was standing and the top of the roof was barely equivalent to a single step. Yet as Ellie tried to turn, her joints locked into place, frozen shut and worn into position by the vibrations of the craft. Ellie fell forward with a surprised start.

Jake caught her hand as she stumbled down, pulling her upright and helping her get her feet under her. Ellie looked up, their eyes locking. Concern was etched into his features, but also a look of self-assuredness. Despite everything, he held himself confidently and hadn't hesitated or floundered as he'd helped her. His presence caused something to stir in her chest, and her panic died a little.

The moment passed quickly. Jake let her go and turned back to Alayna, leaving Ellie to try and tame her heartbeat.

"Come on, Spitfire, let's get you inside."

"I... I can't. I can't move my..." Alayna trailed off. The small girl was tugging at her wrist, her left hand still wrapped around a small metal strut she'd been using as a handhold. Ellie gasped to see that the fingers on Alayna's left hand were a deep maroon, her nails having taken on a purplish tint.

Jake stepped up onto the skid behind Alayna, raising an arm to hold onto the craft and bracing his feet along the outside of hers.

"Don't try to move them, okay? Just keep still and relax your muscles," Jake said in a reassuring tone. Raising his hand to his mouth, he bit down on the tip of his glove and pulled it off. Only now did Ellie realise he wasn't wearing the hard, Conviction-styled armour from before. Rather, he was cloaked in a dark, soft-bodied flight suit.

"Easy for you to say!" Alayna grimaced with an accusatory tone. Yet she didn't resist as Jake reached up and carefully worked her frozen fingers loose from the metal strut, gently worming them free as she winced. The moment her last finger was freed, Alayna fell backwards, her back impacting Jake's chest. Placing his free hand across her, Jake stepped down from the metal skid and leaned over to sweep the small girl off her feet, carrying her in both arms.

"Don't *touch* me!" Alayna snapped before rearing back, headbutting Jake square on the forehead.

"Alayna!" Ellie shouted in shock and horror.

Jake was forced back a step from the impact, standing stunned for a long moment, recovering. Finally, Jake shook his head as if to clear it, still holding Alayna.

"It's all right, I didn't ask permission; that was my mistake," he said, carefully lowering Alayna to the ground.

Alayna's whole body was shaking in the cold, but she was able to walk herself past Ellie and towards Jonathan. The two locked eyes and seemed to have a wordless exchange back and forth as they started huddling together.

"Anyway, let's not just stand here in the cold. Let's head inside," Jake repeated, seemingly no worse for wear.

Ellie shot Alayna a disapproving look. The two of them would have to have a talk later. But right now, Ellie was freezing, her own skin too cold against her as she held her arms tightly against her chest.

Jake walked towards a cylindrical column that pierced the centre of the roof. A door slid open at their approach, spilling yellow light across the flat rooftop. Ellie quickly ushered Jonathan and Alayna forward. Together, all four of them crowded into a small elevator built within. Ellie was immediately happy to be out of the biting wind.

Jake tapped at a control console and the door slid shut, the sudden silence deafening. The loudest noises in the small space were their shivering and ragged breaths.

They rode the elevator in silence, save for their shivering and the quiet hum of the magnetic track. When the doors opened again, Ellie's breath hitched as warm air flooded in, surrounding them like a blanket.

"Come on, all of you need to be warmed up. This way," Jake said, stepping out and beckoning them to follow. Ellie was just glad to be out of the cold, but as she stepped out to follow Jake, her eyes widened.

They stood inside the large open space of the round spire. Thick red carpet squashed beneath their feet and tall, floor-to-ceiling windows ringed the outside wall, through which Ellie could see the entire valley. In front of the windows, to her right, a large circular area had been sunk into the floor. Thick, velvety sofas lined the rounded edges, broken by a few sets of short stairs between levels. A large, circular fireplace made of black anodised metal stood freely towards one side of the dropped floor. A wood fire burned within, and a low hood caught the smoke, disappearing into the ceiling.

A ring of thick glass prevented any embers or ash from being thrown out.

"Excuse the place for being a bit disorganised; it was only put together *today*," Jake said, stepping down the stairs and turning back to them as they followed him down. "Or, well, yesterday now, technically. But the place is less than a day old in total," he said with a grin, waving his hand in the air to dismiss his own argument.

Jake motioned towards the fireplace.

"Please, please, get yourselves warm, make yourselves comfortable."

Alayna and Jonathan moved to sit on the sofas closest to the fireplace without any further prompting, dropping heavily into the velvety cushions, sinking in considerably. Both pulled forward to the very edge of the sofa and held out their hands. After a moment, it was clear Alayna still wasn't satisfied. She lowered herself to the floor and scooted even closer. The young girl rested her toes on the metal base and held her fingers right up to the air inlets, the flames burning just centimetres away. Jonathan followed almost immediately, and the two sat together on the sunken floor, pressed shoulder to shoulder.

Ellie reached up to catch the edge of Jake's flight suit as he began to move away.

"Thank you," Ellie said quietly, unwilling to look directly at him. Already her fingers and other areas were beginning to tingle with pins and needles, becoming progressively more painful, but it was a pain Ellie was grateful to be feeling, given the alternative.

Even if she wasn't looking directly at him, Ellie could feel Jake's eyes focus on her before his head turned towards Jonathan and Alayna. He seemed to appraise them for a long moment too, then turned quietly back to her.

"Hey, don't worry about it," Jake said softly, laying his hand over hers. The warmth of his bare skin against hers was so hot it was almost as though it was burning.

"You should have seen the expression on their faces when they thought they'd dropped you. Go, look after them, and yourself. Those two would break without you."

Ellie looked up to meet his eyes. Jake's words struck a chord. Her eyes began to sting, and she screwed them shut.

"You're too kind," she said. "First Hunter, then the Rike, now this; I don't know how to repay you." And it was true. How many bullets and missiles had it taken to rescue them? How much fuel, time and effort? What was the value of the craft he'd risked in landing to pick them up? How many problems had he caused for himself by snapping Hunter's arm on his first day in the colony? Ellie didn't have anything left. Her home was gone, her farm too.

She had nothing of value left to give. How was she—

Her thoughts were interrupted by a weight pressing down on her hair. Ellie slowly opened her eyes to see Jake had placed his hand on her head. His eyes brimmed with a kindness that made her want to simultaneously dive into his arms and pull away completely.

"For now, you can repay me by focusing on getting through tonight with everyone's fingers and toes intact. And not thinking about anything else besides that."

Ellie stared at him for a long moment. A kind face, a strong jawline, an almost playful smile.

Sulaya help me.

Closing her eyes again, Ellie took a deep breath, straightened her back a little and swallowed the lump in her throat. Jake lowered his hand, and she opened her eyes to face him head-on.

"Okay," Ellie said with a sureness she didn't quite feel. Jake nodded as she reluctantly turned away and walked towards the fire. Ellie heard Jake move away and looked over her shoulder as he disappeared into a darkened area behind her.

As she looked around properly for the first time, Ellie saw most of the room was hidden in darkness, lit only by the flickering light of the fireplace.

Ellie sat on the sofa directly behind Alayna and Jonathan, feeling her joints creak as she lowered herself into the soft cushions. By now, her face, ears, toes and especially her fingers were pounding, feeling swollen to three times their usual size though they looked no different to her naked eye beyond being flushed a light red.

Ellie leaned forward, resting her elbows on her knees, and laying her wrists on Alayna and Jonathan's shoulders. She let her sausage-feeling fingers drape over them to steal a little bit of the warmth for herself, though stealing wasn't necessary given the impressive heat the fireplace was putting out. It made sense as Ellie thought about it. The space in which they were sitting was vast, even with most of it hidden away in shadow. If the fireplace was the only source of heat, it would need to be strong to fend off Adroa's intense winters.

But what was more critical to Ellie, as her heart sought to repair itself at least a little bit, was that neither Jonathan nor Alayna was shivering anymore.

They stayed like that for what felt like a long while. Given the chaos of what they'd just gone through, Ellie's perception of time had grown skewed; the colour of the sky outside hadn't even changed at all before she sensed Jake approach.

"Here, I brought you some hot water," he said.

Ellie looked over and saw him standing there with several steaming bowls, one in each hand with another balanced along his forearm. Jake lowered himself to his knees, careful not to let any spill and drench the carpet. Jake placed one next to Alayna and held another out towards Jonathan.

Jonathan hesitated, looking to Ellie. She nodded with a small smile, and Jonathan took the offered bowl off Jake with a grateful nod. Jonathan carefully placed it in front of himself, but otherwise made no move towards it.

Placing the other to the side, Jake sat cross-legged, facing Alayna with a bowl between them.

"May I?" he asked, holding out his hand towards hers.

Alayna frowned, her mouth taking on a pouting shape. She seemed to consider for a long moment before placing her hands in his and turning her body towards him.

Jake gingerly lowered her hands into the bowl. Alayna winced as her skin made contact with the water.

"Don't worry, it's not boiling, even if it feels like it. See, my hands are in here too."

"That still doesn't stop it from hurting," Alayna grumbled.

"No, no it does not," Jake replied with a wide smile. "But you're supposed to say reassuring things when someone's in pain and you're trying to make them feel better, right?" He looked up to meet the face of Alayna, who just glared daggers at him. The action only succeeded in making Jake's smile widen even more.

"Either way, thankfully this doesn't look severe," Jake said, returning his attention to Alayna's hands. "Though much longer and you would have started to lose things permanently. Sorry I kept you out there in the cold for as long as I did. As it stands, I think you should fully recover, though they'll probably throb pretty bad for the next few days. Let me see if I can do anything to help with that."

Jake began to slowly and gently massage Alayna's fingers beneath the water. Ellie's head tilted slightly as she tried to understand his purpose, guessing he was trying to get Alayna's blood flowing back to the damaged areas before they got any worse.

Ellie subtly cleared her throat, causing Alayna to look over.

Ellie pointedly looked towards Jake, then back to Alayna, motioning with her head. Alayna visibly bristled, but Ellie glared directly at her, nonverbally putting her foot down before the girl could argue.

Alayna averted her gaze, sulking momentarily, before turning her head towards the fireplace.

"Thanks for, well, everything, I guess," Alayna said slowly. "And sorry for...you know, headbutting you, or whatever."

Jake looked up at her, a wide, amused grin spread across his face.

"Not a problem, Spitfire. I don't know your boundaries, so if I ever *do* make you feel uncomfortable, feel free to let me know," he said good-naturedly. "Well, of course, I already know that you will do so."

Alayna turned her head back towards him.

Jake chimed in. "Just you know, try using words first, skull bashing second. I don't want to end up like those, what, *three* other guys you messed up today?"

Ellie almost fell to the floor flailing when Alayna actually smiled.

"They should have known better!" Alayna said haughtily, raising her nose in the air.

"Oh, I'm sure. I'll bet everyone in this little colony knows who you are and to get out of your way when you're on the warpath, just like I'm sure everyone knows who you are too, hey, big man?" Jake said, shifting his gaze to look past Alayna towards Jonathan.

"M-me?" Jonathan stammered in surprise. "No, no I don't think so…"

"Oh, come on. I saw you cannonball right into the side of a man five times your size, and you can't tell me that kind of bravery doesn't leave an impression on people," Jake encouraged. " I think it also shows strong character that you were willing to put yourself in harm's way when your girlfriend was in danger."

Ellie closed her eyes, wincing. A silence settled on them, drawing out for a long moment and causing a confused look to cross Jake's face.

"Sister…" Alayna hissed the word low and venomously, snatching her hands away from Jake.

"Oh... My apologies," Jake said awkwardly.

The silence continued for a moment longer. Ellie was holding her breath, and needed to make a conscious effort to breathe in.

"Regardless, though," Jake started, seeming eager to move past the subject. "That was a brave thing you did. The both of you. And if I recall, even if you were able to pull yourself off the side of my LAC, your fingers weren't looking too good either." Jake switched to addressing Jonathan.

Jake rose, stepping around Alayna and picking up Jonathan's bowl to hold it out to him. Jonathan seemed hesitant to take it at first. But as his shaking hands closed around the warm ceramic, he quickly changed his mind. Taking the bowl into his lap this time, Jonathan dunked his fingers in the steaming water, just as quickly jerking back with a wince.

"It's fine, just put up with it for a minute," Alayna said, a note of annoyance still in her voice as she took hold of one of Jonathan's hands and plunged it beneath the water.

Ellie watched his back arc in shock or pain. She was about to tell Alayna to let Jonathan move at his own pace when she saw him slowly relax, delicately placing his remaining hand atop Alayna's. The two now sat with their backs to Ellie as Jake stepped over, holding out the remaining bowl. His gaze moved from Jonathan and Alayna to her as his expression changed, lingering on their hands.

I'm confused, his demeanour seemed to say.

Don't worry about it. Ellie thought back immediately, again surprised by how easily it came to mind as she took the offered bowl.

Stabs of pain went shooting through her fingers and an almost overwhelming heat followed as she let her hands sink beneath the surface of the hot water. Her instincts cried out to withdraw, but she persisted. Ellie had seen first-hand the results of frostbite and gangrene, and had no desire to experience either. She tried to wriggle her fingers, but her joints were stiff, her poor muscles crying out against her orders. Ellie couldn't help but wince just as Jonathan had.

"May I?" Jake asked gently.

In being absorbed by the heat and pain, Ellie hadn't realised he'd sat beside her. Her cheeks immediately flushed at his unexpected proximity.

Why? He's not doing anything; he's just sitting there.

Still, Jake was holding out his hands, motioning to her bowl. Ellie nodded, turning slightly so she was facing his direction, allowing him to reach out. With his gloves removed and the sleeves of his flight suit pushed halfway up his forearms, Jake could dip his hands in without risk of wetting his sleeves.

A nervous flutter came to Ellie's chest as his hands closed around hers. The sensation of touch was unfamiliar, yet surprising herself, she realised it wasn't entirely unwelcome.

"Relax your fingers for me," Jake said softly.

Ellie did so, and relief washed over her almost immediately. The feeling of his hands brushing over her skin was enough to quiet the nerves that had thought they were being burned. The muscles in her fingers ceased complaining once she stopped trying to move them herself. As Jake slowly flexed her fingers back and forth, her joints seemed to loosen.

The temperature of the water still felt far too hot, and a dull, deep ache permeated both her hands. But as the minutes ticked by, the fiery stabbing pain subsided, allowing Ellie to take a deep breath in relief which only served to set her heart racing once again as the breath brought with it a new scent smelling faintly of woodsmoke, leather and something vaguely sweet.

Ellie was suddenly keenly aware of Jake's proximity. His flight suit was thick and heavy, its folds and creases hugging his lean shape. His eyes were bright and focused as he worked life back into her frozen hands. Just how long had it been since she'd found herself this close to someone? Certainly, there were the hugs she gave out during her performances with the Slackvore and his crew. And the occasional greetings from her neighbours like Mr Tannis' crushing bear hugs. But beyond that, she couldn't remember a time since landing on Adroa.

"Ellie?"

"Hmm?" She snapped back to reality as Jake spoke to her.

"I said, try clenching and unclenching your fists for me. Let me know if there's anything in particular that hurts." Jake said.

"Right, y-yes," Ellie stammered, clenching her fists. "It all feels fine, just a little sore."

"Okay, good. Then just like Spitfire, you should be fine," Jake said, standing up towards the fire. His back arched, causing Ellie to flush on noticing she was getting a good look at his proportions from behind.

"That said, we should start thinking about the sleeping arrangements. It is…" Jake trailed off momentarily, checking a small display built directly into his suit. "Wow, almost 2 a.m."

"Oh, no, it's okay; you don't need to do anything special for us," Ellie said quickly, placing the bowl to one side and standing. "The room is plenty warm, and we couldn't impose any further. We'd be happy just to sleep by the fire. You'd be surprised how comfortable carpet can be."

Jake looked at her, cocking his head with an amused and slightly concerned expression.

"Don't worry about it," he said kindly, looking directly into her eyes. "This is the whole reason I have spare rooms in the first place. I can put you up tonight, no strings attached. And in the morning, when we're all not quite so exhausted, we can discuss what to do from there. Please." He motioned outside of the sunken lounge area and into the darkness.

Before Ellie could respond, Alayna snorted, "And what do you get out of it? We don't have anything to repay you with." Her voice was thick with suspicion. "Or let me guess… Hmm, I don't suppose you are hoping for some sort of *alternative payment,* are you?

"As I said, no strings attached. How could I expect you to sleep on the floor when I have empty beds available?" Jake replied.

"Yeah, whatever. Nothing is free, and you still didn't answer what *you* get out of it."

"A world in which being kind isn't considered a weakness," Jake snapped abruptly, an edge to his words that hadn't been there previously.

Ellie watched as the two locked eyes, staring each other down, Alayna backed by the fire shining through her long red hair, looking all the world like some kind of phoenix or ancient fire spirit, righteous and indignant. Jake, in his dark, militaristic flight suit, was backed by the surrounding shadow that whisked away any light falling on him. Silent and immovable.

Where beforehand Jake had seemed eager to lead with respect and compromise, he now stood with his feet planted. An air of intimidation extended from his stern expression as it became clear this was not a point he was willing to yield. Yet Alayna, stubborn as ever, seemed unwilling to back down just on the principle of having been challenged. The moment continued to stretch out.

To Ellie's surprise, it was Alayna who blinked first, facing away and crossing her arms over her chest.

"You're an idiot," she accused.

"Alayna!" Ellie scolded immediately. But Alayna's insult only served to spread an endeared grin across Jake's face.

Just like that, the air of tension evaporated. Jake was laughing, a calm chuckle almost to himself.

"Come on, let's all call it a night before someone starts to think they're going to have to pay for the air they're breathing," Jake said in a slightly exasperated tone, turning to lead the way up the short stairs and into a darkened part of the tower.

Ellie paused a moment before following in his steps. Looking over her shoulder at the other two, Alayna's face was scrunched up in a displeased expression. But she lifted her hands and gave them an aggressive flick, water droplets spitting as they hit the hot metal of the fireplace before following.

And where Alayna went, Jonathan would predictably follow, falling in behind her.

Jake led them down a short, curved hallway with a handful of doors lining either side. As they walked, smooth, metallic ovals protruding from the wall by about the width of Ellie's finger lit up from behind, throwing light back onto the wall while keeping its source hidden. It gave the area a soft, indistinct glow. There were no direct lights anywhere, so did it serve some specific purpose or was it simply a stylistic choice on Jake's part?

"Bathroom here," Jake said, knocking on a particular door. "Guest room one," he continued, knocking on a second, before pointing down the hallway to a third. "And guest room two. Sorry, Ellie, you and Alayna will need to share a bed in here. The other room only has a single, so—"

"Jonathan and I will take this one then," Alayna asserted, cutting him off.

Jake blinked. He looked to Ellie, confusion on his face.

Am I still misunderstanding their relationship?

It's... complicated, Ellie thought back.

Alayna scoffed angrily, stamping her foot.

"Jonathan can't sleep alone; he has night terrors," Alayna explained in an indignant tone, picking up on Jake's confusion. "Plus, he's a light sleeper, so if there's ever a threat, he wakes me up and I can defend the house. This is how we normally sleep."

"Right…" Jake drew out the word in an unsure tone.

Alayna threw her hands up in frustration and grabbed Jonathan by the wrist. Pushing past Jake, she opened the door and pulled Jonathan in after her.

Ellie spied several large boxes littered around the room and a bare double bed with what looked like several sheets and blankets vacuum-sealed in a soft storage bag.

"Goodnight!" Alayna asserted before closing the door in their faces, leaving Ellie standing in the hallway alone with Jake.

"Should I ask?" Jake said carefully, a hint of concern in his voice as he indicated towards the closed door.

Ellie took a slow, deep breath, weariness suddenly threatening to overcome her.

"I'm sorry for Alayna and the way she's been acting. She's a good girl, but very strong-willed and prideful. She's also quite protective towards Jonathan, and she doesn't like new people. But…" Ellie trailed off quietly, raising a hand to tuck some loose strands of hair behind her ear, looking down and putting on what she hoped was a thankful expression. "I appreciate all you've done for us. I don't know where we'd be now if it weren't for you."

Jake was shifting his weight, prompting her to look up and meet his eyes. He wore a sympathetic expression.

"Best not to think about it. You, Alayna and Jonathan are alive; that's what's important. And please, I did nothing but the bare minimum any decent person would do. You don't owe me any thanks," he said gently.

Ellie swallowed. How could she tell him that billions of people back on her home world wouldn't have done even the 'bare minimum'? How many of them would have let her little farm be overrun with her inside without lifting a finger, just so they could pick over the broken scrap after it had been ground into the dirt. That what Jake considered the floor of human decency sank down infinitely further. And even though Adroa was far beyond the Conviction, populated by mostly good people who greatly cared about their neighbours, every bullet, every bomb and every litre of fuel had its cost. Eventually, the price of saving someone might become too high, regardless of whether it was right or decent.

"But, either way, you look exhausted. Let me show you to your room, please," Jake said slowly, breaking Ellie from her thoughts and stepping back farther down the hallway.

Ellie followed, entering a separate room as Jake opened the third door and held it for her. Inside, Ellie was almost taken aback by the view. Like the living room, the entire far wall was floor-to-ceiling glass, only now brought much closer.

Sulaya was bright and magnificent in the sky, covering the landscape in a pale light. Ellie looked out over the rolling hills, rivers and forests she knew so well from a height and angle she'd never seen before. Heavy curtains hung to either side, where internal walls came out to reach the external edge. Here too were some large boxes, and a single bed along the far wall.

"Please excuse the mess; I wasn't expecting guests quite this soon. This doesn't even feel like my house yet." Jake chuckled nervously. "I'll get the bed made, then leave you to it. You've had a worse day than some of the soldiers I used to fight alongside. And I'm including the ones who were shot," he said, moving towards the bed and slipping the covers out of their packaging. The soft material began to inflate the moment Jake broke the seal.

Ellie cocked her head momentarily at the slight mention of his past, but hurried forward as he threw out the bottom sheet.

"Please, let me help with that."

Jake turned slightly towards her.

"Are you sure? Your fingers must still be hurting."

"They're fine," Ellie insisted, grabbing one end and tucking it in. "Besides, even if it's some small gesture that means nothing in the scheme of things, please let me do something to help after everything you've done."

Jake paused, but didn't protest, giving her a moment to catch up.

Together, they made short work of the task. In doing so, Ellie couldn't help but take note of the clean softness of the sheets and blankets. Jake finished by placing a thick pillow beneath the covers and stepping back.

"There we are, all yours," he said. "Do you remember where the bathroom and the other guest room are?"

Ellie nodded, sitting on the bed and sinking further into the thick covers than she'd been expecting as Jake moved towards the door. Fanning her hands out, Ellie ran her sore fingers over the layers of fabric, a strange sense of nervousness creeping up her back.

"Okay. In that case, get some rest. We'll talk everything out in the morning, so don't let uncertainty keep you up tonight. Oh, and one more thing," Jake said, turning back into the room. He paused until she looked up to meet his gaze.

"I knew when coming here that the Rike were going to be a threat. This place is a fortress. The sensors are online, the guns are up, and I'll be sleeping right next door." He accentuated his words by knocking twice on the wall. His face took on a determined expression, but his eyes remained kind as they looked at each other across the room.

"You, Spitfire and the big man are all safe here tonight. I promise."

Ellie's jaw hung open just a moment, her mouth moving but no words escaping. Standing there, tall, dark, and resolute, framed by Sulaya's light, he almost looked like a knight just stepped out from some long-forgotten fairytale. Nervousness mixed with exhaustion kept her from making a sound. But as Jake turned to leave, she managed to pull out one last ounce of strength.

"Jake!" she called, an unintended note of urgency in her voice.

He leaned back into the room, now half obscured by the doorway.

"Thank you," she said sincerely.

Jake smiled at her. Nodding politely, he withdrew, closing the door with a metallic *click*.

Ellie continued to sit for several long moments. The quiet of the night made her slowly realise she was once again all alone. Her chest fell as her nervousness at Jake's leaving gave way to near exhaustion. She fell sideways, her head impacting the thick pillow with a *whump*.

Weeks of careful harvesting, running their stall on market day, the stress of Jonathan's inadequate provisions... Alayna ripping men apart, swindling a dangerous pirate captain and his mountain of a quartermaster, losing her home, fighting then running from a Rike swarm, and now a kindness she had no way of repaying. Despite everything she should probably be feeling, Ellie was numb. She just wanted to close her eyes, wake up, and realise it was all a bad dream.

Pulling the covers up, she slipped between the sheets. Any other time, she might have marvelled at how the mattress rose around her form, and at the weight and warmth of the thick, feathery blankets atop her. Or the complete absence of the crack between the cushions into which her hips would always fall when she slept on the sofa.

But, perhaps as one small mercy from the universe, her thoughts began to drift the moment she settled, and she fell asleep within minutes.

Eight: More than Our Lives

Ellie cracked one eye open, the feeling dry and scratchy. With a groan, she slowly raised one hand to rub at the caked sleep encrusting her vision. Her muscles ached and a thick fog had spread through her mind, making thinking slow and difficult.

She had no idea how long she'd been asleep, but it felt like an age. She was sure she'd got up at some point in the night but could barely remember. Ellie sat up, blankets falling off her, their warmth a siren's call to lie back down and sleep for another year or two. But as she stretched and tried to shake the fog from her mind, she became very aware of some bodily needs that required urgent attention. Her throat was parched dry, her belly rumbled, and her bladder was fit to burst.

Reluctantly, Ellie swung her legs out over the side of the bed. Still wiping at her eyes to clear them, she could see early morning light reflecting off the walls around. It couldn't have been more than an hour after dawn, which by her admittedly unreliable maths meant she could have only got about five or six hours' sleep.

"Still, needs must," she said to the quiet room, forcing herself to her feet. Stumbling out of the room, Ellie groggily made her way to the bathroom and closed the door.

After taking care of the most immediate concerns, Ellie propped herself up against the generous sink, wiping her face down with water blissfully hot straight out of the tap. Finally clearing her vision, Ellie sniffed and looked into the mirror set into the wall. Her eyes widened slightly.

Just how long had it been since she'd seen herself this close up? Their little ensuite had had no mirror. Her long, wavy blond hair was dishevelled from the events of the night before. Bright blue eyes stared back at her, and she could see the bags forming beneath them from exhaustion. Her pale skin on which so many people usually complimented her looked sickly, and her slender face seemed even gaunter than she remembered.

Was this how she had been looking to everyone? Was this the face she thought she could use to flirt her way to better prices and special treatment? Was the power of her still ample chest really that strong, or was everyone just taking pity on the pallid girl whose skin had begun to hang from her frame?

Ellie sighed hard as she leaned heavily on the sink; this was not just the kind of tiredness that came from a short sleep, but a deep, permeating exhaustion born from relentless year after relentless year. And now even her beauty, her main advantage that had carried them this far, seemed to be fading.

And I'm only meant to be turning twenty-one this year… I think.

Ellie ran the sink again and wiped her face down one last time. Trying to put her worries to the side, she stood, dreading the thought of having to come up with what to do next, wanting nothing more than to return to the soft bed still calling her name. If it was just herself, she might try just throwing herself at Jake as he surely wouldn't mind having her around. But it was not just herself, was it? She had Jonathan and Alayna to think about, and she'd learned a long time ago they couldn't survive on someone else's mercy.

Ellie shook her head. Besides, everything she had seen of Jake so far led her to believe he wasn't the kind of man to take advantage of her like that. Taking a deep breath, she opened the bathroom door and stepped outside.

As her feet moved from hard tile to soft carpet, voices carried down the hallway towards her, intermingled with faint, boppy music. The sounds of conversation and laughter tickled her ears as she moved forward.

As Ellie rounded the bend, smells greeted her, ones that instantly made her mouth tingle. The hallway emptied into the main living area from the night before, with the sunken lounge and fireplace to her right. But to her left, hidden in shadow previously, a long breakfast bar stretched out from the wall. Alayna and Jonathan sat atop two thickly cushioned stools, plates resting on the bar before them as they ate.

Jonathan was the first to notice her approach.

"Effie," he said in surprise through a mouth stuffed with food.

"What?" Alayna said before turning. "Oh, *Ellie,"* she clarified.

Jake's head appeared around the corner, leaning over the opposite side of the bar.

"Well, hey sleepyhead, get over here; you must be starving," Jake said welcomingly before disappearing again. "Sit down. I just about have something ready, so you'll be able to eat right away," he called.

Ellie walked forward; her surprise must have been evident on her face as both Jonathan and Alayna fixed her with coy smiles. The pair were still in their pyjamas while Jake had changed into a collared shirt with short sleeves. A sweeping, in-reaching pattern helped accentuate the broadness of his shoulders and the muscles along his arms.

As Ellie entered the room proper to take a seat at the far end, Ellie saw Jake moving about in a well-appointed kitchen. Standing over a six-burner stove, he was managing multiple frypans, each having a hissing sizzle emanating. The sweet scents of meats wafted to her, causing even her dry mouth to water.

The clink of ceramic mingled with the splat of hot oil as Jake turned and set a giant breakfast sandwich in front of her, a thick English muffin stacked with cheese, eggs, bacon, a spicy-smelling sausage patty and a hashbrown, dripping with a rich-looking brown sauce and still bubbling, only just removed from the heat.

"For me?" Ellie squeaked out, her eyes going wide. "Jake I couldn't! This is too much—"

"Ellie *please*." Jake interrupted, pushing the plate closer to her. "You can't tell me you're not starving. Stop thinking, eat, then we'll talk, okay?"

Ellie hesitated. She wanted to argue, to insist. But her stomach protested, growling at the prospect, and she was picking up the sandwich with shaking hands before she realised it. She took the briefest moment to smell the aroma before taking an enormous, unladylike bite. Flavour exploded in her mouth, juices immediately dripping down the bread and onto her chin. The warm sauce mixed with oil and a perfectly runny egg yolk made a delicious mess she slurped up loudly. Realising just how famished she was, Ellie couldn't get it inside her fast enough, taking another monstrous bite and cramming it into her cheeks.

She suddenly froze, coming to the horrific realisation she was scarfing it down like an avaricious, emaciated beast. Her hand came up, slapping wetly over her mouth to cover her animalistic chewing. Her eyes met Jake's in a moment of hyperawareness.

"Oh, I'm—I'm sorry!" she somehow managed between chewing down on the food with which she had stuffed her mouth. The realisation seemed to have appalled her.

Jake burst out laughing at her horrified expression, both Jonathan and Alayna joining in immediately. The three looked like a gang of cackling birds, doubling over the bar the way they were. Jake went as far as to rest his forehead against the counter and beat down with his fist. The bright, beautiful sounds of their laughter resonated within her chest, easing the tension in Ellie despite it clearly coming at her expense.

"I'm sorry, I'm sorry…" Jake managed to choke through fits of laughter. "By the wars, don't hold back on our account. I'm glad to see you eating something substantial," he said, straightening up to wipe tears from his eyes before facing her, leaning back against the bar. "Besides, I can't tell you how good it is to see you enjoying my food so much. I bought quite a lot of fresh produce when I landed," Jake began to explain. "I was thinking I could hold a housewarming party or barbeque or something to introduce myself to the neighbours.

"Lure them in with free food before talking their ears off about my security services. I didn't realise how spread out everyone was though. So, before you worry about repayment, please, I've got more than I can possibly eat before it goes bad. You'd be doing me a favour by not letting it go to waste. On that note, who wants more?"

"Bacon please!" Alayna shouted immediately.

"Can... can I have some of that sausage mixed into your cheesy scrambled eggs?" Jonathan said louder than expected, his words carrying easily over the music playing nearby.

"You got it, second breakfast coming up," Jake said with a wide smile, twirling a spatula between his fingers.

Ellie was surprised by how easily and enthusiastically the two had answered. Yes, Jake had insisted, but it was only yesterday that Alayna had been headbutting him for helping her off his aircraft. Jonathan, too, had been half convinced Jake was only here to conquer them in the name of the Conviction.

Yet as she watched, the three spoke back and forth like old friends, all smiling and joking as Jake worked the stove.

Ellie's stomach growled again, and she quickly demolished her extravagant breakfast. The weight of it hit her insides as a warm lump. She could almost feel her stomach quiver, unsure of what to do with such a bounty.

A clinking sound drew her attention sideways as Alayna put down a glass next to her, pouring in a bright orange liquid.

"It's full of pulp because I just squeezed it but drink it anyway. You look dehydrated," Alayna said, pushing the glass towards her. A thought seemed to cross Alayna's mind before Ellie could take it and the redhead quickly snatched the drink back.

"Wait… should I be giving her orange juice if she's dehydrated?" Alayna directed the question to Jake.

"Actually, you know what? I'm not sure," he responded over his shoulder as he cracked a number of eggs into a frypan.

"House," Jake said loudly. The music immediately lowered. "Can you give orange juice to a dehydrated person?"

"Yes, that is acceptable," a cool, feminine voice responded. "Most juices contain approximately 85% water as well as various other vitamins and minerals. As long as you are using 100% real fruit juice from a trusted source, it is safe to give fruit juices to someone suffering dehydration."

"There you go, go ahead," Jake finished as the music returned to a normal volume.

Alayna handed the glass back to her. Ellie raised it to her lips, immediately taken aback as the strong, sweet, tangy flavour hit like a punch to the mouth, causing her to cough and get some of it caught in her throat.

"It's delicious," Ellie managed to wheeze out after a few moments. "Thank you."

"It's fine," Alayna said, rolling her eyes and moving to sit back down.

"But what have you three been talking about while I was asleep?" Ellie asked, curious as to what subject could have brought them so seemingly close in such a short period.

"The beach, and the coast..." Jonathan answered. Ellie wasn't sure what precisely, but something in his tone made it seem as if he was deflecting her question. "Jake wanted to know why we live so far inland on an uninhabited planet when Adroa has such nice beaches."

"And I was telling him," Alayna interjected with some snarky remark directed towards Jake. "Because Sulaya is so big and so close, the tides come and go more like a tsunami. And if you're standing at the water's edge at low tide, a human can't run fast enough to beat the tide back and they'll be swept away, but he doesn't believe me!"

"That's because you said you've never seen it yourself and besides, it makes no sense," Jake responded. Turning away from the stovetop, he leaned one hand on the bar. "If Adroa had such extreme tidal forces, it would also affect the wind, weather, and tectonics. Cyclones, tornadoes, or volcanic eruptions would have destroyed the colony before it was properly established. How do you explain such calm weather when we're talking about forces on literally a celestial scale?"

Alayna's expression turned indignant at being questioned. How dare he?

"I don't know, do I? I'm not a meteorologist or climatologist or whatever you call a weather scientist. I just know it from somewhere. And Adroa *is* volcanic; that's why the soil is so fertile. We have ash storms every so often and they're a huge pain!"

"Right, okay then. In that instance, who's the faster runner between the two of you?" Jake asked, flipping between the two with his spatula. "I can drop you off at low tide and we can see if you make it back in time before being swept away."

Ellie blinked at the conversation.

"How long have you all been awake?" Ellie asked.

The three of them stopped to look at her, before all sharing a conspiratorial grin.

"Well, I mean, *today,* I think we've only been up the past hour and a half," Jake answered with unnatural smoothness. They were all smiling at her as if they knew something, and Ellie couldn't help but feel she was the butt of some inside joke.

Not that she minded, considering how glad she was to see them all getting along so well, but what were they hiding? Her eyes narrowed in suspicion as she looked from one to the other. Even ever-loyal Jonathan seemed to be enjoying being part of the gang. He was emerging from his shell all of a sudden.

"Okay then. How long have *I* been up?" Ellie asked.

Jake looked to Jonathan. Jonathan looked to Alayna. Alayna to Jake, Jake back to Alayna.

"You want to tell her?" Jake asked.

"You do it," Alayna said, looking directly at Ellie with a grin.

"Well then," Jake began, propping his hip against the side of the bar. "I think the question isn't so much 'how long' as 'when'. Since by your clock, tomorrow is now yesterday. And yesterday, you missed out on all the fun," he said with a smile that lit up his eyes.

Ellie, suddenly determined not to be distracted by his charm, cocked her head.

"I don't understand?"

"Ellie," Jake said. "It's the day after tomorrow. You've been asleep for about twenty-eight hours," he finished before turning to the other two. "I'm pretty sure that counts as a coma, right?"

The pair gave him the same *I don't know* gesture.

"Twenty-eight hours? Really?" Ellie said in shock.

It immediately began to fall into place. The time she had spent asleep seemed far longer than she would have thought, explaining how she had woken up completely parched and famished, as well as the various fades in and out of consciousness. How had she managed to sleep that long?

"Yes, really. We all came in to check on you but figured you really needed the rest. If you hadn't woken up by the time I'd finished making breakfast this morning, though, we were going to come in and shake you."

Ellie was still shocked. She didn't think she'd ever slept that long before in her life, but it was all making perfect sense.

"Now please," Jake said, interrupting her thoughts as he placed a large plate of hash browns topped with scrambled eggs in front of her. "Do your poor body a favour and *eat.*"

***

Ellie tried to remain in a dignified pose as Alayna lay splayed out over Jake's lounge, groaning. Their stomachs filled to bursting, this was a marvellous sensation; had she ever felt this full? Not of late, anyway. Certainly, on the rare occasions they'd visit the Lindens for dinner, they always put on a good feed. But none of her nearby neighbours raised herds of cattle, so their meals were mostly practical and vegetable based whereas Jake's breakfast had been thick, rich, and heavy. Lots of meat, cheese, and sauce, all with a very high fat content. Even the bread and buns had been slathered in a thick layer of sweet, warm butter.

Ellie hadn't even been aware of shutting her eyes until she felt herself begin leaning to one side. She caught herself, straightening and arching her back as she corrected her posture.

Trying to fight off the food-induced tiredness, Ellie stood, moving to the windows so she could walk along the curved outer edge of the room.

Her movements hitched as her eyes naturally gravitated over the landscape beyond, landing on her hill.

From this distance, any details were difficult to make out. If she squinted, Ellie thought she could just make out some brown marks surrounded by scorched, blackened borders. The wet grass had seemingly smothered the flames once the initial weapon propellants had been spent.

What screamed out to her more than anything was what was missing. At the crest of the hill, where she expected to see their home's small yet familiar shape, was simply a smudge against the landscape.

"I'll take you to have a look if you like."

Ellie let out an involuntary squeak and spun around as she was torn from her melancholy thoughts.

"Oh, Jake…thank you," Ellie said slowly. "Though I'm not exactly sure what might be left."

"Not much, I'm afraid," Jake said cautiously. "I did a flyover yesterday with Jonathan and Alayna and…it's probably best if you go see for yourself."

Ellie's heart jumped, a nervousness spreading through her chest. She set her jaw, trying to summon her strength before nodding.

"When do you think we might be able to leave?"

"Well," Jake said as he crossed his arms over his chest, cocking his head in consideration. "It's early morning, and we have a full, sunny day ahead of us. Unless there's anything you need first, I don't see any reason we can't head out now."

"Oh," Ellie said, somewhat surprised. "Yes, if that's all right."

What exactly had she been expecting? But facing the aftermath of the swarm suddenly seemed like a runaway train rushing towards her.

"Alayna, Jonathan, could you—" Ellie leaned over to call past Jake's shoulder, and stopped mid-sentence.

She had intended to ask the two to clean up and change clothes. The realisation that they no longer *had* any other clothes hit like a slap to the face.

"...could you get ready, we're leaving."

"Ugh, why?" Alayna let out as a long, low moan from where she lay as she sluggishly extracted herself from the sofa. Jonathan obediently made his way over and stood by her. Eventually, all four of them gathered in Jake's elevator.

Ellie blinked as they began to descend rather than rise towards the roof.

"Are we not flying?" Ellie asked Jake in confusion.

She immediately smacked herself, feeling as though she'd sounded expectant or ungrateful.

"Oh, we are," Jake said reassuringly. "Just not on the LAC Weapons Platform you rode before. It *is* designed to carry external passengers, technically, but the other night was a bit of a desperate scenario. I've got something a little more comfortable in mind."

The elevator came to a halt with a quiet sigh. The doors slid open, and now, Ellie was staring into the vastest internal space she had ever seen. A single, enormous room with a curved ceiling held a pair of unidentifiable aircraft, the first one four or five times the size of her house, obscured by a large protective covering that reflected the light. The other was much smaller, yet still equal in size to any of her neighbours' mechs. Both looked like toys in the cavernous space.

"Welcome to the hangar," Jake said, stepping out and gesturing to the enormous area. "I know it might not look like much, but it's everything I need, and it's *mine!*"

Ellie looked up as he emphasised the last word, witnessing pride burning in his eyes. There was a spark of happiness for Jake. Ellie knew the feeling of having struggled through life, knowing better than many how the heart of a person sang to behold something they truly owned in a climate where true commodities were scarce.

"When you're ready, we'll be taking that one," Jake said, pointing to the smaller of the two.

"Whoa-ho-ho, yes!" Alyna exclaimed, running forward.

Ellie was again taken aback as they followed. The aircraft Jake had used to save them the night before— *the night previous to the night before*, Ellie corrected herself—had been blunt, angular, and almost aggressively utilitarian.

The craft Ellie was looking at now was wide, sleek, and beautifully thin, its pointed nose quickly expanding into a wide central chassis. An angular glass cockpit held two rows of seats in a plush-looking interior, while a pair of graceful, forward-swept wings extended from the main body, tipped in two hard-edged, teardrop-shaped nacelles.

A rotating, twin-barrelled turret sat tucked behind the back seats, poking out of the roof. Several discreet inlets cut into the main body towards the back, before flaring out into an enormous bank of geometric engines around which the rest of the craft seemed purpose-built.

It hovered in place, its lower edge about knee height from the floor. Ellie crossed the space and looked closely at the glossy, dark red paintwork. The quiet, tell-tale vibration of a gravity repulsor gently reverberated in the air. This was not a short-haul ground hopper meant solely for in-atmosphere flight. No, Ellie recognised the purpose in its design as a full-fledged *spacecraft*.

"This is Lara. Be nice to her; she's my favourite girl in the whole wide world and she's saved me more times than I can count," Jake said, affectionately running his hand along one of the spacecraft's angled surfaces.

"You know, now that I think about it, the three of you will be the first passengers she's carried in quite some time," Jake continued thoughtfully.

"Why Lara?" Alayna asked, fascinated as Jake walked around the craft to the far side.

"Long Range Light Assault Fighter," Jake answered. "Technically, LRLAF, but I think that sounds ugly, so I just fudge it a little and call her Lara."

Jake grabbed onto the side of Lara and hauled himself upwards, Ellie watching as the whole craft dipped slightly under his weight. Holding his wrist up to the canopy, a small holographic symbol flashed over the surface of his hand and the canopy began to lift away, hinged towards the back of the craft to grant them easy access.

"Neat!" Alayna exclaimed as she grabbed the edge of the cockpit and lifted her leg, searching for a foothold.

Ellie quickly grabbed Alayna's shoulder and gently, but firmly, pulled her backwards.

"Hey, what are you doing?" Alayna protested loudly, causing Jake to lean over from where he'd already climbed into what was presumably the pilot seat.

"Jake…" Ellie said softly.

"Ellie," Jake replied patiently.

Ellie had to pause a moment to gather her thoughts, to arrange them in a way that might be understandable without causing too much offence. She took a deep breath.

"This is worth more than our lives."

Jake's brow furrowed, a look of concern on his face.

"*Nothing* is worth more than your lives, Ellie."

"Jake!" Ellie snapped a little louder than she had intended. "You're very sweet but be practical. I appreciate you saving us, I really do. And sheltering us and feeding us. But all of that, I might, *might* be able to pay off someday. But this?" Ellie said as she gestured to Lara. "If we damage this. If we break this…"

She grabbed the hair on top of her head in frustration.

"I would never be able to repay this, Jake. Not if I were to be given ten lifetimes. Not if I were given a *hundred* lifetimes."

Silence fell over the enormous room. Jonathan may have been his usual quiet self, but even Alayna stood still, unsure what to do.

Jake looked down at them for a long time, his mouth working in deep thought. Eventually, his weight shifted, and he vaulted over the edge, landing directly in front of her. He straightened slowly, and Ellie raised her chin, dragging her eyes to meet his.

"What do I need to do to make you comfortable, Ellie?" Jake asked quietly, voice thick with sincerity as his eyes pierced into hers.

"I don't… I don't know, Jake. Just, maybe consider the value of the things you're offering before you offer them so easily." Ellie looked away. She couldn't adequately give voice to the feelings raging around in her chest. Nobody offered these things so freely, so easily.

It could only make her wonder again about what he was expecting in return, what his end game was. No one so genuinely kind could have survived this long, certainly not in the Conviction. The contradiction between this fact she knew too well, and his seemingly selfless actions were leaving Ellie's thoughts in a destructive loop as she struggled to reconcile the difference.

"You know..." Jake began slowly. "It's unfortunate I don't have a tragic backstory I can tell you. I can't point to some grand action, event or epiphany that might explain things. I was fortunate, born into a…*community* of sorts. One that held a set of values that made life…well, quite beautiful to live really." Jake spoke in a low, almost embarrassed tone, appearing to half lose himself in memories as he continued to explain. Ellie couldn't help but raise her head to watch him as he began to pace back and forth.

"I had loving parents, multiple brothers and sisters. I knew all of our neighbours and they knew us. It was a very close-knit community. We looked out for each other. We were beyond the Conviction, but we weren't isolationist. Whenever someone would come to us, we'd do our best to help, show them a level of kindness most people had never experienced before. Most of the people who found themselves on our doorstep eventually decided to stay, and they'd become part of the community. They would, in turn, learn to be kind themselves, and give back ten times what they originally took. Everyone uplifted everyone. But occasionally, someone would leave. And as you can imagine, sometimes word would get out about a group of kind souls and, well.."

Jake shook his head, a strained smile spreading as a dark look came over his eyes.

"Some people believed they could take advantage of that kindness. And why wouldn't they? Truly kind people can be kind to the exclusion of all else. They believe in the good in people too much. They're either too naive, or too weak and end up getting consumed, and in this way, the universe loses a rare and beautiful thing."

Jake's expression became downcast at his last words, a sorrowful tone entering his voice. He was quiet for a long moment, closing his eyes before straightening his back again and looking forward.

"I believe an ancient philosopher once said, 'Speak softly, and carry a big stick'. I *refuse* to live in a system where kindness is a weakness or in which each time we are kind, everyone must call the act into question. That is madness, don't you think? If I have to be the change I want to see in the world, all on my own, then so be it. I will be kind. I will assume the best in people. I will do my best to ensure we can all live long, happy lives beside each other. And when someone comes along who mistakes that kindness for weakness..." Jake's brow furrowed, and a hard light shone in his eyes. "Well, then I'll grind them into a bloody paste beneath my boot and make room for someone who might show a little more *basic human empathy*."

Jake's tone rose as he became more animated. At his last declaration, Ellie couldn't help but picture his ruthless efficiency when taking on Hunter and his gang.

"Ellie," Jake said, causing her to jump as she hadn't realised he'd stepped in so close.

"I can tell you've had a hard life. You may very well have good reason to always assume the worst. But there is nothing I will be able to say that can change that. No promise I can make that will put you at ease if you are one who is filled with suspicion, and doubt, and fear. All I can do is the total opposite, to ask you to put yourself at even more risk…" Jake raised his hand to her. "...and trust me."

Ellie's heart began pounding in her chest. When Jake spoke, it was with such a fiery passion that she couldn't help but feel overwhelmed. His stunningly green eyes seemed to see right through her. This impossible, handsome, passionate stranger had almost fallen from the sky. In the mere span of a day, Ellie could already feel herself being swept off her feet, a sensation she had never expected to experience and with which she had no idea how to deal.

All she had been through, everything she knew was screaming at her to back away, that it was all too good to be true, that it had to be a trap, had to be a trick, a con or a dirty scam.

She couldn't take his hand.

And yet, when she looked into his eyes, seeing the fierce determination and his strong jaw set in a resolute line, Ellie was unable to believe anything else. She so desperately wanted it to be real, wanted to believe such a thing could exist outside of fairy tales.

But how could she be so stupid as to get swept up by this? To be won over by a single passionate speech delivered in a near-empty hangar on the edge of the known universe? She had Alayna to consider, and Jonathan, and their futures and...

And...

And she'd already taken Jake's hand.

He smiled at her, and her heart skipped a beat.

Shit, Ellie thought.

Jake drew her forward, stepping back to place her hand on Lara. The surface was surprisingly cool beneath her skin.

"You'll believe me, will you, when I say that I won't ask you to repay me for anything I freely give to you? Breakfast, a ride, or otherwise?" Jake asked softly.

Letting out a long, shuddering sigh was about the only reply Ellie could manage. So instead, she just nodded.

"Great!" Jake exclaimed, clapping his hands together and causing all three of them to jump.

"Change of plans then. We're going to Tropicalia."

Nine: The Redhead's Not Helping

Ellie gripped the handle beside her seat for dear life as they rocketed forward.

She had flown before, and she knew the gut-tingling feeling of repulsors firing and the hard, jittering shock of entering an atmosphere. But always it had been in large freighters or cargo haulers. She'd rarely even had a window as the massive, three-million-tonne behemoths would bull their way through any obstacle with little regard for wind or gravity.

Not so with Lara, and certainly not with Jake at the controls as the devil that was Alayna sat on his shoulder.

"Again! Do it again!" Alayna screamed.

Jake hauled back on his control stick and Ellie's stomach attempted to turn itself inside out as they inverted. Hanging completely upside down, the centrifugal force pushed Ellie down into her seat so tightly she may as well not even need the harness strapped across her chest. They hung at the peak of the loop-the-loop for what seemed to be an age, before finally coming down the other side and levelling out.

No sooner was she able to suck in a desperate breath than she heard Jake speak.

"Hey, d'you know what an aileron roll is?"

The question must have been rhetorical as Jake yanked his control stick sideways without waiting for an answer. Ellie was slammed against the hull as the world outside the cockpit dissolved into a blur. Alayna screamed in delight. The sound devolved into a cackling, maniacal laugh as the girl was clearly having the time of her life.

"Jake!" Ellie screamed as she hit her limit, quickly clamping both hands over her mouth as the bile rose in her throat.

"Oh crap, sorry!" Jake said urgently as he immediately straightened out.

The sensation came as little relief as Ellie hitched forward, fighting the sensation with everything she had, determined not to spray the inside of Lara like a human sprinkler. But such a heavy breakfast combined with being tossed around like a ragdoll at what felt like supersonic speeds was threatening to overwhelm her. Even in the now calm flight, Ellie could almost feel the air moving over the hull as Lara cut through it, picking up on every dip and rise as they moved through the eddies and currents. Each one sent a wave of nausea through her.

Ellie struggled, clamping her hands down as hard as she could, driven to the precipice, and her stomach already beginning involuntary movements. Ellie forced her tongue to the top of her mouth and willed her throat to close. This was the best damn breakfast she'd had in her entire life, and she wasn't letting it go without a fight.

At the last moment, with a final, colossal effort, Ellie was able to fight it back, swallowing hard and letting out little more than a still-too-loud burp.

"Oh, come on, it wasn't that bad!" Alayna exclaimed as Ellie fell back into her seat with an exhausted sigh.

The fiery redhead seemed completely unaffected by the wild flight, having gone as far as to undo her harness and grip the back of Jake's headrest with both hands, half standing in her seat. How the thin girl had not been thrown about like a leaf in a tornado was beyond Ellie as Alayna glared at her for having interrupted her fun.

"I think you might be a natural-born pilot, Spitfire," Jake said, amused as he turned to fix Ellie with an apologetic look. "Not everyone can handle that right away though; cut those two some slack. Remind me at some point to take you out of atmosphere, and we can pull some high-G manoeuvres."

"Wait, really?" Alayna exclaimed in shock as her head snapped back to Jake.

"Of course! Though be warned." Jake paused as he turned in his seat to meet Alayna, a wolfish grin spreading across his face. "Exospheric flight and hard vacuum don't have this big, soft air cushion to keep you safe. You can easily smear yourself into a thin layer of human jam if you're not careful. Are you sure you can handle it?"

Alayna bristled, her eyes going wide at Jake's challenge.

"Jonathan, are you okay?" Ellie asked, cutting off any response Alayna might have.

Ellie sat in what she assumed was the co-pilot's seat, a centre console extending down into a pair of smooth, plush armrests separating her and Jake. Alayna sat in the back row directly behind Jake, whereas Jonathan was sitting behind Ellie, beyond her field of vision.

Ellie carefully leaned to the side, still mindful of her own delicate state. Behind her, Jonathan was stiff as a board and white as a ghost, holding a handle built into Lara's hull in a vice-like grip. His eyes were startlingly wide as he trembled slightly.

"Oh, Jonathan," Ellie said sympathetically. She reached around to place a hand on his knee, stroking it with her thumb.

"Ugh, he'll be fine, he's just a wet blanket, that's all," Alayna grunted. Yet, despite her apparent displeasure, she sidled over on her knees and began running her fingers through his hair. The movement closely mimicked Ellie's habit, and, slowly, Jonathan began to soften, letting out some of his tension.

Satisfied, and still a little queasy herself, Ellie turned back around. The hitches and bumps of their flight were starting to fade, and as Ellie looked out of the cockpit, her breath caught in her throat.

"That's... beautiful," she said.

Outside, the vast, black expanse of space stretched to infinity above them, thick swaths of stars shining with colours more vibrant than she'd ever seen from the surface. Before them, the daylight side of Adroa stretched away in an enormous, distinct curve.

The green of her landmasses and sparkle of her oceans appeared encapsulated in what seemed an impossibly thin layer of light blue atmosphere.

Ellie had seen pictures and videos of planets before and caught distant glimpses during their transit from her homeworld of Praxis, but nothing like this. The sheer *scale* of what was before her was astounding. Their beautiful planet seemed both impossibly huge and impossibly fragile at the same time. Adroa had one colony on her, one small colony that was far behind them. What stretched out before her was a vast, unexplored landscape begging to be experienced. The strangest sense of gratitude filled her. Despite how hard life could be, here she had a whole world effectively to herself. Even the Rike centred around their preferred food source, the colony, and once you were past their mountainous nests, there was little here to harm you.

With Jake steady on the controls, Alayna and Jonathan quiet behind her and the rush of air dissipated, Ellie sank into her chair and sucked in a large, calming breath.

"I've seen a lot of planets, and Adroa is definitely one of the prettier ones," Jake said, seemingly reading her mind. "There's just this strange sense of being so… *alone* out here. I don't think I can remember a time when I haven't been crammed shoulder to shoulder against other people. Where no matter how far you'd walk, or run, or fly, the only thing you'd find beyond the horizon is *more* people."

Jake's words echoed Ellie's feelings as she turned her head toward him.

"Have you ever been to the frontier before?" Ellie asked.

"Well, yes," Jake replied carefully. "But it wasn't exactly under amicable circumstances," he finished, poking at a few spots on his instrument panel.

Ellie wanted to ask more but was left wondering as he changed the subject.

"Have you ever entered slip-warp in a low-tonnage vessel before?" Jake asked.

"Can you define 'low tonnage'?"

Naturally, they'd travelled through slip-warp before, the method of faster-than-light travel that allowed short-lived humans to cross exceedingly vast distances in a comparatively reasonable time frame. However, Ellie was unsure about the scale to which Jake might be referring.

Ellie had heard most non-military slip-warp capable ships were vast, hulking behemoths, built to take advantage of the economy of scale as the cost of running smaller vessels across thousands of lightyears would supposedly become astronomical. She was reasonably certain the smallest vessel on which they'd ever transitioned was the Blister Fang when first coming to Adroa.

Even then, that ship was still large enough to flatten half the colony if it smacked into the ground a little too hard.

Jake looked at her, slightly confused.

"A vessel like Lara then, if that makes it clearer."

"Ah, no, in that case," Ellie answered.

"Well, it's not too bad, but something you need to be prepared for. It can be a little disorienting without sheer mass helping absorb the forces of being forced into a theoretical quantum state and back. Spitfire…" Jake said, turning back around. "Strap in please. Everyone, cross your arms over your chests and place your hands on your shoulders."

Behind them, Alaya let go of Jonathan and began strapping herself back in. Ellie was surprised the girl so readily followed Jake's request, especially without a single gripe or complaint. When they were all in position, Jake continued.

"Everyone experiences it a little differently but the first time is always the worst. Most people feel as if they're falling or having a moment of extreme vertigo. Some experience an immediate and powerful panic attack as their brains struggle to cope with the sensory transition. Just remember you're as safe in here as in any giant starliner. Lara is not going to break apart, your body is going to remain in one piece, and if you do start to panic, just focus on your breathing until the moment passes. I promise you; you'll be fine."

Ellie looked at Jake as he spoke, his attention primarily focused on Jonathan and Alayna, allowing her to study his movements. His voice was calm and reassuring and he moved slowly, with ease. His words and gestures held no edge or worry. Ellie couldn't help but feel calmed by his presence. Whatever they were about to experience, she felt herself trusting him when he promised she would be okay.

"Everyone good?" Jake asked, to be met with a trio of nods and calls of 'yes'.

"Okay then. Remember what I said, and we'll be transitioning in 5… 4… 3…"

Ellie gripped down onto her shoulders and brought her knees together, leaning forward, bracing for some sort of impact.

"... 2…1," Jake finished, sliding his throttle forward.

A rush of terror flooded in; Jake must have accidentally triggered some kind of eject function. Ellie rocketed up and away, swearing she'd heard the canopy explode as she hurtled into the dark void. She couldn't tell which way was up anymore as her senses blurred, losing all point of reference. She sucked in a deep breath to scream and…

Wait…

Ellie exhaled and sucked in another, shuddering gulp of air.

But how, how was she breathing in the vacuum of space?

It was on this thought that the world began to re-materialise around her. She could feel where her harness was constraining her chest as she sucked in deep, long breaths. The interior of Lara materialised back into view, a warmth developing and spreading on top of her hand where her nails were digging into her shoulders. Ellie looked over to where Jake had placed his hand atop hers. Heat rushed to her face as he smiled at her, raising one eyebrow.

"You okay?" he asked.

Ellie let out her breath again, smoother now her senses were returning, and she was beginning to calm. "That was a little more intense than I had expected," Ellie answered earnestly. "Alayna, Jonathan, how are you two doing?"

"I'm fine," Alayna answered, nonplussed. "I felt like I had to pee for a second. But it's gone now."

"Kill me," Jonathan quietly whispered.

"Oh, grow up," Alayna said, shoving Jonathan's shoulder. "Everyone pees. Even you."

Relieved the two were still in one piece, if a little shaken, Ellie turned her attention forward. She had to blink several times before her mind could process what lay before her, a sense of wonder quickly overcoming her. Outside the cockpit, translucent colours of all kinds rushed past in long, undulating ribbons. Layer upon layer of aurora-looking streams stacked atop one another until whatever may have lain behind them was completely obscured. It was a beautifully vivid, living rainbow of such intense colour Ellie was struggling to focus her eyes on any single point.

She opened her mouth to speak, before pausing, unable to think what to say before Alayna undid her harness, leaning forward around Jake's chair and into the space between him and Ellie.

"So, what's so important about Tropicalia that we have to head there in our pyjamas?" Alayna asked Jake.

"Tropicalia's a fairly well-developed colony that's a massive trading hub for this part of the frontier. It's well beyond the Conviction's borders and has a free trade market; you can get practically anything you'd want there. Why? Still haven't figured it out yet?"

"No," Alayna replied in a sour tone.

Ellie's insides flipped as Jake suddenly fixed her with a wide, mischievous grin.

"I'm taking you shopping."

***

"Okay, and we'll be transitioning back in about 3...2...1..."

Ellie felt as though Jonathan had suddenly kicked the back of her chair, causing her to lurch forward. The sensation lasted barely a moment as they transitioned back into real space.

"See, I told you the first time was always the worst. After a few transitions, you'll barely feel it anymore," Jake said.

Ellie leaned sideways to look back at Jonathan.

"Did you kick my chair?" Ellie asked gently.

"W-what? No!" Jonathan responded, confused.

"It's okay, just checking," Ellie said comfortingly, glad it had just been her false sense and not Jonathan involuntarily reacting to the transition.

Ellie had wanted to draw attention to the stunning light display directly before them during their travel, but she seemed to be the only one who'd noticed it. Jake barely registered any change whatsoever, and

Jonathan and Alayna appeared nonplussed as they looked out the windows.

Am I the only one impressed by the living rainbow just beyond the glass? Ellie thought.

"Huh…" Jake muttered.

Ellie's attention was drawn back to him at the note of concern in his voice. Jake's attention was focused on a large screen inset into the centre console, displaying a three-dimensional map, various objects labelled and highlighted in an array of colours. Ellie was trying to read what they might be, but Jake was manipulating the map, rotating it, zooming in and out of various points just a little too fast for her to keep up.

"Is something the matter?" Ellie asked apprehensively.

Jake, in response, moved the map around and zoomed in until a ship was highlighted against the backdrop of stars. Ellie's eyebrows rose as she looked at it. A large ship, long, wide and flat. It was dark in colour and bristling with cannons along every surface. Multiple levels were tiered back in set intervals like flattened blades stacked atop each other as they reached back from a wide central plane. It boasted a vast bank of engines nested into a cut-out section on the back end. It almost looked to Ellie like an enormous, overwrought spearhead that had fallen out of the twisted imagination of a guild of maddened smiths.

The shape and slopes of the ship had the same angled, geometric design that shared a family resemblance with Lara and the armour Jake had worn. It, too, looked aggressively utilitarian. But the main hull, with its layer upon layer of spearheads stacked up and hammered down upon each other, had surely been chosen with intimidation in mind, an effect it was doing well to accomplish as Ellie shifted uncomfortably in her seat, the unconscious awareness setting in that the ship was undeniably Conviction.

"That is a Conviction LD-class patrol boat," Jake confirmed without prompting. "The 'LDPB Conglomerated Affinity', apparently. Twenty-four heavy anti-ship cannons, an orbital lance, a small fighter squadron and, for its size, quite a mean primary accelerator. A crew of about six hundred if memory serves, and I have no idea what it's doing out here," Jake said.

Ellie was sure he had explained for their benefit, but it sounded almost as if he was talking to himself.

"Are they invading?" Jonathan asked in sudden apprehension, he and Alayna leaning forward to look at the screen. Ellie could see nothing outside the canopy except the vast starfield and empty blackness of space. Had it not been for Lara's sensors, Ellie wouldn't have known they weren't alone out here.

Jonathan's question caused Jake to turn around, an expression on his face that was amused but seemingly wondering if Jonathan was secretly daft.

"Not likely," Jake said slowly, turning back to the screen. "It's just sitting in orbit, no scans or aggressive posturing. Even if it were in full combat stance, it's not a landing craft. Conviction naming conventions are usually pretty simple," Jake explained. "They need to communicate a lot of information in as little time as possible. A primary role, followed by a specialisation, if any, followed by a specific designation, usually condensed into an acronym.

"LD stands for 'Light Defence', PB for 'Patrol Boat', and 'Conglomerated Affinity' is the name of that specific ship. Vessels like this normally putter about already secure systems, chasing off wannabe pirates and running down smugglers. They're built for efficiency and taking the little jobs so that the real heavy hitters don't waste their time bringing artillery to a knife fight. It might be Conviction and still able to stomp anything you'd find out here without breaking a sweat, but trust me, it's not a particularly impressive vessel."

"And how would you know?" Alayna asked, a note of accusation in her voice.

"I've…reason to be familiar with Conviction fleet operations," Jake said, deflecting.

Ellie had no reason to believe Jake was lying, but nothing about the ship on screen looked 'light' or 'defensive' to her, barrels jutting from every layered back surface and a mean, aggressive styling with its weapon-like silhouette. She had to agree its presence here was a mystery.

"Then how come you don't know what it could be out here for?" Alayna pressed Jake.

"Because we're not anywhere near the Conviction's borders where it might be feasible the ship crossed over to check in on the local neighbourhood. The frontier is vast, and the borders are far, far back from where we are. Tropicalia is about as far out as civilisation extends. The only things beyond this point are little colonies like Adroa, on the edge of explored space. Even the automated exploration probes haven't ranged much farther than that." Jake explained. "I can't tell you why it's out here, only that it's strange to see it is."

Alayna crossed her arms and grumbled something incoherently.

"It might also interest you to know, our good friend is loitering about as well," Jake said, continuing.

Jake moved the map again and zoomed in on another ship. This time, Ellie recognised it almost immediately.

"The Blister Fang?" Ellie said in surprise. "Captain Slackvore is here? Why?"

Ellie was shocked to see Slackvore out and about. Of course, he had to exist elsewhere and have his own life. But in Ellie's mind, he was someone showing up on export day, fleecing everyone out of all their harvests and just disappearing until the following year.

"Well, this is the closest major trading hub. It's not all that surprising," Jake explained. "Even if he doesn't sell everything here and carts it farther in where the demand and prices are higher, Tropicalia still has the infrastructure for refuelling large haulers and anything else he might need. It'd be a good pit stop at least."

"We're not…we're not going to run into them on the planet, are we?" Ellie asked nervously. She wasn't quite sure why, but running into Slackvore or any of the crew, inadvertently letting them know they no longer had the total monopoly on Adroa's space-capable technology, would only end poorly.

Jake poked around the screen a bit, Ellie watching a dotted line draw itself out in front of the Blister Fang as it curved towards Tropicalia. Jake frowned.

"No is the short answer," Jake answered, somewhat distracted.

Ellie paused as he seemed engrossed in thought. She waited, but Jake just kept staring at the screen.

"Is there something else?" Ellie prompted.

Jake hummed distractedly, pointing to the dotted line, and tapping the screen for emphasis.

"Slackvore is trying to avoid the patrol boat for whatever reason. But the way he's chosen to do it is…" Jake trailed off, making a circling motion with one hand. "Not how I would have done it, to say the least. He's either stupid, a cheapskate, or has a dramatically overinflated sense of bravado. There are always pirates hanging around the outer edges of systems like this, looking to score a nice, fat trader running heavy with goods and materials.

"Most traders will burn hard and juke their courses about randomly, making it difficult for smaller ships to jump in on top of them and board. Slackvore, though, is taking this long, slow line down, keeping the planet between him and the patrol boat the entire time. It'd be a cheap run that would keep him hidden from the Conviction ship, but such a predictable course would make it easy for anyone else to plan an ambush."

Ellie cocked her head in interest. During the long transit from their homeworld, she'd learned just how cut-throat intergalactic travel was outside the Conviction. However, she'd never been on the bridge or privy to any special information. All she knew, she'd gleaned from the mutterings and complaints of various crewmembers throughout their journey.

Sitting at the forefront and learning about the manoeuvres and decisions captains had to make was fascinating.

"Aren't there any wardens? Maybe that's what the patrol boat is here for?" Ellie offered.

"Wardens? No," Jake replied. "They're exclusive to the Conviction and don't run battleships. If anything ever shows up in orbit that's more than their small inspection craft can handle, the wardens call in the fleet proper. The Conviction isn't going to spend resources to send a ship all the way out here to an unaffiliated system for a policing action. And if they wanted to flex some muscle to remind the locals who's in charge, it certainly wouldn't be done with a dinky little patrol boat. Tropicalia has some orbital security that would make a show of responding to any attacks in the system so the other traders don't get scared off. But Slackvore is allowing any would-be attackers to pick their engagement, maximising the response time from orbital security and minimising the time he has to react."

Ellie tilted her head slightly in the other direction. She didn't believe for a moment that Slackvore was in any way stupid. But a cheapskate with an over-inflated sense of bravado? Definitely.

"Is he likely to be in any danger?" Ellie asked nervously. If the Blister Fang and its crew were destroyed, the entire colony could wither and die. Excluding Jake who had just arrived, Slackvore was their sole link to space.

"I'm sure Slackvore will be fine. I was given to understand he and his crew have been running through these sectors for years now," Jake said.

"But still…" Ellie pressed nervously. Why was she so unsettled? Slackvore may pull stunts like this all the time for all she knew. But a nervousness was nagging at her, seeing Slackvore acting so careless. Perhaps he didn't realise just how important he was to the colony. Or perhaps he just didn't care.

"Okay, look," Jake said reassuringly. "The Blister Fang is a moderately capable ship for what it is. It can defend itself, and there's not likely to be anything out here large enough to flat-out destroy it. The danger comes from some opportunistic gutter snakes boarding and taking over the ship. But Slackvore has a large, fairly competent crew that wouldn't give up without a fight.

"On my way to Adroa, I got the distinct impression Slackvore was more of the type to order a boarding than suffer from one. Out here, he's a big fish in a small pond. Which is probably exactly why he's hiding from the patrol boat. I'm guessing it'll have been the first thing he's come across in a long time that's capable of giving him a proper smackdown. At least, that's my best guess."

Ellie nodded slowly as she listened, unable to help but picture a local gang of malnourished spacers making hard dock with the Blister Fang, only for the airlock to open and them to be facing down the veritable juggernaut that was Breacher. She had to admit, those poor spacers wouldn't stand a chance. It still felt to Ellie like an unnecessary risk, though.

"Why didn't he just jump in closer to the planet to begin with?" Ellie asked. "If fuel and safety are important, why not make the trip shorter from the start?"

"That is an excellent question with a long and complicated answer," Jake replied, a small grin spreading across his face. "It's not that I think you wouldn't understand, it's just that quantum mechanics is tricky to get your head around because it deals with some mind-bending concepts, and things get out of hand quick."

"W-would it be okay if you tried to explain it?" Jonathan piped up, leaning forward beside Ellie.

Ellie watched Jake look around at the three sets of eyes staring eagerly at him. He breathed out a huge sigh, his grin only growing.

"Okay, the short, short version is this. At its most basic level, the universe exists as a series of probabilities. When we enter slip-warp, we're using our technology to exit real space and transition into an infinite number of possible states. For a split second, we *could* be anywhere in the universe. This is what's known as a superposition. But the number of possible states we could be in decreases as soon as we interact with anything in real space. Particles, gravity, energy, it doesn't matter.

"If we let the number of probabilities get too low, they'll collapse, and our position in the universe will be set. Once our position is set, we're forced back into real space. It gets so much more complicated, but that's the gist of it. To try and answer your question directly, the bigger the ship is, the farther away it has to exit from something like a planet or another ship. The universe won't allow you to occupy the same space at the same time as another object, so your probabilities will collapse before you reach that point. Does that make sense?"

Ellie blinked.

"It makes a certain amount of sense," Ellie said, uncertain. "It's interesting. I've never even thought about these types of things before. Never had to."

"Well, don't think about it too hard, or you'll be filled with existential dread," Jake said with an amused tone. "Though once Spitfire starts flying about, she'll need to know all this—"

"Wait, you really mean it?" Alayna piped up with a tone of excited awe.

"…so, there's no reason I can't teach you about it at the same time if you like," Jake finished as if he hadn't been interrupted.

It wasn't something Ellie had considered before, and it made her realise just how much she didn't know about Jake. She'd just accepted that he knew how to fly ships and jump to slip-warp and navigate around the frontier and its many dangers. Each of these were skills and even trades in their own right. She couldn't help but feel a deep curiosity about him take hold within her.

"Either or," Jake said. "Slackvore can make his own choices. It's time we set our own course and headed in for a landing. I'm actually quite looking forward to today." Jake's voice betrayed an edge of excitement.

Ellie saw his grin as they began to accelerate forward. A small smile spread across her face that she hoped he wouldn't notice.

Curious indeed.

Ten: City Views

Ellie marvelled at the sights before her.

As Jake helped Jonathan and Alayna out of Lara, Ellie couldn't stop her head from turning every which way. The city that stretched out before her was as magnificent in scale as it was beautiful. Tropicalia was a tropical world consisting almost entirely of scattered archipelagos. The oceans were shallow, and the weather was gentle year-round.

With a lack of solid land, infinite space and a seemingly unlimited budget, the architects and designers appeared to have had a field day designing the city of their dreams.

All around her, broad, curving terraces rose from the electric blue water, tiered back and stacked atop one another, almost looking like the lines of a topographical map. Every building was made of a smooth, rendered white polyplast that shone brilliantly in the sun, matching the startlingly white beaches rising to their edges in certain places.

Dark filtered windows sat back beneath the overhangs in stark contrast to their surroundings. Not a single straight line could be seen anywhere as people moved about the wide paths. Nearly every balcony and ledge was exploding with plant life as lush gardens spilt out over the edges, many long trails of leafy vines reaching all the way down to the levels below. Tall palm trees and other beautiful plants Ellie couldn't identify swayed in the slight breeze.

Vast parks resonated distantly with chatter and music from below as Ellie placed her hand on the railing. The entire place seemed to have been designed as a pedestrian city.

No roads or ground vehicles were anywhere in sight. Instead, the air was abuzz with life, and with the gentle hum of gravity repulsors as ships took off and landed on hundreds of small landing pads identical to the one Lara sat on. In the far distance, much larger cargo haulers lined up in the sky, forming long lanes as they came in to land on the outskirts.

The light breeze tickled Ellie's hair and brought to her the natural perfumes of the trees, oceans, and flowers. Stalls, restaurants, and cafes lined the promenades as people moved with a relaxed purpose between the many, many shops and their extravagant displays.

It was unlike anything Ellie had ever come across. Not a moment went by where she couldn't hear some distant laughter. In almost every definition of the word, this world looked to Ellie like an absolute paradise.

"It's so bright," Alayna said, coming up beside Ellie to look out over the city, shielding her eyes.

"Yes, but thankfully, there's very little UV to worry about," Jake said, joining them. "Tropicalia has a distant orbit around a relatively dim star and a thick atmosphere. So, it might look bright, but it's safe to open your eyes. That's also partly why the sky's like that."

Ellie turned her eyes skyward; it was as if she had vaguely registered the sky previously, but her mind now had so much information to process, it had put the sky to one side.

It was a completely cloudless day, and while the water was so electrically coloured that it could be confused for a sugary sports drink, the sky was a much deeper, vibrant blue. It had a depth and uniformity to it such that, if Ellie looked high enough to remove all the buildings and points of reference from her field of vision, then her eyes couldn't even focus. Just an endless expanse of a single, rich blue that made her head spin.

"Hmm, I didn't think it was *that* noteworthy," Jake said, seeing her expression and turning his gaze upwards.

"Sorry," Ellie said, quickly looking away and feeling slightly abashed. "I didn't see the sky until I was fifteen; it still catches me off guard sometimes. How beautiful it is, I mean."

Jake kept his eyes skyward, suddenly looking as if force-fed a spoonful of a hive world's waste treatment water.

"Are...are you sure it's okay for us to walk around like this? Everyone else is so well dressed, and we're..." Jonathan said nervously from behind Ellie, holding up the collar of his pyjama top.

Jake jumped at the chance to change the subject and looked at Jonathan with a sympathetic expression.

"Well, if that's something you're worried about, I'd say that's where we begin," Jake finished as he took

Ellie's hand, causing her to jump as if she'd been electrocuted. Jake put his arm around Jonathan and led them towards the nearest promenade. This left Alayna, miffed, to follow behind.

The next few hours blurred together in Ellie's mind as Jake took them from shop to shop in the seemingly endless stores that lined the multiple, curved levels of the city. Ellie still hesitated at everything they were going through, trying to stress to Jonathan and Alayna to focus only on the bare essentials. But Jake's exuberance seemed to be rubbing off on the pair as they slowly became more and more excited throughout the day.

The stone of worry sitting in Ellie's gut dissolved a little as she saw Alayna start to show excitement about trying on various clothes and dresses. The girl normally so quick and resolute in her decisions, who usually become infuriated with even the smallest amounts of deliberation, was almost paralysed with indecision, spoilt for choice for the first time in her life.

Besides, Ellie thought. *He's offering, and we don't have anything left besides the clothes on our backs.*

And it was true. Even if she hadn't visited their hill yet, Alayna had quietly let her know the situation was bleak. Ellie strongly doubted anything of their home would remain after it'd been crushed under thousands of feet of a Rike swarm. Ellie had put up enough of a fight that if Jake ever did turn around and demand some kind of repayment, she could turn back and say that he had insisted, and she owed him nothing at all.

It wasn't as if Jake wasn't capable of simply taking anything he may want from them anyway. So, if he was going to insist on helping them survive, who was she to argue? She may as well get everything out of him as she could; they would need it in the long run.

Yet, as Ellie watched Jake follow an excited Alayna around with an enormous 'maybe' pile in his arms, she couldn't help but feel he would stand by his word and never ask for anything in return. But how could he have got this far in life with the way he was? The man was, honestly, an idiot. A kind, well-intentioned, lovable idiot, one who seemed so genuine in everything he did that people couldn't help but get swept up by his enthusiasm.

Wait, loveable? Ellie clued in on the errant thought, shaking her head. It was far too soon to be thinking of him in such familiar terms.

Why the hell does he have to be so damn endearing?

The day continued like that, moving from store to store until they finally broke for lunch.

Ellie sighed in relief as she slumped into a padded chair. It was late afternoon by now, and they'd been on their feet all day. They'd stopped at a little open-top cafe on one of the higher levels, providing a beautiful view of the city and the ocean just a few kilometres away.

Ellie sat across from Jake, each with a cool drink in front of them as Alayna and Jonathan, overcome with an energy Ellie couldn't quite explain, ran about nearby. It almost looked as though the two teenagers were playing as they darted back and forth, pointing out various points of interest and talking excitedly.

Something that amazed Ellie was precisely how the shopping had worked.

Ellie assumed they would be dragging around bags all day, or Jake would have to hire a porter bot to carry it for them. Instead, for anything they hadn't changed into and walked out with, Jake had given the store their pad number. Supposedly, they were going to deliver everything directly to Lara. That would explain the number of drones quietly zipping by on occasion.

So far, they'd purchased a few bare essentials. Jake had broken off at one point to grab something he needed. He was cagey about it when Ellie asked so she let the subject drop. While he was away, she, Jonathan and Alayna had been idly browsing when Ellie had been confronted with just how much of a stranglehold Slackvore had over the colony.

She'd come across a set of brand-new wind turbines. Three of them together, clean, modern, and likely far more efficient than the one she'd bought on export day. A deep rage was still boiling inside her at the price.

Twenty dols. Twenty! Breacher, you arsehole! Ellie thought. She'd always believed the man had rocks for brains, and she was running circles around him. Maybe it had turned out she was the one being danced around and was too naive to see it.

Although…

Ellie had to admit she was probably misplacing her anger. At least towards Breacher, specifically. It was most likely Slackvore dictating to the slab of a man what the prices had to be, and she really had got

Breacher to lower them significantly. Still, he had to know the value of a dol and that the price she was paying was outrageous. Surely Breacher couldn't be *that* thick?

Well... Ellie thought, weighing it up in her head. In all honesty, it probably came down to a coin toss about whether Breacher truly understood or not.

Regardless, Ellie had slapped down her own dols on those turbines so fast the clerk jumped. She'd had to struggle so hard for so long to earn enough for the bare minimum when in reality, she could have bought the set of *three* she'd come across ten times over. Ellie could have been swimming in wind turbines and had not the slightest care in the world about how much power she used in the morning. It was only due to the fact neither she nor anyone else on the colony had a slip-warp capable ship, that they had to rely on Slackvore and his obscene profiteering.

Ellie made a note to speak to Jake about it later. She didn't know how much it cost to run Lara about, but surely Jake could make far more as a simple courier than by putting his life at risk to fight off the swarms.

"So. I've had some thoughts I wanted to run by you…" Jake began slowly, breaking Ellie away from her intense musings.

Ah, here it comes, the shitening, Ellie thought as she deflated a little.

There was a mild disappointment in Jake. She'd been ignoring her misgivings all day yet despite her best efforts, she'd begun feeling a little hope, growing more trusting of him. Deep down though, there was a sense it had to be too good to be true. Contemplating all this,

Ellie was suddenly very aware of the new dress against her skin, the one he'd bought and paid for earlier in the day.

"Of course," Ellie answered with a forced chipperness. "What were you thinking?"

Jake cocked his head slightly, picking up on the strain in her tone. He seemed to consider his next words very carefully, taking a long moment before speaking again.

"Well," he began. "When we came here this morning, I'd had the vague idea that I could pick you up a tent, or some kind of disaster shelter depending on what was available. But after we landed, I started seriously putting together a list. If you're in a soft-walled tent, you'll need extra protection. That's a turret or two at least. That also means you won't have house power, so that's a set of external solar panels that you're going to need along with stand-alone mountings and energy storage. You'll need a water tank, a filtration system, and some kind of toiletry solution beyond a composting toilet or a hole in the ground. A separate transmitter to call for help, extra bedding and food storage and the list goes on and on."

Jake twirled his hand in the air for emphasis.

"And I know you're already uncomfortable accepting breakfast from me, let alone letting me set you up an entire new home. On top of that, you'll need to replant your fields and re-establish your crops, so who knows what kind of harvest you'll have next year?"

As Jake continued, Ellie remained still and quiet. All of these were things she was painfully aware of as she waited for him to get to the point, not so much as touching the drink in front of her. Even with the sudden relative jump in the value of what dols she did have, it was still far more than Ellie could afford on her own.

"It's dangerous with the Rike around. Then you factor in having to protect Alayna and Jonathan. And don't even get me started on the likes of *Hunter…*" Jake spat the last word with venom, a fierce look coming over his face.

Jake paused, taking a sip of his drink before calming down and continuing.

"It would be much better if you could just stay with me. But I can't put you up forever, at least, not for *free…*"

And in 3…2…1… Ellie thought, pensive.

"So, I was wondering, if the three of you might like to come work for me?"

Ellie blinked.

"I'm sorry, what?" Ellie asked in surprise.

"Well, this is the solution I came up with. You need to rebuild your fields, but that won't take up all of your time, especially not with all three of you there to work them. I knew Adroa was an isolated farm colony from the beginning, so I'd always intended to grow a few crops myself. Not anything in the order of magnitude to sell commercially, mind you. Just enough to be self-reliant as I earned an income protecting others from the swarms.

"I made sure I had enough stores to get me through a few failed attempts while learning the nuances of getting things to grow and bear a usable harvest. But you've already been farming for years. I could use you to leap-frog over that learning stage and establish my fields. In return, you get food and board, and I'll even pay you a small wage. This way, you get all the benefits of staying with me, earning your way without imposing on my kindness, and work towards getting back on your own feet at the same time."

Ellie's heart began to beat faster, her eyes dropping from Jake to stare at the table for a long moment. Eventually, she picked up her drink and threw her head back, downing it in one go. The feeling of the cold liquid hitting her stomach helped undo the knots that had tied themselves there. It was a good plan. A wonderful plan, one in which it was difficult—or impossible—to uncover any flaws.

Ellie struggled to point out anything specifically 'wrong' with Jake's idea. It was just, she still felt as though she was imposing on him for a favour, that somehow, he had come up with something to save her from this mess she would otherwise have. He hadn't been planning to employ anyone, had he? So why now, and why her? Or to put it more accurately, why the *three* of them? As for herself, sure, she could see why he might value her growing skills. But who in their right mind would employ Jonathan and Alayna when setting up a new venture?

It would also mean they'd have to be careful not to step on his toes in his own home.

Yes, these were the objections to the plan. Yet as Ellie lowered her eyes to carefully study his, despite all the apprehension in the moments leading up to Jake presenting his idea, she didn't feel they were in danger of him suddenly snapping and throwing them out.

Importantly, she could actually do what Jake was asking.

She could prove herself capable at it. She might primarily be a melon farmer, but she'd learned how to grow multiple crops by helping her neighbours and as a backup should their melons not work out. Jonathan and Alayna also knew enough to pull their weight. And with Jake coming from a place of ignorance, maybe Ellie could actually add value in this arrangement, helping him navigate the nuances of Adroa's rich soil and sometimes too-heavy rainfall.

She could easily imagine Jake literally drowning his first few growing attempts.

Or maybe he'd space his plants far too close together, leading them to compete and strangle each other, affecting their yield. His was a sound plan, a logical plan, and she'd be crazy not to jump at it.

And yet…

"Jake," Ellie said quietly. Moving her focus from the depth of his eyes to look at him as a whole, she could see she had his full attention. The seriousness of her tone seemed at odds with the beauty of their surroundings.

"I know you said I'd be earning my way. But…you're still asking me to put Jonathan and Alayna's safety in your hands indirectly. It's a generous offer, and, honestly, it's one I think I'd like to agree to. But…I need assurances. I can't risk the two of them. It might sound stupid, but from my experience, sleeping in an open field, exposed to the elements and the Rike…as long as we're doing so on our own terms, which will always be better than living on someone else's mercy."

Her insides twisted; in reality, they'd starve to death long before they'd be able to regrow any substantial harvest. Marshweed could sustain them only for so long, and with no shelter to get them through the winter, she could only appeal to her neighbours' mercy. Ask to stay with the Lindens or the Mathews. Ellie could probably even convince one of their sons to marry her. There weren't exactly a lot of eligible partners in the colony, and if she bedded one of them for a few nights, taking him around the world a couple of times in the process, she was sure he'd be only too eager to offer her a ring.

But then she'd be right back where she didn't want to be, living on the mercy of her 'husband' and his family, stuck with a man she didn't particularly love and just buying her place with her body. At that point, she may as well just whore herself out; the pay would certainly be better.

Ellie's legs began to tremble beneath her seat, the dark thoughts and enormity of the decision before her taking their toll. It had been a calamitous week, and she might be nearing her breaking point.

But just at the right moment, Jake's hand closed gently but firmly around her wrist—the kind of clasp that said, *I hear you and I've got you. You're safe.*

He lifted it up between them, clasping her hand with both of his.

"What assurance can I give you then, Ellie?" Jake's voice was soft, but his tone was serious. His eyes once more pieced into her, making her feel as if she were stripped down so naked that nothing was left but her soul. A soul he could see right through.

"I don't......I don't know, Jake." Ellie tried to keep her tone even, failing miserably as her eyes began to burn. "I just don't understand..."

Ellie trailed off, squeezing her eyes shut and dropping her head a moment. What was she even trying to say? She wanted to trust him, already knowing the answer was to take the opportunity presented and just go along with it. But her trust had been broken in the past, and she would be leaving herself vulnerable. Leaving Alayna and Jonathan vulnerable, more to the point.

Ultimately, she barely even knew Jake.

He was charming and seemed genuine. Ellie would even go as far as to say he was utterly disarming. But that was over the course of how many interactions? What would happen when they were under one another's feet, in close confines and in the depths of a bleak period before the first harvest came along fo the taking?

Jake leaned back into his chair, lowering her hand. He let go to drum his fingers on the table.

"Well..." he began slowly. "I think your main concern is security. And please, correct me if I'm wrong but it seems you're worried that if you become reliant on me, I'll have power over you. That I'll be able to throw you out on a whim and in the end, your choice will either be to do whatever it takes to please me or for you all to die a slow death of starvation and exposure. Sounds about right?"

His tone was thick with sympathy, but his eyes showed no condescension as he regarded her. How could he be so empathetic and understanding, especially when she was struggling to process her own thoughts and feelings?

"So how about…" Jake drew out, rolling the words around in his mouth. "I pay you a full year's wage, in advance, for all three of you. Then you're simply honour bound to stay and do the work I've paid you for. But if you feel the situation becomes untenable, you can leave and already have the money in your account. Maybe board with your neighbours for a while or not, but the point is you'll have the resources to stand on your own for a good length of time."

Ellie's head shot up, her eyes going wide. This was actually getting worse, wasn't it? Not better. Because now, she'd be beholden to him for a whole year and there had to be something more to it than him needing employees. It was a strange offer, too generous by far, and there had to be something hidden… Something she would come to regret later. Otherwise, the deal was all on her side, nothing in it for him given that they could up and leave at any point, leaving him high and dry. Whatever was in it for him, he was reluctant to talk about that aspect.

She couldn't help but feel she was staring at Jake as if he'd just grown a second head.

"Jake!" Ellie exclaimed. "Why would you suggest that? What's to stop me from accepting and then leaving the moment we get back to Adroa? Or just running off right here? I'm sure I could get a job as a shop assistant or something. I've just never had the resources to afford rent, or to even reach a planet like this. I could completely take advantage of you!"

"Yes," Jake answered calmly, a smile spreading across his face. "You could. But I believe it was only this morning you took a leap of faith and allowed me to whisk the three of you away to some far-off planet, sight unseen. You decided I could be trusted, Ellie. So let me take that same leap, and ask the question…"

Jake raised his hand between them, holding it out to her.

"Can I trust you?" he asked.

Ellie stared at Jake, thoughts and emotions rampaging through her head and in her chest. Her mind worked so fast to try and get a handle on things that she didn't even know what she was thinking. Ellie looked up to meet his eyes once more.

Ellie yearned to take his hand but a wisp of hesitation held her back; there was one more thing she needed to be clear about.

"So I understand, you just want us to farm for you. There are no other duties you'd expect?" Ellie asked. The turmoil inside disconnected from the seriousness of her tone. Jake frowned in a confused sort of way.

"I mean, we'll be living together, so I'd hope you'd do me the courtesy of cleaning up after yourselves and helping me with cooking and general housework—"

"Not what I'm referring to." Her heart was beating faster. This wasn't a conversation she wanted to have, but this was their future with which she was gambling. "Are you expecting any… night-time activities?"

Jake's frown deepened, a touch of exasperation entering his tone.

"Ellie, you're clearly after something specific, but I genuinely have no idea what you're talking about," Jake said before pausing. Taking a long breath, his frown lifted, and when he spoke again, his voice was full of sympathy and reassurance. "Please just come out and say what you mean. I know that may not have gone well for you in the past, but I'm my own person, and I want you to be able to be honest with me. Please."

Ellie eyed Jake up and down, his hand still outstretched. Butterflies were swarming about inside her and her heart was pounding. Ellie closed her eyes, drew in a deep breath, and when she opened them again, she looked Jake dead in the eyes.

"Jake," Ellie said coolly. "Am I going to have to sleep with you for this?"

She was glad of being able to keep her voice level but the strange stillness was at odds with how she was nearly vibrating in her chair.

Jake flinched as if he'd just been struck, his eyes widening, a look of abject horror crossing his expression. He looked all the world as though he'd been thrown backwards out of an airlock. After a long moment of staring at her, something changed in his expression. His jaw clamped shut, the muscles on the side of his face tightening visibly as his lips set in a firm line. His eyes hardened and he fixed her with a steely gaze.

"Ellie," Jake said. His voice was deeper than before, rougher, carrying a note of authority. It lacked the playfulness with which he usually spoke as his gaze bore into hers. "I swear on my life, you will never have to do anything you are not one hundred percent eager to do.

"Nothing that is not completely consensual in the truest sense of the word. I'm doing what I can, so you won't have to resort to that. I respect you, Ellie. And no, not the food, not the job, not the roof or anything else comes with the expectation or unsaid implication that you'll have to sleep with me or indulge any other carnal fantasies. If you stay with me, I want you to feel absolutely safe and comfortable. I promise, you'll never have to fear me stealing into your room one night, looking for...*compensation*."

Jake slowly spat out the last word as if it passed a toxin over his lips as he did so. Even here, a shiver darted up Ellie's spine as Jake referred back to what had happened on export day. But along with the memory came a swelling in her chest, a deep relief as she realised she probably wasn't being fair to compare Jake to the likes of Hunter. Why would she do that?

Ellie had no doubt if the same offer had come from that slime ball, she'd be spending almost every night on her back or on her knees. Again, she was reminded that what Jake considered the floor of human decency actually sank so much lower. She'd need to try and open Jake's eyes a little to repay him, or at least get him to see around his own filters.

Ellie felt a weight being lifted from her, and a fierce protectiveness towards Jake beginning to form. The universe needed more people like him in it. He was strong, masculine, but also young, and strangely innocent. Ellie would need to ensure he didn't get taken advantage of.

"You're mad. You're absolutely mad, do you know that?" Ellie said in complete disbelief.

The mad, endearing man that was Jake only smiled wide at her as his eyes lit up.

"Oh, be honest, you like it that way," he said knowingly, the playfulness re-entering his voice.

Ellie, unable to think of anything else she might have left to say, slowly reached up to place her hand in his.

Her heart nearly jumped to her throat when the thin blue holographic rings appeared above their hands and hundreds of dols began flooding into Ellie's account.

She froze, her hand hovering in midair even as Jake lowered his. She may as well have been one of the mannequins in the nearby windows for all outer appearances.

Jake cocked his head again, still smiling.

"I mean, don't get too excited; that's the combined wage for all three of you, not just yours."

He'd misunderstood. Ellie was beginning to hyperventilate, darkness quickly creeping in from the edges of her vision.

"Ellie…Ellie are you all right?" Jake's tone had an edge of concern that turned into one of urgency as he leaned forward.

"I'm fine," Ellie said breathlessly, her vision swimming. "I just need a minute."

Ellie desperately wished for a distraction, so she'd have a chance to pull herself together. Anything to take Jake's attention off her while she tried to come to terms with how fast things were moving. Like an angel sent from on high, Alayna appeared beside Jake.

"Umm…" Alayna said slowly, uncharacteristically hesitant as she held something behind her back. "Jake?"

Jake shot a look at Ellie as if to confirm she wasn't going to be blown away by the slight breeze, before turning to Alayna.

He sat there a few long moments as Alayna fidgeted, swinging her hips distractedly as a range of emotions played across the girl's face. Annoyance, anger and frustration in equal parts as she tried to speak a few times but seemed unable to get the words out. There was a general nervousness to her movements that Ellie hadn't seen before.

"I uh… I mean, this is…it's not…" Alayna struggled. As she spoke, hesitating repeatedly, she seemed to grow more agitated with herself.

Jake calmly stood, placing his hands behind his back and giving Alayna his full attention. He wore a patient expression, waiting for her to find the words in her own time.

Ellie half expected Alayna to bristle as someone taller than her rose up in such close proximity. Yet oddly, his placid and always calm demeanour seemed to have the opposite effect, Alayna taking a shallow but determined breath. She took whatever she had behind her back and showed it to Jake. It was an expensive-looking hairbrush, still on its placard.

Alayna pointed to her head as if that might help clarify the situation. She struggled to meet his gaze as she made eye contact before quickly looking away.

"My hair, it gets… And I think this would…'cause it's a *smart brush* but I…and I don't want to ask but…and it's just… Oh, forget it."

"Alayna," Jake said soothingly, smiling at her in a reassuring way. "What exactly were you trying to ask me? And no, I won't 'forget it'. I'd very much like to know."

Jake sounded as though he already knew the answer but wanted Alayna to tell him, nonetheless.

"Could… *would* you, maybe, get this for me? Um…please?" Alayna asked in a surprisingly small voice. She still struggled to meet his eyes, looking every which way except directly at him. Eventually, as she finished, Alayna was able to drag her chin up and ask Jake directly.

Jake beamed down at Alayna.

"Spitfire, I would *love* to buy you a brush for your hair. Which shop did it come from?"

Alayna sheepishly pointed towards a store slightly down the way. Jake took the brush from her and moved off, a spring in his step as if buying a hairbrush for a girl was the highest thing on his list of priorities. Alayna's cheeks flushed red as he headed off. Ellie might not be the only one dealing with new thoughts and feelings.

"So. A brush, huh?" Ellie asked softly, still not confident in being able to say much more but grateful for the distraction.

"Shut up," Alayna said in reflex, but it lacked any of the usual steel or venom for her to mean it.

"Are you embarrassed about asking Jake to buy you something?"

"NO!" Alayna snapped as she sat in Jake's chair.

"... Yes," she admitted after a moment. Alayna looked conflicted, almost distraught, emotions still playing over her face as she refused to look at Ellie. She let her speech carry her away…

"I don't know, it's just…I don't get it. There's been lots of things I've seen today that I wanted. I would have walked away with half the things in this city, but I wasn't going to be indebted to him like that. I don't want to give him anything to lord over me, to let him, to always know he has one over on me, to make me have something to repay. He wanted to buy me a dress, and I needed a dress, that's fine, that's one thing, but I could have easily continued in my pyjamas, it's not like I care. But when I saw that stupid brush in that stupid display, I had this…*flash* in my brain that I really wanted it. I might actually be able to brush my hair without ripping half of it out and walk around with nice, straight, brushed hair instead of the birds' nest it usually is.

"And, I don't know, as I was thinking about it, I didn't even really consider that Jake *wouldn't* buy it for me. Even though he has no reason to."

Alayna was becoming more animated as she spoke. A note of agitation rang in her voice as she gesticulated with her hands for emphasis.

"I could picture myself asking him and he'd just get that stupid dopey grin on his face and wouldn't even ask for anything in return. Like, he wouldn't try and bargain for something or make a big show over how big of a deal it was that he was getting it for me or anything like that. I don't know, it's like he'd be happy I asked him to get me something, and that made me feel—"

Alayna cut out in exasperation, throwing her hands skywards in a dramatic huff. Slowly, she lowered them to her lap, turning her head side on towards Ellie.

"—*not* angry," Alayna finished, struggling to find the right words to convey her emotions. It seemed as if even she was surprised to hear the words that came spilling from her lips. That she would allow Jake to buy her something and not be worried by it, not be scared. But somehow, just like Ellie, she couldn't believe how easy it all seemed either. Where was the catch? It was as if she wanted to feel aggrieved at Jake. For something. Only, she had no idea for what.

Ellie was still reeling from her own discussion with Jake. But hearing Alayna explain what was going through her head helped Ellie to come to some of her own conclusions. Ellie held her hand across the table. Alayna hesitated a moment, then took it without a fight.

"I think..." Ellie began, squeezing Alayna's hand. "We've had a very specific set of experiences. I'm only just realising this myself, and I'm not exactly sure how to explain this concisely, but we haven't had an easy life. I mean, just look around us!"

Ellie gestured to the beautiful architecture, wide streets, and calm atmosphere around them.

"Can you imagine even a few dozen of the hive rats we used to deal with daily making their way here? They'd rip this place apart. They'd rob everyone blind before murdering them for the clothes on their backs, or even just for 'fun'. They'd break all these glossy windows and scrawl their gang signs all over these nice clean walls. They'd set the gardens on fire and generally just ruin everything nice about this place. The people here aren't expecting to be attacked on their way home. I doubt they've ever leaned out from their front doors to make sure the coast is clear before leaving their house. But *we* have. We've only been in the depths of Praxis, a few cargo holds during transit, then Adroa. If I try to take a step back…"

Ellie let go of Alayna's hand to make a pushing motion in the air. Then she carried on.

"I think I'm just starting to realise how limited our view may be. We've always considered it normal because that's all we've ever known. It's not as though we had reason to think otherwise either. There were billions of people back on Praxis living just that same way. It's sad."

Ellie could feel herself getting a little exasperated as she spoke. Alayna was watching her closely, so Ellie took a deep breath to calm herself before continuing.

"We've always been on our guard, Alayna. And that has served us well and for so long, because it's what we needed to survive in the environment we were in. But it *only* serves us well in environments like that, where everyone is out to get us. It leaves us unprepared for someone like Jake. Someone who doesn't have all the suspicion, and cynicism, and meanness in him."

Ellie couldn't help but briefly flick her focus over to the corner of her vision showing the number of dols in her account.

"I think Jake is just genuinely a kind person. And he likes you, and me, and Jonathan. I think he can see how guarded we are, so he's happy when you ask him for a brush because it shows that you trust him. And I think…"

Ellie trailed off to take Alayna's hand once more, looking into the girl's eyes sympathetically.

"You might like the idea of having someone around who isn't going to throw you to the wolves the moment it's convenient for them. Which, I believe, is a new experience for you. Well, for us both really. For us all. What do you think?"

Alayna stared at her for a long moment. At first, Alayna looked annoyed, then thoughtful. Ellie's heart panged as she saw a sad, almost downtrodden expression settle on the girl. An exceedingly rare vulnerability from someone who usually refused to show any weakness, to anyone, ever.

"Dad always said he was just going to cut my hair off," Alayna said quietly. "It'd make me stand out, and it took Mum ages to get rid of all the knots... And he'd rather she spent that time doing whatever *he* wanted. It's not like we ever had anything to clean it with anyway, so it'd just get tangled again. I never would have believed Dad, *my* dad, would get me something like that brush, not in a million years. So, I don't understand why I thought a stranger like Jake would be so happy to. Or even why he'd care about what I'd want or why I might want it. And then that he'd actually *get* it for me, himself, and go and sort it out—"

She seemed almost breaking, tearful, a fragile young thing about to fracture on account of an unexpected kindness. It all made sense to Ellie. Right now, it made more sense than anything else buzzing about her mind. *Jake* made sense for all three of them, it seemed, though they would all struggle with it in their own ways.

Ellie squeezed Alayna's hand sympathetically, rubbing it gently with her thumb. For Alayna to even bring up her father, Ellie's stepfather, Ellie knew the girl must be deeply affected as she wrestled with all her thoughts on Jake.

"It's just so…everything that's happening feels so *weird* right now," Alayna growled, the sad look evaporating as she returned to her usual indignant self.

"It *is* weird," Ellie agreed earnestly. "Couldn't put it better myself. And I'm not saying we let our guard down, not completely. Let's just acknowledge our view might be a little more limited than we think, and at least try to give Jake the benefit of the doubt. For now, anyway."

The girl scowled but didn't argue. Ellie almost jerked, recognising she'd forgotten something. Her movement drew Alayna's attention, and Ellie tried to play it off casually.

"Hypothetically though," Ellie said, coyly. "Would you be opposed to staying with Jake a little while? Or do you think that would make you uncomfortable?"

Alayna's eyebrows shot up in surprise before a look of confusion overtook her expression.

"What? Why? We've been there for days already. If we keep trying to stay, he's going to want something in return, and I don't know what we have left to give."

"And what did we just talk about, Alayna?" she asked softly. "Didn't we just say that we thought Jake might just be a giver, a kind person, someone untainted by the greed and the selfishness among which we've been living for so long before coming here? So, let's assume that isn't an issue," Ellie replied, trying to wave it off with one hand. "Would you like it if we were to live with Jake for a few months?"

Alayna's eyes narrowed in suspicion, and she snatched her hands away from Ellie, crossing her arms over her chest. She had still missed the point.

"Not so much that I'd want you to go warming his bed for it," Alayna said pointedly. She evidently hadn't soaked up a word of what Ellie had said.

"Oh, no, it's not that," Ellie said, chuckling nervously as she dropped her head in embarrassment. "I know it won't be that!" But Alayna was a clever girl, and Ellie could tell she wasn't going to be able to get away with not sharing the details.

"Jake has asked if we could stay and help him grow his own crops while we get back on our feet," Ellie said, looking back up to the fiery redhead. "But I wanted to get your and Jonathan's opinion on it. We don't have to stay if you don't want. Of course, we don't. I'd never, ever, want to put you two in any kind of an uncomfortable situation. You know that, don't you?"

"So, wait. Jake wants us to stay with him?"

"Yes."

"In his house?"

"Yes."

"The one with the nice beds, hot water, and amazing food?"

"Yes."

"And all we have to do is the same farm work we'd be doing on our own fields anyway?"

"More of it, but yes."

"And you won't have to sleep with him?"

"Not if I don't want to."

"And *do* you want to?"

"I…"

Ellie had to pause as she caught up to Alayna's question.

"What? Shut up!" Ellie exclaimed.

The mood suddenly flipped onto its head as Alayna broke out into maniacal laughter.

Ellie gathered the remaining condensation from the outside of her glass and flicked the little water droplets at her sister. The heavy feeling that had settled over the conversation lifted at Alayna's teasing. Ellie wasn't sure if the sun had come out from behind the non-existent clouds or if her mood had improved, but the day seemed a little bit brighter.

"Well, I guess I don't mind." The girl tried to sound disinterested, but she'd already tipped her hand, and Ellie could see right through her.

From behind Alayna, Ellie saw Jake and Jonathan making their way back over. The two looked deep in conversation, leaning closely towards each other in an almost conspiratorial manner.

Their heads quickly snapped back up as they saw Ellie and Alayna.

Ellie kept quiet just long enough to allow Jake to sneak up behind Alayna and tap the girl on the shoulder. Ellie couldn't help but feel a twinge of satisfied vengeance, watching Alayna jump suddenly.

Alayna almost looked taken aback as Jake held the brush out to her. Her face once again went through a gamut of emotions as she stared at the offered object. The girl looked like she might have a lot to say, but she stamped it down at the last moment.

"Thank you," Alayna said simply as she took it from Jake, an edge of embarrassment in her voice.

"You're very welcome, Spitfire," Jake replied.

His smile was infectious, and Ellie found herself hiding a slight grin behind her hands.

Jake pulled up two more chairs for Jonathan and himself from a neighbouring table before sitting down. "Now come on, let's eat something; I'm starving." He raised his hand to signal to the wait staff.

"*More* food?" Alayna asked in surprise, still holding the brush in both hands.

"Uh, yes," Jake said, an amused look coming over his face. "You realise you should be eating at least three times a day, and we've been here for hours," Jake finished as a waitress walked over and handed them all menus.

Ellie couldn't help but notice the waitress was quite pretty, with a half-length apron around her waist and a bright smile. This wasn't the male waiter who'd initially served them their drinks. She had a sunny lilt to her voice as she read off the daily specials. Ellie was somewhat shocked and bristled slightly, wishing the pretty waitress would go away.

"I'll let you get familiar with everything on the menu but is there anything else I can help you with first?" the waitress asked them.

Ellie was about to say no when Jonathan spoke up.

"Umm…did you know there's a Conviction ship in orbit?" he asked nervously.

"Oh that? Yes, it's all anyone's talking about!" the waitress said, letting out a light, trill-like laugh. "It's so strange; I've never seen the Conviction out this far," she continued without letting anyone else get a word in, speaking directly to Jonathan.

Gossip was clearly the waitress's hobby as now she'd got started, the cadence of her speaking increased, falling over herself to get the words out.

"One of my friends had to cross over the border recently and she said all the checkpoints this side of

Hector Station were unmanned. She even heard some people talking about all the garrisons being emptied."

"That's...not possible," Jake said, a deep frown furrowing his brows.

"That's what I said!" the waitress exclaimed excitedly. "But my friend swears it. She only just got back a week ago and now we have a Conviction battleship in orbit. All the way out here. Isn't it exciting?"

"Not a battleship," Ellie heard Jake mumble to himself, too quiet for anyone else to hear.

"So, what, are they just floating there?" Alayna asked.

"No one knows, that's the thing. I've been keeping my eyes open to see if I could see any troopers walking by, but there haven't been any official statements or anything. All of my friends are trying to work it out. One of my friends, Damian, he's into all these conspiracy circles, and they're all convinced something has come out of Null Sector and he thinks—"

"I'm sorry, would it be possible to order?" Ellie said, trying to sound polite but also wanting to stop the waitress standing there with her hips so close to Jake's head, even if he seemed completely oblivious.

"Oh, sorry, of course," she said with a laugh. "What can I get you?"

Truthfully, Ellie hadn't even looked at the menu yet, so just ordered the first thing she saw. Everyone else seemed to have picked something out specifically. Jonathan needed a little more coercing, but Ellie watched as Jake calmly and confidently convinced the boy to order.

Alayna spun around to Jake once the waitress left.

"What was she talking about with the garrisons and the checkpoints and 'Null Sector'? What's going on?"

Jake cocked his head. "What makes you think I'd know?" he asked coyly.

Alayna growled at him, leaning down close to the table as if about to pounce. A wide smile broke out across Jake's face at the theatrics.

"Don't put any stock into what she says, Spitfire. I think she's a little overly fond of rumours. I know the ship in orbit would cause a stir, but everything else seems like wild speculation.

"The Conviction might move some troops around if they needed to stomp out a local warlord or some frontier planetary governor who thought he could declare independence. Abandoning whole garrisons though? Especially from as deep in as Hector Station? Not a chance.

"Why would they even do that? There's no shortage of manpower and no force in the universe that can compete with the Conviction as a military power. And even when someone is dumb enough to challenge them, the fleets are more than capable of dealing with it without dredging up an invasion force's worth of backline ground pounders. I know it's odd there's a ship in orbit, but I really wouldn't worry about it, especially since it's *just* a patrol boat," Jake finished.

Alayna frowned.

"But, what if there's a war on, and we don't know about it? What if the Rike evolved a new species, or we encountered aliens, or some splinter group rebelled within the Conviction itself?" Alayna persisted.

Jake looked at Alayna with a sympathetic expression. When he spoke, Ellie was surprised by how much encouragement he could inject into his tone.

"Spitfire, there's always a war on. That's why each fleet has enough firepower to storm the gates of heaven. Null Sector has always attracted mad theories because, on the surface, it's exactly what conspiracy theorists want. A dark region of space that no light can escape from or pass through. Most probes and ships that enter mysteriously disappear, and an occasional burst of electromagnetic radiation is detected emanating from its centre.

"They all conveniently ignore that some ships have returned with nothing to report but flatlined sensors for the whole trip. It's a scientific anomaly, but if the Ostronous hadn't come drifting back out with all its crew missing, I doubt most people would even have heard of Null Sector.

"Beyond that, the Trinity is careful who they place in positions of power, and even if someone as high as a Grace Admiral went rogue, several other fleets would combine and put them down. You're dramatically underestimating the size of the Conviction. Not once since the founding has the Grand Armada ever been marshalled.

"If it were, our hulls would blot out the stars. 'Neither men nor beasts nor gods shall stand against our Conviction'," Jake said, his eyes shining, sounding as though he was quoting a passage of which Ellie wasn't aware.

"I know it may be tempting to picture some spunky young rebels overthrowing a military-industrial complex, but the reality is something altogether different."

Alayna clearly wasn't happy with what Jake had to say. She crossed her arms over her chest and pointedly looked away.

"You don't know; it could happen," she griped.

"Naaw, what's the matter, did you want to run off and be a rebel?" Jake asked in good-natured ribbing as he delicately poked Alayna's shoulder. "Going to fly around with a band of misfits and fight with the wind in your hair and a dramatic sunset in the background?"

Ellie couldn't help but let out a small smile which she promptly hid behind her empty cup.

Alayna slapped Jake's hand away after the fourth or fifth poke, the two devolving into a back-and-forth, Alayna full of sarcasm and Jake clearly enjoying getting a rise out of the young girl.

Ellie also had to admit to a small amount of satisfaction at seeing Alayna meet her match somewhat. Jake wasn't intimidated by her, and Alayna couldn't steamroll over him the way she did with almost everybody else. It would be good for Alayna to learn how to deal with people besides just being louder than anyone else in the room.

It was several minutes more before the food was brought to their table. The moment the scents reached their noses, everyone forgot about the ship and the Conviction, and dug in wholeheartedly.

Eleven: No Substitute

Despite all that had already happened in the day, it seemed as though they weren't quite done.

Ellie sat on a raised bed in the middle of an immaculately clean room, the smell of strong disinfectants permeating the space as gentle music drifted down from small speakers embedded in the ceiling. It sounded to Ellie as though it may be a harp or some similarly stringed instrument. She supposed it was meant to ease nervous patients, but it was doing little to allay her awkwardness.

Jake had insisted they stop by a clinic while they were on a developed world, for a checkup. Ellie had only been to a doctor once, before Jonathan and Alayna were born, to get her long contraceptive. She remembered with disturbing clarity the fear that overtook her when the doctor offered to purchase her from her parents. Understandably, they never went back.

When the four of them arrived, they'd been split up and taken to different rooms. Ellie had baulked, nervous at the prospect. But this was a different world to Praxis, and who knew when this opportunity would come again.

A particularly eloquent nurse had brought Ellie here, asking her a few questions, poking swabs into some sensitive areas and then placing a small device against her arm. It had hissed with the release of compressed air, and a slight pinch on her skin. She expected there would be a mark or drop of blood afterwards, but when the nurse took the device away, her skin remained smooth and unbroken. She'd then been told to wait, and the doctor would be in to see her shortly.

Ellie kicked her legs nervously, unsure what to expect, but she couldn't imagine the life they'd led would be particularly conducive to good health. She'd known they'd have to cross this bridge eventually. Ellie wasn't aware of any significant issues with her or her siblings that needed a doctor's intervention, so it had always been something that had fallen by the wayside. Besides, there wasn't a doctor on Adroa she could access even if she wanted to.

A few farmers happened to have autodocs that the rest of the colony might borrow in emergencies, but they were no replacement for a human doctor.

Ellie flinched as the door opened, a tall man holding a tablet walking in.

"Ah, Ms White, is it? Wonderful to see you. Would you prefer 'Ellie' or something else?" he asked.

The doctor had a soft, handsome face and appeared quite young, though still older than Ellie by a decent margin. Maybe in his thirties if she had to guess. Crows' feet were just starting to form at the corners of his eyes as he fixed her with a welcoming smile. The lines on his face fell easily into shape, showing he used that smile often.

He was smartly dressed and wore a long white lab coat over his clothes. Everything about his movements and facial expressions gave the impression that he was a kind, caring and attentive person. Some of her nervousness washed away.

"Ellie is fine, thank you," she replied softly.

"Perfect. Ellie. I've just spoken to your younger siblings, and they have quite a lot to say about you!" He chuckled openly as he sat in a rolling chair and scooted his way over to her, his tablet lighting up.

"I have your results here. There are a few things to discuss, but, it's mostly good news, especially for your first-ever medical appointment!" he exclaimed, throwing his arms wide as if tossing confetti to a crowd.

Ellie was beginning to get the distinct impression he might be very popular with children, unable to contain a small smile herself.

"I'm Dr Douglass by the way," he said, reaching out and offering his hand. Ellie reached out gingerly, giving his hand a few polite pumps before returning it to her lap.

"Now, I can see the nurse has already asked you a number of questions, and you lack any formal education or experience with the medical profession. So, I'll give you a high-level view of everything I have here and everything you need to know, but if you're confused at any point or would like me to explain anything further, don't hesitate to ask. And if there's anything that's making you uncomfortable or uneasy, please let me know; I'm here to help. Is that okay?"

Ellie nodded. Dr Douglas' tone lacked any kind of accusatory or exasperated notes. Given how amazing a city they were in, Ellie was half expecting her hive-born, farm-girl self to be met with some level of derision. But he seemed both patient and happy to be talking with her.

"Excellent. So, let's start with the big things and move on to the littler ones. First off, you have impeccable genes, Ellie. From a genomic perspective, you're about as healthy as you could hope to be, especially considering the contaminated environments to which you've been exposed. Immediately, what that tells me is we want to rule out any gene therapy, and we want to stay as far away from germline editing as we possibly can. We haven't done a genealogical trace, but I wouldn't be at all surprised if you had a strong, direct line back to Unification Era ancestors."

Ellie was somewhat surprised to hear that. She knew next to nothing of her family history. Given they had lived on an older hive world, she'd always assumed their line originated with the same recompiled colonist stock most of the old expeditions had used.

"Now, given your history," Dr Douglass said a little more delicately. "It's essential you remember that. There are quite a few less scrupulous organisations or 'medical professionals' who may try to talk you into expensive gene treatments, either with the promise of gaining some supernatural abilities or because of some purported critical flaw that must be corrected.

"But I'm here to tell you not to believe them, and definitely don't let them touch your genes. If you ever have any doubts or concerns, either come back here or seek out another credible, licensed clinic. Okay?" He gently tapped his tablet, looking directly into her eyes for emphasis.

"Yes, thank you, doctor, I appreciate it," Ellie said earnestly. She resolved to put what he'd just said into a box and keep it somewhere safe in her mind. She knew too well from her own failed experiments the disastrous effects rogue gene editing could have.

"Excellent." He looked back to his tablet. "Moving on, you are, unfortunately, quite malnourished though I'm fairly sure you were already aware of that coming in here. You have significant deficiencies across the board, especially in iron and vitamin C. Do you have bouts of weariness or lightheadedness? How about feelings of tiredness even after a full night's sleep or aching in your joints?"

Ellie had a strange feeling of embarrassment, taking in the fact she was experiencing everything he was describing. She'd always thought of it as an extension of her permeating exhaustion.

She simply nodded.

"Okay, that's good to know," Dr Douglass replied, scribbling a note onto the tablet. "Nothing too life-threatening at the moment, but it has the potential to develop into a multitude of issues further down the track. It's something we'll want to get on top of. But despite this, your kidney and liver functions look good, your thyroid function looks good, and your red blood cells and platelets are… okay, we'll need to test again once we've got rid of those deficiencies.

"Your white blood cells are functioning perfectly, but their count is low. Again, that's something we'll need a follow-up on. The important takeaway is that it doesn't appear to be caused by a viral infection or any disruption in your bone marrow," Dr Douglass continued, flicking his wrist as if tossing something over his shoulder.

"In fact, I have excellent news in that you don't appear to have any disease, virus or other bacterial infection, but I am seeing antibodies for most everything I'd be worried about for someone your age. That means you've been exposed to the pathogens in question, but your immune system has been able to fight them off and develop the appropriate response. That's an encouraging thing to see. I'm also not seeing any signs of STDs or other venereal diseases or infections, which is also good. However…"

Dr Douglass lowered his tablet again to look at her as he explained.

"While you may not be suffering any infections currently, I am seeing an imbalance in the gut and vaginal microcosms we looked at. Try not to think of this as an active attack on your system, but it can cause issues. Our bodies are ecosystems in and of themselves. Residing within us are trillions of beneficial bacteria and harmful bacteria. Then you have opportunistic pathogens and bacteria that are generally neither helpful nor harmful to you directly but will take the side of the dominant bacteria. Good for when you're healthy, bad for when you're not. I don't think we need to go that far into our immunology theory, though," he said with a wink.

"What all this means is that right now, you have more bad bacteria than good bacteria; thus, you have an imbalance. This can have a host of associated problems, but it also leaves you susceptible to more serious infections if left untreated. Do you understand?"

"Yes, I think so," Ellie responded.

"Good. Again, the silver lining is that it appears to be caused mostly by environmental factors, for which we can correct. Luckily, you currently have no infections we need to worry about. So, here's what we're going to do," Dr Douglass said as he leaned back into his chair, crossing one leg as he scribbled away.

"I don't believe an antibiotic or bacteriophagic treatment will be necessary at this stage. I'm going to prescribe you a complex multivitamin and multiprobiotic to take together. I'll give you the complex multivitamin as a powder to make it a little gentler on your system. Mix one sachet a day into a glass of water and take it with breakfast. The multiprobiotic will come as a capsule. Swallow it whole at the same time as breakfast, being sure to keep the multiprobiotic chilled as it contains live bacteria that will die if left out. Will all of that be okay?"

Ellie almost hesitated, unsure if their cold box would be up to the task of keeping her medicine chilled. Then she remembered she didn't have a cold box anymore and would be using Jake's powered refrigerator.

"Yes, that will be fine," Ellie said thankfully, feeling somewhat relieved, even with the slightly overwhelming information dump.

"Wonderful. Now there shouldn't be any side effects but given your body may not be used to this sudden flush of nutrients, you might have a bit of an upset stomach to begin with. That should be fine, but if it doesn't disappear after a few days, or you feel it's particularly affecting you or especially if you have any pain around your kidneys, I want you to stop immediately and come back. Understand?" He showed where the kidneys were, moving his hands to the spots.

"Yes," Ellie said again.

"Then, finally, you need to know that while these will help with many of your deficiencies, you still need to increase your caloric intake. Specifically, protein. You need to eat more meat, once a day at least, and lots of fresh fruit and veg. If meat isn't available to you, the next best thing will be beans, and lots of them, then eggs. If you're struggling to find either of those, you can resort to a dehydrated whey powder. Just bear in mind the whey powder is meant as a supplement to an existing diet and not as a full protein replacement. Any questions?"

"N-no," Ellie stammered, struggling to keep up as the information was heaped upon her.

"Then is there anything else you'd like to discuss before we wrap up?"

Ellie hesitated. Should she bring up her headaches? Ellie had been mostly fine since landing on Tropicalia, despite the population. She had less of a headache and more of a general buzz vibrating in the back of her head. Besides, Ellie had doubts there would be a medical reason behind crowds giving her headaches. It was more likely to be psychological.

"No, thank you, Doctor Douglass."

Dr Douglass smiled at her, his eyes shining with a kind light as he stood to shake her hand again.

"It's a lot to go through all at once. I'll have this all put onto a printout for you, so you don't forget," he said with a bright smile. "If there's nothing else, head out to see the reception staff; they'll have everything waiting for you. Book a follow-up appointment for three months from now and I'll see you then."

"Yes, of course, thank you, Doctor," Ellie said gratefully as she rose to shake his hand again and exited the office, closing the door behind her.

Ellie paused to take a deep breath as she stood in an equally spotless hallway. She could feel the heat radiating from her face as she fought the flustered feeling. It was a lot to take in so quickly. But Dr Douglass had been surprisingly supportive, and the news about her health hadn't been nearly as bad as she was expecting.

Ellie thrust her hips back slightly and pushed off from the door, walking back to the reception area. She felt a twang of curiosity about the origin of her line, something she hadn't really considered before. For her ancestry to extend back to Unification Era humans, while not exactly rare, also wasn't common when considering the entirety of humanity. It was something she'd like to know more about if she ever had the chance.

But Ellie put that aside for now. Digging into her past wouldn't matter if she didn't focus on the present and the future. She needed to remember a lot already and hadn't even heard what Jonathan and Alayna might need.

As Ellie rounded the corner into the reception area, she saw the pair chatting together with Jake. They all turned to her as she approached.

"How'd it go?" Jake asked.

"Umm, good genes, lots of vitamin deficiencies and a gut bacteria imbalance? If I understood that right?" Ellie said. She certainly wasn't about to go discussing her vaginal ecosystem with Jake. The mere thought of it made a hard blush rise to her face.

"That's pretty much the same as me," Alayna said. "Except he was also saying something about hormones I didn't understand. I need to take *east-row-gin* medicine until it fixes itself."

"Oestrogen." Jake clarified. "That would probably also have come about due to your poor diet."

"Wh-what? Screw you!" Alayna said, taking offence at his use of 'poor' diet.

"Don't worry, Spitfire; I'll make sure you're fed," Jake replied, grinning.

As the two dissolved into a tit-for-tat argument, Ellie turned to the frail boy sitting quietly beside Alayna.

"How about you, Jonathan?" Ellie asked gently.

"A-a lot more of the same, I think," he stammered. "He talked a lot about malnourishment, and he kept mentioning my thyroid? He seemed to be really worried about it. He hasn't given me any treatment for it yet, not until I've been taking a multivitamin for a while, but he wanted me to know in case we ever went to another doctor. He wants me to make sure they check it."

Ellie nodded, filing that information away so she could remember it in future.

"Well, not as bad as I was worried about. It all seems to boil down to 'Eat more, eat better'. It's not like we didn't know that already," Ellie said with a small smile as she walked over and began straightening Jonathan's hair.

Jonathan went to speak, then hesitated. After pausing for a long moment, he continued.

"Alayna said we're going to be staying with Jake?" He worded it as a statement but asked it as a question.

"We might," Ellie said slowly. Jake and Alayna seemed engrossed in their conversation, but she took Jonathan's hand and led him towards the reception desk regardless. The boy stood without complaint and obediently followed.

"What would you think about it if we were?" Ellie asked gently, once out of earshot of the other two.

"I think, I think it would be nice," Jonathan said quietly. "But will you have to…*do anything*, for it? I'd, I'd rather just go dig a hole into our hill and live in that if staying with Jake meant you had to do something you didn't want to."

Ellie blinked. She leaned down to kiss the top of his head. Jonathan was a good soul.

"No, Jonathan. We will be helping him get his crops established, and *nothing else*. I promise."

She felt Jonathan nod below her.

"If that's the case, I'd be happy to stay. You, you deserve to sleep in a real bed. And I don't mind working someone else's fields if that's what it gets you."

A brief stab of gratitude made its presence felt for her younger brother. Jonathan was always selfless in his considerations, even in such an unexpected situation. She hoped she'd eventually be able to have him consider his own wellbeing in future.

"Ugh, can we go home now?" Alayna whined loudly, walking up behind them.

"Actually, there is one more thing I'd like to show you. If you wouldn't mind?" Jake asked, approaching Ellie with an odd look of excitement and pensiveness.

Ellie blinked.

"We've been all over the city today, just for *our* benefit. How could we say no if there was somewhere you wanted to go?" Ellie said slowly, unsure as to where the situation was heading.

"Well, see, the thing is, I'd need you to... Close your eyes, Ellie," Jake said, becoming surprisingly bashful, the attitude at odds with the strong figure standing before her. "Alayna and Jonathan can keep their eyes open, of course. It will all make sense if you go along with it, but I understand I'm asking a lot."

A long pause hung in the air.

Ellie couldn't help but cock her head to one side as she thought furiously as to what he might be thinking. Before she could give voice to her thoughts, Alayna spoke up.

"That's weird," Alayna said in a low, drawn-out tone, an edge to her voice. "You're weird. This is weird. Why do you need—"

"Umm…" Jonathan, of all people, suddenly interrupted just as she was starting to wind up. "It'll be fine," he finished. "This is Jake…"

Ellie looked to Jonathan. The small boy kept his head cast downwards as he shuffled his feet. Alayna gaped openly at him and his interruption. He wouldn't meet Ellie's eyes, and there was a general sense of nervousness in his movements but she knew him well enough to tell there was nothing uneasy about how he shifted his weight or moved his gaze between the sparklingly white floor tiles. The boy knew something she didn't, and if he wasn't concerned, then she had no reason to be either.

Ellie took a deep breath, moving to meet Jake's gaze directly.

This is the part where you lead Little Red Riding Hood off the forest path and reveal you're the big bad wolf, isn't it?

A smile broke across Jake's face.

You'll have to find out, won't you?

Jake turned slightly side-on. That stupid, charming grin took over his expression and made something flutter inside her.

Goddammit, Ellie thought as she closed her eyes, keeping them shut.

The butterflies inside her burst into a brief flurry, tickling her insides as a warm, firm grip closed around her hand. Ellie didn't resist as Jake gingerly pulled her forward.

She was allowing herself to be led.

Alayna let out an indignant scoff. Ellie wanted to turn back and open her eyes to ensure the wilful girl was following. But a moment later, Ellie heard a lowly muttered curse and the sound of an extra set of footsteps as Alayna followed behind.

Ellie let herself be led outside. With her eyes closed, she could more easily feel the sun on her face and hear the wind in the trees. She was hesitant in her walk, unsure if she would run into an obstacle or encounter an unexpected drop. But Jake's grip anchored her, guiding her every step. Ellie couldn't help but feel something swell within her chest.

How long had she been dreaming of a hand in the darkness? Someone reaching out to help, to offer some kind of guidance, or comfort. Ellie had been standing on her own for so long. She'd fought off terrifying dangers and survived so many hardships, but always, always it felt as if it wasn't enough. She'd been forced into a corner and was always just reacting as best she could; she had no real idea what she was doing.

Ellie had always felt so unrelentingly inadequate as she'd been forced to watch herself and her family slowly waste away. Then Jake came in, almost falling from the sky. Strong, handsome, confident, and kind. Was it so wrong that, deep down, she wanted to hand the reins over to someone else? To not have to face off against the entire universe all on her own? Surely, she deserved to not be the one responsible for everything that ever went wrong, even if just for a moment?

Ellie was glad she had an excuse to keep her eyes screwed up as her head bowed. She reached her arm up, gripping Jake's hand with both of hers, desperate to not let the feeling of holding onto him slip away. There came a comforting squeeze in return. Ellie's arms and shoulders shook for a few moments before she could get her emotions under control. A hand in the darkness. A little more literal than she'd been expecting. But at that moment, she'd let Jake lead her through the gates of hell if only he'd keep a hold of her.

She lost track of time as they navigated through the city. Jake would curve around obstacles and help her down the wide stairwells as they moved forward. The soundscape around her was rich, allowing her to identify cafes and shopfronts by the difference in music and conversation. A dull, distant roar had been slowly building as they progressed; it was beginning to drown out most other sounds.

"We're just about there. One more big step in front of you. Make sure you keep your eyes closed for this last bit," Jake said.

Jonathan and Alayna were strangely quiet from where Ellie could feel them beside her. Holding her foot out, Ellie began slowly lowering it, unsure how big of a step it might be. It was less distance than she expected as her foot hit the ground. Confident she had her bearings, Ellie stepped forward, before crying out in shock. As she'd moved her weight, the ground shifted beneath her, turning her ankle, and throwing her off balance.

Jake's arms closed around her as she fell forward, catching her in a firm grip. Ellie braced against him, her head against his chest. Some distant part of her mind registered she could hear his heartbeat. Another, louder part of her mind was flustered by the sudden proximity, by the feeling of his warmth and the strength with which he held her. But with her eyes screwed shut, it paled compared to the feeling beneath her feet. Ellie had lowered her other foot to try and steady herself, but the ground was incredibly soft. It seemed every tiny movement, every slight shift in weight would cause the ground to morph its shape. Ellie wobbled and clung to Jake as she tried to step forward. She began to feel it solidify the more it gave way. It was taxing her ankles, causing them to roll at awkward angles.

The nearest description was that it was like trying to walk along the most freshly fallen snow, but denser, grittier somehow. Where Ellie might expect her leg to disappear up to her knee in the snow, this soft ground barely rose around her shoes before compacting to something more solid.

"What *is* this?" Ellie asked, totally unable to place what they might be walking across.

"You'll see; we're just about there," Jake answered, a smile in his voice.

A slight crunch sounded with every step as the material gave way. Ellie could place her steps along with Jake's. Extra sets behind her also sounded unsure but they still felt more confident in their movements than Ellie's as she heard a muttered curse from Alayna. The girl, along with Jonathan, seemed to be managing fine since they had the use of all their facilities.

Ellie became aware of a cool breeze ruffling her hair, a strange scent that had permeated the city since landing even stronger now. A dull roar she had thought belonged to the distant sound of large gravimetric drives coming and going was louder, more consistent.

"Okay," Ellie heard Jake say close to her ear. "Open your eyes."

Ellie did so. At first, she was blinded, having to screw them shut immediately to block out the light. Slowly though, with a fluttering of eyelashes giving her a chance to adjust, Ellie was able to open her eyes fully, and gasped.

Twelve: Making Waves

A breath caught in Ellie's throat. All around her, as far as she could see, electric blue waves rolled in to crash against pure white sand. The ocean seemed to extend forever. No building or trees rose above her, no distant movement or marred spots sullying its surface.

Ellie had never experienced Casadastraphobia, but with the endless expanse of space ahead of her, Ellie's head swam with a sense of vertigo. Her hand unconsciously tightened around Jake's arm. Even standing on the upper levels of the city hadn't provoked this feeling within her. Seeing manmade structures gave a scale to things, a way to gauge distances and quantify area. Whereas space had the opposite problem, the distances so vast and the size of things on a cosmic scale so massive one couldn't possibly hope to fully understand it. Space might technically have been larger, but this *felt* larger to Ellie, falling along a cognitive line that threatened to break the limits of her perception, without crossing over into the incomprehensible.

Here, she was unable to tell the size of the waves as they rose and fell, spreading out to impossibly thin lines that came to a stop just before her feet. They stood on a small peninsula of land that jutted out into the ocean where the beach was wide, smooth and almost empty. They were effectively alone, barely a handful of people in her entire field of vision until she turned back to the city proper.

"Jake, this is amazing," Ellie said breathlessly. "I've never…I've never been to the ocean before. Honestly, I never thought I'd see it in real life. Only in the daydreams of a girl stuck buried in the bottom of a hive world."

When she turned to Jake, Ellie almost jumped. For a brief moment, she caught him looking at her in total awe. The shine of wonderment sparkled in his wide eyes as he stared at her. As quick as she noticed it, the look disappeared, a fleeting moment that set off a fresh wave of fluttering inside her as he caught himself and returned to his usual smile.

"You certainly have a way of making people appreciate the little things, Ellie; I'll give you that," he said in an almost embarrassed tone, averting his gaze to look down.

Ellie's heart beat faster. She wanted to reach out despite already holding him. A movement to her side forcefully dragged her attention away as Alayna moved forward.

"Is it safe?" Alayna asked.

Ellie saw the girl had removed her shoes, standing barefoot on the soft sand with the bottom hem of the skirt she had eventually decided on hanging just below her knees.

"The water?" Jake asked, before a grin spread across his face. An almost goading tone entered his voice, egging the redhead on. "Yes, Tropicalia was lifeless before colonisation. There's nothing in the oceans apart from human-introduced coral and parrot fish. You can have as much fun as you want without worrying."

Alayna rose to the bait, glaring at Jake. She grabbed Jonathan's hand and pulled forward the nervous boy who had already removed his shoes. Together, they stepped into the surf. Frothy white foam washed around their feet and splashed up their ankles. Ellie saw Alayna shiver at the sensation. After a few moments, the girl began to delicately kick the waves as they came toward her, sending a shower of water droplets skyward. Jonathan, for his part, crouched down, pressing his knees together to let the water flow up his legs. Jonathan's clothes were immediately soaked, but he hardly seemed to notice as he reached down into the bright, shallow water and buried his fingers into the wet sand.

"Jonathan!" Ellie called in shock, surprised the usually mindful teenager would let his new clothes get drenched in salty seawater.

Jonathan's head shot up at her call. He looked confused for a moment before dropping his head to look at his wet clothes. A look of horror overcame him as he shot straight up, letting go of Alayna's hand and sprinting back towards Ellie. Jonathan's footfalls made enormous splashes that reached up to further soak his clothes. The final nail in the coffin was yet to come, though. Ellie watched as the wave pulled back, sucking the water with it. The panicked boy, rushing on unsure footing, tripped and fell forward, faceplanting into the water. The retreating wave flowed over him, dragging sand and water along with it. If any part of Jonathan's outfit hadn't been thoroughly soaked, it was now rendered entirely waterlogged.

Ellie and Jake rushed forward immediately, clomping over the wet sand as the next wave rolled in. They each grabbed one of the boy's wrists, Ellie pulling him forward while Jake hauled him upwards. Together, they rushed back past the tide line, the wave lapping at their heels.

"Sorry, I'm so sorry!" Jonathan half shouted as tears welled up in his eyes. Not that they were easy to see as the boy was dripping with water. Ellie could see the sand had got everywhere, clinging throughout his hair and sticking to his face. Ellie tried to gently wipe away at it, but rather than clearing any space on Jonathan's skin, it only seemed to multiply and cling to her instead.

"It's okay," Ellie began softly.

"No, it's not! I've ruined my new clothes!" Jonathan wailed. "They're the first new clothes I've had in so long, I'm so sorry, I'm so, so sorry—"

"Easy, big man, easy," Jake interrupted, a chuckle in his voice as he cut off Jonathan's panic. He slapped a hand down on Jonathan's shoulder and turned him around. "They're not going to disintegrate because of some seawater."

"But wet clothes catch and rub and rip. They'll stretch all out of shape and the salt will make the fibres brittle!" Jonathan persisted as great sobs wracked his body. Ellie began to move, but Jake held up a few fingers for her to stop.

Give me a minute.

He's sensitive, Ellie thought as she hesitated.

I know, I've got this.

"Tell you what, look at this sun!" Jake said, motioning toward the late afternoon sun shining down on them. "Take your clothes off and we'll let them dry up where the waves won't reach them. They'll be done quick in this weather, and then you can even go swimming if you like."

"What? They'll get stolen," Jonathan protested.

"No, they won't", Jake replied with a wave of his hand, unconcerned.

"Yes, they will!"

"No, they—" Jake was about to reply when he seemed to catch himself, pausing a moment in consideration.

Jake placed his hand gently on Jonathan's shoulder again. He knelt, bringing his eyes level with the shaking boy. Something in his gaze was causing Ellie's breath to hitch. No anger or annoyance, only a tender compassion.

"Jonathan, there's no one here; we have this whole beach to ourselves. We won't be any more than a dozen meters away, and anyone who tries to steal them will have to deal with all four of us. And the moment they see a beast like you come rising out of the water, they'll just drop everything and run," Jake said with a wink. His tone was reassuring, and Ellie could see a conflicted look come over Jonathan as he considered.

"But…they'll just be sitting there all on their own. I couldn't stop anyone if they wanted them…" Jonathan said in a small voice.

Jake blinked.

"Well, tell you what," Jake said, standing as he reached his hands up.

Jake undid the three buttons near his collar. Reaching back down, he grabbed the bottom of his shirt with both hands. Ellie's heart skipped a beat as, in one fluid movement, Jake pulled both his shirt and undershirt up over his head. Jake was lean, trim, and had a beautiful shape to his body from which Ellie couldn't tear her eyes. His skin was light and unmarred, rolling over distinct musculature. The late afternoon sun caught the smooth shapes, casting soft shadows across his body, further accentuating his fine form. She watched his pronounced muscles move together like a symphony as he balled up his shirts and tossed them away from the water.

"I'm leaving my clothes here and going for a swim. You're welcome to do as you like."

Ellie suddenly had to force herself to about-face, spinning 180 degrees as Jake began to undo his pants, heat rising to her face. Her resolve lasted all of a few seconds before she couldn't help but look over her shoulder. Jake was standing there in a pair of fitted boxers, tight over thickened thighs and a distinctly full bulge between his legs. Ellie was incredibly grateful Jake's attention was still on Jonathan as she had to fight to raise her gaze.

"What are you doing!" Alaya shouted in shock as she stomped forward, splashing water as she went.

"Jonathan and I are about to go swimming," Jake answered smoothly. "You're welcome to come. I can even teach you if you don't know how."

Alayna stopped short, sputtering a moment.

"I-I know how to swim!" the girl exclaimed, which Ellie knew was a complete lie. "But...but we don't have any swimsuits or anything!" Alayna crossed her arms over her chest, satisfied she'd found an excuse that wouldn't require her to prove her claim.

Jake laughed, loud and good-naturedly. The sound rang across the bright day and mixed with the backdrop of the clear blue ocean, tickling Ellie's ears.

"The only difference between underwear and a bikini is consent, Spitfire. If you're uncomfortable stripping down or scared of getting washed away, you don't have to do anything you don't want to. But Jonathan here needs to dry his clothes, and I haven't been to the beach in an age so we're going regardless."

Jonathan hadn't actually agreed yet. But as Ellie turned her attention to him, she saw the frail boy hesitate before walking over, delicately peeling the wet clothes off himself. He laid them out carefully next to Jake's crumpled pile, maximising their exposure to the sun.

Next to Jake, Jonathan looked skeletal. His ribs were visible, and his arms stick thin. But this didn't seem to be bothering the boy at all. Jonathan did look vulnerable for a long moment as he returned, stood there in nothing but his loose, worn boxers. Jonathan kept looking over his shoulder at his exposed clothes until Jake slapped him on the back and leaned in close.

"Race you," Jake hissed with a wild grin, before turning about and tearing off in a run towards the water.

"W-what?" Jonathan exclaimed in shock. Whether it was a conscious choice, or the boy was following some long dormant instinct to chase, he too began to move. His first few strides were half-hearted and hesitant but as the distance between him and Jake rapidly grew, Jonathan seemed to find himself and opened the taps, breaking into a full sprint and sending cascades of water forward as he pumped his skinny legs.

Ellie and Alayna were left standing there, gawking at them as they ran.

"Boys!" Alayna shouted in frustration. She glared at their backs as if she might burn a hole right through them, willing the pair to return and grovel at her feet.

Ellie reached out to say something as Jonathan caught up to Jake, both now waist deep and jumping into the incoming waves. Both excitedly flailed as they rode the swells upwards, splashing each other and trying not to get bowled over. They looked as though they were having incredible fun.

"Screw it," Alayna hissed, throwing her clothes into a heap alongside Jake's, causing Ellie to pull her hand back. Alayna took a moment to ensure her brush was secure in one of the dress pockets away from the sand, before standing. Alayna wore a mismatched pair of black panties and a red bra, her bones equally visible as Jonathan's. Without a word or second look to Ellie, Alayna sprinted off, kicking up sand as she did so, determined to catch the other two as they continued farther into the surf.

Ellie watched as the redhead wadded into the water. She would plant her feet as a wave approached and lean forward, forcing the wave to break around her. Alayna's hair quickly became drenched, darkening and hanging heavy. Yet despite the darkening in colour, it still shone bright in the sunlight. Jonathan and Jake both turned to her and threw their hands up in welcome as she approached. Ellie could hear their shouts and laughter drifting back towards her.

Gosh, that looks fun, Ellie thought.

There was a strong and very real temptation to join them. But as she pictured herself taking off her dress, a hard blush rose to her face. If it had been just Jonathan and Alayna, she might have gone in. But the thought of revealing herself to Jake in nothing but a bra made her grab her cheeks in embarrassment. She just wasn't ready to do that. And even if she had been, a niggling line of worry ate at her. Ellie didn't know precisely what Jake thought about her, but she'd learned from repeated, harrowing experience that simply having such an ample chest brought sexual attention down on her, whether she wanted it to or not.

It was not that she thought Jake would do anything uninvited, but she worried if he came to consider her as a sexual being, whether he already did so or not, it might change something about their relationship. Ellie couldn't quite pin down what exactly she was worried about.

She'd done her best to weaponise her breasts as assets before, putting them on display for Slackvore,

Breacher, and a few other young men around the colony. That had always been a means to an end, though. Life or death. She'd had a clear goal or outcome in mind and was using what she had to improve her odds of success. When she thought about doing the same to Jake, it was just different. Ellie wasn't ready to let him ogle her yet.

Plus, her own ribs might stick out once she took her dress off. Even Alayna's hip bones had been clearly visible, probably meaning that Ellie's were as well. She didn't think she had to be beautiful to satisfy the world. But Ellie also didn't want to *not* feel attractive.

With a sigh, Ellie tried to let go of the urge to join them all. It was a shame, but it was hardly worth getting upset about with everything else that had happened. Instead, Ellie sat down briefly to remove her socks and shoes. Leaving them with their other clothes, she looked back one last time to make sure they were secure and not about to be robbed.

There was no one within kilometres of them in any direction. Satisfied, Ellie stepped forward into the leading edge of the surf. The water broke over her feet and swirled around her ankles. She stumbled as the wave pulling back washed away the sand from beneath her heels, catching herself at the last moment.

The water was surprisingly warm, a strange sensation. Ellie could tell it was just cooler than the ambient temperature, but after letting it envelop her for a few moments, it felt warmer than the surrounding air, and intriguing. She walked along, feeling her feet sink into the sand and relishing how it shifted with the direction of the waves.

Ellie walked back and forth several times in long, slow, meandering tracks, ninety degrees off from where the other three were playing in the water. She swerved in and out of the surf, leaving long trails of footprints that would get washed away. She was fascinated by the shape of the waves and the power it must take to move so much volume. If she could harvest the energy it took to move the waves, even for a fraction of a second, they'd never need to worry about power again. She watched the patterns on the ocean floor shift and morph as the sun shone through the water above.

Eventually, Ellie returned to their pile. There she sat, just far enough down that she could bury her feet in the wet sand, but not so far that the waves would reach her rear. The entire time, as the sun had continued to sink in the sky, the sounds of excitement and laughter hadn't ceased.

As Ellie watched, Jake cupped his hands and bent down low in the water. Ellie was startled as Alayna placed her hands on Jake's shoulders, stepping in close, very close. A moment later, Jake launched Alayna upwards, the girl seeming to jump off him as she was thrown clear out of the water. The height of Alayna's arc took her well above Jake's head and gave her enough hangtime in the golden hues of the sunset sky to cartwheel her arms and legs in all directions. Alayna came crashing down into an oncoming wave with a delighted scream, bobbing back up to the surface and wiping the water away from her face after barely a moment.

Jake seemed to offer the same to Jonathan, but the boy didn't appear interested. Instead, Jonathan held his hands above his head, bringing them flat together before plunging forward, disappearing into the trough of an oncoming wave. Unlike Alayna, Jonathan vanished for a long time as he dove beneath, long enough that Ellie felt a pang of worry forming before he finally resurfaced, shaking the water from his hair.

It didn't look as though Alayna was done as she badgered Jake to toss her again, which he seemed only too happy to oblige. Alayna's distant, gleeful cackle made its way to Ellie as she was thrown high once more. Ellie marvelled at the sights in front of her.

Neither Jonathan nor Alayna had ever interacted with anyone like this before. They'd been too young to leave the house on Praxis, and Ellie had made sure to keep them well hidden during their transit. Not that the wilful Alayna had made it particularly easy for Ellie to do so. Once they reached Adroa, there were a few more people their age with whom they might have made friends. Jonathan had always been too nervous to make friends on his own, though. A few had approached him, but none were ever comfortable enough with his neurotic tendencies to really try and get to know him.

Alayna, on the other hand, couldn't seem to stop many of the young lads in the colony from trying to strike up a conversation with her. However, few escaped with their souls in as many pieces as they'd begun with, let alone their egos. There had been some who were braver, or stupider, and tried to persist. Those usually left with a little less blood in them as well. Alayna had not only never shown an interest in developing a friendship with anyone, but also, she seemed all too happy to actively drive them away with a fierceness bordering on zealotry.

Yet here they both were, Alayna letting Jake bodily toss her about like a ragdoll, and Jonathan not only allowing Jake to talk him down to his underwear but also trusting him enough to actually try something new and go diving beneath the waves.

What the hell is it that's made them trust him so quickly?

Then Ellie remembered she was the one who'd let him bring them here, buy them things, stay with him and lead her through an unfamiliar city blind.

Ellie drew her knees up to her chest, a range of emotions swirling around inside her. Worry about the future, hope for something better, and a desire but also a reluctance to trust, all these emotions bringing a sense of apprehension—and oddly, of hope at the same time. Frustratingly, whenever she tried to pin down any of the feelings to flush them out, they'd slip away, only leaving her with a vague sense of uncertainty.

Ellie was deep in thought. Only at last moment did she register the wet smacking of footsteps approaching. As she raised her head, a dripping wet Alayna seized her wrist and pulled her forward. Ellie lurched and had to quickly stand to avoid faceplanting into the sand.

"Alayna! What are you—"

"Shut up and come swim with us," Alayna growled. "We came all this way just for you, so you can't just sit on the beach looking all moody."

"Wh-what! Alayna, s-stop," Ellie protested as the smaller girl kept pulling her along, keeping Ellie off balance as they entered the water.

"Alayna, my dress!" Ellie cried in desperation as the water rose above her knees.

"Just wear it, it'll be fine!" Alayna grumbled, not letting go.

The water was already up to her waist by the time Ellie got her feet under her and regained her balance. Alayna wasn't giving her any time to think or room to argue.

"You need to learn to respect other people's decisions, Alayna," Ellie chided.

"Not when they're stupid!" Alayna shot back indignantly.

Ellie wanted to respond, but her attention was stolen by a massive wall of water heading toward them, her eyes going wide. The wave had yet to break and was simply an enormous swell of water rising above them. They hadn't looked nearly this big from the shore. Now she was up close, Ellie could see it reached well over the height of her head. The roaring of the waves was suddenly terrifying; what was she supposed to do? She wanted to turn and run but ended up digging her feet in, freezing as the wall of water loomed large above her, coming in fast.

"Come *on*, don't be a wuss!" Alayna exclaimed in frustration, turning back to grab Ellie's wrist in both her hands and haul her forward. Ellie was pulled off balance in a terrifying moment of clarity as the wave impacted Alayna's back. The girl disappeared into the water for just a fraction of a second before it hit Ellie full force in the face.

An explosion of sound rocked Ellie's hearing as she was lifted off the ocean floor. She felt herself get swept backwards as the water rushed past relentlessly. She was going to be blown back halfway to the shore! But no—there came a brief tug against her wrist. Alayna was still holding tight and had somehow anchored herself to the ground, leaning back hard. No sooner had it begun than Ellie felt herself being lowered back to the soft, swirling ground.

Ellie's head broke the surface first, and she gasped in a great heave of air. Water was pouring down her body and her hair had been blown out of its ponytail, left to stick wetly all over her face and shoulders.

Now able to breathe, Ellie stood there for a long moment. She eventually turned to look toward Alayna before bursting out into laughter.

The moment of approach had been terrifying, and the panic once her face had gone beneath the water had been very real. But now it was over, Ellie felt exhilarated. She'd never felt anything like the sensation of the wave picking her up and the water rushing around her head. It had almost felt as if she was flying.

"Just plant your feet and push back against it, it's not hard," Alayna said with a grin.

"Smart-ass!" Ellie exclaimed excitedly and with as much mock anger as she could muster. She dove her hand into the water and tried to grab a fistful like she would a snowball.

She threw it at Alayna, but the action only managed to splash her with a few large drops of salty water. It was still enough to get the girl to flinch, dropping Ellie's wrist as she raised her hands to protect her face.

"It'll show you what's not hard," Ellie continued, placing her hands on Alayna's shoulders and pushing downward. Alayna let out a surprised cry, her head disappearing beneath the water. She struggled against Ellie's grip as she tried to rise. It wasn't until she finally tapped Ellie's arm twice that Ellie let Alayna come back up. Alayna broke the surface gasping for air, coughing and sputtering as great rivulets ran down her face.

"By the wars, don't kill me for it!" Alayna sputtered.

"Serves you right!" Ellie exclaimed, but there was no venom or spite in her voice, only a wild kind of excitement.

The two of them laughed together under the golden sky, Ellie feeling her chest swell with love for her sister. The girl wasn't subtle, but she meant well in her own way.

Ellie supposed she might have a habit of getting lost in her own musings sometimes, and it took Alayna's crassness to break her out of it. She could barely even see Alayna's eyes under the wet curtain of hair that had folded forward over her face. She would do anything for this ridiculous girl.

Alayna retook Ellie's hand, much gentler this time, leading her forward as the next swell began to build.

"This time, jump just as it hits," Alayna said.

Ellie wasn't quite sure why, or even exactly how she was supposed to 'jump' in the water. But as the next wave approached, Ellie braced herself, bending her knees and lowering slightly.

Just as the wave's leading edge hit, rising to her chest, Ellie jumped. Elation overtook her and she cried out in delight, carried upwards against gravity. Ellie felt she'd done some kind of super jump as the force of the wave picked her up once more, though this time, it seemed determined to lift her up rather than bowl her over. The water still engulfed her to her shoulders, but Ellie's head was clear as they hit the wave's crest. Alayna was cackling beside her, and Ellie had a beautiful moment of clarity. On top of the wave, she was the highest thing around, able to see much farther out than before, seeing the golden sunset reflected off the rippling water reaching out to infinity. The sky was turning pink, and the clash of the two colours was as breathtaking as it was spectacular.

They'd ridden the wave so high that Ellie would have been terrified to jump from the same height if they'd been on terrestrial footing. But as the swell continued to flow past, it gently lowered them, placing Ellie and Alayna back in almost the exact spot from which they'd leapt, if back a pace or two.

"See! Aren't you glad I dragged you out here?" Alayna exclaimed, shaking Ellie's arm.

"Okay, okay, you win. Thank you," Ellie relented as the excitement in her chest settled merely into a frantic buzz.

"You can thank me later," Alayna said in a tone indicating she was very pleased with herself.

Alayna continued to pull Ellie forward, jumping another few waves until they made it out to Jake and Jonathan. The water this far out was just below chest height, even between waves.

"ELLIE!" Jonathan and Jake both shouted in excitement as she approached.

Jonathan waded up to her first. "Ellie! Look! I can swim, I can swim! I didn't know I could swim!" he shouted, exuberance bubbling over as he immediately dove into the water, paddling a slow circle around them with an awkward gait that nonetheless managed to keep his head above water the entire time.

"Indeed," Jake agreed as he approached, chuckling. "I didn't have to show him anything. He just took to it. So now it turns out we have a flier, and we have a swimmer." Jake pointed to Alayna and Jonathan in turn, his voice much calmer, but he still carried a smile, enjoying himself too.

Ellie hadn't quite been prepared for his approach. Jake was standing very, very close to her now, his waist hidden, and his chest bare. Water was dripping down along his body, the sunset behind him causing his edges to glow. His bleach blond hair was radiant as he reached up with one arm to sweep it wetly out of his eyes.

Ellie couldn't help but notice the shape of his biceps and all the muscles over and around his shoulders working together. The nail in Ellie's coffin came when he cocked his head and fixed her with a wide, inviting grin.

Ellie felt herself quiver, heat rising in a very unexpected place.

"Throw me!" Alayna exclaimed, letting go of Ellie as she rushed forward.

With a lack of hesitation that surprised Ellie, Alayna ran up to Jake and wrapped her hands around his neck. Jake smiled wide and cupped his hands, leaning down the way Ellie had seen him do before.

"*Cshht*. Launchpad to mission control, permission to begin liftoff sequence, over," Jake said, looking up at Alayna as she placed one foot into his hands. Jake spoke out of one side of his mouth in a deliberately muffled imitation of radio chatter. Ellie felt as though she'd just been bowled over by a surprise wave as Alayna not only smiled back, but joined in.

"*Cshht*, Mission control to launch pad. Rocket has been loaded, you are clear for takeoff, over," Alayna replied, following Jake's lead.

"*Cshht*, Roger mission control, we are prepared for launch. Takeoff in T minus five…four…three…two…one…" Jake said.

Just before he hit *one,* Ellie saw both him and Alayna brace. Alayna leaned forward and moved her hands flat on Jake's shoulders. Meanwhile, Jake's back, smooth up until now, suddenly had much more definition rising as he flexed. As the countdown hit zero, Jake hauled up hard as Alayna pushed down with her bent knee, jumping out of his cupped hands.

Ellie had seen them do this from the shore, but from that distance, she hadn't realised just how high Alayna was being thrown. The girl squealed the entire way up, spinning in the air before she came crashing down with an enormous splash. Jonathan paddled over just as Alayna was resurfacing. When she saw him, she immediately splashed him. Jonathan turned away quickly under the assault, but rather than run away as Ellie had expected, he grabbed Alayna by the shoulder and hauled her to one side. Alayna, surprised, grabbed his shoulders in return, and the two skinny teenagers began to wrestle.

"Do her. *Do her!*" Alayna screamed to Jake over her shoulder as she fought Jonathan for a dominant position.

By the wars, phrasing, Alayna! Ellie thought as a wild heat burned its way to her face.

Ellie almost jumped as she felt Jake come up beside her.

"Entirely up to you," Jake said with a wide smile. "But my skills as a launch pad apparently come highly recommended."

"I-Is it dangerous?" Ellie asked nervously as a way to stall for time rather than from any actual fear of being thrown. Alayna was making the whole thing look amazingly fun, and with the elation she'd experienced riding the wave, Ellie really did want to try it.

Jake threw his head back and let out a bright, beautiful laugh.

"No, it's not dangerous," he said, wiping at his eyes. "Just keep your eyes and mouth shut as you hit the water and try not to knee yourself in the face. You'll be fine."

"Oh, okay then," Ellie said lightly, excitement rising as she realised she was actually doing this. "If you don't mind."

"Not at all, you just let me know if you want to go higher," Jake said with a wide grin.

Following what she'd seen from Alayna, Ellie waited for Jake to cup his hands together and bend down, offering the foothold to her. Ellie stepped up, letting out a small giggle before she could stop herself at the feeling of his fingers on the soles of her feet. Jake crooked one eyebrow as his grin widened further.

"Sorry! I-I don't normally have people touching my feet!" Ellie tried to explain in embarrassment as her flush intensified. Jake shook his head, looking as though he was trying to suppress more laughter.

"*Cshht*, Mission control to Ellie, are you prepared for your maiden voyage? Over," Jake said, an amused tone thick in his voice.

Ellie tried to resist the smile, but couldn't. The whole thing was entirely silly but also such honest fun. Surely, she'd earned the right to enjoy herself a little.

"Uh…I mean, *Cshht*," Ellie said as she tried to imitate the sound. "Ellie to mission control, you are clear for launch?"

Ellie began in her normal voice before remembering to act as though speaking through a radio. She didn't quite have it down like Jake or Alayna, but she was having fun playing along.

"*Cshht*, Acknowledged. Lift off in T minus ten…nine…" Jake began to count down, and Ellie realised she was just standing there with her foot in his hand. Quickly trying to make up for it, Ellie slapped her hands down on his shoulders and leaned in, trying to position her legs in a way that would let her jump off without kicking him in the face on her way up.

"Two…one…"

Ellie felt Jake's shoulder muscles tense a fraction of a second before his hands began to rise. She took that as the signal to jump up as hard as she could. Everything happened almost too fast to process as surprise exploded in her mind. She hadn't expected it to be this effective or have this much force behind it as her and Jake's strength combined to send her flying upwards, throwing water in all directions.

Ellie screamed in shock and delight, her heart jumping into her throat. The sensation was incredible, excitement threatening to blot out all other senses. The world was a blur as it tumbled around her, and Ellie felt she must have spun head over heels at least twice before she impacted the water. It sounded more like an explosion as the water gave way before immediately rushing back in to fill the void she had left behind. The water slowed her down, but she felt her rear impact the soft sand before she began to rise again, pulled upward by her buoyancy.

As Ellie breached the surface, she began shouting in incoherent delight, losing her senses a little. She was sure she was trying to say something, but couldn't think what it might be, only managing a few half-formed words before dissolving into open laughter. Her head was still in a spin and her stomach felt as though it was fizzing. Ellie looked around to thank Jake and beg to be thrown again when she came up short.

"Oh! Jake! I'm so sorry, did I kick you?" Ellie asked in sudden horror, Jake leaning over, doubled at the waist as he rubbed at his eye. Ellie rushed forward.

Before she reached him, he looked up at her.

"Hmm? Oh, no, not even close," Jake responded nonplussed, taking his hand away from his eye and looking at it. "I think the bottom of your dress whipped my eye on the way up and maybe put some sand in it, but I think I've got it," Jake said, unconcerned as he rubbed his eye one more time before blinking rapidly, seemingly no worse for wear.

Ellie stopped and considered for a moment. Truthfully, she'd even forgotten she was wearing the dress. Everything Ellie had been thinking as she sat on the beach came rushing back, the thoughts bringing with them a sense of nervousness. But now, Ellie felt her blood was up. She clamped down on the anxious feelings and made a decision.

She was having far too much fun, and trusted Jake. She wanted to keep playing around, and certainly didn't want to take his eye out in the process. Besides, in this moment, it seemed her previous thoughts were probably just her overthinking it.

After a final moment of hesitation, Ellie reached down. Grabbing the hem of her dress, she crossed her arms over her chest and pulled it over her head. It was a struggle as the fabric clung wetly to her skin, but it came away after a few gentle tugs. Ellie lightly spun it into a long roll and tied it around her waist.

"Is it okay if we try again then? Maybe higher this time?" Ellie asked, thankful he hadn't been hurt and wanting to get back to it.

"Of course," Jake said with a smile. "Let's go," he said, finishing his rapid blinking and turning in her direction.

Excitement was running wild in Ellie's chest as he brought his arms together.

Ellie realised too late that she might be a bit too excited as, in a moment of perfectly poor timing, she stepped up and wrapped her arms around his neck just as he was cupping his hands, the result of which had her step inside his reach as his hands closed around the small of her back.

Ellie's eyes widened as time suddenly froze. The roar of the ocean seemed to fall silent as she came face to face with Jake, taking in its happening and its meaning, the sides of their noses touching as they held tight to each other. Their lips were barely a hairsbreadth apart.

Jake's eyes widened along with hers. Ellie now so close she could see his pupils dilate, suddenly very aware that she was pressed wholly against Jake, neither of them wearing much of anything. His skin was warm against hers, and the expanding of his chest as he breathed squashed her softer assets against him, bra or not. Ellie realised with horror that he might not have known she'd taken off her dress until now.

He'd been distracted and facing away. But the thoughts melted into an incoherent slurry as a new sensation pushed its way to the forefront of her mind. They stood so close, Jake's scent was wholly flooding her nostrils.

By the wars, I could get drunk off his scent.

Ellie felt with some trepidation the unexpected heat from before rising anew. Almost in answer, a pulsing pressure from Jake was beginning to press against her inner thigh.

Ellie froze, her mind screaming. Should she acknowledge it? Ignore it?

Jake wasn't moving either, appearing to be caught in the same spell. They just stared at each other.

Without any conscious direction on her part, Ellie's knee twitched upward slightly, rising along the outside of Jake's leg. His body seemed to answer in kind as the grip along the small of her back tightened, pulling her in that much closer, pressing their bodies together.

The unintentional movement was enough to break the spell. Ellie finally felt she was back in charge, yanking on the controls. She immediately placed her hands on his chest and pushed away, putting space between them.

"Sorry!" Ellie shouted at the same time as Jake.

Ellie caught a glimpse of his face, now burning red. She couldn't turn towards him enough to read his expression, an embarrassment unlike anything she'd ever experienced overtaking her. It only became worse the longer she had to process. She'd sent a signal, accidentally or not. And he'd responded, hadn't he? Or was that also an accident? Ellie just wanted to sink beneath the ocean waves and disappear. Surely, she could live out the rest of her days as a mermaid. Forget farming and space travel, she'd just cover herself in seaweed and spend the rest of her life luring innocent sailors to their doom.

"Uhh…" Ellie's head shot up at the sound of Jonathan's voice. "Would…would you like to try swimming?"

Jonathan! Sweet, wonderful Jonathan had come to her rescue.

"Yes, yes I would!" Ellie said desperately, grabbing his hands and walking in the opposite direction of Jake. "Show me how to dive, Jonathan."

"Uh, okay."

Alayna was only a few steps behind Jonathan, Ellie's little sister looking up at her with a curious and somehow immediately irritating expression, a mix of smugness and something else vaguely haughty and self-assured that Ellie couldn't quite read.

"What?" Ellie asked. Alayna's only response was to raise an eyebrow, emphasising her expression. Combined with the embarrassment Ellie was already feeling, the move brought a very rare sense of infuriation.

"What!" Ellie snapped again. "Go play with Jake. I want to spend some time with Jonathan."

Alayna, again, said nothing. After a moment, she began to move off. A coy smile spread across her lips as she passed Ellie, a smile that made the older girl want to dunk the smaller girl's head beneath the water.

As Alayna moved on, Ellie kept her back to Jake, feeling as though turning around now would cause her to simply drop dead from embarrassment. Once Alayna had gone, Ellie took a deep breath to try and calm herself.

"Okay," Ellie said more evenly to Jonathan. "Show me how you swim."

Thirteen: FFSA-2217

Ellie and Jake stayed in that separated arrangement until the golds of sunset turned to the deep purples of twilight, approaching dusk. A cool breeze began ruffling Ellie's hair, bringing with it the scent of night. Jake, Jonathan and Alayna simultaneously came to the same conclusion without so much as a word between them. Ellie followed as they went stomping out of the water, all shrivelled and wrinkled, and exhausted.

Nothing had been said, but as they continued to spend time in the water, the awkward distance between her and Jake had begun to shrink. Ellie was back walking beside Jake, acting as if nothing had happened. She had already discreetly put her dress back on, a change that went unacknowledged by everyone present.

"I think that might be enough to call it a day," Jake said, half chuckling, half panting as he collapsed to the sand. Ellie had to carefully turn her head away, trying not to study the muscles of his heaving chest.

Jonathan and Alayna followed suit, falling to the ground, and splaying across the sand.

"Why didn't you join us?" Alayna asked Ellie, half scolding, half knowing, the harshness of her tone tempered by her exhausted panting as she lay there, eyes closed.

"I…wasn't ready to, yet. And now it's too late," Ellie deflected.

"We can stay longer if you still want to swim. Jake has his own ship; we can come and go whenever we like," Alayna shot back, eliciting an exhausted laugh from Jake.

Even as Alayna said the words, she began to shiver. Dripping wet, with the light fading and night rapidly approaching, the temperature was starting to drop.

"It's okay. Next time. We really should get going," Ellie insisted as she reached over to pull away some of the girl's wet hair from where it clung to her face.

"Fine," Alayna griped, not even bothering to open her eyes or swat Ellie away. "Just, in a few minutes."

They proceeded to lie there until the last light of the sun faded completely. Behind them, streetlights turned on all over the city, light reflecting off the walls while upward-pointing spotlights embedded in the gardens lit the trees and leafy plants from below. The lights made the city look even larger than before, stretching away into the distance and causing the night to glow.

"Okay, come on, time to get up before we all freeze to death," Jake grunted as he rolled over, getting his arms beneath him and pushing himself up. Alayna groaned loudly. Jonathan half crawled a few paces, before doggedly rising to his feet. He was letting his arms dangle as he walked with jittering steps, all his energy completely expended.

"Umm…" Jonathan let out as he picked up his clothes. As Jake had promised, they had indeed dried in the afternoon sun. Jonathan was now the wet one, white sand clinging to him all over.

"I don't know if I should put these back on?" Jonathan stated as a question in his usual habit.

Jake blew out a breath of air slowly as he considered.

"There'll be freshwater showers lining the first promenade off the beach. You can wash the sand and salt off there, though obviously, that'll get you wet all over again. We could—"

"Ugh, I don't care!" Alayna growled, rising to her feet and grabbing her clothes.

"Alayna!" Ellie exclaimed as the girl balled her clothes under one arm and stomped back toward the lights, still in her underwear.

Alayna didn't respond, leaving Ellie to gape at her retreating back. Ellie turned to Jake, and the two locked eyes.

"She really has no shame, has she?" Jake asked rhetorically, a smirk spreading as he balled up his clothes and followed after Alayna. Ellie had to pause a moment. Now out of the water, she was given her first natural look at Jake's backside. It took considerable effort to look away as the wet fabric clung tightly to his form.

Ellie instead let her eyes fall to Jonathan, who was still standing there holding his clothes, looking entirely unsure. Ellie let out a little huff at Alayna's theatrics and placed her hand on Jonathan's shoulder.

"Come on, I'm sure it'll be fine; we need to be getting home," Ellie said, turning the boy away from the water and urging him forward.

The walk back through the city was more straightforward than Ellie had expected. She'd thought that the sight of the four of them would draw attention, but even with Alayna out front, leading the way in her underwear, they barely attracted a glance. As Ellie paid closer attention to the crowds they were passing, she began to see that many people were wearing similarly revealing clothing. Short shorts and bikini tops seemed the most common, though there was a wide variety of attire in styles and patterns ranging from the risqué to the relatively conservative.

The city at night was even more bustling than during the day. People were finishing work and heading out to dinner, the restaurants filling up and short lines beginning to form near their 'Please wait to be seated' signs. A mixture of human and robotic attendants guided people to tables, taking orders and running out delicious-looking meals that steamed in the night air. The atmosphere was calm and easy, with people too engrossed in their conversations to notice the four of them walking by.

Ellie was still people-watching when they slowed. A large group had crossed in front of them, causing Alayna to wait indignantly as they cleared.

'...so strange. I must have passed a half-dozen checkpoints on my way. All deserted..."

Ellie's ears perked up as she unconsciously caught the fragments of a conversation between a pair of men sitting beside them. Their clothes were businesslike but their shirts were unbuttoned at the top and their sleeves were rolled. Each cradled a drink in one hand.

"You're joking? I'd heard garrisons were going quiet, but I'd thought they were just rumours. Did you see any troopers during your trip?"

"Not one. It was all wardens and auxiliaries. We weren't even inspected on our way out. I'm telling you, it was freaky to see everything so empty—"

"Hurry up, Ellie!"

Ellie jumped as Alayna shouted at her; she had fallen behind the others.

They continued through the night, heading back towards their pad and leaving the bustle behind, bringing a certain relief to Ellie when they made it all the way back to Lara without so much as a cat call though she struggled to get what she'd heard out of her head. The waitress they'd spoken to earlier was undoubtedly a gossip, but this was the second time she'd heard the same sentiment.

A niggling nervousness began worming around in the back of her mind despite Jake's earlier assurances. Ellie wasn't exactly sure why she cared what the Conviction was doing; it had certainly never done her any favours.

Yet at the same time, the Conviction had always been a vast, immovable monolith as permanent and resolute as the mountains. Hearing about it moving was like hearing an ancient titan was awakening, threatening to darken the skies and crack the continents asunder.

The walk had dried them off considerably and Ellie began fussing over Alayna and Jonathan to try and distract herself, attempting to brush as much of the sand from them as she could before they got into the ship. Even Jake took a few moments to thoroughly brush himself down. A stack of boxes sat next to Lara, their deliveries from earlier in the day. Ellie was surprised they hadn't been stolen as they were simply sitting on the ground, completely unguarded. Jake didn't even consider it as he opened a side panel near the bottom of Lara to reveal an ample, empty space within. He loaded their deliveries as Ellie tried to finish cleaning the other two. Ellie thought she could recognise the size and shape of what most of the packages might be, but there were a number of them she couldn't account for.

Are those what Jake bought when he went off by himself? Ellie wondered.

In the end, Ellie wasn't able to get it all off, but if Jake had any complaints about sand in his spaceship, he didn't say anything as they all climbed in. A strange sense of quiet settled over Ellie as Lara's canopy closed with a final *thunk*, cutting off the sounds of both city and ocean.

Jake yawned, stretching wide beside Ellie, taking a moment to settle before reaching over to power up Lara. He'd put his shirt back on, but his pants lay crumpled to one side of his footwell. The slight hum of the gravimetric drive increasing in power was strangely soothing to Ellie. She'd loved the trip, but she'd been outside in the crowds and wind and noise all day. By contrast, Lara's soft, plush interior was an intimate, still, protected space all their own like being sequestered in a private bubble. If that bubble was climate controlled and armour-plated.

Ellie clearly wasn't the only one comforted by Lara's rhythm. As Jake lifted off from the pad, the ground falling away outside as they rose into the air, Ellie watched Alayna's head loll to one side. Jake gently pushed the throttle forward, and they began accelerating away from the city. The dampened bumps and low hum put both Alayna and Jonathan to sleep in the back seat, Ellie smiling as the two teenagers leaned against each other in a picturesque scene she wished she could capture.

"Thank you," Ellie said quietly to Jake, turning to the front. "It's so easy to forget that they're both just fifteen and sixteen sometimes. I'm glad they were given a day to just act their age."

"What do you mean?" Jake asked, equally as quiet. "They both seemed to be acting the same to me."

Ellie shook her head in amusement.

"Not really. Alayna would normally be caught dead before letting anyone know she was having fun. And Jonathan usually just… hides." Ellie paused as she considered a way to describe Jonathan's behaviour. "I've never seen him take off and chase someone like that. Especially not into a new environment like the ocean. He'd normally just stand behind me and worry about everything. About drowning, about someone seeing him undressed, about crabs or small critters in the sea biting him… About everything really."

Jake worked his mouth a little as he considered.

"I think he has a lot more strength and confidence in him than he lets on. Or at least, he has the desire for it. I think he and the rest of you have been living so close to the edge that he's never really had a chance to be any different. I think today shows what their 'normal' is once the pressure's off, and they've been given a chance to breathe," Jake said.

Ellie blinked. She hadn't considered that line of thought before.

Jake's perspective as an outsider was new. While Ellie wasn't totally sold on how accurate it might be, she had to admit her siblings had experienced more new things today than at any point in the past. Was this really who they were when not just waiting around for their next thin meal?

"I feel you might still be underselling how big a deal it was that Alayna actually asked you to buy her that brush," Ellie whispered, cautious not to wake the girl.

A wide grin spread across Jake's face.

"Maybe, and I feel so honoured she did that. It's almost like when an angry cat decides to crawl into your lap for the first time."

Ellie broke out into a smile she tried to hide behind her hand. She knew exactly what Jake was referring to.

"The fact I am sitting on you means nothing, human. It's not as if I like you or anything," Ellie said, laughing.

Both she and Jake had to stifle their laughter, clamping down hard so as not to wake the other two. After a few moments, Ellie drew several long breaths as Jake wiped at the corners of his eyes.

She felt a strange sense of closeness to Jake right then, as if a distance between them had been crossed, and they were becoming more comfortable with each other. She remembered hearing somewhere that mutual traumatic experiences sometimes helped people bond. Did almost dying of embarrassment count?

"You are an amazing person, Ellie White," Jake said, turning to her. "At some point, I would love to sit down and hear your story."

Ellie turned to regard him, her breath hitching in her throat. Jake sat there calm and confident. A beautiful smile and bright eyes sat under his tousled hair. His buttons were undone, and his shirt hung loose, framing the muscles of his arms and the top of his chest. The atmosphere had long faded behind them, and he was lit in the dark cabin entirely by Lara's instrument panel. In this light, he looked absolutely gorgeous.

Shit, Ellie thought as her heart immediately began hammering.

"I mean, I might tell you at some point," Ellie managed to get out bashfully, surprising herself that she actually meant it. She reached up to stroke her hair and used it as an excuse to look away. Ellie was sure he'd be able to hear her thundering heartbeat in the small space, but he seemed completely oblivious.

"I'm glad," he said with an earnest smile.

The two of them settled into a comfortable silence, the gentle hum of the repulsors and the quiet breathing of Jonathan and Alayna behind the only sounds in their private little world. Ellie eased back into the cushy seat, the plush material soft against her skin.

As she closed her eyes, a faint warmth seemed to be emanating from within her chest. She was calm, content, feeling safe in their little bubble, with Jake watching over them as they flew deeper into space, completely disconnected from everything. Right then, Ellie had no desire to be anywhere else. She couldn't quite place the warmth as it felt like more than all of this combined. It was confusing for several long moments, until she realised what it might be. Was she…happy?

Opening her eyes slowly, Ellie looked out into the vast starfields ahead. The smallest of smiles played across her face.

"Ellie…we might have a problem," Jake said, a concerned tone in his voice.

Because of course, Ellie thought with a sigh. The universe really couldn't give her a moment, could it?

She turned to Jake.

"What is it?" she asked. But her question answered itself as Jake had already pulled up a picture of the Blister Fang on the centre screen.

Multiple ships were swarming around the Blister Fang as it listed to one side, flames belching from one of its flanks. Several small, agile fighters dodged cannon fire and large, rectangular barges had already connected. Some looked as if they'd rammed the larger ship, punching holes in its outer hull and half burying themselves within. They looked like fat, elongated ticks clinging to some poor wounded animal. In the distance, a much larger ship, about half the size of the Blister Fang, was approaching from behind. Scrappy, mismatched turrets raked the Blister Fang's engines with streams of weapons fire.

Alarm rapidly began to creep up Ellie's spine.

"What's happening?' she asked with urgency.

"It's as I said. Slackvore's course was too predictable. Those barges are boarding craft. They'd have never made it through the guns if they approached from any distance. I'm guessing they dropped out of slip-warp right on top of the Blister Fang before they had a chance to lay down any serious fire. The fighters would be there to snipe any craft Slackvore might try to send out to scrape them off the hull. The big one behind is keeping away from the primary accelerator and trying to shred the engines. If they succeed, they'll likely try and tow the Blister Fang to another system where they can take their time picking it apart," Jake answered. His tone was cold, his eyes never leaving the screen. This wasn't the Jake she had seen before.

Ellie's heart began to beat faster. Surely, Slackvore couldn't be overcome. He was fierce, and he had Breacher and the rest of the crew. He wouldn't let his ship be taken from him, would he?

"How much of a chance do you think the boarders have?" Ellie asked, trying to control the quiver in her voice.

"From the looks of it, I'd say they pretty much have it won," Jake answered.

The floor of Ellie's stomach dropped out and her head snapped to Jake.

"What do you mean? How could you possibly know that?" Ellie exclaimed.

She heard Alayna and Jonathan stir in the back seat, but she ignored them. Jake pointed to the screen, singling out one of the barges that had punched its way through the outer hull towards the front of the Blister Fang. The visage reminded Ellie of a wolf, jumping up and clamping its jaws onto the neck of a bear.

"That barge punched through right below the bridge," Jake said. "They could have hard docked but chose not to. That's too precise to be random; it had to have been a deliberate target. Which means they know the layout of the ship and its critical systems. The others have made hard dock or rammed through all over the hull, aiming to split the crew and prevent them from defending any one system or choke point. Pirates usually rattle their sabres from a distance or go in guns blazing, untrained and undisciplined. This is more organised than that. This is either a mercenary outfit, or they happen to have a very competent commander. Either way, Slackvore will be cut off from his crew, facing a capable, armed, organised force, and no amount of bravado will save him once they cut through the bridge doors."

Ellie's breathing became harder. How had the moment turned from calm to panic so quickly?

"Is there anything we can do?" Ellie grasped. "Lara has weapons, and you're a pilot!"

Jake turned to Ellie, looking her up and down. His gaze wasn't without sympathy, but it was cold. "You're asking me to fly into combat with two kids in the back seat?" Jake asked evenly, though his tone could be taken for implying she'd said something ridiculous. It was a total shift from his softness toward her until this moment. It was not a nice shift to witness.

Ellie stopped short, fear and frustration building up in her mind. Jake was right; she was panicking, not thinking. They couldn't fly into battle with her entire family aboard. She had no idea what the situation truly was, what their odds might be or what could happen. If what Jake had said about space flight earlier was true, Ellie wasn't even sure they'd survive Jake's flying if he was forced to push it to the limit.

But still, Slackvore was their one link to space. Their one exporter. Even if he was a manipulating, profiteering bastard.

 "Jake. Is there anything we can do?" Ellie asked desperately, tears welling. "I don't know if the colony will survive without him. Everything we have. The Mathews, the Lindens, our friends and neighbours, everyone who has built a life on Adroa will lose it all. And *we* don't have anywhere else to go either. Please, is there anything? *Anything?"* Ellie was choking on emotion. Her eyes were burning, and a desperate fear was taking over her.

Jake's face was ashen, something guilty in his movements. He remained silent, refusing to meet her gaze.

"Jake, please!" Ellie cried desperately, reaching across the gap between them to grab his arm with both hands.

He finally turned to look at her but his expression was unreadable, his facial muscles pulled taut. Sadness showed in his eyes as they met hers. For a brief moment, Ellie thought she caught a shadow of fear moving across his face.

"Ellie," Jake said after a long moment. "There…would be a cost."

Dead silence settled over the cabin, flashes of weapons fire lighting up the screen as the Blister Fang continued its fight. Jonathan and Alayna were keeping quiet, feeling the tension stretching the air tight.

"Whatever you want, Jake…" Ellie said slowly, a forced calm settling on her.

She had to save the colony. Even if it meant…

"No, no…." Jake said quietly, closing his eyes. "Not a cost to *you*. You don't understand."

Jake looked away. Ellie saw his knuckles were white on the control stick just before he let go, raising his arm to place his hand on her shoulder. He turned back to her, leaning in close. His eyes were stern, but she could feel him shaking.

"Ellie," Jake said in a severe tone as his eyes bore into hers. "If I save Slackvore, it might endanger Jonathan and Alayna. Are you absolutely certain that's something you want?"

No, Ellie thought immediately.

But as he stared into her, Ellie could picture nothing but them being stranded, harvests going uncollected, ammunition depleting. Mechs would be breaking down as their parts failed and went unreplaced and eventually, a swarm of Rike would flow over everyone and everything. In the long run, they might die screaming anyway.

"Do you have a freighter?" Ellie asked with a dry mouth. "Or can you promise you'd be able to get another freighter to make the run? Can you guarantee everyone I know isn't going to die because you didn't want to get involved here today?"

Jake's mouth set in a hard line. He said nothing.

"We need him," Ellie whispered. "Please…"

Jake's eyes shifted back and forth as he studied her face. Slowly, without a word, he drew back. Ellie watched as he closed his eyes and took a long, deep breath.

Something subtle about him changed, his posture becoming ramrod straight in the chair, his chest puffing outward, shoulders pulling back. Jake's eyes opened, and any fear or sadness that had been there previously was completely removed. His expression was stern, his eyes were fierce. Ellie felt herself let go and shrink back a little as he moved, his every action quick and definite, each click as he flipped through instruments carrying a note of finality to it. Pulling back, he began to speak, his voice loud, ringing clear in their little space.

"FFSA dash two two one seven to LDPB Conglomerated Affinity. How copy, over."

Ellie jumped as, after barely a moment, a disembodied voice with slight static reverberated around the cockpit.

"Two two one seven, this is LDPB Conglomerated Affinity, copy five. You are broadcasting on a restricted channel. Confirm FFSA designation."

"Affinity, confirm, Foxtrot Foxtrot Sierra Alpha. Requesting to speak to Affinity actual. You will comply." Jake responded immediately. His tone was stern, professional, carrying an undercurrent of command that brokered no argument.

"Stand by."

Ellie understood the words but had no idea what they may mean. She felt completely out of her depth; what might she have got them into? This was a different Jake, the one who had shattered Hunter's arm without so much as flinching, the one exuding an aura of intimidation and steel. Ellie quickly looked back to Jonathan and Alayna. Jonathan was curled up into a ball, pressing into the side of the hull, eyes downward. Alayna was leaning forward, her eyes on Jake, cautious. A new voice came over the link, older and gruffer than the one previous.

"Two two one seven, this is Affinity actual. You mind telling me what a First Fleet asset is doing all the way out here?" There was a tone of annoyance in the voice.

"Do I wish to discuss the intricacies of First Fleet intelligence with the captain of a rusted shit bucket so low on the chain that he gets sent out to the arse end of nowhere with barely enough time to scrape his underperforming crew out of the local dives? No, no; I do not. Confirm copy."

Ellie's eyes widened at Jake. His tone was the same as before, but a definite note of condescension had entered his voice, one on which the captain of the Affinity had obviously picked up. When his reply came, it sounded like he was trying not to fly into a blind rage.

"Confirmed," the captain choked out.

"Affinity actual, you are to go to full battle stations and move at emergency speed to assist a friendly freighter currently under assault by known seditious forces, callsign Blister Fang. Two two one seven will remain on station to coordinate fighter squadron, callsign Bluebird one. Scramble fighters and engage immediately. Seditious forces are to be executed without remorse. Confirm copy."

"Confirmed. Authorisation?"

"Niner, niner eight-two, betray eternal light," Jake responded, a fierce look coming over him.

A long pause... In the sudden quiet, Ellie became aware of how her shoulders were subconsciously straining under the thick tension.

"FFSA authorisation confirmed, Affinity moving to intercept, fighters launched, flight of twelve, callsign Predator. Break. Predator one, confirm copy. Battlestations!"

The voice cut out a moment too late. Ellie heard the captain roar out his battle cry as the wail of an alarm began to rise in the background before the transmission ended.

"Predator, copy five, over," a new voice sounded, much younger than the captain's.

"Predator, set bullseye to galactic centre, prep bruisers," Jake responded.

"Copy, request bogey dope braa."

"Multiple hostiles, bearing one nine five by negative two zero zero, range sixteen kay, altitude eight five kay, mixed aspect. Predator cleared hot, weapons tight."

"Roger, weapons tight, cleared hot, proceeding."

"Hold on," Jake said to the three of them.

Jake hauled on the control stick without waiting for an answer, pushing forward on the throttle. A muffled boom sounded as Lara's main engines engaged and Ellie was pushed back hard into her seat. For whatever reason, Jake was no longer willing to coast along on the gravimetric drive.

Lara's instrument panel suddenly lit up and several alarms began blaring. Jake spoke up loudly, a cold note in his voice as he leaned forward slightly.

"Buddy spike, buddy spike! Bluebird fast mover, braa zero niner zero for angels, eight two zero flanking, confirm!"

"Clear copy, bluebird angel eight two zero, nails on raygun, over."

Ellie was rapidly losing track of the conversation but the pressure on her body was growing as they continued to accelerate, the air being squeezed out of her lungs. Her heartbeat began pounding in her head and she was beginning to think she would pass out from lack of breathing before the pressure finally eased.

"Look out to the right," Jake said.

Ellie did so, fighting the weakening forces pressing against her. The planet was dark below them. They were barely out of the glowing atmosphere. At first, Ellie wasn't sure what she was looking for when movement caught her eye. There was a star, brighter than the rest and moving fast across the sky as it came about the planet. As Ellie worked out the direction, she realised it was heading towards them, rapidly growing in size and brightness. The indistinct star morphed into a long engine plume. As it dissolved into more detail, Ellie could see that it was not one, but multiple lights streaking across the darkness. One large plume being led by a dozen smaller streaks.

Ellie was entirely unprepared for the scales and speeds involved. No sooner had she made out the details than the smaller ones shot past far above them, unidentifiable as anything other than streaks of light, followed a fraction of a second later by the much larger plume that left a trail of swirling, nebula-like gasses in its wake.

"Sloppy," Jake said.

Whether he was referring to the captain of the Affinity, Slackvore, the attackers or even himself, Ellie couldn't tell. Jake was looking at the screen again. He prodded it before making a flicking motion with his wrist. The picture on the screen was thrown up onto the inside of Lara's canopy, expanding to take up the available space and blocking their view of the stars. Ellie could see in much more detail as the attackers seemed to realise what was coming. The fighters veered off, their engines burning bright as they screamed away from the Blister Fang. One of the barges disconnected, reverse thrusters firing as it tried to move its bulk and turn away.

"It's about to get real, no one speaks unless I tell you to, clear?" Jake asked, quickly looking to each of them.

Ellie didn't have time to respond as all at once, the Conglomerated Affinity was on them. The streaks Ellie had seen before slammed to a halt, dissolving on the screen into a series of Conviction fighters. They shared a distant resemblance to Lara. They had the same forward-swept wings and large rear engine banks. But where Lara was wide and flat, these were pointed, angled, almost needle-like. Their styling made them look like angry, armoured hornets. Voices exploded in Ellie's ears, Lara's cockpit filled with the overlapping chatter of multiple voices.

"Hostiles locked, Predator merging." "Hostile tally, fox-three!" "Chaff, chaff, gunt! Splash one." "Fox-two." "Aspect hot!" "Splash two hostiles." "Bruiser launched!"

Fireballs erupted over the screen as the Conviction fighters began chasing down the attackers. Ellie looked on in horror as the fleeing pilots tried to turn, spin or manoeuvre any way they could, but it was like watching a cast of hawks descending upon a rabbit warren. The Conviction fighters flew faster, turned sharper, and each bright streak of weapons fire seemed to find a target. Ships were blown apart into shrapnel and gas without the Conviction fighters taking so much as a single hit. It was a slaughter.

The Conglomerated Affinity itself entered the frame against Ellie's expectations, a little smaller than the Blister Fang, but infinitely more intimidating. The attacker's main ship peppering the Blister Fangs engines had already begun veering off to one side. As the Affinity entered the scene, dark spots started appearing all over the attacker's hull.

Jake suddenly shouted, "Affinity break right! Ripple, bearing zero seven zero. Vampire! Vampire! Vampire!"

The Affinity's engines lit up as lines of burning fire flew from the dark spots of the attacking ship. With rising panic, Ellie realised they were tipped with the long, silver forms of missiles. They flew wide from their ship, turning to converge toward the Affinity from multiple angles.

The chattering voices devolved into chaos as the surface of the Affinity erupted with streaking trails of weapons fire. Some missiles exploded as they were hit, others dodging out of the way. The Affinity's guns spun, attempting to track them, leaving curved, glowing paths expanding into the darkness of space.

The missiles were rapidly closing the distance, a few more knocked out closer and closer to the Affinity until suddenly, they were through.

Ellie had to squeeze her eyes shut as Lara's canopy whited out, the Affinity disappearing behind a series of catastrophically bright explosions.

The image stayed like that for several long moments, the light flooding the interior of the dark cockpit.

"Did...did the Affinity just lose?" Alayna asked, uncharacteristically subdued.

"No," Jake answered flatly.

Ellie began to shake as the screen cleared, showing the Affinity hovering in space. Mean, angry, and just a little more ragged than before. Black scorch marks covered its hull, the centre of a few craters glowing a dull orange. Every barrel along its surface rotated towards the attacking ship, small ruptures appearing along the attacker's hull. Small, rounded objects began launching, long engine trails extending behind them as they screamed away.

"More missiles? After all that?" Alayna almost whispered, looking to Jake.

"Escape pods," Jake responded in a cold tone.

None of the pods made it very far. As the last of the Affinity's barrels were brought to bear, it disappeared beneath a level of fire of truly staggering proportions. Every surface of the Affinity erupted in swerving trails of repeating weapons fire as its cannons expelled enough ordinance each second, to keep Adroa safe from the Rike for an entire year.

The attacker's ship didn't explode so much as it vaporised, enormous chunks blown off in every direction until its keel resembled shredded paper. The larger chunks were targeted and repeatedly broken apart until it looked as if its individual pieces were smaller than the glowing rounds rushing in to destroy them. Adding a final insult to injury, the long, expanding gas trails of the Affinity's own missiles— that Ellie hadn't even seen launch—came roaring in, exploding amidst the cloud of atomised particles that was once a ship. There was no doubt as to the fate of all those who had been aboard, escape pods or not.

Ellie's hands were shaking. She'd just witnessed the deaths of who knew how many people. Years of life, memories and experiences ended in a flash, having taken just moments.

The ships on screen were just metal. They had no faces, no body language or personalities of any kind.

But Ellie swore she could see in the Affinity's actions the same cold lack of hesitation she'd seen in Jake when they first met. Everything of the Conviction seemed to carry a unified attitude towards violence that was terrifying.

The shaking spread to her arms, so Ellie wrapped them about herself. She thought she knew the Conviction. She had been born amongst it, taught to fear the sight of its troopers since before she could remember. She knew it controlled hundreds of thousands of worlds, keeping them all in check with a military as brutal as it was absolute. It was the single greatest superpower in the known universe, uncontested by all the trillions of people whose lives it dictated on a daily basis.

Jake had even given her the impression the Conglomerated Affinity was a runt, nearly a joke. Yet, it had just shown a level of power more incredible than anything else she'd witnessed in her life. Now she'd seen it first-hand, Ellie had a much better understanding of why the Conviction had stood for so long.

"Bluebird one to Blister Fang, come in, over."

Ellie flinched as Jake spoke; she had been completely engrossed in the screen and her thoughts.

"What? Bluebird? Ardent, is that you?" Slackvore's voice asked over the link, hoarse and raw. The sound of a hacking cough and blaring alarms sounded in the background.

"Confirmed, Slackvore. The Conviction forces are there to assist. When they ask questions, you tell them you are a loyal Conviction sympathiser and under no obligation to explain your mission to a lowly patrol boat captain. Do you understand?"

A pause followed, then a low chuckle from Slackvore.

"Understood. How much is this going to cost me?"

"It's not *me* you need to thank," Jake responded, motioning to Ellie.

Ellie blinked. Her arms shot up to her face. He was asking her to speak.

"Oh, C-Captain. Are you okay?" Ellie said, wheezing past the thick lump in her throat. So much for not letting him know she was out here.

"What? Who's this?" Slackvore responded.

"It's Ellie. Ellie White," Ellie tried again.

"Wait, Melon girl?" Slackvore shouted in disbelief. "What in the two-fanged, arse-up, seven-bitten hells are you doing out here! Actually, forget that, how the hell were you able to call in a damned Conviction battleship! Did watermelons become the new Atronite while I wasn't looking?"

"Not a battleship," Jake murmured. Ellie looked at him briefly but had to turn her attention back to Slackvore.

"Oh. It's a long story," she said, unsure how else to explain. "How's the damage to the Blister Fang? Do you think you'll be able to make next year's harvest?"

The Blister Fang looked primarily intact, especially compared to what had happened to its attackers. Even as they spoke, larger, slower ships than the fighters began exiting the Affinity. They flew across the distance and attached themselves to the clinging barges. But for all Ellie knew, the Blister Fang could be a total write-off. She was glad Slackvore hadn't been killed, but she needed to know now whether to expect him or not.

There was a long pause before the line erupted in hoarse, raucous laughter.

"Melon girl, if it's you I have to thank for this timely intervention, I'll be sure to give you an extra special deal come next harvest even if I have to get out and drag this slag heap there myself!" Slackvore said with amusement.

"Although…" He trailed off briefly, the usual slime slithering back into his voice. "I am going to have to cover quite a number of repairs, and I'll naturally have to adjust my prices accordingly. I suppose in that instance—"

"You're welcome, Slackvore. Bluebird out," Jake interrupted, reaching over and cutting the link. He shook his head. "Unbelievable."

Jake's tone had softened. Ellie carefully looked over to see if *her* Jake was back. He was sitting easier, his eyes no longer having that ruthless look to them. But his movements were stiff, and there was something generally unhappy about his manner.

Have I crossed a line? wondered Ellie.

"Jake…" Ellie said delicately, still tussling against the fear of watching the Affinity fight.

"Don't," he interrupted immediately, not looking at her.

Ellie felt as though she'd been stung. Her mouth opened, but she closed it again. She bowed her head a little and faced back towards the front, wrapping her arms around her waist.

"Two two one seven to Affinity actual," Jake said loudly.

"Affinity copies, proceed," the gruff voice of the Affinity's captain responded over the link.

"By my authority under the first article of the Fleet Intelligence Operations Charter, you are ordered to purge all logs, entries and evidence of this operation once complete. A lifetime silence order is now placed upon you, your crew and any associated auxiliaries under penalty of death. Confirm copy, over," Jake said in a cold tone.

"Confirm copy, will comply with all orders, over," the captain responded, a grave tone heavy in his voice.

"Two two one seven, out," Jake finished, cutting the link.

"We need to get out of here; Slackvore's on his own from this point. Prepare to jump to slip-warp," Jake said coldly, not bothering to turn and address Ellie or the others.

Fourteen: Think Better of Me

The trip back to Adroa was made in total silence. At first, they'd transitioned into real space with nothing in sight, only to transition back to slip-warp almost instantly. Jake made several hops like that, carefully checking Lara's sensors each time.

Ellie lost count of how many hops it had been before they finally appeared over Adroa.

The steadily increasing vibrations of air against the hull was the only sound as they flew through the atmosphere. Jake was clearly upset, and at least annoyed. However, Ellie couldn't tell—was he truly angry or was it something else? All the men Ellie had known in the past would scream in her face when they'd been angry. They'd beaten the walls, letting her know precisely what they were feeling in no uncertain terms. Ellie was used to that; she could manoeuvre around their explosive moods and temper tantrums.

What she didn't know, however, was how to deal with Jake as he quietly piloted them home. No hint of violence or passive-aggressive stomping or thumping about. It rather seemed as though he just shut everyone out. Or perhaps she was the one to notice it most for some reason…

The roof of the hangar began closing behind them as Lara lowered to the ground. There was a *clunk*, and the cockpit opened. Jake vaulted over the edge, the sound of his feet impacting the hard floor shaking something inside Ellie. She took a deep breath. This was the type of thing she had been fearing. It was one thing to offer something when you were in a good mood, and another when encountering adversity.

Ellie needed to gather her strength, her nerve. She needed to be able to send Jake packing as much as she didn't want to. Not that Ellie really believed she could if she even tried. But she also knew she owed him an apology. She might not fully comprehend the details, but she'd asked something enormous of him, and he hadn't turned her away.

Ellie had felt a tinge of guilt for those who'd attacked the Blister Fang. She didn't feel right, thinking they deserved to die for what they had done. But neither could she be overly sympathetic towards them. Everyone had to make their own way in the world and play the cards they'd been dealt. Their own choices had led them to attack the Blister Fang, and it was down to them to deal with the consequences.

Climbing slowly out of Lara, Ellie straightened her dress and walked towards Jake.

"I'm sorry," she began.

"That was a trump card," Jake interrupted, his back still to her. He was quiet, and Ellie was shocked to hear a quiver in his voice.

"A one-time use, world-ending trump card. And I just spent it saving a goddamn pirate!" Jake suddenly spun to face her, his voice rising. "Do you have any idea what using that might have brought down on our heads?" he demanded. "What I might have to do now to keep you safe? You have no idea what could be coming!"

Ellie was taken aback. She'd been expecting an outburst. She'd been expecting to deal with anger. She'd expected screaming and raging and resentment. She had expected everything—but just not this. Jake's eyes were wide, his shoulders and hands shaking, and his mouth was turned downwards. Ellie's stomach flipped. Jake wasn't angry; he was *scared*.

"And what makes you think you can talk to Ellie like that?" Alayna demanded to know, venom in her tone. She walked up beside Ellie as if to show solidarity.

Ellie put her hand on the girl's shoulder to try and control her, but the redhead shrugged it off immediately, stepping forward to square up against Jake.

"You might have been Conviction but that doesn't mean you get to treat Ellie that way," Alayna continued, putting her hands on her hips and leaning forward, accusation spitting free. "You think you know everything, but you don't. You think we're ignorant but we're not. We've already worked out your *big scary secret,* as if it wasn't already blindingly obvious."

"And what would that be, Spitfire?" Jake's eyes dropped to Alayna. He was still shaking, but as Ellie watched, his jaw set. An icy tone permeated his words as he slowly spoke.

Alayna scoffed, indignant.

"That you're nothing but a coward. A runaway. A deserter—"

"I AM *NOT* A DESERTER!" Jake suddenly roared, rounding on Alayna.

Even the dragon of a girl unconsciously took a half step back from the fierceness in Jake's face. His teeth were bared, and he loomed over the much smaller girl. His expression was contorted into one of rage. Silence fell as everyone was frozen in place.

Ellie thought she would have to put herself between Jake and Alayna, but she stopped when she saw the wet shine in his eyes.

Jake raised a shaking hand to plant one finger against Alayna's chest.

"I do not…" Jake's voice was strained, his jaw clamped shut, and he spoke through gritted teeth. "…abandon the things that I care about. Not my squadron, not my ship, and not *you.*"

He spoke pointedly, his voice thick with emotion. Alayna was pushed back another step, her eyes widening in shock.

"I am not a deserter. And if you knew anything about me, that would have been the first thing you realised." Jake straightened, turning his shoulder away.

"Think better of me, Spitfire."

Ellie saw the corners of Alayna's eyes tighten as Jake walked away. She continued glaring at him the entire time he went. He stepped into the elevator and kept his back to them until the doors slid shut, silence once again settling on the three of them. Ellie slowly moved forward as Alayna offered a death stare to the elevator door, yet her scowl was undone by a momentary quiver of her lower lip before she could stop it.

"He's an asshole," Alayna said, sniffing as she quickly wiped her eyes with the back of her hands. "He *is* a deserter. He's totally a deserter. And a liar. What else could he be? He has to be projecting. Why else would he care what I think of him?" She tried to spit the words out in a harsh tone, but they came out wobbly, lacking any conviction.

"Shhh," Ellie hushed as she gently took Alayna's head and held it against her chest. The girl didn't resist but crossed her arms, trying to scowl or frown but unable to keep her mouth from turning downwards.

"It's okay to cry," Ellie soothed.

"I'm not crying. *You're* crying. Shut up!" Wet streaks began to run down Alayna's cheeks.

Ellie held one hand out to Jonathan, the boy's head bowed as he stood there shaking like a leaf. When he saw her, he slowly walked over and pressed against Ellie's side. She put her arm over him and held him close.

Ellie was shaken by the outpouring of emotion. What could have Jake so scared? And what had she done in saving Slackvore? Well, never mind. Right now, she needed to comfort her siblings. This was the only thing that mattered.

The three of them stayed like that for several long minutes, until Alayna started growling to try and summon her anger, pushing away from Ellie. The fierce girl dried her eyes completely and resumed her usual, displeased-at-everything look.

"Do you think dinner's an option tonight?" Alayna asked pointedly, not wanting to discuss what had happened further.

"I'll work something out," Ellie said gently, placing her hand in the small of Alayna's back. "Why don't we give everyone a chance to breathe first? Could you help me figure out how to unload Lara?"

Alayna rolled her eyes but turned around without further complaint. Ellie took a deep breath, trying to stamp down on the emotions swirling within and satisfy herself with a distraction.

Ellie approached Lara and searched around the compartment door she'd seen Jake open before. Thin lines ran along Lara's surface, cutting into the craft's body. Ellie found what looked like a recessed handle. Reaching her hand up, she pressed in with the tips of her fingers, expecting it to pop out. A flash of surprise passed through Ellie as the blue holographic ring appeared over the back of her hand, and the compartment door cracked open. Had Jake already added her to the household, and by extension, to Lara?

A small bloom of sadness mixed with a touch of guilt; Jake was trusting them to an almost ludicrous degree and asking little in return. Ellie sighed. She didn't deserve to be the focus of his anger, but she resolved to try and understand his point of view when they spoke again.

"Okay, help me with these please," Ellie said.

Unloading Lara took longer than expected. Ellie had Jonathan and Alayna treat each package as the most fragile object they'd ever held. Likely unnecessary, given the forces they'd experienced during their flight from Tropicalia. The packages had shifted and tumbled about in the large hold, so Jonathan had to climb inside until only his feet were visible, intent on extracting the last of them. Ultimately, he was successful.

With the packages carefully stacked and time wearing on, Ellie ushered Jonathan and Alayna into the elevator.

Once inside, Ellie reached for the console. She didn't know which floor to go to. The screen displayed each floor numbered one through twenty-one, excluding three at the bottom that read 'Ground', 'Basement' and 'Shelter'. Taking an almost blind guess, trying to determine the main floor by how high it looked through its windows, she pressed for floor eighteen. The selection lit up and the doors sighed shut. The elevator set off rising.

After a few moments, she felt the elevator slow. When the doors opened, they led out into total darkness. Ellie's brow furrowed in confusion as she stuck her head out. From the light spilling out of the elevator, she could make out shapes in the darkness, none of which corresponded to the sunken lounge, fireplace or breakfast bar she had expected.

Ellie filed away a note to see what this place was later, feeling Jake might not appreciate them exploring at this exact moment. Retreating behind the doors, she would try working backwards. Perhaps floor twenty-one may lead to the roof, so she pressed for floor twenty instead.

When the doors opened this time, Ellie saw what she'd been expecting and hoping for; they were engulfed in warmth. The lounge room with the fireplace already lit sat directly in front of them, the kitchen to the left, and the hallway leading to the bedrooms curving away to the right.

Stepping out, Ellie could hear the sizzle of cooking and smell a rich aroma in the air. Cautiously, Ellie moved toward the kitchen and saw Jake at the stove, four plates set out along the bar, and a range of ingredients neatly laid out on the work surfaces. He was always immaculate in everything he did, even cooking, apparently. Jake looked up as Ellie approached. They locked eyes for a long moment.

"Sorry," Ellie said at the same time as Jake.

"Oh, I didn't mean—"

"No, please, you go."

Ellie tried to talk, then give way as Jake tried to speak simultaneously. They managed to keep doing it until Jake held up a hand.

"Sorry, let me," he said. "Look, Ellie. I may have got a little too…emotional, before. I put you on the spot, Ellie and asked you to make a decision out of nowhere without all the necessary information, and I'm the first to acknowledge that. I don't blame you and am certainly not angry with you. I'm sorry if I gave you reason to believe otherwise. I overreacted, and I apologise."

Something in her chest lightened a little, a cautious feeling of relief spreading through her. How refreshing it was to deal with someone who wasn't too proud to admit fault.

"It's been a bit of a roller coaster these past few days," Ellie admitted earnestly, a grateful smile spreading across her face that it seemed as though this wouldn't be nearly as awkward as she'd feared. "I'm sorry if we seem ungrateful for anything you've done, Jake. You see, we're not. I can't tell you how much of a difference you've made to us, to me. It's just—"

"Not at all," he replied, a small smile playing across his lips, his own sign of relief escaping him. "Can we put a bookend on the situation for now and sit down for dinner together? We can discuss everything later. But for now, we can say we're two stubborn people who butted heads."

Ellie let out a relieved breath.

"I'd like that," she said.

As a way of apologising, Jake cooked them all a fantastic dinner. There was still much to be resolved, but being all high-minded about it wasn't going to get them fed.

When Jake placed a plate of shredded chicken breast in a heavily spiced orange sauce, with rosemary roasted potatoes and a tall glass of fizzed apple drink in front of her, Ellie quickly resolved to enjoy the little things while she could and tackle the dramatic discussions later.

She was still entirely unused to this level of decadence. But she had to admit, she undoubtedly was enjoying it. Very much so.

Ellie, Jake and Jonathan were eventually able to make conversation. It was stilted at first, but they quickly fell back into their comfort zone after a few minutes. Alayna, however, refused to participate, pointedly looking away whenever Jake turned to her, an indignant expression on her face. Ellie's heart went out to him as he looked downtrodden whenever Alayna did so, but he didn't push the issue.

After they'd eaten and were loading the dishes into the automatic washer, Alayna finally spoke up.

"May I please use the shower?" she asked pointedly, a note of passive aggressiveness in her tone.

Ellie and Jake both jumped at her unexpected interruption.

"Oh, of course, Spitfire, it's—"

"I know where it is," Alayna snapped before Jake could finish pointing, moving off around the bar.

With that, she was gone, Jake huffing a big breath out from his cheeks as he watched her go.

"Sorry," Ellie said quietly. "Alayna's a little…" She trailed off as she tilted her hand from side to side.

"I know, I know," Jake replied. "It's been a hell of a week. I didn't exactly help things earlier, either. Well, I guess that gives us some time together, huh, big man?"

Jonathan jumped as Jake suddenly turned to him.

"Oh, uhh... uhh," he stuttered.

"Come on, I've got something I wanted to show you," Jake said as he closed the washer and started the cycle. "Go sit down on the sofa; I'll meet you there in a sec."

Ellie stepped to one side to let Jake pass as he exited the kitchen. He waggled his eyebrows at her as he did so, clearly up to something. Ellie couldn't help but smile and shake her head at his ridiculousness. They'd swung from drama to play so quickly that she found it hard to believe. She was still reeling at just how easy things were with him. A moment later, she heard the sound of his bedroom door opening and closing.

Stepping down into the sunken circle with Jonathan, Ellie sat near the fireplace, closing her eyes momentarily, revelling in the heat against her skin. She opened her eyes again as she heard Jake return, carrying a strangely shaped object in each hand. Ellie noticed one seemed much older or more heavily worn than the other. They were made of rugged, glossy black material with matte grey accents. Jake held out the newer looking one to Jonathan.

Jonathan looked to Ellie first. She twitched her eyebrow and smiled, trying to give no indication whether she was giving permission or not, hoping the young boy would make his own decision.

Jonathan looked a little distraught, but with Jake still standing there, he carefully took the device from his hand. Jake sat down next to Jonathan, on the other side from Ellie.

"Have you ever played a game console before?" Jake asked.

"N-no, I don't think so," Jonathan answered hesitantly. Jake's face lit up immediately.

"Oh, boy, you're in for a treat," Jake said earnestly. "The TerraSphere Eight, and the TerraSphere Nine," Jake continued, indicating first to his older version, then to Jonathan's cleaner, but still slightly worn one.

"And yes, I'm aware they're no longer spheres. The internet has beaten that particular horse to death, so just roll with it. I'll let you use the nine since it's the newer one. Even though they're different generations, we can still play together," he said with a wink before turning to Ellie. "Sorry, Ellie, I only have the two. I'm happy to take turns if you like."

Ellie smiled and cocked her head, just happy to see Jonathan taking an interest in something. Now the device was actually in his hands, it had clearly caught his attention. Jonathan was turning it around and prodding it from all angles. If it had come from anyone else, Ellie was sure he would just sit there frozen, holding it as if it were made of eggshells.

"I'd like a shower as well, so I'll just wait until Alayna is out and watch you in the meantime," Ellie said as she regarded the two.

"If that's what you prefer," Jake answered before turning his attention back to Jonathan. "Watch this," he said as he leaned over and gingerly grabbed the top of the device. With a pull, it smoothly opened out like a clamshell, revealing the devices were a pair of controllers with screens that folded down over the top of them. Asymmetric thumbsticks, lots of colourful buttons with varied triggers along the top and paddles along its underside.

Ellie watched as Jake began showing Jonathan the features, and before long, both were engrossed in their screens, heads almost pressed together as they played. As near as Ellie could tell, the two were working together to pilot a sizeable military walker during a beach assault. The music and sounds emanating from the little devices were as dramatically heroic as they were intense.

Boys, Ellie thought, a small smile playing across her lips.

Ellie sat and watched for a long while as the two of them cooperated. Jake, more experienced and knowledgeable, guided Jonathan, emphasising the impact the boy was having and how valuable his assistance was. Jonathan, for his part, began beaming under Jake's constant praise, quickly learning and becoming eager to share every victory.

Ellie eyed Jake. He was warm, encouraging, and supportive of Jonathan, letting him choose their missions and weapons and make other decisions. Her feelings were still mixed. But as she saw Jonathan begin to open up, Ellie found herself wishing Jake had come along for him a lot sooner.

As the time drew on, Ellie began to wonder what was taking Alayna so long. Standing up, she crossed in front of Jonathan and Jake. The two didn't seem to notice her passing. Walking up the small stairs out of the sunken lounge area, Ellie walked down the corridor and around the corner until she approached the bathroom, the wall lights illuminating as she passed.

Ellie knocked gently on the bathroom door, hearing running water within.

"Alayna?" Ellie called softly.

"What?"

"May I come in?"

"I'm naked!" Alayna shouted, sounding scandalised.

"I know, but I feel a little silly talking to you through the door," Ellie said, turning the handle and cracking it open about half the width of her face. "How about this?"

The door opened inward with the shower positioned against the wall behind. Ellie would have to open the door fully and step into the room before she could see even a sliver of Alayna.

"Ugh, fine. What do you want?" Alayna grumbled.

"You've been in there a while. I just wanted to check you were okay," Ellie said, telling a half-truth.

Alayna *had* been in the shower for quite a while. But the girl was also known to get into periods of intense brooding, such as when she'd ridden the cart back on market day. Sometimes, Ellie needed to leave the girl alone, and sometimes, she needed to pull Alayna out of it.

"I'm fine," Alayna answered, somewhat annoyed. "This is the hottest shower I've ever been in. I'm just enjoying myself."

"And you're not upset about anything?"

"Upset about what?" Alayna snapped with some cynicism.

"Well, you had to watch the Conviction destroy the people attacking Captain Slack—"

"Pfft, they were idiots, they deserved it," Alayna interrupted, not the slightest hint of pity in her voice.

"And then you got upset when Jake—"

"I was not upset!" Alayna snapped. "He's an arsehole and I hate him."

Ellie closed her eyes and sighed.

She's only sixteen, Ellie reminded herself.

"Well, he certainly doesn't hate you," Ellie said calmly. A long, drawn-out silence followed as Alayna didn't respond.

"I appreciate you standing up for me, Alayna, even if I disagree with how you did it. But please try to realise that you upset each other, and it wasn't only you or only him. I don't think either of you would have got that upset because of hate. You only get that upset when you care about someone," Ellie said softly.

There was a long moment of silence before Alayna replied.

"Go away," the girl said solemnly.

"Okay," Ellie replied. "But only stay in for a few more minutes. I'm worried you'll dehydrate or give yourself heatstroke."

Ellie waited again for a reply, but none came, only the splashing of the water sounding off the walls, so Ellie drew the door closed. She walked back to the lounge and sat across from Jake and Jonathan, the angle letting her see behind them. The two hadn't moved and seemed just as oblivious to her arrival as to her departure.

A few minutes later, a lithe figure made her way out of the hallway. Alayna stood, hair still wet and wearing a set of new, clean pyjamas, glaring at nothing in particular. She didn't acknowledge Ellie as she walked down the steps and crossed over to the other two.

With a level of presumption only Alayna could manage, she took one of Jake's hands and forced it to the side, causing him to let go of the controller and open his guard. He looked up at Alayna with a confused, but not hostile expression. Ellie nearly fell off her chair when she saw what happened next; Alayna turned around and, delicately, sat down onto his lap.

What? Ellie screamed internally.

Alayna pulled her ankles up until her heels touched her rear, both knees to one side. Taking Jake's empty hand, Alayna forced her smart brush into it until his fingers closed around the handle. Jake's expression was confused at first, until it suddenly erupted into a look of such complete and utter joy that Ellie's heart launched into a flutter.

Jake looked to her, and their eyes met in a moment of magic, a shaft of sunlight after a storm.

It was as though he could hardly believe what was happening but was so amazingly excited about it no matter how shocked he may be. Indeed, Ellie had to force her jaw shut from where it had more or less fallen to the floor. She might have nudged the girl towards being a little more honest about her feelings, but Ellie certainly hadn't expected this.

Look. By the wars, look! Jake thought.

I know, I see it, I can't believe it either! Ellie thought back.

Jake consciously lowered his controller as if any sudden move or hitch in his movements would scare the girl off, like approaching a frightened deer in a forest clearing. With all the care of a giant trying to pet a tiny kitten, Jake oh-so-carefully lifted a lock of Alayna's hair and began to delicately brush it.

Ellie could hardly believe what was happening right in front of her. Her amazement must have been evident, Alayna catching her eye. The girl immediately looked away, raising her nose and taking on a haughty look as she let Jake run the brush through her long, beautiful tresses. The heated bristles moved about of their own accord as Jake drew the brush down, detangling knots and straightening her hair at the same time.

They all stayed like that for several long moments, no movement in the room except for the crackle of the fire and Jake's long, slow, careful brushing.

Ellie almost had to do a double take as she finally looked over to Jonathan. He sat locked still, as if all his joints had been welded shut. His fingers had stopped moving over the buttons and he could have been mistaken for a lifelike statue except for the tremble in his upper lip. He wore an expression Ellie had never seen on him before, the muscles around his eyes tight, and his mouth turned in the shallowest of sneers.

A look of hurt, betrayal and anger was subtly etched across his features.

A hint of worry flashed to life amidst the astonishment Ellie was still processing. Jonathan and Alayna had been inseparable since birth. He'd had a complete monopoly over her time and attention all their lives, so it would only be natural for him to feel a certain amount of jealousy. She would talk to him about it later.

Ellie remained deep in thought until Alayna, sick of the continuing silence, huffed indignantly.

"Oh, for war's sake. Go have a shower!"

Ellie jumped, so tense she nearly lifted off her cushion.

"Manners, Alayna. It's rude to go ordering people about like that," she chided. But her heart wasn't in her words; she was still coming to terms with her own disbelief.

Alayna frowned, an annoyed expression coming over her face.

"You haven't showered in three days. We went all through export day, then all through the Rike attack and all your sleeping before walking all over Tropicalia and getting dunked in salty sea water; you're beginning to stink," Alayna said accusingly.

"Alayna!" Ellie snapped, suddenly very conscious of herself.

Ellie resisted the sudden urge to turn her head and delicately sniff herself. Alayna might have horrible tact, but the girl wasn't a liar. And horribly, she was right. It *had* been several days since she'd bathed.

"Just go," Alayna said, exasperated. "Jake's being so slow anyway. It's going to take him forever to do my hair."

Ellie's eyebrow twitched. The faintest inflection in Alayna's voice made it sound as if she was trying a little too hard to make them believe she was dissatisfied with how long it was taking. Jake, wisely, kept his mouth shut.

"Fine, but we *are* going to talk about the way you speak to people, Alayna," Ellie said pointedly, rising from the sofa.

Alayna didn't respond as Ellie walked past and up the short stairs, doing her best not to look rushed, but a bubbling embarrassment at the bottom of her stomach was trying to urge her on faster. Ellie was highly grateful once she rounded the corner and her line of sight with the others was broken. She kept up the smooth walk until she could duck into the bathroom and close the door behind her.

Fifteen: Cleans Up Pretty Well

Ellie let out a huge sigh leaning back against the door, feeling the heat in her face. Now alone, she turned her head and took a long sniff of herself. Her nose crinkled. Though it was only very light, there was the unmistakable scent of the sea and stale sweat. Thinking about it, Ellie could still feel sand in her joints and throughout her dress.

Grabbing it by the bottom, Ellie peeled the dress off, careful not to stretch the fabric too much as it stuck to her in several places. Looking around, she saw a small wooden bench tucked neatly behind the shower. She folded the dress up and laid it down on the wide slats, doing the same with her underwear before walking around and stepping into the shower.

The space was large, far more expansive than the little coffin they'd had in their ensuite. It was built into a corner, two tiled walls meeting at ninety degrees, a third curved glass wall reaching far into the room before curling back around. Ellie had enough space to hold her arms out and spin without brushing the edges.

For a long moment, she marvelled at how much room she had before turning back to the task at hand.

"What the…" Ellie said aloud.

Ellie was unable to find either the showerhead or the taps. A stainless-steel device dropped out of the ceiling high above, but it was a wide, flat square, offering no angle except straight down. Against the tiled walls, two vertical rows of flat, silver disks extended up from knee level, each disk spaced about a hand's width apart. A larger disk sat embedded to one side on the wall closer to the glass. This one was glossy black and appeared to be made of glass.

Beyond that, the space was featureless, no fixtures or controls, not even a drain hole in the floor, leaving Ellie with no idea where the water would come from or go.

A twinge of fear tracked up Ellie's spine. She didn't want to go ask Jake how to use his shower, bare and shivering. Surely she couldn't be that stupid. Besides, she knew the shower worked; she'd heard Alayna using it!

Determined not to embarrass herself any further than she already had, standing naked and confused in an unfamiliar shower, Ellie looked around and decided what to try.

Reaching up, Ellie pressed firmly on one of the silver discs on the wall. It was cold, chrome-like metal, smooth beneath her hands. She felt at a ridge etched into its centre, but beyond that, nothing noticeable happened.

Ellie blinked.

"House, shower on?" Ellie asked, unsure.

"I'm sorry, I cannot help you with that," the feminine, disembodied voice answered.

"Great," Ellie muttered.

Since the silver disks were a bust, Ellie pressed on the black glass one instead, flinching as it lit up unexpectedly. The disc was a screen. It had two empty bars, one labelled 'Temperature' and one 'Pressure'. Curious, Ellie dragged her finger up on the temperature bar, and it started displaying numbers in degrees Celsius. Ellie set it to fifty and waited. Nothing happened.

Still confused, Ellie began to drag up on the pressure bar, jumping as multiple hot water jets struck out at her, each of the silver disks as well as the flat square overhead spraying out simultaneously. Curious, Ellie increased the pressure, the spray becoming a blast.

Ellie shuddered in satisfaction, the water impacting her body from so many directions all at once, firing at her with a significant level of force. Closing her eyes, Ellie raised her head and let the near scalding hot water wash down her hair and over her face. Ellie turned, feeling the jets massaging her suddenly aching muscles as she did so.

This wasn't anything like their old shower.

"Umm...shampoo?" Ellie asked in hope.

Almost immediately, the water turned a frothy white, and a lather began to form over her.

"By the wars!" Ellie sighed in relief as she began to scrub.

This shower was nothing short of glorious, the powerful jets burnishing her, stripping away dirt and the top layer of dead skin with it. The beautiful heat didn't waver or slow for a moment. It was as though she was being violently scoured as she scrubbed through her hair.

She'd never encountered a shower this hot or with this much pressure. By the time she stepped out, dripping wet and having steamed up the entire space, Ellie felt she must have been glowing red with her raw skin. Her knees were weak, and she had to push her dirty clothes aside to sit on the bench. She didn't think she'd been cleaned quite that thoroughly in her entire life. They might have started off on the wrong foot, but she and this shower would become best friends.

But as Ellie sat curled, head hanging forward almost to her knees, an issue occurred to her. She hadn't brought any clothes into the room!

Aren't all my other clothes still down in the hangar?

She lifted her head as it spun slightly, taking large, deep breaths of the misty air. She looked to the side at her old, stinky clothes.

The thought of putting them back on was borderline revolting. That may have been who she'd been twenty or thirty minutes ago, but she was a whole new person now. She'd been blasted clean, turned fresh and new into the world. The shower had uplifted her, washing away all past sins as well as the dirt and grime of who she'd once been.

She let out an exhausted giggle at her own ridiculousness, though the shower had been really, really good. Maybe she'd have to dress in the smelly gear, get fresh clothes, then shower again. Well, anything to get another shower like that! But those smelly clothes… *Really?*

She stood, walked over to the bathroom door and leaned close, listening. She heard nothing beyond, so turned the handle and opened it a crack, poking her head out into the hallway. The coast seemed clear. She really didn't want to put her old clothes back on, and the door to her room was only a few steps away. If she could make it in there, she could dig through the boxes and hopefully find some of Jake's spare clothes to put on. She was sure he wouldn't mind, just this once.

Stepping carefully out into the hallway, Ellie held one arm across her chest as she closed the door behind her. Dashing down the hall, fearful she might be caught at any moment, Ellie kept vigil over her shoulder as she quickly turned the handle and pushed the door open, slipping inside.

"Whew," Ellie said in relief as the door clicked shut. She lowered her arm and pressed both hands flat against the door behind her, leaning against it.

It looked as though she'd got away cleanly.

Ellie shivered. The air outside the bathroom was frightfully cold in comparison, water still dripping down her body as she stepped forward.

"Oh. Well, that solves that problem," Ellie said quietly, her eyes falling to her bed. One of the others must have already unpacked their shopping and laid out the clean set of clothes Ellie had picked out earlier in the day. A beautifully thick turtleneck with long sleeves lay atop a pair of dark pants. The turtleneck had rows of thick, patterned stitching along its length and was glowing white in the low light of Sulaya that shone through the windows. Ellie wasn't sure what the pants were made of, but they were warm and stretchy. They clung to her form like leggings, and the inside was lined with an ultra-soft, faux fur-like material.

Ellie noted with some embarrassment they'd included a fresh pair of underwear and socks. She hoped Jonathan or Alayna had laid it all out for her instead of Jake.

She walked up to them. Ellie was still wet, but there was no towel, and she'd likely dry quickly if she stood next to the fire. With a shrug, Ellie dressed, pulling down the woolly turtleneck last, her head popping out of the tall collar as she seated it around her waist and tugged at the wrists.

Everything about the outfit was warm, soft and immeasurably comfortable. Ellie was going to go very soft, very fast if she continued to live in this level of luxury.

Flicking her hair up, Ellie let it fall wide down her back rather than putting it up in its usual ponytail where it would take longer to dry. With a last breath to steady herself, she stepped out of her room and walked back towards the lounge.

To her surprise, everyone still was right where she'd left them, so who had left the clothes for her?

Stepping into the sunken area, she walked over and backed up against the fireplace, at first carefully pressing her rear against the black anodised metal. The heat quickly soaked through her clothes and became dangerously hot. Pulling away, Ellie contented herself with leaning forward slightly, ensuring none of her hair would burn without her noticing.

Jonathan was still in the same position but seemed to have loosened up. He was moving about a little, tilting his controller slightly as his fingers worked the various buttons and triggers. His brows were creased as he seemed determined to focus on his screen and ignore all of them. To the right, Alayna was—

Ellie gasped.

As her gaze fell on Alayna, Ellie's eyes misted.

Alayna still sat, letting Jake tend to her, but the girl was almost transformed.

Her hair glowed in the firelight, hanging down straight and voluminous. It had a sheen that caught the light, making it look as though it was made of satin or silk. It draped beautifully, hanging in a long curtain that framed her slender face.

Her fringe rose away from her hairline slightly before curling back down to rest just above her eyebrows in a neat row. Her skin was clear and unmarred by dirt or grime, her eyes bright and alert; the dark circles she usually carried beneath them already seemed to be fading. The young girl looked for all the world like some beautiful goddess just stepped out of the myths of old.

Alayna looked over at Ellie's gasp, doing a double take as she saw her elder sister's face.

"What?" she asked.

"Nothing," Ellie replied, unable to keep an airy crack from her voice as she fanned her face.

Alayna's eyebrows stitched together in confusion.

"Well…those clothes look good on you," Alayna said slowly, her eyes searching Ellie's.

"Oh, they do? Thank you," Ellie said, letting out a forced giggle before sniffing loudly.

Alarm began to overtake Alayna's expression and she stood, rising out of Jake's lap and walking over. The moment she was in range, Ellie grabbed the girl.

"What—" Alayna let out as Ellie pulled her into a tight hug, wrapping her arms around the girl's neck and burying her face against the side of her head.

Alayna stiffened but didn't fight, and Ellie felt her slowly lower her arms from where she'd raised them, her hands eventually resting hesitantly atop Ellie's hips.

"Are you okay?" Alayna asked earnestly, an edge of worry in her voice.

"Yes," Ellie whispered quietly. "You just, you look……*healthy*." Ellie screwed her eyes shut, unable to contain the wetness forcing its way out.

If Alayna was bothered by the small amount of dampness spreading into her freshly brushed hair, she kept it to herself.

The two stood there for several long moments. Eventually, Ellie felt Alayna begin to fidget, the girl growing uncomfortable with the extended display of affection. Ellie released her hold, wiping at her eyes as she regained control, letting out a shuddering breath.

Alayna fixed her with a sideways stare.

"It's late…" Alayna began slowly. "I'm going to bed." Turning, she grabbed Jonathan by the wrist. "You too," she said.

"What!" Jonathan exclaimed, an annoyed tone in his voice as he was suddenly pulled up and dragged off.

"What's wrong with *you?*" Alayna demanded, turning as she pulled him up the stairs.

"Nothing," Jonathan responded, turning his head away.

Alayna snorted.

"Whatever," she said. "Eww, actually, you stink too; go have a shower." Alayna's voice echoed back to Ellie as she pushed Jonathan towards the bathroom, the two disappearing around the corner.

Ellie watched them go, feeling the turmoil in her chest abate a little.

Ellie had to close her eyes and resist the urge to chastise Alayna at her sudden proclamation. She raised a finger to her lips and scrunched her face a moment, fighting the sudden swing from calm to tears. Regaining control a second time, Ellie drew in a deep, calming breath, lowering her hand back down, only for her stomach to flip as her eyes fell on Jake.

He was looking at her with an expression that took her totally by surprise. His eyes were wide and his lips parted, with eyebrows raised high in a look of complete and total awe. A hard blush forced its way into her cheeks. He was looking at her as though she was the beautiful one, as if he hadn't just had Alayna literally sitting in his lap.

"Is-is something the matter?" Ellie asked as she quickly ran her hands over her face and patted down her head, suddenly desperate for something to take the attention off her.

The fire was directly behind her, casting her shadow over Jake. She was suddenly terrified her hair might have been set alight, or her new clothes had melted, or something equally disastrous.

Jake's jaw slammed shut, and he seemed to snap out of it.

"Sorry. It's just you're…you are…" Jake paused and shook himself. He bowed his head, an embarrassed-looking smile spreading. "How did you get here, Ellie White?" he said softly.

Ellie paused a long moment.

"How did *you* get here, Jake Ardent?" Ellie asked back just as softly.

Jake chuckled nervously.

"I don't think my story would show nearly as much strength of character as yours," he said.

Ellie's stomach flipped as he raised his head. Gorgeous green eyes that danced in the flickering light fixed on her, rooting her to the spot.

"You're beautiful, Ellie. That's obvious enough for everyone to see. But I don't know how many people will have been lucky enough to see how strong you truly are. I'm glad I get to count myself as one of those privileged few."

Ellie felt her breath hitch.

Sulaya give me strength, Ellie thought in exasperation, heat radiating out of her face as her heart began to hammer in her chest.

"I don't know what you mean, Jake," Ellie said quietly, diverting her eyes.

Ellie's insides exploded into a flurry of butterflies as Jake stood, walking over to her, and stepping in close.

"Come on, Ellie," Jake said with an amused tone and a grin. "Even Alayna touched on it earlier. You worked for months cultivating your harvest. You were back and forth to the spaceport for market day, then export day. You fought off Hunter and dealt with Slackvore.

"You survived losing your home and escaping a Rike swarm. You let a stranger take you away to a far-off planet and immediately started to rebuild. You stood firm when the decision to throw a Conviction patrol boat after a mercenary outfit was sprung on you, even weathering me when I lost myself a little. Throughout everything, the only things you've cared about were Jonathan and Alayna. Each obstacle you've dealt with would have been enough to crush so many other people. Yet you've handled each of them with nothing short of grace. I've known soldiers, officers and commanders who didn't remain as cool under fire or show such devotion to duty as you. You are amazing, Ellie, and I wish you could see that."

Ellie felt the floor open up beneath her. She raised her head to look at him as he spoke, transfixed by his gaze. How to handle this? Nothing he was saying was nearly as big of a deal as he was making it out to be. Yet at the same time, she couldn't argue that those things had happened. Something welled up inside her as he spoke. Something that was causing her core to shake.

"You're wrong," Ellie said, tears welling up. He was so far off the mark that she wasn't even sure how to correct him. Her words started pouring from her without much thought.

"Jonathan and Alayna are almost skeletons. My tiny farm was the best I could do, and even then, it wasn't enough to support us. You and Alayna were the ones to fight off Hunter, and I paid Slackvore thirty times the price for a broken-down old wind turbine, thinking I was somehow pulling the wool over their eyes. I didn't do anything but run from the swarm, and how many people died because I thought I could help save the Blister Fang? And now I've unleashed something even the bravest person I know is afraid of!"

Wet trails were running down her cheeks. She hadn't felt the tears come, but now she could feel her body being raked with great rasping breaths. Any semblance of composure was lost as Ellie was forced to face what she'd so desperately tried to turn from.

"You asked me how I got here. You wouldn't be saying any of these things if you knew! I'm a fraud, a pretender. And I can't *stand* the way you're looking at me like I'm something special!"

Ellie raised her hands to cover her face. She couldn't deal with this anymore.

"I'm just a girl, Jake," Ellie pleaded as she shook her head. "I'm not a superhero or some character in a fairy tale. No matter what I do, it's never enough. No matter how fierce Alayna is or how supportive Jonathan is or how hard I try, it didn't matter in the end. If you hadn't dropped out of the sky when you did, we would all be dead by now."

Ellie choked, her throat constricting, and her voice was becoming a desperate wail.

"All you do is give and give and give, so much that I'm never going to be able to repay you. They already trust you, Jake! Jonathan takes shelter behind you, and Alayna sits in your lap! And after everything, you still turn around and say *I'm* the special one. Well, you're wrong. You are so, so wrong—"

Ellie's throat gave up on her, tightening to the point it strangled her already struggling voice.

Strong arms closed around her, a warmth radiating from them as Jake drew her in tight. Ellie felt her face fall into the shelter of his neck, a soft, rhythmic heartbeat grounding her as caring hands stroked her head, running fingers through her hair.

Ellie didn't resist; she couldn't. It was finally too much, and her dam broke. The ups and downs, the terrors and joys of the past few days and weeks finally overcame her, grief and loss and hope all mixed together. Everything she had put aside to process later finally pushed its way to the forefront of her mind, and she could no longer hold it back. She wasn't invincible.

Ellie cried hard. Harder than she had at the end of market day. She lowered her hands from her face and gripped onto Jake, wanting to disappear, to undo every horrible decision she'd ever made and let the story of the universe play out without her. She wouldn't have to be responsible for it then, couldn't be accused of not doing enough then either. She'd tried.

What more did the world want from her?

Ellie continued to cry, everything pouring out of her with no hope of her holding it back. Moments turned into minutes, and minutes stretched into what felt like hours. Ellie was racked with great heaving sobs and barely subdued wails.

When she eventually devolved into dry hitches, it wasn't because she was done, but because her body had run out of fluids.

The entire time, the embrace that held her hadn't wavered. Jake hadn't pulled away or made a single complaint. He just held her. Warm, comforting, immovable as the mountains. Ellie was slowly beginning to calm down, a great stillness entering her chest as her breathing evened out.

Jake pulled her in, his embrace tightening. It was just a little *too* tight, in the best way possible. For the briefest of moments as she buried her head against the crook of his neck, Ellie felt safe. It was as though she'd found shelter in the storm, no longer cast out into the cold, hard rain.

Blinking, Ellie slowly began to pull her head back. Long, wet strands connected her face to Jake's mess of a collar.

"So much for strong and beautiful," Ellie tried to joke self-consciously, not knowing what else to say as she wiped a hand along her face.

A finger under her chain raised Ellie's head. She was met with a pair of piercing green eyes that saw right through her. What could Jake be thinking? Her eyes were puffy, her face a mess. And yet he was so close.

"You're as strong and beautiful now as the moment I met you, Ellie," Jake said. His tone was direct, steely and sounded one hundred percent earnest. Ellie's heart skipped a beat.

A tingle of confusion worked its way up her spine and heated her face. Why was he doing all of this? Jake didn't need to go to nearly so much effort if all he wanted was to get her into his bed. There surely wasn't any other reason he would be so kind towards her.

"What do you want, Jake?" Ellie asked desperately, at an utter loss and struggling to deal with it. Anyone else would have dropped the hammer by now and revealed their end game. She had to know why he was doing all this.

"Nothing, Ellie. I want *nothing*."

"Then why—"

"Because you're worth it," Jake interrupted, throwing an arm out and sweeping it across the view of the surrounding landscape. "Because you deserve it. Because you should be able to look across beautiful sunset fields and see more than bare survival. Because you shouldn't have to wait until you're a teenager to see the sky, or the ocean, or anything else the universe has to offer. You shouldn't have to carry the weight of the entire world all on your own. You're a good person, Ellie, and I don't *need* something in return to want the best for you!"

Ellie stared into Jake's eyes. This close, she could see patterns in the green, now growing acutely aware their lips were barely any distance apart, their breaths already intermingling. It would take just the slightest push to connect...

"You're mad," Ellie said in complete resignation. "What am I supposed to do with you?"

Something shifted inside her chest. At first, it was difficult to identify. As she processed it, a realisation began to dawn, that Jake really wasn't like anyone else she'd ever known.

"How about for now…" Jake sighed, his gaze losing its intensity, to be replaced with a look of exhaustion as he straightened his back and rolled his shoulders. "We call it a night? And tomorrow, we tackle the day together?"

Silence stretched out between them for several long moments. Ellie was beyond much thought. She moved without thinking as she slowly raised a hand, to press it gently against the side of Jake's face. He didn't pull away. Ellie delicately pressed her forehead against his. If she could steal a moment, just one more moment…

It was as though someone had pulled a plug inside her, all her energy and thoughts swirling around and emptying into a dark, bottomless pit, leaving her exhausted, sore, and drained.

"Would you…stay with me tomorrow? When we go see what's left of my house?" Ellie asked in a whisper. She didn't know why, or what he could do to help, just that she wanted him there.

"Of course," he said quietly. "Whatever you need."

Ellie opened her eyes. She'd never been this close to someone, certainly not willingly. His face was soft, shoulders steady, a rock she could cling to as she cobbled herself back together.

"You really do look exhausted, Ellie. Do you need me to help you to your room?"

"No," Ellie responded, pulling her head away from his. "You've done enough, and I can see myself to bed. But will you come wake me in the morning?" she asked, looking to him.

"I'm sure I can work something out," Jake responded, a small smile spreading across his lips as he let go of her completely.

"Then…goodnight, Jake," Ellie said.

As she turned to go, Ellie couldn't stop herself from lightly grabbing his forearm and giving him a short squeeze. Somehow, she hoped she could communicate all her appreciation through that one slight touch. It seemed laughably inefficient, yet the smile on his face grew that much larger.

"Goodnight, Ellie," Jake said simply.

Ellie didn't let herself look back as she walked up the small steps and moved down the hallway. She opened the door to her room, stepping in without breaking stride. She didn't pause as it closed behind her with a faint click. Ellie felt as if she was standing on the edge of a cliff, about to fall over the edge and if she stopped, she might just pass out where she stood.

Ellie reached down to pull her top over her head. She stepped out of her tights and threw back the top corner of her blankets, considering putting on pyjamas just as a wave of weariness overtook her, forcing her to sit down on the edge of the bed.

Ellie leaned forward, taking a deep breath.

What is happening?

Ellie didn't know what she was feeling. She'd become so familiar with Jake so fast. Was she unconsciously clinging to him just because he offered stability right after she'd lost her home? Was there actually something there, or was she being swept away by some imagined fantasy?

Ellie held her head in her hands.

There was so much for her to think through but she was exhausted. Taking a second, deeper breath, Ellie held it for a long moment.

Tomorrow, they'd finally visit their home, so any conclusions or solutions she could come up with might change before she could do anything about it.

Mentally throwing her hands up, Ellie let out the breath. She lay down, head sinking into the thick, soft pillow as she pulled the covers over her. A beautiful, merciful warmth enshrouded her, banishing any doubts or drawn-out musings.

Deep in her chest, a small flame of hope was burning. Ellie tried to ignore it, as if simply acknowledging its light might snuff it out. But still, her mouth formed into the smallest of smiles as sleep rapidly approached.

For all her dark musings and nervous uncertainty, Ellie couldn't deny that, right now, she liked being exactly where she was.

Sixteen: Contradictions

"We can tackle this another time if you're not ready. There's no rush anymore," Ellie heard Jake say from a million miles away. Her attention slowly pulled back to reality. She sat inside Lara, the canopy still sealed. They'd landed on the crest of her hill.

Ellie had kept her gaze averted, not wanting to look out as they flew across the distance. Now they were on the ground, she only had to turn her head by a fraction, and she would finally be face to face with the aftermath of the Rike attack.

Ellie took a deep breath, a nervousness bordering on dread causing the pit of her stomach to undulate like the waves of an ocean. So much had already happened since then that Ellie thought she might be able to get away from ever having to face it. To take Alayna and Jonathan and jump into some fairytale ending with Jake where they would fly around the universe living happily ever after.

But now here she was, separated from the reality of the situation by a thin glass dome.

"It's okay, Jake," Ellie said calmly. "We can do this."

Jake's mouth set into a worried line, eyebrows pulling together into a sympathetic expression. After a moment, he reluctantly leaned over, pressing a button, causing the canopy to rise open.

Ellie closed her eyes, taking one last, long breath. This would be the closing of a chapter in her life.

But also, the beginning of a new one, Ellie reminded herself.

Pulling herself up, Ellie stood and opened her eyes. All around Lara was nothing but churned earth, dark brown mud that had solidified into peaks and troughs, uniform in its inconsistency. Ellie knew their home well enough that even with the landmarks removed, she could tell they were right in the middle of what was their field. They were floating right where the broad green leaves and long fuzzy vines of the melons she'd spent so many years cultivating should be.

Ellie leaned down, placed her hand on the edge of Lara's cockpit and vaulted over the edge. She distantly registered that she'd copied Jake's practised movement without thinking about it. Her feet impacted the ground, and the dried mud cracked and crumbled under her weight.

There were no signs of green beneath her. No identifiable husks of shattered melons or even twisted remnants of vines. In the back of her mind, Ellie had secretly hoped she could recover some seeds, to find a wayward plant that had survived just enough to shelter some of the precious objects, particularly from her butterfly melons.

She'd worked so hard and had no other way of reclaiming them. Those plants had been unique in the universe, and even if she chased down Slackvore to buy back the fruits she'd sold him, she'd cultivated them specifically to reproduce outside of the fruit. Getting her snow melons and modified strain of watermelons would have been nice as well. But despite the greenery of the surrounding landscape, the top of her hill looked like scorched earth, leaving nothing but desolation.

Ellie heard footsteps approaching as Jake, Alayna and Jonathan came around from Lara's far side. She began walking forward without acknowledging them, sure they would try to say something supposedly comforting, but she didn't want to hear it. Ellie was strangely still inside.

She walked up their field, eying the ground as she went, hoping to find something, stopping when a jagged, broken shape entered her vision. It was so caked in mud that she almost couldn't differentiate it from the dirt until she nearly stepped on it. Despite wearing her white turtleneck, Ellie reached down into the dried mud, grabbing the long, broken shape and firmly pulling it up. The ground crumbled away as she lifted the form free. Their loyal little turret's fractured, twisted barrel was released from the earth, still connected to its shattered housing.

Perhaps it could be repaired! Maybe something about it could be salvaged or somehow saved!

But the thought was short-lived. Ellie lifted it higher, not feeling right letting it lie buried. The barrel wasn't just bent, it was wholly destroyed. Collapsed inward, twisted and folded over itself in a dozen different places, wires hanging out of its housing like spilt innards.

None of its processing boards were intact. It was completely shattered, nothing remaining for her to save but a few strands of copper.

She wanted to toss it like the junk it was. At the very least, to let it slip from her fingers and crash back to the ground from which she'd pulled it. But something within her just couldn't let it go. It didn't feel right to do it.

"Thank you," Ellie quietly whispered to the inert, twisted metal. "You saved us, all of us. We made it because you stayed behind until the very end."

Ellie felt strange. If viewed from the outside, she must look ridiculous. But the words were flowing from her without any real thought on her part. The eulogy for her little turret was coming as easily as breathing.

"I wish there were something I could do for you. I know you were never really alive, but you still kept us safe. You fulfilled your purpose, and I don't think there is any other turret I could have got that would have done a better job than you. You sacrificed yourself for us. For what it's worth, I don't think I'll ever forget you. Please, rest now, you did your duty wonderfully."

Ellie lowered herself to her knees, ignoring how she was dirtying her clothes, and gently placed it down. It was silly; the turret was in no better a position than before, but a feeling of peace spread throughout her chest.

After a moment, Ellie stood, feeling the other three closing behind her, keeping quiet. She didn't turn around, not wanting to look at them just yet. If that was their turret, then the mess just beyond had to be the remnant of their home.

A pile of flattened, muddy metal spread out before her. What were once walls looked as if they'd been pounded upon by some great, angry giant. The edges were split, the surface was warped, and it had been punched clean through in several different areas.

"Can you help me with this?" Ellie asked, not bothering to turn around.

After a quiet moment, the others approached. Without a word, they helped Ellie pick up one end of the wall, lifting and pushing until it was vertical once more. There it stood, for the briefest of moments, before crashing down in the opposite direction. A harsh, reverberating *clang* sounded as it hit the ground, bouncing and twisting several times before stopping.

Ellie saw the wall had acted as a sort of shield. For beneath, she could just make out some shapes in the mud. Crumbled, shattered pieces of ceramic from their bowls. A twisted quarter of a shutter. Even the dirtied, shredded fabric of their sofa.

Jonathan slowly stepped forward, carefully placing his feet as if his minuscule weight might break something more than it already was broken. He squatted down, poking through the rubble and the layer of dirt and mud that still encrusted everything. Ellie had no idea what he hoped to find, but the small boy looked so forlorn Ellie couldn't leave him on his own. She moved over, wiping down her knees as she squatted beside him.

Jonathan looked to her, and just as he would hope, she tried to fix him with a comforting smile.

Ellie was enfolded in a strange sense of calm as they picked over the remnants of their life. It wasn't quite as though she was picking through a stranger's belongings, more as if looking through someone else's eyes. She wasn't just calm, however; she was almost unbothered.

In the days leading up to this moment, Ellie had expected to be openly weeping by now, having lived in fear of finding the crushed housing of the turbine for which she had fought so hard. But now, even though it was all right in front of her, pressed into the dirt, there was a strange sense of alienation from it, a sense of distancing. Oddly, perhaps her long, heartfelt cry into Jake had helped her come to terms with everything that had happened.

It was the only way to comprehend things.

Alayna and Jake joined her and Jonathan. They were soon sorting out what might be salvageable from what was not. They hadn't had much to begin with, so there was little point in Ellie's mind in trying to find something they could actually use. But at the same time, a great sense of catharsis washed over her. And surely, Jonathan and Alayna must have been feeling something similar as they moved about, focused on their task.

Ellie wasn't able to find much. She'd moved over to where the living room's far wall would have been, hoping to find the remnants of their heater so she could plug it in and leave it running for no other reason than the principle of the matter.

Of course, she had to have a heater for years, keeping it inert, only for the universe to destroy the thing as soon as she had the power to get some use out of it.

Jake called out occasionally as he found something, unable to tell whether it might hold any sentimental value. It seemed obvious to Ellie that a bent fork was not the most valuable of things, but she appreciated the effort on his part, so she encouraged him.

It was hard to tell in the mud, but pulped, splintered firewood showed Ellie she'd passed onto the outside of their wall, meaning there'd be nothing left to find. She stood, straightening out and brushing the dirt from her pants. As she did so, a dark patch, out of place in the surrounding mud, caught her eye.

Ellie reached down, grabbing the object and pulling it loose from the dirt. Like everything else, it has been crushed and trampled, but given its size, had remained relatively intact, a small black box that fitted the palm of her hand.

Ellie's eyes narrowed. *I don't remember owning anything like this; what could it be?*

Yet still, a spark of recognition ignited somewhere deep within her mind. She'd seen something like it before, but where?

"Melon girl!" A harsh voice caused Ellie to jump, almost tossing the small box into the air.

"Oh, Mr Magonihue!" Ellie exclaimed as she spun towards the sound.

The grumpy old man sat atop one of his pigs, just beyond the boundary of what used to be their house. The fat, floppy-eared beast grunted with a rhythmic oinking as its wet nose searched along the ground. Even as Ellie watched, it reached forward with one of its stumpy hooves, digging in the dirt before plunging its snout downward, treating the earth as though the most prized delicacy lay underneath its hooves.

When it pulled back, it had the torn, desiccated remains of a melon vine in its mouth and began to chew. Maybe there was a small hope of finding some seeds after all?

Mr Magonihue snorted loudly.

"Yep. Nothing gets past you, does it?" he said in an unimpressed tone.

Ellie blinked.

"I'm sorry, Mr Magonihue. I just wasn't expecting to find you…well, *here,*" Ellie said, motioning to the destruction surrounding them.

"I've been looking out for yer return," he said as if in explanation. "Heard yer farm got destroyed."

"Well, yes, unfortunately," Ellie replied, motioning to the space around them for a second time. It was a strange thing he'd said, wasn't it? Couldn't he see the destruction with his own beady little eyes? What did the old man want and why was he here?

Jake approached from behind.

"Good morning, sir. What can we do for you?" Jake said, his voice raised to carry clearly. Almost as an aside, he discreetly held out a crushed box with colourful printing on it up to Ellie. "What's this?" he whispered quietly to her.

"I weren't talking to you!" Mr Magonihue snapped at Jake. "I don't know *you!*"

"Ah, that! It's my old genetics kit. It's what I used to modify my melons," Ellie said quickly to Jake before turning back. "Then, what can I help you with, Mr—"

"I came to offer yer lad a job. Figured with yer farm gone, yer could use a neighbourly helping hand. But I ain't giving it out for free!" the old man grunted aggressively.

"What, Jonathan?" Ellie asked, turning. *What could he want with Jonathan?*

Jonathan's head perked up at the mention of his name, looking over to them.

"Ellie, this is just a *children's* toy," Jake exclaimed in a hushed whisper.

"I don't know what to tell you, Jake; it's what I had, and it's what I used," Ellie responded, feeling a touch of annoyance at having to manage two separate conversations simultaneously.

"I'm not sure what use he might be to you, Mr Magonihue," Ellie responded to the old man. "He is but a small boy, not very strong yet, and a little shy. And fearful."

Mr Magonihue's snouts were huge, the tops of their backs easily coming up to Jonathan's chest. She didn't imagine the small boy would be particularly useful when it came to corralling them.

"He'll collect the slop, throw it to the snouts, hose 'em down when they're done. Though looks like yer doing plenty fine without gainful employment," Mr Magonihue grunted, pointing a craggy finger at Ellie's new turtleneck.

"The centrifuge is elastic bands and cardboard!" Jake exclaimed in the background.

Ellie ignored him. "That's very generous Mr Magonihue. But—"

"I'll do it!" a small voice interrupted.

Ellie turned to see Jonathan standing behind her.

"Jonathan," Ellie said gently. "You don't have to."

"I know," Jonathan replied, his lower lip quivering.

Ellie watched as the small boy looked over his shoulder. Alayna was still digging through the rubble, determined to ignore the sour old man. Feeling their gaze, she looked up, meeting Jonathan's eyes and cocking her head quizzically.

Jonathan turned back, looking towards the snout as it stood there, still loudly chewing the dried vine. Finally, he turned to Jake. Jake, seemingly just as adept at feeling their gaze on him, finally lowered the box and raised his head as he turned to look back at them.

A strangely determined look came over Jonathan's face. He straightened as his shoulders drew back in a rare show of posture. For possibly the first time ever, Ellie saw Jonathan's eyes harden somewhat, his brows coming together and his jaw setting.

"I'll come work for you, Mr Magonihue, if you're willing to provide fair pay for fair work," Jonathan called out as if he'd become a young man overnight. His voice still emerged uncertain, still holding an undercurrent of hesitation. But no one knew him the way Ellie did. She could hear, buried, his voice held the faintest touch of steel.

"You'll get paid exactly what you earn and not a dol more!" the old man snapped back, his bulldog-like face wobbling as he sneered.

"Jonathan, why—" Ellie began softly.

"Because you're always doing *everything,* Ellie," the small boy replied, not taking his eyes off the old man sitting atop the fat pig. "I can be strong too. I know I've never had a job before, but I-I'll make you proud. I'll still be able to help you with our farm and Jake's farm and everything else. I'll show you I can earn and buy Alayna's brushes and look after us just as well as Jake!"

Jonathan was shaking. Ellie regarded him with surprise, looking him up and down. They'd never really had an opportunity like this before. Their family might have been a particularly extreme example, but everyone on Adroa lived close to the edge. Despite his grumbling and foul attitude, Mr Magonihue really was giving them a generous offer.

Ellie doubted that Jonathan would earn anything significant. But as she looked at the thin, frail boy, finally standing with his back straight, she doubted that was his real motivation anyway. He might be worked a little too hard though. Ellie looked to Jake.

I don't know about this, she thought.

Jake's eyes shifted to focus on her.

It would be good for him to get out from under your skirt and gain some independence.

Ellie lowered her head back down to Jonathan. She reached up to stroke his hair slightly.

"If it's what you really want…"

"It is," Jonathan said immediately. "Th-thank you, Mr Magonihue. When would you like me to start?"

Mr Magonihue grunted in the displeased fashion he usually did.

"Come by the stye tomorrow at sunrise. Yer better be prepared to work, lad. I ain't no charity."

With that, he kicked his heels into the snout's flanks. It let out a squeal in protest, before turning around. The sight of Mr Magonihue seated atop the snout as it waddled away on stumpy legs would have been almost comical in any other circumstance. But Ellie had to admit, if there was ever a person perfectly suited to snout herding, it was that grumpy old man.

"Oh, and water yer fields!" Mr Magonihue suddenly called over his shoulder. "If any seeds survived, you'll want to give them the best chance of pulling through. Better than panning through the dirt hoping to find one on yer own."

Ellie blinked. *Oh! Oh!*

The thought hadn't occurred to her, but it made sense that if any had survived, she'd be better off trying to grow them in place than digging them up! The Rike may have dragged off their dead to be consumed, but plenty of nutrients would have soaked into the soil from their blood and bones.

"Thank you, Mr Magonihue! I'll try my best!" Ellie called, waving a hand high over her head. The old man didn't turn or acknowledge in any way, simply continuing to plod along on his way down the hill.

Thinking of the Rike caused something to tickle in Ellie's mind.

"Jake, come here!" Alayna called from the far side of the kitchen, where their small pantry would have been.

"Oh, is that the new way we get people to do what we want now? Just scream demands at them?" Jake called back, a rueful smile on his face.

"Ugh, *please*," Alayna griped, sounding as though she'd been asked to bathe in a septic tank.

Jake chuckled, shooting a bright smile to Ellie before moving off, leaving her alone with Jonathan.

Ellie raised her hand from beside her, uncurling her fingers to look down at the little black box again. A sense of frustration was creeping through her chest; something was beginning to bother her about it.

"Will you be okay working for Mr Magonihue, Jonathan?" Ellie asked, still not taking her eyes from the device.

"I-I'll be fine," Jonathan answered assuredly, trying to keep the quiver from his voice.

"I'll be sure to make you a big boxed lunch, okay?" Ellie said, finally taking her eyes off the device and looking at the frail boy.

Jonathan didn't acknowledge her, his eyes also focused on the device.

"What is that?" he asked.

"I honestly don't know. I feel like I've seen it before, but don't remember us actually owning something like this," Ellie said, frowning.

"It…it kind of looks like a lure…"

A LURE!

The world snapped into hyper-focus, realisation exploding in her mind.

Ellie's mouth dropped open.

"It is, it is!" Ellie hissed quietly. "But why… who…?" Ellie looked up as the pieces began to fall into place. She had helped with the logistics of a big lure several years ago. These little devices were the ultrasonic lures that enraged the Rike and drew them en masse from their hives. She'd prepared several of these throughout the night, so that was where she recognised it from. It would also explain why the swarm that had attacked them retreated rather than flowing over the hill after them. It also explained the timing of the attack.

"Hunter!" Ellie pretty much snarled the name, a hot rage bubbling up inside her.

He'd taken their home, their livelihood. He'd tried to kill them, and for what? Because he'd assaulted Alayna and hadn't liked it when she'd stood up for herself? It was wishful thinking, but in the moment, Ellie was sure the next time she saw that fat slimeball's face, she'd—

"Or Jake," Jonathan said coldly.

It was as though Ellie had been punched in the gut, all the wind blown out of her.

"What? Jonathan, how could you say that?" Ellie spat though hushed tone, rounding on him.

Ellie shot a look over her shoulder, but Jake and Alayna were busy digging something from the ground, out of earshot.

"You should know better than that by now. What possible reason could Jake have for putting a lure on our house?" She baulked at the tone of accusation in her voice, not meaning to round on Jonathan the way she did, but the boy's response had shaken her.

Jonathan didn't answer, just trembling where he stood but meeting her gaze straight on. That same look of anger from the night before stitched his brows together. He was pointed and deliberate in his movements, looking from Ellie's eyes down to her chest, then back again, his meaning clear.

"Jonathan…" Ellie began, exasperated. She raised one hand to rub her eyes with her thumb and forefinger before regarding him again.

"Jake has had more than enough opportunity. If that's what he wanted, he could have just… I know you worry about it, and I understand, but I really don't think that's it," Ellie said, struggling to find the words and cutting herself off mid-sentence. "What could he possibly hope to gain?"

Surely, Jonathan was allowing jealousy to cloud his judgement.

"He gets to ride to the rescue of the most beautiful girl in the colony and have her fall all over him for being a hero. Then sweep her off her feet by flying around in his spaceship and taking her for a shopping trip. He gets to be the most attractive man in your life by default!" Jonathan answered.

Instantly, heat rushed to her face. Jonathan had never argued back like this before.

"I'm not the most beautiful. And even if I were, I don't think any of that's even remotely close to the truth, Jonathan," Ellie said earnestly.

"Of-of course not. It's not like he had you moved in and all over him in about a day, is it?" Jonathan said pointedly. "Can you think of any other reason why he would be so kind and spend so much on us?"

Ellie went to speak, but suddenly came up short.

"He's...just a kind person," Ellie said quietly, but even to her ears, it sounded almost pitiful. What Jonathan asserted was true. The timing *had* been perfect, and they *had* already moved in with him after just a few days. Now dragged out into the cold light of day, Ellie had to admit, she had been rather...*friendly* towards Jake.

Ellie's eyes burned, and she screwed them shut. Even with all of that, surely she couldn't believe Jake would be capable of doing something like that. She remembered his smile, his laugh, how he was always so quick and happy to uplift them whenever he could. She remembered his look of joy when Alayna had sat in his lap and how encouraging he'd behaved towards Jonathan.

But then the cold look on his face as he ordered the deaths of countless mercenaries entered her mind, the look of stone as he shattered Hunter's elbow, wearing the black, bladed armour that still caused her to shrink back in fear. Jake had to be Conviction, and that was almost impossible to deny. And high-ranking Conviction too if the impression she got from the

Conglomerated Affinity's captain was anything to go by. He could be capable of more than she could imagine.

Ellie didn't want it to be true. She desperately wanted to believe it was just good luck or fate that had seen their suffering and kindly dropped a strong, rich, handsome man into her lap for the low, low price of growing a few plants for him. But even as she fought it, all the selflessness, all the kindness, Ellie just couldn't genuinely explain it. People just weren't that good. At the very least, not to her. She wasn't special or important, and no way could someone like Jake be genuinely interested in someone like her. She'd be fooling herself to think otherwise.

"By the wars, I'm so stupid," Ellie sobbed, hot, angry tears forcing their way free.

"It's okay," Jonathan said quietly. "I've got a job now. There might still be some surviving plants in the field. And if not, we can swipe some of Jake's seeds. We'll be able to get away from him. I promise."

Jonathan's voice had a crack in it, his small hands closing around her wrists. He was trying so hard to be brave for her. All Ellie could think about was the mess she might have got them in.

"What did you do?" Alayna's harsh accusation caused Ellie to open her eyes, and Jonathan jumped.

"N-nothing," Jonathan pushed back, trying to put strength into his voice.

Alayna's cold, blue eyes turned to him, and Ellie watched as poor Jonathan wilted like a flower under an orbital death ray.

"Then why is Ellie *crying?"* Alayna spat.

"Sorry," Ellie said, wiping the few tears from her eyes and sniffing hard. "Just a little overwhelmed with…everything."

Ellie watched a concerned look come over Jake's face from where he stood beside Alayna. A cold doubt was blossoming in Ellie's chest at having believed she was so good at reading Jake. It appeared to be just like the time when she'd thought she was running circles around Slackvore and Breacher, only for them to have been in control of her the entire time.

Jake reached out a comforting hand to grip her arm, and before she could stop herself, Ellie flinched away.

Jake's hand pulled back as if struck. Was that a hurt expression flashing across his face? But then it was gone, his expression changing to what seemed to be a forced neutrality.

"Sorry," Ellie said again. "I'd just, like to go if that's okay."

"We only just got here!" Alayna exclaimed, throwing her hands up. "Of course, you're upset, but that doesn't mean we just run away."

"Easy, Spitfire," Jake said calmingly. He crossed his arms behind his back and avoided making eye contact with Ellie. "Remember, not everyone is the same as you. I've no doubt you can handle being here, but that doesn't necessarily apply to everyone."

Alayna crossed her arms over her chest and *harrumphed.*

"Fine," she growled angrily. "I'm going back to Lara then, since there's no point sticking around here. You too." She finished by pointedly addressing the comment towards Jonathan.

"Um…" Jonathan spoke up, looking as if he was going to object.

Alayna half spun, fixing him with a glare that could strip the paint off a freighter and Jonathan jumped, immediately hopping to and falling in behind Alayna, who stormed off.

Jake began to move off. Ellie looked to him. The sight of his back to her, moving away, triggered something deep inside. Just as she couldn't stop herself from flinching, neither could she stop her arm from shooting out and grabbing his wrist.

He turned to regard her patiently, his expression still neutral.

"I'm sorry. I just…" Ellie trailed off.

Emotions raged within her. She kept seeing Jake's smiling face, feeling his warmth and strong arms around her. Everything she knew and felt about him was screaming at her that he couldn't have been the one to plant the lure. But her mind was trying to exert its cold, unforgiving logic. She could be deceived; her feelings weren't necessarily a reflection of reality. She had to at least consider it a real possibility.

How could she communicate that she wanted to trust him, but couldn't? At least, not yet. Not until she knew who had planted the lure, and why.

As her grip shook around Jake's wrist, his expression softened. The kindness she was so used to seeing in his eyes returned, and he slowly let his arms fall. Carefully, he worked his fingers into hers, until they stood there, holding hands. The butterflies that rose up in her chest didn't help calm the storm inside her.

"I can't imagine what you're going through right now, Ellie. But I'm here for anything you might need," Jake said softly, a small, compassionate smile spreading across his lips. "I know this whole experience must have been horrible. Let's go home."

Ellie's head shot up.

It would have been worse without you. She tried to think.

Ellie wanted to tell him what she'd felt earlier. Where she'd been surprisingly okay picking through the rubble, and how she was sure it was because of all he had done for them.

But Jake was already facing the other direction and didn't see her expression.

He stepped away, their arms stretching out as their hands stayed clamped firmly together, neither letting go. Ellie took one last look around them, seeing the fields, trees, rivers and mountains, also Bellator Peak in the distance, the radiant sky above and the churned earth of what had once been her home.

There was still so much to do. So much to process and uncover, but for now, she was out of time.

With a final, deep breath, Ellie pocketed the lure. She stepped forward, grasping Jake's arm and resting her chin atop his shoulder. She didn't know anything for sure. But for now, Ellie decided to side with her heart as she closed her eyes and drank in his scent.

She would figure the rest out later.

Epilogue

High Commander Perseus Laquarious Onronovich tramped down the hallway.

He'd never thought of himself as a vain man, certainly not one who would sacrifice practicality for needless frivolity. Yet he had to admit to some moderate satisfaction level as the harsh thumping of his footfalls transitioned to a muffled *whumph* on turning the corner, the stark metallic hallway yielding to ornate gilded columns and thick velvety carpet.

Perseus loved visiting this part of the ship partly because of its opulence, relishing how its rich pile sank beneath the boots he kept polished to a mirror shine. Something about this section's perfect finish and attention to detail mesmerised him, speaking to his nature.

His dark, bladed armour also looked spotless despite being concealed beneath a long black trench coat held around his waist by two intricately wrought silver buttons, parting at the front to allow the fabric to flow about his knees.

His uniform was a point of pride, framing his shoulders and hugging his chest, setting him apart as a true officer of the Conviction. As long as he lived and breathed, he'd see to it that every fibre of his garments remained meticulously pressed and maintained, not a single crease or loose thread daring to mar its magnificence. A man's presentation showed the state of his inner mind, he believed, so showing up smartly turned out was an intrinsic part of winning the upper hand.

A pair of troopers stood guard ahead, sequestered in their own little alcoves like the toy soldiers they were. As he approached, they both stood straighter, saluting at his passing.

It took Perseus all he had not to sneer at them since the troopers didn't belong in these surroundings, clearly having spent too much time amid trenches and battlefields.

To his immense chagrin, they had acquired slovenly habits, their clumsy attempts to polish their armour having left streaks along their surfaces that caught the light at certain angles. Faint remnants of mud and stubborn dirt stuck in their recesses, indistinguishable to all but Perseus' trained eye. He was sure he even spotted a few flecks of dust sitting atop one of their helmets!

No, rabble like these might well be good for fighting and dying, but they didn't belong here. This was where true power lay, where only men such as Perseus should tread—educated and well-bred men, ones with finesse, who appreciated the sumptuous surroundings in which they were most fortunate to find themselves. But this was a difficult scenario, and well he knew it.

Who was he to tell the Lord General who he could keep as his guard within his own personal quarters? Perseus did not possess the rank to make such an audacious suggestion.

At least, not yet.

In any other fleet, he might not have been so proud to be standing at its seat of power.

Perseus wasn't here riding some wave of nepotism or political favour. Politics might well infect the other fleets like a malignant cancer, but not this one. Here, each man must earn his place and his status, deserving his rank. No number of family ties or backdoor deals would get a man anywhere with the Lord General. No, in this fleet, you were raised up solely on ability and skill, earning your stripes the hard way, and High Commander Perseus had certainly earned his.

Of course, all the Conviction's assets were considered equal, the Trinity showing no favouritism amongst its competing fleets. It was merely a coincidence that his fleet had been tasked with elite problems at which none of the others had a hope of succeeding.

It was a coincidence that his fleet always received the benefit of taking first choice of all the young officers graduating from military academies throughout the Conviction. And it was also a mere coincidence that when the Trinity needed something done, when failure was not an option, it was always his fleet that they sent. Yes, all the fleets of the Conviction's Grand Armada were equal, and this fleet was first amongst those equals.

Perseus stopped, spun, and brought his feet together with a clack. He stood outside a wide metal door, the same one you would find in any of the other corridors, separating compartments, each one acting as an impromptu airlock in the event of a hull breach.

Everything on this mighty ship had been built to see combat, to take hit after hit and yet to keep on fighting through them all. It was just that this door also had an intricate wood overlay, beautiful, artistic patterns flowing down before flaring away into a myriad of designs, a level of artistry difficult to surpass even by the great manors of the High Estate Lords themselves.

It was a style that spread from the door and onto the bulkheads, continuing down the hall, along the ceiling and over every pillar, reaching back to where the carpet began.

Reaching up a supple, leather-gloved hand as clean and manicured as the rest of him, Perseus rapped his knuckles against the surface five times, a backwards gesture, given the call button was sitting illuminated in its cradle directly beside the door. But as with the guards, the Lord General insisted. And one did not disobey the Lord General on his own ship if they expected their career to survive the next ten minutes.

"Come in!" a harsh, grating voice called.

The door, with all its intricate carvings, slid open.

Perseus stepped into the lavishly appointed stateroom in which tapestries, statues, and trophies from across every conquest and victory in which the Lord General had fought lined the walls. Luxurious sofas surrounded a faux fireplace to one side, and a glittery chandelier hung from the ceiling. No, he might not be a vain man, but as Perseus stood with his back just a little straighter, he felt these surroundings far better suited him than anyone else on this ship.

He found Lord General Carter seated behind an ornate, ludicrously expansive desk, its dark, polished surface inlaid part with a sumptuous leather and part with carved stone depicting scenes of battles fought long past. It was large enough to easily serve as a banqueting table if Carter ever cared for such things.

Carter sat side on to Perseus, his face half concealed by a high-collared jacket. A black beret leaning to one side covered Carter's bald, wizened head. The effect was supposed to be intentional, but it just looked dramatically crooked in Perseus' opinion. He wisely kept his mouth shut. Reclined in his tall leather chair, Carter's eyes closed as a wet slopping sound emanated from below the edge of the table, beyond Perseus' line of sight.

"What do you want?" Carter grunted unhurriedly, his voice sounding like a metal scouring pad scrubbing against an old pan. It had been rendered permanently hoarse and ragged by many long years inhaling gunpowder and chemical propellants, also screaming orders at the top of his lungs as he'd carried forward the glorious will of the Conviction.

"A first fleet designation pinged toward the far edge of the frontier, sir," Perseus answered. He always liked conversing with the Lord General. Not for any particular love of the man himself, but because next to Carter's rusty hack, his own voice sounded buttery smooth.

"So what? One of the long-range scouts get lost and fail to report in?" Carter asked, unconcerned.

"Sir," Perseus said. "The designation was FFSA dash two, two, one seven."

Carter's eyes snapped open as he finally turned his head to acknowledge Perseus.

The general lowered his hand beneath the table. There was a pained choke, and the head of an attractive young comms officer appeared over the edge of the table. Perseus recognized him as being from the bridge crew's second watch as the man was dragged up by the hair.

"Get lost," Carter growled into the young man's face before throwing him backwards.

The desk was so large that he disappeared from Perseus' view.

He heard the comms officer floundering on the ground until he was finally able to stand.

The young man hurried past Perseus, avoiding eye contact. His head was bowed, and a wet sheen clung to his chin. The man's only crime was being young and handsome, at least where the Lord General could see him. But that was no excuse for not acting with a little decorum, even though Perseus was sure the young man had had no desire whatsoever to be here.

For war's sake, clean yourself up! Perseus thought aggressively, narrowly resisting the urge to physically spit out the words at the young comms officer.

The sound of the door closing echoed through the atmosphere of the stateroom, the temperature of which seemed to have suddenly dropped several orders of magnitude. Carter pulled at something below the edge, making no attempt to hide his movements from Perseus as he got himself situated. Once done, Carter placed both elbows on the table before intertwining his fingers beneath his chin.

He slowly closed his eyes again, just for a moment looking almost serene, like a grandfather who'd simply nodded off. Perseus knew better.

"Tell me we have him," Carter said quietly.

"Unfortunately, sir, there was a delay. He'd commandeered a local patrol boat and ordered the captain to destroy all evidence of his presence, claiming intelligence operations."

"And that worked?" Carter spat.

"Yes sir. The captain complied, and we were only passed the information as they had a Blackwatch operative on board on special assignment. We've only just received his communication. The incident occurred three days ago—"

That was all Perseus got out before Carter erupted, slamming his fists down on the table so hard Perseus felt it reverberate through the deck. Carter screamed a series of expletives so foul it could have curdled fresh milk as he launched from his chair. Objects started flying across the room, the Lord General's infamous temper hitting at full steam.

Perseus remained where he was, standing at rigid attention, eyes locked forward as hurled objects shattered around him. It always struck Perseus as a little maniacal that Carter would go to such trouble to collect artefacts from his victories, only to inevitably smash them to pieces. But it was good that he usually stuck to smaller *objets d'art,* not great hulking statues.

He supposed Carter thought there would always come more victories, more conquests, so plenty more opportunities to replace anything he might destroy.

After several minutes, Carter slumped heavily in his chair, chest heaving and hands shaking. An eclectic scowl caused the lines on his face to run so deep Perseus was surprised his head didn't crack wide open. He was sure Carter's face only held together because his tanned skin was so thick and leathery it would need a diamond-tipped blade to cut it.

"Have that shit-for-brains captain removed from command!"

"Aye sir."

"I want his entire bridge crew thrown in the brig!"

"Aye sir."

"Have our friendly Blackwatch agent start breaking fingers bone by bone until I get a damned good reason as to why they obeyed orders coming from a flagged designation!"

"Aye sir."

Carter was breathing heavily. Perseus had always thought of the Lord General as looking like an angry bull when he began huffing the way he was doing now.

It certainly didn't help that Carter was an enormous man to begin with, having been a soldier for decades before rising to command. Age and privilege were doing little to slim down his frightfully broad shoulders or thick, meaty neck.

When Carter's voice came again, it was cold, smoldering.

"Divert the fleet. I want us at his last-known location at emergency speed. And I want a full search pattern ready to deploy the moment we exit slip-warp. I want every backwater town, every mudball colony and dusty station scoured until we find him."

"Sir," Perseus began, a fear welling up from the pits of his stomach as he shifted uncomfortably. "Even if we limit our search to the local celestial neighborhood, the process could take weeks. We've no guarantee he's even in the vicinity. The Trinity—"

"FUCK THE TRINITY!" Carter roared at ear-shattering volume, rattling the bulkheads as he surged to his feet. "Carry out your orders, High Commander, or I'll have you strung up on the outer hull and flown face first into our next engagement. You won't be handed back to your family in a box so much as a damned juice bag. Am I making myself clear?"

"Yes sir, right away sir!" Perseus answered quickly, ducking his head to hide behind the polished brim of his cap and backpedalling as fast as he could.

The ornate door closed in his face just in time to block some unidentified candelabra as it smashed against the wood-covered surface, right where Perseus' head had been a moment ago.

Perseus stood in the deafening silence of the hallway. He took a moment to pointedly straighten his already straight coat and brush off some non-existent dust. When he raised his right hand to speak into his wrist, he pretended he didn't notice it shaking.

"Bridge, priority orders from the Lord General."

As Perseus relayed Carter's instructions, the ship's background hum changed in pitch.

Outside, ships of a scale unmatched by anything short of celestial bodies, possessing such raw destructive capability as to singlehandedly keep an entire sector in line, began to turn. Weapon barrels large enough to accept landing shuttlecraft all angled toward a single point, hundreds of thousands of souls and millions of tons of steel moving with a singular purpose.

Shining, rainbow ripples began to appear across vast hulls as mighty reactors bent spacetime to their will. Ships began to disappear as they jumped to slip-warp, heading with all speed toward Tropicalia.

The legendary First Fleet of the Conviction was on the move.

Afterword

Wow, what a ride, am I right, dear reader? If you ever wondered if authors go through the same swath of emotions writing a story as you do reading it, the resounding response is yes!

I can't thank you enough for sticking with me, especially as this is the debut novel from an otherwise unknown author. I truly do appreciate you taking a chance on my book and allowing me to wrench you from one emotion to the next. I sincerely hope you enjoyed reading at least as much as I enjoyed writing.

If it wasn't obvious already, Ellie and the gang will be returning in the following titles of the Trials of Conviction series. There are so many reveals I can't wait to share with you. I hope you'll support me in purchasing the sequels to find them out!

If you read my acknowledgements, then I would finally like to thank you properly, dear reader.

We each have a tragically limited amount of time in our lives, and your choice to spend some of yours reading my story is the highest compliment I could possibly imagine. I hope my writings have left you more enriched and fulfilled than when you started. Whether you walk away with a new meaning, quote, or having just been entertained, I hope my stories were worth the time you spent reading them.

So, from one mind to another, across time, distance and media, again, I thank you.

If you would like to keep up to date on the series and new releases, I can be reached and have a mailing list at CJWatson.info

Finally, if you would like to leave a review for me to obsess over, you can do so on Amazon or by scrawling inside your copy's cover and throwing it over my back fence. Readers' reviews really do an amazing job of keeping authors motivated.

Until next time, dear reader. It's been a pleasure to write for you.

About the Author

Christopher is an author, cosplayer, wargamer, ravenous reader and all-around avid imaginer.

Writing stories since he was five, he decided sometime around 2018 that he should actually kick them out of his mind and into the world before they completely took up his rapidly diminishing head space.

Having grown up on hard SciFi stories and grand space operatics, he hopes to pay homage to the great authors who influenced his developing years and, in turn, write stories to inspire the next generation of bright young thinkers.

When he's not running various I.T. departments for his day job, Christopher can be found spoiling both his partner and their many, many cats somewhere around the desolate hellscape of Sydney, Australia.

www.ingramcontent.com/pod-product-compliance
Lightning Source LLC
Chambersburg PA
CBHW030807260626
47169CB00001B/220